FAULT LINE

FAULT LINE

Sarah Andrews

ST. MARTIN'S MINOTAUR ✸ NEW YORK

This is a work of fiction. All the characters and events portrayed in this novel are either fictitious or are used fictitiously.

www.minotaurbooks.com

Grateful acknowledgment is made to Edward Christopherson to quote from *The Night the Mountain Fell: The Story of the Montana-Yellowstone Earthquake,* copyright 1962.

Library of Congress Cataloging-in-Publication Data

Andrews, Sarah.
    Fault line / Sarah Andrews.—1st ed.
        p. cm.
    ISBN 0-312-25350-8
    1. Hansen, Em (Fictitious character)—Fiction.   2. Government investigators—Fiction.   3. Salt Lake City (Utah)—Fiction.   4. Forensic geology—Fiction.
    5. Women geologists—Fiction.   6. Earthquakes—Fiction.   I. Title.

PS3551.N4526 F38   2002
813'.54—dc21

2001048664

First Edition: January 2002

10 9 8 7 6 5 4 3 2 1

For Frankie Brown,
with lots of love

Acknowledgments

Once again I heartily thank M. Lee Allison for providing the central inspiration for my story (sorry you had to do it the hard way this time, bubba, and I'm glad you're in Kansas anymore).

My thanks to the many people who contributed their special earthquake stories, which appear as epigraphs in this book.

I wish to thank the legion of geoscientists who helped me approach technical accuracy. They include Walter Arabazs, director, and Sue Nava of the University of Utah Seismic Station; Marjorie Chan, professor, Department of Geology, University of Utah; Sarah George, director, Utah Museum of Natural History; John Middleton, geographer; Edward A. Hard, Timothy A. Cohn, and Kathleen K. Gohn, U.S. Geological Survey; Vicki Cowart, director, Colorado Geological Survey; John Nichols, Mid-America Earthquake Center, UCIC; and Michael Malone, consulting geologist, Sebastopol, California (a man of sterling professional character, not to be confused with the shlub named Malone in this book). I am also indebted to the authors of a great many geoscience publications, particularly *Prediction: Science, Decision Making, and the Future of Nature*, edited by Daniel Sarewitz, Roger A. Pielke, Jr., and Radford Byerly, Jr., *Waking the Tiger: Healing Trauma*, by Peter A. Levine, and *Paleoseismic Investigation of the Salt Lake Segment of the Wasatch Fault Zone at the South Fork, Dry Creek and Dry Gulch Sites, Salt Lake County, Utah*, by Bill D. Black, William R. Lund, David P. Schwartz, Harold E. Gill, and Bea H. Mayes. I wish to acknowledge the expert assistance

viii   ◆   Acknowledgments

of Robin Wendler, structural engineer, ZFA Santa Rosa, and Lee
Siegel, freelance science journalist, Salt Lake City. I thank Salt
Lake City's mayor, Ross C. ("Rocky") Anderson, and his building
guards for their kindness in providing tours of the Salt Lake City
and County Building.

I thank Kelley Ragland for her superb editorial advice, and I am
indebted, as always, to the Golden Machetes critique group, in the
persons of Mary Madsen Hallock, Thea Castleman, Ken Dalton,
and Jon Gunnar Howe. Special thanks to Jon for several extraordinary assists when I painted myself into corners.

My thanks to Andrew Hanson and his Grace Connection Seventh
Day Adventist congregation in Chico, California, for inviting me
to address their gathering, thereby inspiring me to cogitate more
coherently about certain issues that are central to this book.

My special thanks to one of the finest geologists I know (lucky me,
he is also my husband), Damon Brown, principal geologist, EBA
Engineering, Santa Rosa, California, for vastly improving my understanding of the fields of earthquake prediction and engineering geology, and for staying up late many nights to talk through the ethical
issues spawned in the oftentimes cramped meeting place between
geology and public policy. And I thank my young son, Duncan, for
charming Salt Lake City's mayor into that tour by telling extra-
good cow jokes, and for his enthusiasm while accompanying me to
the top of the clock tower. He was a sport then and continues to be
so as I spend too much time writing these books.

FAULT
LINE

❖
❖
❖

I was driving down the Fell Street ramp off Highway 101 into San Francisco. It was like skiing down a mountain made of Jell-O.

> —*Larry Yurdin, describing his experience of the October 14, 1989, magnitude 7.1 Loma Prieta, or "World Series," earthquake that rocked northern California. The ramp was one of many sections of elevated highway around San Francisco Bay that, as a result of damage from the earthquake, were condemned and later demolished. Larry was fortunate to have been on the Fell Street ramp rather than on the Cypress structure of Interstate 880 across the Bay in Oakland, which collapsed, crushing sixty-three people.*

THE EARTHQUAKE THAT SHOOK ME AND THE REST OF SALT Lake City awake at 4:14 A.M. that wintry Monday measured 5.2 on the Richter scale. That's a modest quake by California standards, and if you live in Japan, or Mexico City, or Turkey, or in any other place in which violent shaking of terra firma is more common, you'd be done chatting about it by lunchtime. It would linger in your thoughts only if someone mentioned it again, or if you lost a favorite knickknack in the fracas, or if you saw the follow-up in the next day's paper.

But in Salt Lake City, Utah, some of us thought life was ending. The girls who lived across the hall from me greeted the experience with screams of terror and a great deal of howling about Armageddon and other biblical references of doom. For them, the Earth had just become a place that had to be reconsidered: a place that might drop them, or cause something to drop *on* them.

Being a geologist, my experience of the event was somewhat different. I found it exciting, once I got over the disappointment of waking up from the dream I was having about my boyfriend, Ray. That dream and I didn't want to let each other go, so it translated the motion Salt Lake City was experiencing into the bliss of rolling around on that bed under entirely different circumstances. Or at least, I presumed such circumstances would be blissful. Ray's a devout Mormon, and, as we weren't hitched, his policy was to say good night after the lingering tease of a smooch. But my body, having more elaborate ideas, hated to wake up. I can be forgiven for hoping, I trust, because stranger things have been known than for a handsome, healthy thirty-two-year-old male to finally decide to toss policy aside and just plain go for it.

But the earthquake did finally wake me up. Something deep in my brain stem got through to the pleasure section of my gray matter and said, *Hey, honey, this isn't just someone bouncing the springs next to you, and aren't those your neighbors screaming?*

As I surfaced fully from my dream, I heard not just my neighbors losing their wits, the rattling of books, jam jars, and pot lids, and the crashing of other miscellaneous chattel falling off of shelves, but the sound of my slatted window blinds slapping against the glass. And then it was over. Perhaps ten seconds total.

There were a few seconds of complete silence; then Greta and Julia, the college girls who lived across the hall, caught their breath and started in again with their howling.

I rose up onto my elbows, my heart racing with both the happy and unnerved varieties of adrenaline, still struggling to sort out what my neighbors were trying to tell me. Had the house just been hit by a Mack truck, or were they flipping with jealousy because they'd somehow gotten a glimpse into my dream?

I switched on my reading light and discovered that I was indeed alone. And that the shade on my desk lamp was swaying, all by itself, and my jacket was sliding off the chair onto which I, tired from the previous afternoon's solo cross-country skiing, had dumped it. A pencil rolled off the table that doubled as a dining surface and desk. Then there was more silence, except for the otherworldly ruckus of my panicked neighbors.

The racket suddenly got louder as the door beyond mine crashed open and Greta and Julia thundered out into the hall. They took the stairs at a gallop, ululating like a couple of banshees and wailing prayers to Jehovah. Their voices streamed off in a wild Doppler shift of terror as they flung open the street door and hurried out onto the frozen sidewalk.

I swung my legs out from under the covers and lurched onto them. One leg twanged with pain, and I wobbled, arms whipping around in search of something to grab hold of. I cursed. I had only days before gotten that leg out of a walking cast. It had been broken during a mine cave-in, and I had overdone it with the cross-country skiing, trying to convince myself that I was whole again. But that's another story.

I staggered across the small bed-sitter I was renting and opened the front window, letting in the biting breath of winter, and hollered, "It's all right! It was only an earthquake!"

Greta and Julia reeled back in terror, as if I were some hideous gargoyle come to life.

Which got me to wondering what in hell I was saying. *Only? An earthquake? Hey!*

I suddenly felt a little exposed there hanging out of the window. So I backed off and slammed it shut.

On brief reflection, I understood their concern perfectly. Those of us who grow up in the great solid interiors of continents tend to think of the Earth as something that holds still. Oh, the ground might crumble underneath our boots as we climb a steep hill on adobe soil, or the passage of a summer's cloudburst might carve a steep gully through it, and we have the occasional landslide, but on the whole, our experience is that, at depth, Mother Earth stays put. Which is good, and comforting. Floods we've got, and tornadoes, and plagues of locusts, so who needs earthquakes? Those are for idiots who live by volcanoes and steep coastlines, right?

Wrong. Salt Lake City was built right on top of the Wasatch fault, and the Earth had just awakened from a half century's nap.

The phone rang. *Ah*, I thought. *Ray, calling to check on me. How dear. Kind of makes up for his distance lately.* I picked it up and said, "Hi, sweet pea."

A female voice on the other end shrieked, "Jesus! What was that?"

I let out a laugh, embarrassed to be caught spilling my love name to the wrong ears, but relieved that it was, at least, a very close friend who had gotten to hear it. "Oh, ah . . . hi, Faye. What's up? Certainly not you, at this hour?"

"The hell! That was an earthquake, right?"

"No, just a routine bit of maintenance on the Earth's substructure, the laws of thermodynamics bringing about a little reapportionment of stress translated to its crust, as it were. Yes, that was an earthquake. What's the deal—you got to call up a professional to have it certified?"

"Em, my dear," Faye intoned frostily, "I am a pilot, not a geologist. I know air turbulence. When the Earth shakes, that's *your* department." Muttering, she added, "Leave it to Em Hansen to intellectualize a near-death experience."

I realized that I was grinning into the phone. I whooped, "Wasn't it great?" Because it was. I had just experienced my first earthquake. I felt excited, even gleeful. I suppose that's part of what sets a geologist apart from normal people: We find natural disasters stimulating. From a professional standpoint, riding out an earthquake is a rite of passage.

"*Great?*" Faye said. "Woman, you are insane. My favorite Acoma water olla just bit the dust. Or turned to dust."

"Sorry to hear." Much as I admired Acoma pottery, I was

certain she could afford another twenty like it. Faye Carter was filthy, stinking rich. She flew a half-million-dollar airplane on errands at break-even rates for her buddies and called it a delivery service.

"You don't sound suitably sympathetic," she growled.

"Hey, any geologist worth her salt wants just four things in life. One is to witness a volcanic eruption, another is to see a flash flood, a third is a landslide, and a fourth is to feel a real live earthquake. Coming from Wyoming, I've seen a flash flood already, and now here's my earthquake. So that means I'm halfway there."

There was a moment of silence at the other end of the telephone line. I expected that she was preparing some spicier rejoinder about finding a saner profession, but instead, very softly, almost at a whimper, she said, "Em, can you come over?"

It was not unheard of for Faye Carter to sound grumpy, but nervousness was not in her nature. "Are you okay?" I asked.

"Of course I'm okay!" she shrieked, which was also out of character. She was silent for another long moment, then said, "I . . . aw, hell, Em, the earth just kind of wound up somewhere different, you know? I mean, not all of us find this sort of thing as entertaining as you do! I mean, is it done? It could be a foreshock, right? There might be something bigger coming. Should I run outside? Should I—"

"Is it a foreshock? I have no idea. Not my specialty. More likely there will be aftershocks, but small ones. Very small. Your olla collection won't so much as jiggle."

"You need to get out more," she grumbled, then added something about scientists having been fed turpentine with their pablum.

To which I replied, "I went into geology precisely because I could be outside more. And it's just your house jumping around on you that made the earthquake feel so big. If you had been outside, you—"

"Rm, you're sick," she muttered, then gasped, "I wish I hadn't said that," and dropped the phone. It hit something hard with a deafening *thunk,* and a moment later, I heard the distant but unmistakable sounds of vomiting. I heard also a man's voice: "Faye? You okay, love duck?"

Love duck? Well, that puts sweet pea all in perspective, I decided, *but Tom Latimer, Zen FBI agent and curmudgeonly cradle-robber, calls Faye "love duck"?* I decided to revise my diagnosis. There had been no earthquake. Instead, my species had gone collectively insane.

I waited for the phone to be picked up again. Waited two minutes, because I was, in fact, concerned about Faye, and not for the more altruistic reasons alone. I had been living in Salt Lake only a few months, she was the closest friend I had in the city, and, love between a hardheaded cop like Ray and a harder-headed geologist like me being what they sometimes were, she topped a short and essential list that might be entitled "Without These People, I Implode." Funny how something like a little natural disaster can leave you feeling more dependent than you had previously been willing to admit.

While I listened to Faye's distant vomiting, I walked around my apartment, switching on lights, inspecting the place for broken crockery. I sniffed slightly over the shattered saltshaker I found in the kitchen and put away my jacket. I glanced out the window to make sure Greta and Julia weren't freezing to death on the front lawn, and saw that our landlady, Mrs. Pierce, was out there wrapping quilts around them, fussing over them like an old hen pecking at june bugs. I waved to let her know I was all right. Finally, I gave up and put the phone back on its cradle. Tom was with Faye, so I could relax and go back to sleep, right?

Wrong again. It was too early to be up, but it was also too late, and I was too wired, for getting back to sleep. I thought of phoning Ray, then remembered that he was out of town, down in Saint George with his mother on family business.

Which means that Ray doesn't yet know about the earthquake. . . .

I stopped short in the middle of the room, wondering how I'd known that. *Well, because Saint George is at the opposite corner of the state is why. He would not have felt it.*

But how did I know that the shaking would not be felt that far away? How did I know that it wasn't a bigger quake centered near him?

Because the motion was sharp, chattery; a quick jolting followed by a high-amplitude rolling sensation.

I have this kind of conversation with myself all the time. Geologists are emotional introverts, which means that they like to keep to themselves, but intellectual extroverts, which means that we like to think out loud. Which frequently results in our . . . well, talking to ourselves. But abstracted or not, I knew—instinctively, intuitively—that I was very close to the epicenter of the earthquake. I had made a kinesthetic evaluation of the amplitude and frequency of the vibrations, and had intuited that the initial chattery vibrations would attenuate over a very short distance, leaving only the big rollers, and even they would feel more liquid, less jolting the farther I was from the epicenter.

I tried to remember the lectures from my freshman Physical Geology course, in which the professor had described the kinds of shock waves set off by the slippage along fault planes that we call an earthquake. I remembered that they had differing senses of motion—some push-pull, some side to side, some up and down. First came the fast, short-amplitude P waves (for primary), then the slower but bigger S waves (for secondary). But there my memory fizzled out. It had been too long since college. I couldn't recall which wave was which. One propagated along the surface of the Earth and another traveled at depth, but . . .

But I trust my gut sense, I decided. *The shock waves might have been felt ten miles away, but not one hundred, and certainly not as far away as Saint George. I am a geologist down to my deepest neurons, and I believe my observations.*

About then, certain possibilities began to hit me. Geology had just happened in a big way, and right under my feet. *Perhaps, in the aftermath of this event, there will be work for me! Maybe the Utah Geological Survey will need me part-time, even, so I can keep going to school. Enough of this job-hunt merry-go-round! If—no, when—I find work, I can even tell Tom Latimer to take a hike with this training he's putting me through.* This thought in particular appealed to me. Tom and I had been getting together on the odd evening and weekend. He was training me to be a detective, or operative, or whatever he liked to call himself. He was teaching me how to detect things formally, through the old-fashioned routes, and without risking my foolish neck. But I was beginning to think that low risk meant life in a laboratory, looking at bags of dirt shipped in from the remote places I'd prefer to be, and old-fashioned seemed to mean the same thing as tedious. I'd begun to tire of the whole idea. "Give me a good field job in geology," I'd told him. "Out there by myself. Working out geological puzzles, not human ones. That will keep me out of trouble." For the first time that day, Tom had laughed.

Laugh while you can, cloak-and-dagger boy, I told him now in the privacy of my own head, *because the earth has moved, and I am going to do some geology!* I grabbed my jeans, some wool socks, and a pair of boots—my favorite old pair of red ropers, for luck—and wiggled into them. *Did the rupture come to surface?* I wondered. *Will I be able to see the scarp? No, it wasn't that big. Well, maybe some chimneys have fallen, or maybe there's even a house off its foundations!*

I stopped, my right boot halfway on my foot, chagrined at what I'd been thinking. I was a student of the Earth, but Faye had been right: My excitement was everybody else's tragedy. I began to wonder about the damage in a different way. Wondered if anyone had been hurt. Wondered if any cornices had fallen on people's heads. These thoughts kept me frozen for several seconds.

Well then, I'll just go out and see if I can help, I told myself. I pulled my boot the rest of the way onto my foot, slipped into my down parka, checked its right-hand pocket for my keys, and hurried out the door.

I was in a liquor store in Santa Cruz. Glass started raining off the shelves. I made it out the door and did some Tai Chi break-dancing in the parking lot. When it was over, I turned around and looked back inside the shop. The place was shin-deep in broken glass.

—A young man, describing the 1989 magnitude 7.1 Loma Prieta earthquake as he experienced it in Santa Cruz, California, a lovely coastal university town founded in the 1800s by retired sea captains. Many of the fine old commercial buildings downtown were constructed of unreinforced brick. As buildings collapsed, there were fatalities. Many businesses, while nominally insured, could not afford to rebuild, and so went out of business, permanently changing the prized character of the central business area.

I WAS HALFWAY DOWN THE STAIRS WHEN I REALIZED THAT underneath my jacket I was wearing only my flannel nightshirt. This fact suggested to me that I was a little more jangled by the earthquake than I had previously been aware. I ran back upstairs, rigged myself up with proper long-john shirt, turtleneck, and sweater, once again donned the down parka, grabbed a wool cap, and tried again.

Down on the lawn, Greta, Julia, and Mrs. Pierce were still staring at the house as if it had grown fangs, though their way of expressing their thoughts and feelings had subsided from screams to a gentle sobbing. They were still huddled together under Mrs. Pierce's quilts. "Are you frightened, dear?" Mrs. Pierce asked, her beetle-bright eyes measuring me for damage.

A thick fog was visiting the predawn darkness. The chill, damp air bit into my nostrils and swirled over the street, evoking a movie set for the remaking of *The Hound of the Baskervilles*. I exhaled. "I'm fine, thank you, Mrs. Pierce. I'm just going for a little drive."

Mrs. Pierce gave me a look that suggested that she thought that I, too, had just sprouted fangs. I briefly considered trying to explain the workings of my mind, but, having struck out with as close a friend as Faye, I decided to save my breath.

The old woman's eyes narrowed from anxiety to distrust. She said, "You're a geologist, hmm? So you know a little more about this than some folks. I see you're taking off here. Is there something you're not telling me?"

I thought, *What's this? You think I'd just run for it without passing you a warning?* but my training kicked in again and immediately started spewing scientist hem and haw talk, full of qualifications. I said, "Well, first, earthquakes aren't my specialty, so I really don't know that much more than you do. But I think the first shock is usually the largest. Although there is no way to predict what will happen next."

Mrs. Pierce's eyes narrowed down to slits. She was not enjoying this taste of the kind of sidestepping geologists get mired in when they're trying to answer such questions.

It was not the moment to try to explain the limits on predictability and the slipperiness of nonquantitative confidence intervals to my landlady. I threw scientific caution to the winds and said, "If I had to guess, I'd say that was as big as it's going to get, but there will probably be several littler ones over the next few hours. And in that time, you're infinitely more likely to die of exposure if you don't go back inside than from falling masonry if you do." I was unable to say this without looking somewhat apprehensive. My apartment was in Mrs. Pierce's big old two-story unreinforced brick house on Douglas Street, up near the University of Utah, within a block of the line where the ground suddenly steepens as it ascends the buried scarp of the Wasatch fault. You'd think a geologist would live somewhere other than smack-dab on top of a fault, but hey, it's cheap housing, and while house hunting, I'd used the same brand of denial that seems to work for everyone else: I'd told myself it wouldn't happen while I was living there.

I stood a respectful distance back from the facade, inspecting it as best I knew how. I couldn't see any new cracks in the ancient mortar. The chimney was still standing. All was quiet. But was there something obvious I had missed?

A moment later, I heard a siren, far in the distance. Somewhere in the back of my brain, it rang like a call to action. I scanned the wall again, my mind reaching into it, Em Hansen waking up once again in the skin and skull of the geologist. Giving Mrs. Pierce a pat on the shoulder, I said, "Go back inside and keep warm. But don't sit next to a bookshelf, or under that chandelier you have in your dining room. Turn on the TV, get some early news; they'll have interviewed some seismologists by now, and they'll have an advisory for you. I'll go scout the area and let you know what I find out."

I got into my truck and drove through the predawn city, marveling at how many lights were on, but as far as I could see, each house appeared to be still firmly mounted on its foundation. After a five-minute tour of the avenues, I had spotted only one fallen chimney, and for all I knew, it had been sent to its doom by the freezing and thawing cycles of Salt Lake City's temperate winter weather, not by the renegade shifting of the Earth's crust. *Or by a combination of factors*, I reasoned. I had read that earthquakes could be as quixotic as tornadoes when it came to the damage they did; one house might be leveled, while the one across the street could suffer only a few broken dishes. It was all a matter of the quality of construction and the angles at which shock waves struck solid and not-so-solid objects. Like the 1989 Loma Prieta quake out in California: Structures close to that Richter 7.1 event were snapped off their foundations unless bolted down. The farther away a building was from the epicenter, the less damage was done, until the shock waves reached the forty-miles-distant cities of Oakland and San Francisco. There, a bridge fell, and elevated highways built below current codes collapsed.

But that was a really big quake, I reminded myself. *This one here is really only moderate, and the amount of energy released as the Richter scale numbers get larger is logarithmic. Loma Prieta was probably a thousand times larger.*

I decided to go back to my apartment and get some breakfast, then head up to the University of Utah to dig into some textbooks on seismicity and structural geology. *Go on home,* I told myself. *Emergency over.*

But then I saw another pile of brick that had once been a chimney, and another, and then an ambulance hurrying north toward Holy Cross Hospital, and I wanted to be with friends. I remembered that Faye had asked me to come to her house. I decided to go there and, like Mrs. Pierce, watch the news.

Faye's house lay to the south and uphill. It was a big thing on a choice bit of real estate, set up above the city on a topographic bench carved by waves that had rolled ashore eleven thousand years ago, when Great Salt Lake filled the whole desert like a chamber pot. Being a pilot, Faye liked altitude and long views, and, being a trust-fund baby, she could afford to pay for them. Sadly, my ancient truck did not and could not. It conked out about four blocks short of her house, declaring its intentions by belching up a cloud of stinking smoke with a horrible grinding noise.

I climbed out, slammed the door, and jumped up and down on the empty street in frustration, which is not something I recommend if you're still getting back in shape after wobbling around in a walking cast for four months. A nasty jolt went up the still-healing muscles of that leg. But I wasn't worrying about bones and flesh just then. That truck and I had gone a lot of lonely miles together, and this time, I could not afford to fix it. I was, as was not unusual, a touch underemployed. I had enough money squirreled away to pay my rent and feed myself for about four more months, but another round of automotive repairs would sink me. I closed my eyes, threw back my head, and whispered, "Why me?"

The cold air kissed my face. Not getting an answer and not expecting one, I heaved a deep sigh, turned my back on the truck, and trudged the rest of the way up the hill to Faye's house. As my leg now felt like I'd been hitting it with sledgehammers, I took the shortest route, which cut straight through a few acres of other people's landscaping. The most recent snow had melted sufficiently so I left no obvious footprints, I awoke only one dog, and I had to climb only one fence, so by the time I got to Faye's, I felt once again almost in control of my destiny.

I found my way to Faye's back door and knocked loudly. Abruptly, the light that had been burning in the bedroom wing winked out. I knocked again. Nothing.

Perhaps half a minute later, I became aware that a volume of space beyond the window to my right had grown slightly paler.

"It's just me, Tom," I announced to the ghostly accumulation of molecules. "I came in the back way because I had to walk the last four blocks. My truck bit the big one again. Let me in, okay?"

The door swung open to a dark kitchen. "How'd you know I was here?" Tom asked, still not showing himself, his voice low.

I stepped inside. There was just enough illumination cast by the galaxy of light-emitting diodes on the electronically controlled coffeemaker, the microwave oven, and all the other labor-saving wutzitses and widgets that decked the room that I could discern his face if I looked out of the corners of my eyes. He was not smiling.

"You always dodge to your left," I said. "So I looked to my

right. A white boy like you shouldn't try to skulk in modern kitchens, or you should at least put on more than just a pair of blue jeans. You glow like a beluga whale basking under a full moon."

"Spent a lot of time watching whales on that ranch of yours?" he asked dryly.

"How I do wish it was mine. Right now, I'd sell it and buy myself a new truck."

Tom was still not smiling. "Somehow, I don't see you doing either."

I said, "It suits my personality to keep duking it out with that same old heap of rust. But hey, we've had an earthquake. Now maybe there'll be a little extra work for this girl geologist."

"Girl detective," he replied.

Like I said, Tom was trying to marry my skills as a geologist to my raw talent for forensic work. Part of our agreement was that I didn't have to take any crap from him. I popped him in the gut with a loosely balled fist and was surprised to discover how firm it was. He smelled of sex. "Go take a shower," I muttered.

He chuckled under his breath and padded off toward the bedroom. While he bathed, I sat on the edge of Faye's bed, trying to discover what had moved her to demand my presence. She lay in bed facedown, with a pillow over her head, refusing to explain herself.

"Come on, Faye," I said. "I sacrificed a perfectly good twenty-year-old pickup truck getting here. Now tell me what's got you playing ostrich or I'm leaving."

"Take my car," she groaned. "My keys are on the table by the door into the garage."

"Your four-by-four? Didn't you say that the clutch on that 'miserable bucket of bolts' is slipping like it's on banana peels? I don't mean to be picky; it's at least fifteen years younger than my truck, and the leather seats are oh so cushy, but I just got my leg out of a cast, and—"

"I meant the Porsche. The clutch is stiff, but you won't have to ride it."

"I can't take your Porsche. What will you drive?"

"The four-by is going into the shop on Wednesday," she muttered. "I won't need it before then. If I live."

"You sick, huh?"

She didn't say anything for a while, then, "Yeah."

"Stomach flu?"

Pause. "Yeah."

"Oh. So I guess you don't want me to get you anything. Cup of ginger tea?"

"Nooooo . . ."

"But really, I can't take your car."

"Take it, please. I. Am. Going. Nowhere!"

"No, really, Faye. There's open season on cowgirls driving sports cars. Someone would take a shotgun and—"

"Then we'll both be out of our miseries."

Now, that sounded a little bit nasty. Not like Faye at all. I yanked the pillow off her head. "Hey, what's going on?"

She cringed.

I was just about to say something else when Tom came out of the bathroom, buttoning his shirt. He gave me a stern look and flagged me toward the door that led out into the hall. "Come," he said. "She wants to be alone."

I opened my mouth to protest, but Tom drew me out the door by my arm. I followed along, figuring I'd wait until Tom went to work, then try again. *Maybe they had a spat, and she's just waiting for privacy.* Faye and Tom were the odd couple, he being over twenty years her senior and obliged to work for a living, but otherwise, they were both intellectuals, and as such, they got along like a couple of . . . well, intellectuals. They did their fighting abstractly, and in private.

Tom dragged me back down the hall into the kitchen, turned on the lights, and began to rustle up some breakfast. He set to making the coffee, which he ruined by adding milk, and sicced me on the eggs. Sneering as he pulled the carton out of the pristinely clean refrigerator (oh, to be able to afford Faye's housekeeper), I said, "Where's the bacon?"

"Let's not fill the house with the smell of frying meat, okay?" He tipped his head toward the bedroom and did his impression of a vomiting gecko.

"Mm. Forgot."

When we had our breakfast ready, we settled at the kitchen table. Tom switched on the television on the counter to get the early-morning news coverage of the earthquake. The top of the news was the scene outside the emergency room at the hospital half a mile from my house, where anguished relatives were gathering to await news on an infant boy named Tommy Ottmeier, who had been badly injured when a heavily laden bookcase fell on him during the quake. Tom whipped his hand out and had the channel changed in a blink. "I just can't stand this kind of thing," he muttered, looking anywhere but at me.

The fragile moon-shaped face of the Utah state geologist now filled the television screen, floodlights glinting off her glasses, her elegantly cut graying hair glowing in the lights like frost. She stood hunched up against the cold in front of the massive concrete rampart of what looked like the outside of the new sports arena. "The good news is that the quake was as small as it was," she was saying.

The TV camera shifted briefly to a studly young reporter who was soberly nodding his head as if agreeing with her on every point. "What we're all wondering is, Dr. Smeeth, is it safe to go back into our homes?" he asked importantly. "Aren't aftershocks likely?"

The camera shifted back to Dr. Smeeth. Her hands danced, proving that, like every other geologist, she was incapable of speaking with her mouth only. "It's always important to remember that it's not earthquakes that kill people, it's collapsing structures that kill people. As I was saying, the good news is that the quake was no larger than it was, but we don't know yet if this morning's shaking was a foreshock or the main event. We simply don't have enough records from previous seismic events in this area. In the meantime, Caleb, we need to mobilize our crews to inspect buildings that may have been damaged. Much of Salt Lake City is built on soft sediments, which tend to liquefy when shaken, intensifying the destructive force of any quake."

The reporter's voice cut back in. "You asked us to meet you here at the new sports arena. It's built to the latest standards. Do you really anticipate any problems here?"

Dr. Smeeth said, "Caleb, I am concerned. The fault zone responsible for this morning's earthquake runs right underneath the city, and because most of it is buried, we don't even know the exact locations of many of its branches. You see, it's not just one line on the map. Part of it may run right underneath our feet, and when it comes to buildings, the best and the latest can also mean the least tested. So it is crucial to make certain that the ground accelerations involved have not caused critical damage to any of our public or private structures. And we should start with this building here."

The state geologist drew herself up as if girding for a street brawl. "I chose this stadium because in just a few short weeks, Salt Lake City will host the Olympic games. Every hotel and every city service will be filled to capacity, and, as I've been telling the governor—"

The view suddenly cut to a reporter at another location. He looked surprised. Caught unprepared, he fumbled with his microphone. He fingered the wire that led into his ear, his eyes wide with astonishment, as if he were receiving advice from a miniature oracle. "Ah . . . thank you for that report, ah . . . Caleb. Now . . . I'm here with Fred Bower at Temple Square. Fred, what's the condition of these famous structures?"

Fred Bower popped his eyes at the camera, giving the impression that he had a thyroid problem. He smiled unctuously. "Good. Heavenly Father is merciful. Everything is fine. Nothing amiss. Salt Lake City is ready for the Olympic Games!"

Tom switched off the TV. "Nothing worse than trying to invent something to say," he observed.

"Sounded like the state geologist had plenty to say. Wonder why they cut her off?"

Tom shot me a look. "Getting paranoid, little Emily?"

I narrowed my eyes witheringly. "I know, I know. 'Some days, a cigar is just a—' "

I was interrupted by the distant sounds of Faye once again emptying her already-empty stomach.

"When'd this vomiting start?" I asked.

Tom peered into his coffee like he'd seen something swimming in it. "Oh, she threw up yesterday morning, but she seemed okay last evening. Except that she about chewed my head off." He winced at the memory.

"Why?"

He arched one grizzled eyebrow, making its first few long, twisty hairs dance. "For nothing at all."

"Nothing, Tom? You?"

He took a long draw on his coffee, savoring it, then slowly let it slide down his throat. A mischievous smile flickered at the corners of his lips. "All I did was pat her on her stomach and observe that it looked pleasantly Rubenesque. It was a compliment."

"Are you tired of living?"

Tom knit his brows in a burlesque of defensiveness. "Faye is a lovely, slender woman, and very sure of herself. I was just noticing that she had gained a pound or two, and affectionately suggesting that it suited her. Since when does the Faye Carter we know and love involve herself in such cultural norms as worrying about her figure?"

He was right. At five-ten and a scant, lithe 142 pounds, Faye was sleek as a racehorse. A thoroughbred. A purebred. Muscular and elegant. If she'd had fur, it would have shone like satin. "Nice going, Tom. She may look anorexic to you, but remember that this culture teaches us fool women that Barbie dolls are the ne plus ultra. It's subliminal. We've been brainwashed. We can't help ourselves."

He shrugged. "The Barbie doll is a distortion of everything I love about the feminine sex. Worse yet, the form was adapted from a doll given out by post-World War II German street-walkers to their marks. What self-respecting student of history would want to look like that? Give me the Venus of Willendorf any day. *There's* a woman built to last a hard winter. Or June Cleaver; now, she had hips. To hell with you gen-Xers and your imitations of prepubescent waifs. I want a woman with a little adipose tissue. Nice mama-san with T and A."

Mama-san? Suddenly, things began to come together. I had just raised my coffee cup to my lips, but set it down again with a thud. I opened my mouth to speak, but shut it without uttering a sound.

"What?" Tom demanded.

I had to think fast and cover my reaction. "I—I just remembered what I forgot."

"What?"

"I think I left my door unlocked," I said evasively. "On the truck."

Tom's shoulders relaxed, and only then did I realize the extreme tension with which he had been holding them. "You afraid someone's going to steal that broken-down wreck? In this neighborhood? More likely, they'll ticket you for besmirching their *feng shui*. Eat your eggs."

"Right." I shoveled into them, quickly emptying my plate. "I'll clean up," I said. "You run along down to your office."

"The maid comes in today. I'll see you to the door."

"Maybe she won't come. There's been an earthquake. Remember?"

Tom pointed toward the door to the garage. "March."

My mouth sagged open. I knew now what was really bugging Faye, and I had no doubt that she wanted Tom to leave for work before she would discuss it. She had merely taken advantage of an event that no doubt had awakened me to get me here as early as possible.

I stared at Tom, measuring his resolve. A card-carrying workaholic, he was frequently off to his office by six, and he returned home only after what he termed his "half days—you know, twelve hours." Not a man to love if you needed a lot of companionship. But on this morning, he was sticking to her like glue, or should I say, sticking to me. "Come on, Em, the garage is this way. You take her car, like she said." He tossed me a set of keys off the hall table. "You go on home. Go back to bed. It's not even light out yet. Wait until the birdies start chirping."

I said something like "Yup, okay," and followed him out into the spacious garage, which still smelled of newly laid concrete. It was big enough to play touch football in. Not for the first time, I vowed that in my next life, I, too, would be a trust-fund baby.

Tom hit the lighted switch that triggered the door behind Faye's Porsche and walked out onto the driveway to his own car, a ten-year-old American-built sedan with a bashed front fender. I dithered around with the Porsche, pretending that I didn't know how to get it started, but even this last stall didn't work. Tom leaned patiently against his car, waiting for me to leave. He had even picked up his cell phone and was making a call, talking into the darkness.

I backed the Porsche out next to him and waited, pretending that I was fiddling with the CD player. He finished his call, came over to my side of the sports car, and tapped at the glass. I lowered the window. He bent down and leaned in, bracing his hands on his knees. "What?" he demanded.

"I'm . . . just worried about her."

Tom kissed the end of my nose. "Get out of here," he said softly. "Scram. Faye will be fine. Just needs some sleep." But as he straightened up, he folded his arms and just stood there, watching me, willing me to leave.

I backed the car out of the driveway, but as I pulled away into the street, I glanced into the rearview mirror. He was still standing there, watching me. He looked gruff, but reassuringly solid in the bright light cast from the garage. I hit the remote control to close the garage door, dropping him gently into the deep ultramarine blue that presaged the coming dawn, and wondered if he, a detective of such repute, could miss the symptoms that Faye was displaying. Or did he interpret the signs exactly as I did, and feel an overwhelming need to stand guard over the tiny new life she carried inside her womb?

I heard about a man from Kodiak, Alaska. He saw the ocean pull out miles from the shore. The slope was terribly steep there. He knew what was coming. He ran downhill to get his family, who were down near the water, then ran back uphill with them. [The tsunami came and] the water came up and up and stopped just short of them. He'd run so hard that he had ruptured blood vessels in his lungs.

The official death toll was much lower than the actual, because there were many transients living in hovels by the waterfront.

—Carol Benfell, journalist, recounting events associated with the tsunami that was generated by the magnitude 8.6 "Good Friday" Alaskan earthquake of March 27, 1964

WENDY FORTESCUE CLUTCHED THE MOUSE ON HER COMPUTER much more tightly than usual. From outward appearances, the four-foot-eleven-inch-tall blonde looked her everyday abstracted self, the temple pieces on her glasses askew and her third cup of coffee chilling on the desk beside her. She sat staring into the big, goggling, glass eye of her computer monitor, surveying a long, squiggly line. Across the room, an array of seismograph needles tickled out their giddy record of movement within the Earth on slowly revolving drums. The seismographs were hitched to the data-storage cold room to her right, and to the computer in front of her, and together, the extraordinary cluster of machinery was tallying the few paltry aftershocks of the morning's quake as they arrived, plotting them in time and space. *There . . . that's another one, so small we didn't even feel it.* She shifted in her chair, irritated. Being shaken awake had been fun, and plotting that first big set of shock waves had been exciting, but now things were disturbingly quiet. *C'mon . . . gimme some more here. Gimme enough to plot the fault plane at least!*

Wendy's array lurked deep in an inside room in the engineering building on the campus of the University of Utah. Most days, she was alone in her domain, which suited her fine; her close friends had nicknamed her "the gnome" clear back in high school. Why disappoint anyone by suddenly becoming a social butterfly? *That would shake people up as much as . . . as this morning's quake.* Wendy shook her head at the screen, ignoring the raft of reporters who stood watching her. As a seismology technician, she had known a quake could occur at any time along the Wasatch fault; in fact, she found it more surprising that the human settlement had existed this long in Salt Lake City before experiencing a "big one." *A 5.2 is chump change,* she mused. *A couple chimneys down, grandma's Delft figurines bite the floor. But this fault can deliver a 7.0 or larger, almost 1,000 times the jolt.* She thought it appalling that the news sharks who now circled her could be so blasé about the threat. Hadn't any of them been here in 1983, when a 7.1 cracked off in southern Idaho? *Well, okay, I wasn't here myself; I was just in high school back in Santa Barbara, but hell, everybody knows about the Idaho quake. . . .*

A giddy vibration ran through the room, and Wendy heard several of the journalists suck in their breath. "Another earthquake!" someone said, and the hubbub of voices started anew, swapping speculations on how big that one was.

Three point five, Wendy wanted to say, but she kept her mouth shut. She had long since learned not to say anything she didn't want repeated, out of its proper context, in some damned newspaper. *What do they expect? We're sitting practically right on top of the damned thing.*

A big man with one bushy black eyebrow that framed both eyes strode into the room. "That was an aftershock," he informed the reporters, keeping his voice level. "To those of you who have just arrived, I'm Hugh Buttons, director of the Seismic Center. As I explained earlier, aftershocks are to be expected. It's just Mother Earth's way of releasing the stress. We'll be triangulating responses from several stations to plot the precise locations of these shocks. With any luck at all, this will give us a much-needed picture of the fault trace. Three or more points, or in this case earthquake hypocenters, describe a plane. As you know, the Wasatch fault divides into an array of fractures under Salt Lake City, but until this morning, none of these had produced an earthquake that we can definitively ascribe to the Wasatch fault." He pointed to a map on the wall. "Most people don't realize that the majority of earthquakes do not cause ground rupture—our name for a crack at the surface. As you can see, we've had to infer the precise locations of several of the branches of the fault. This is because they are covered with regolith." He smiled, which produced an eerie, toothy effect on his craggy face. "That's soil to you. Surface cover. Although surface cover includes houses, what we call the 'built environment.' The really large earthquakes that have occurred on the Wasatch fault—those measuring six point five or seven—all of them struck long before Salt Lake City was built. Before white people came to the area. There was presumably nothing here then to fall down. Nothing *built*, you see."

One of the reporters asked a question. "How big an earthquake before we'd see a crack in the ground?"

Dr. Buttons smiled. "That would take one of the big ones. They don't leave cracks, exactly. They leave a 'scarp,' a small cliff, perhaps three to ten feet high, where the valley drops down and the mountains stay high. Another term is *surface rupture*. With

an earthquake of this size—just five point two in magnitude—
the actual rupture and movement do not propagate to the surface.
The area of rupture in moderate-size quakes is relatively small,
and quite deep. Several miles, perhaps ten. The Earth is fairly
elastic, you see."

Wendy shifted again in her seat. Hugh Buttons was her boss.
His name had won him highly predictable nicknames, and the
fact that he was six foot-four-inches tall made them stick. *Huge
Buttons*, Wendy mused, noticing that once again the man had
dressed entirely in clothing that had not one such fastener, not
even a zipper or a snap. *Poor sot. The same assholes call me "Tinker
Bell."*

As Dr. Buttons droned on for the press, the phone next to
Wendy's computer monitor warbled. Automatically, she plucked
it up, positioned it by her ear, and nipped her shoulder in to pin
it in place. "Seismograph Station," she said into it, pitching her
voice into a throaty tenor from the long habit of making herself
sound bigger and more authoritative than she looked.

"Wendy?" The voice was familiar: Ted Wimler, down at the
state Geological Survey. He sounded breathless, as if his asthma
was acting up.

"Speaking," she replied in a voice cool enough to freeze ether.
What was Ted calling about? Looking for juicy tidbits about the
aftershocks? Couldn't the *putz* wait like everybody else for her
to analyze the results and pass them upstairs for the official an-
nouncement? *Male gossips,* she thought disparagingly. *Worst kind.
Gotta have the most about the latest, and the grislier the better.*

"Wendy, are you sitting down?"

Wendy contracted her eyebrows toward her nose, as if something stank. On an ordinary day Ted's tone was melodramatic,
but this time, it was cracking, even shaky. The guy was going
to have to get a life. "Spill it, Ted. I'm busy."

" 'Spill it'? My God, Wendy, it's Dr. Smeeth. She's—"

"Who?" Wendy asked, knowing exactly whom Ted meant.

Sidney Smeeth, state geologist. And, incidentally, her landlady. She glanced at her boss. He was just finishing up with the reporters, now managing to extract himself from the room with the suggestion that he'd be back in half an hour with another report. She gazed at the center drum, checking the latest aftershock. Sure enough, it had again registered the broadest needle sweep of the group. *Same cluster. Ride 'em cowboy.*

In her ear, Ted's voice said, "She's dead, Wendy! Christ, she's the state geologist and we've just had an earthquake! And I mean, you live in her basement! What are we suppose to do? One moment your life is going along normally, you're maybe getting a good night's sleep for a change, you're——"

Wendy shifted her crosshairs and clicked the mouse. She didn't have time for Ted's hallucinations today. On the best of days, she greeted Ted's idiocy with the same affection she would afford the discovery that ointment prescribed for an embarrassing rash was sticky and stank conspicuously.

"State the circumstances," she said abruptly.

"Christ, Wendy, you're like a . . . a navy colonel or something." He repeated her command in a high-pitched, nasal, kindergarten-sassy kind of voice: " 'State the circumstances! State the circumstances!' "

Wendy sighed heavily. So she'd had a little dalliance with him on the AWG raft trip the summer before; did that mean she had to tolerate every little perturbation and fantasy that flitted through his beleaguered skull? Or was he suffering the postquake shockiness that was so often reported? Now, that would be interesting. . . . "For your information, Ted, the navy has commanders. Colonels are with the army or the air force." A moment later, realizing that the obnoxious voice of her one-night paramour was still yammering in her ear, Wendy said, "Ted, get yourself a cup of coffee and go smell it or something. I've got a seismic event going on here, so, like the man said, unless you've got good news or money, get off the line."

Ted's voice rose to an hysteric screech. "Good news? *Good news?* She's *dead,* Wendy, not late for a meeting!"

Mother Smeeth isn't there holding your little hanny, so you lose that itty-bitty marble you call a brain, Wendy thought angrily as she trailed the phone back to its cradle and dropped it with a *thunk. Overdosed on Aspartame at long last,* she decided, settling her mouse-driven crosshairs onto the beginning of the P-wave portion of the newest wiggly line that she had conjured on her computer screen.

Almost instantaneously, the phone rang again. Swearing under her breath, she plucked it back up into position next to her ear, ready to hang up if it was Ted. "Seismograph Station," she barked.

The voice she heard this time was Hugh Button's. "Wendy," he said, his voice gruff with emotion. "I got some bad news. Sid Smeeth was just found dead."

"Yow," she whispered. Wendy's brain rocketed through a series of tight calculations of how this might affect her immediate future, not to mention the closely knit world of professional interaction in which she moved. "Give me a mo'," she said, then rose from her chair and turned to the journalists who stood all around her. She heard a cell phone warble. "That would be your editor calling," she said tonelessly. "I have to clear the room a moment, okay? You take that call out there in the outer room, and take everyone with you. I'll get back to you." She stood up and waved her arms, hurrying them through the door.

Eager but a bit confused, the journalists shuffled through into the outer office, craning their necks to listen in on the conversation their colleague was now having through his cell phone. Another phone rang, and another. Wendy closed the door behind them and returned to her desk. She found that her hand was trembling as she raised the telephone back to her ear.

4

"HOW FAR ALONG ARE YOU?" I ASKED AS I TURNED THE TELE-
vision off again. I had gone back to my apartment and taken a
bath, changed into something a little more organized, and circled
back up to Faye's house. She had greeted me without words and
led me back to the kitchen, where she had taken up a position
in front of the incoming news. She preferred CNN, but they had
passed the morning's event off in sixty seconds at the top of the
hour and were now giving chapter and verse about a prayer
meeting the president had presumed to intermix with international
politics. The local network affiliates were zeroing in on the sobbing relatives of the baby boy who had been injured at the time
of the earthquake—a bookcase holding stone carvings had fallen
on him while he was in his crib.—Faye had watched the ghoulish
close-ups of the unfortunate parents in silence; biting her nails,
tears streaming down her face like rain. It seemed that the trials of
parenthood had taken on greater meaning for her in light of her
recent events.

Faye cradled her head in her arms. "Five weeks."

"So you just found out."

"This morning," she sniffled. "Mere seconds before that
damned earthquake hit."

"You took the test at four A.M.?"

She nodded. "You know, first pee of the morning. Supposed

to make it register more accurately. I'm in there with a flashlight so I won't wake Tom up, staring at the watch, timing the thing. Pee on the stick. Ten minutes, I'm supposed to give it. I'm staring at the watch because I don't want to set the timer and wake Tom. The little LCD is blinking away the minutes, the seconds. Finally—blink—it's four-fourteen. Don't make a noise, I tell myself. Just look at the stick and take it like a grown-up. Don't wake Tom. I take a deep breath, lift up the damned stick, and the whole room starts jumping around on me. Don't wake Tom, *hah!*"

Wow, I thought. *What are the chances of that happening?* "So it kind of shook you up," I ventured.

Faye lifted her head just far enough to give me a dirty look.

"Sorry," I said softly. "Just trying to lighten the mood."

Faye dropped her head back into her arms and began to wail. Let me tell you, it's tough watching your big stoic buddy lose it like that, upset hormones or no. The linen place mat she had her face on was dark with tears. I put out a hand and touched her back, which was heaving with the effort of working her feelings to the surface.

"Sorry," I said again.

"Oh, it's okay," she whimpered. "I—I've always wanted to have kids. I'd begun to wonder if it was going to happen, because I'm such a washout in the marriage department. Now here I am!"

"A washout? What you talking about?"

"High school: Johnnie Edmonds asked me to marry him. I said no. College: Frank Leibowitz and Terry Perry. I said no. Graduate school—"

"Terry Perry? Of course you couldn't marry anyone named Terry Perry. I mean—wait, you've turned down three men and you feel like a washout?"

"Six."

"Six? Darling sweetheart, that's not a washout; that's a flood!"

Faye started bawling anew.

"No! Wait! I said that all wrong! I mean, there's nothing wrong with you; it must be them. I mean, you had good reasons for turning down each one of them, right?"

Faye lifted up one gimlet eye. "I suppose."

"Give me one."

"Well, first I was too young. And then, well, Terry had a little thing about alcohol, and—"

"See? Gotta kiss a lot of frogs before one of 'em turns out to be a prince."

Faye's eyes glazed again. Suddenly, she jumped up and ran for the bathroom, where the now-familiar sounds of Faye Carter tossing her cookies reverberated off the splendid tile job.

"Does Tom know?" I asked as I arranged myself against the doorjamb.

Faye was bent over the toilet. She shook her head dejectedly.

"Let me rephrase that," I said. "Have you told him? Because, trust me, he knows."

A look of panic crossed her face.

"Hey," I said. "Tom's okay. He's not going to run out on you just because—"

"No! You don't understand! If he knows, then that means I no longer have a choice."

"Wait a minute. A choice? I thought you just said—"

"Of course I want this baby!" Faye squealed, her voice tightening up like someone was squeezing her throat. "It's just that— just that—"

"You want it to be you who's deciding, not Tom. And not an accident."

Faye rolled over onto the bath mat and stared at the ceiling, her lips swollen from crying. Tears continued to stream out of the corners of her eyes, descending now towards her ears. "Nooo. It's just that he'd want it sooo badly, and I don't know . . . he's— he's not around a whole lot, you know?"

"Maybe he'd change."

"I make a lousy codependent, Em. I don't suffer the delusion that men can change. And I'm too used to having my own way to even give one the chance to try."

I heard the phone ringing. "Want me to get that?"

"Sure. That'll be him," she said, her voice hollow with fatalism. "Checking on me."

As I rose to find the telephone, I said, "Hey, count your blessings. At least he calls. It's been six hours now since the quake and I haven't heard from Ray yet."

"You've checked your messages?"

"Four times."

"You've called him?"

"No. Fact is, I don't know how to reach him. He went down to Saint George for the weekend with his mother. Just a mo—" I picked up the telephone next to her bed. "Hello?"

There was silence at the other end of the line.

I repeated my salutation, automatically beginning to count the number of times I'd said it so that at three I could feel polite about hanging up, but before I got it out the third time, I heard an exasperated sigh, and then: "I did dial Faye's, right?"

"Yes, Tom, you did."

With heavy annoyance, he said, "Well, it was you I wanted to speak with anyway."

I was taken aback, naturally. "So why are you all pissed off that's you've found me?"

Another pause, then: "Okay, sorry. Can you come down to my office? Meet me in about a half hour?"

"Well, sure. Why?"

"Tell you when you get here." He clicked off without saying good-bye.

I stared stupidly at the phone for a moment.

"Who was it?" Faye asked.

I explained. Faye frowned.

I said, "Well, you didn't like it any better when he hovered."

Faye flopped onto her back on the bed and groaned. "This means he has a new case. He always gets grouchy when he has a new case."

"And he wants me on it?"

"Oh, get off it, Em. The man's been training you for months now. He isn't doing that out of sheer altruism. He's getting older. He's slipping. He needs a fresh new mind to keep him going."

"Now, that sounds just terrific," I said huffily. "I get to be an extension of the great man's eyes and ears. And what's this now? You assigning him to the Alzheimer's ward?"

Faye was staring at the ceiling, her hands folded on her belly, beginning to relax for the first time that morning. "No, but, well . . . he's old enough to be this baby's grandfather! You misunderstand. Tom goes so far into his work that he really doesn't see a big line of demarcation between himself and the rest of the universe. You're an extension of him, yes, but more as a peer than a tool. If he thought you stupid, he couldn't get that Zen about it."

"I think I followed that," I muttered.

"Okay, to hell with it. You were telling me where Ray is, and why the self-righteous SOB hasn't called you."

I dumped myself into the lounge chair that sat ten feet away from Faye's king-sized Arts and Crafts bedstead. "He's been in Saint George with his mother. Family business."

"Which is?"

I thought about it. "I have no idea."

"Really knitting you into that family, ain't they?"

I started to say something defensive—like, Okay, so you're in a big bad mood because you're knocked up, so don't take it out on my sorry love life—but something stopped me. Something that felt like it was surfacing in my consciousness, something I wished would dive back to the bottom and stay there. "You're right," I said. "In the past two months, they've all but closed me out entirely."

"Used to invite you to Family Home Evening, Sunday dinner, all the rest."

"Now I'm lucky to get a glass of lemonade when I stop by to say hi."

After awhile, almost to herself, she said, "I was wondering why he was taking vacation time to go somewhere with her, rather than with you." That's what I like about Faye. She's not just up there looking down; she's down there taking the long walk with me.

"Family business," I said again, so quickly that even I heard the defensiveness in my voice. "He's due home tonight," I added, trying to make it sound like a solution rather than a miscellaneous fact.

"Good."

"He's the man of the family and has been since his dad died, so that's his job, I guess. But I thought he could have asked me to go with them."

Faye turned her head my way, her eyes soft with sympathy. "And you're wondering why he didn't tell you what that business was."

"Yeah."

"Screw him."

I forced a smile. "Nah, I could wind up like you!"

She sat up and threw a pillow at me. I jumped up and heaved it back. She threw me a second one and we fell into a fit of nervous giggles. As they subsided, she turned her head my way again. This time, it was she who was defensive as she asked, "So, what did Tom want?"

"He told me to get my butt down to his office."

Faye gazed fixedly at me, her eyes dark and thoughtful. "Fine, but this time, you keep that butt of yours covered."

5

I believe that there is more danger to be apprehended from the concealment of facts, or the tacit silence of the public press on this topic, than in free and open discussion of the subject and speculation for the future.

—*Bret Harte, 1866; from a newspaper editorial on the subject of public policy response to earthquakes, including the San Francisco temblor of October 8, 1865*

FRANCIS W. MALONE SAT ON THE TAILGATE OF HIS GLOSSY new Ford pickup truck, watching the men in the trench work. He unscrewed the cap of his stainless-steel thermos and poured himself a cupful of his special blend of coffee. He had had the beans shipped straight from Jamaica, and he kept them in the freezer so they'd stay fresh. He knew to thaw just the right amount of beans overnight before grinding them, so that the flavor could reach its full bouquet, and he doused the grounds in a drip brewing system, using only unbleached filters. Life was nicer that way.

He was in no hurry for the men in the trench to complete the job of setting the big steel shores that would keep it open while he got down inside and took a look at the condition of the sediments through which the trench had been excavated. It was cold, and would be colder still down in that dank, cramped space, and even uglier than this beaten-up patch of earth on which these fools planned to construct a new shopping center. Urban renewal, they called it: You could throw a rock and hit downtown Salt Lake. He called it urban removal: Just scrape away the old crap and build new crap.

He unkinked his shoulders and took a sip of his coffee. Up here on his pickup truck, the sun was shining, and he needed this moment of respite to recover from the experience of the earthquake that had so rudely awakened him that morning. Hell, his colleagues seemed to have loved getting knocked awake ahead of the alarm like that, but he had suffered a slight nausea and had been more than a little bit pissed to find that his wine rack had collapsed and dumped two bottles of good California chardonnay onto the quarry-tile floor of his kitchen. The bottles had shattered into a thousand pieces, and not only were their contents lost, but he'd had a nasty job to clean up, as the maid had just been there and wouldn't be back for a week.

Francis W. Malone was, however, prepared to be philosophical. An earthquake was cash on the barrelhead for him as a consulting engineering geologist. He could not ask for a better demonstration of the Earth's disregard for the constructs of human civilization and the resultant need for his services. A nice 5.2 to snap some fear into people, but not the mess that a 6.5 or a 7 would cause. Then, all work would stop for weeks or months as everybody tried to dig the bodies out of the rubble. Of course, there might be even more work for him after that, but it would, in fact, be too much work, and would draw in heavyweight competition from out of state. No, a 5.2 was perfect, just his cup of java.

There was a commotion in the trench, which gaped twenty feet away from where he had parked the truck. He heard hollering in Spanish, a bunch of ripe epithets no doubt, and—whoa, boy—someone was jumping up the ladder out of the ditch in one big hurry. Hell, what was this, a collapse? Shit, okay, nobody hurt. One of the hydraulically operated shores had just let go as they were trying to lock it in, that was all. Scared them. The man was standing up on the edge of the trench now, visibly shaking as he knocked the mucky soil from his brown hands, his ill-fitting hard hat jiggling on his head.

The trench was ten feet deep, plenty deep enough to kill a man if the walls collapsed. Everyone on the site knew that a man had to be buried only up to the diaphragm to suffocate before the dirt could be moved off of him; that was why OSHA required these shores to keep the walls apart. The crossbracing also provided handy supports for the boards on which Malone could stand while he examined the upper portions of the walls.

The site foreman hustled up to him. "Malone," he said, "damned stuff's pretty unstable."

"That's what the shores are for," Malone answered.

"Yeah, well. You gonna feel safe going down in there after we get them set? I mean, I've set plenty of shores before, but this is dicey. We're down below the frost level there, and the ground's really wet. Falling into a slurry. You gonna be able to see what you need to see, even?"

Malone nodded. "You just keep Jaime and Juan at it, okay?"

The foreman's face clouded with anger. "That's not their names."

"Sorry," Malone said, his heavy-lidded eyes telegraphing his apathy. *Guys are making a mint here next to what they get back home in Mexico*, he mused. *What's a little risk?* "Whatever their names are, just make sure they do it right, okay?"

Malone's cell phone burbled at him. He pulled it out of his pocket, told the foreman, "Catch ya in a minute," and said into the phone, "Hello?"

"Mr. Malone? This is Maria Teller in the governor's office."

"Hey, Maria! You can call me Frank." He grinned into the phone. Maria had nice stems. She was short, but that meant she wore those nice high-heeled jobs, little stilettos, gave her that kind of *mm-hm* look, even though she was all upholstered up in a little drab suit because she was playing at being the director of Natural Resources for the state of Utah.

"Frank. Look, what's the verdict out there? As you can imagine, things are getting even hotter up here now with this morning's earthquake. What are you finding?"

You see? he told himself. *One little tremor and they're running for their cell phones to call their geologist. Time to make hay. The green kind that folds up and fits right into the old wallet.* "I'll know more in just a few minutes, Maria. I have the men down in the trench setting the shores. OSHA regulations. Very dangerous. Just as soon as I know, I'll let you know."

"Well, now really, Frank, you give this one to me straight. I want it by the book. The governor's really concerned."

I'll bet the big honcho probably slept right through it and hasn't even bothered to come in yet, Malone thought, but he said, "Of course, of course. I hear you loud and clear. Get back to you soonest."

"And Frank, you know what's riding on this, need I say."

Yeah. Sure. I say something you don't like and I'm not your consultant anymore. Malone let out a grunting laugh. Clients were all alike. They had to make nice in public and look very serious about geologic hazards, but when push came to shove, they wanted only one thing, and that was profit. He wondered who was paying Maria, or the governor, or whether Maria was just fixing to run for higher office and angling for campaign contributions. *Maria isn't stupid. She knows I'm answering her call on a cell phone, and that anyone with a little technology and half an idea of crying foul could tape this conversation.* "I've got everything under control," he told her. "Public safety is priority one."

"Thanks." She rang off.

Five minutes later, the coffee consumed and the shores properly set, Francis W. Malone strolled over to the lip of the trench to take a look.

He could see almost nothing.

Damned if trench walls aren't a devil to read, he told himself. He sighed. The old conundrum faced him once again: how to read the history of the site from a haphazard pile of muck. He scanned the far wall of the trench for any sign of faulting, such as a steeply diagonal line with one kind of soil on one side and another on the other. *Or buried paleosols with the A horizons cattywampus. Or contorted bedding—lines that should be horizontal all humped up and around as a result of slumping or soil liquefaction.* Malone knew that these soils had developed on old lake bed sediments deposited during the last ice age, when Great Salt Lake, which now ended miles to the west, was a big mother pluvial lake that put this spot almost a thousand feet underwater, with beaches miles to the east, up in the ramparts of the Wasatch Range. The sediments here were fine sands and silts fully saturated with water, just waiting to squirt that water skyward whenever they were shaken hard, such as by earthquakes. But Malone could see nothing but smeared muck.

He put his hands on his hips and scanned up and down the trench. *Nothing.* It needed to be scraped clean with a mattock and then picked at with a knife. But that would require getting down inside and exposing himself to the risk. He walked down the hundred-foot run of the trench, around the end, and along the other side. That view was no better. He considered calling a grad student in. *Send him down there. Let him pick at that crap.*

He returned to his truck to think. Poured a second cup of coffee, wishing he'd put in more half-and-half back at the house. He saw the foreman looking his way again. What a pisser; if the bastard had the nerve to push him, he'd tell him he was contemplating the case, which he was. *Foremen have it easy,* he decided. *All they have to do is point and shout and follow someone else's plan. But geology is never cut-and-dried, never obvious.*

And here he was, working on this political hot potato of a project. It could blow up in his face if he didn't watch out. The big boys who held the purse strings would kick him off the field like a lopsided football if they needed someone to take a fall.

He walked back over to the trench and looked in again. "Get someone down in there again with a shovel," he told the foreman.

A moment later, the trembling Mexican was once again back down in the trench, his dark eyes wide with fear. The foreman handed a shovel down to him.

"Cut away that smeared soil there, okay, fella?" Malone told him. He crouched down behind the retaining position of the nearest shore and gestured with one hand, indicating the direction to carve at the wall of the trench.

The man bent to the task, gingerly cutting at the soil with the edge of the shovel. A little of it caved away, revealing much the same effect as he had started with.

The wall is just too sodden, Malone told himself. *We're not going to see anything.* Then as he noticed that his coffee was getting cold, he decided, *If there were anything dramatic, we would see it; it would be obvious. Coarse gravels here and sand there, that kind of stuff.* The foreman was watching him. *Time to put on a show.*

He returned to his truck and opened the toolbox, looking for his mattock. Couldn't find it. Fished out a Swiss army knife instead. Sauntered back to the trench, grasped the top of the ladder firmly with both hands, held his breath, and climbed down to the first set of boards, which the two Mexicans had now set in place. They were wet and slippery. The air was dank with the breath of the Earth. Malone walked along the board to a place where the sediments seemed a little coarser. Picked at it with his knife. Wished he hadn't forgotten his gloves. *Damn the cold.*

"What do you think?" called the foreman from the brink.

"I don't think. I read history," Malone answered. "The story's right down here. Just got to be able to interpret it accurately is all." *Like hell,* he told himself, now picking a little harder. *Stuff's all stirred up. Probably liquefaction. Whole area's subject to it, just like the UGS maps say. The nearest branch of the fault ends half a mile north of here. What am I doing down in this frigging hole in*

*the ground, risking my nuts for some half-witted developer? The
reason I can't see anything is that this shit's all been stirred up half
a dozen times by earthquakes. No news is no news. Liquefaction. All
go home now. Have us a beer.*

But he knew he had to justify his order to dig a test trench
before the foundation excavation was dug, so he kept on picking.
Pick, pick, pick, hands getting chapped, cuticles torn. Sniffing
with self-pity, he decided, *I'm going to have to charge them double
for this job somehow.*

Half an hour later, Malone climbed out of the trench. He drew
his cell phone out of his pocket and punched in the number for
Maria Teller's office. He knew he should call Hayes Associates
first, as they were, in fact, his client on this project, but he'd do
that next, because he knew what Hayes would want him to do
anyway. When Maria Teller's secretary had punched him through
to the woman herself, he said, "Everything's fine, Maria. We're
going to have to put the foundation on piers, sure, but that's just
a technical matter for the engineers. They can build around just
about anything."

Maria enunciated extra clearly, even though the connection was
good. "Let me get this exactly right. You're saying there's no
fault running through the foundation trenches for the Towne
Centre project?"

Malone paused, considering his wording carefully. "That's
right," he said, inwardly congratulating himself on another job
completed. "I see no fault here."

IN A SALT LAKE TRIBUNE MOTOR POOL CAR PARKED A BLOCK
down the street from the spot where Sidney Smeeth had met her
destiny, Pet Mercer sat pondering her next move. Automatically,
she fished out the small pocket mirror she carried in her case
next to her notebook computer and took a squint at herself. She
tugged at the few strands of hair that were long enough to need
combing, making no change to the arrangement she had sprayed
them into early that morning. She had worn her hair this way
since early adolescence; it fitted her face and her personality. It
was pert and easily cared for. It was, in fact, her unchanging
pertness and apparent low need of maintenance that had earned
her the nickname "Pet." Nowadays, her high school pals slapped
her on the shoulder and said, "These days, you even fetch the
newspaper!" Pet would flash a preoccupied smile. Such comments
whipped right past her. She was too busy fetching stories for that
paper to concern herself with other peoples' opinions anymore.

She turned her head left and right, checking things from every
angle. *Makeup holding, hair good. What next? A snack—keep the
blood sugar up. Almonds—good fiber, protein, fat not a problem.
About five should keep me right on plan.* She unzipped a side com-
partment of her case, withdrew five smoked almonds from a
packet, popped them into her mouth, and began to chew quickly,

mechanically. Thus arranged, she clicked open her computer and began, breathlessly, to spew out her story. She wrote, "Today in Salt Lake City, state geologist Sidney Smeeth made an extraordinary exit from the world of the living."

Shit! She hit the mouse with her thumb, highlighted the sentence, and then erased it and stared at the computer, her fingers trembling millimeters above the keys. *Pet dear, that will never do!* she warned herself. *What were you thinking? We must hit this one just right! Okay, I'll write, "In an extraordinary coincidence of events, today in Salt Lake City, just hours after the largest earthquake in written history of the location, Dr. Sidney"—or no! Too dramatic still! This has to have punch, but also dignity, not a dose of P. T. Barmum.*

The fingers of her right hand broke rank and wandered almost independently to the pouch on the other side of the case—where a few closely hoarded raisins lurked—like five busy squirrels looking for a goody. Spotting this action, her left hand rose off the keyboard and swatted the right. The right withdrew into a fist, curled up defensively on her hip, and waited . . . sulking . . . craving. . . . With an effort of will, Pet snapped back into focus, stared deep into her screen, and typed:

In an extraordinary coincidence of events, Utah's state geologist was killed today just hours after the largest earthquake recorded for the Salt Lake section of the Wasatch fault in almost half a century.

State geologist Dr. Sidney Smeeth died instantly following a fall from the deck of her hillside home. Ice had built up along the board flooring of the deck, making it slippery, sources said.

The fifty-one-year-old top administrator of the Utah Geological Survey was found shortly after sunrise. She had just appeared on Salt Lake television station KCTV—

And, having been cut off in midspeech by vested interests bent on keeping her quiet, Pet mused, *she was pissed as hell. . . .*

—and had returned home for breakfast before continuing to an appointment with gubernatorial staff at the state capitol. Dr. Smeeth served at the pleasure of Utah governor Rowdy Thomas.

In the wake of the early-morning earthquake, which measured 5.2 on the Richter scale, Dr. Smeeth faced a full day of meetings with aides to address the geologic event, which startled Salt Lakers awake at 4:14 A.M. She—

She what? Pet sat back and stared at the screen. This was not deathless prose, but she reminded herself that journalism was not meant to be that. It was meant to communicate, in the quickest way possible, and in terms that any eighth-grade graduate could comprehend, exactly what had happened.

She snorted. Exactly? That was a laugh. Yeah, exactly how had that railing come to find itself torn out, and couldn't the person or persons who had done it think of a better way to bump off a busybody like Screaming Sidney than to pull the old "slippery deck with the railing out" routine?

Pet's busy fingers drummed the air above her keyboard. *So what am I going to do?* she asked herself. *Sit on my tight little butt and write lukewarm drivel about it? Or am I going do just a little tiny bit of digging, find out who killed this woman and why, and pluck me a wee little Pulitzer this time?*

Pet slapped the notebook shut. After first extracting one celebratory raisin from the side pouch, she zipped up the case and slid it onto the seat beside her, chewing happily on the concentrated sweetness of the dried grape. "Pulitzer, here I come," she said out loud as she fired the ignition. " 'Cause this little digger knows just where to dig!"

7

February 20 [1835]. This day has been memorable in the annals of Valdavia, for the most severe earthquake experienced by the oldest inhabitant. I happened to be on shore, and was lying down in the wood to rest myself. It came on suddenly, and lasted two minutes, but the time appeared much longer. The rocking of the ground was very sensible. The undulations appeared to my companion and myself to come from due east, whilst others thought they proceeded from the southwest: this shows how difficult it sometimes is to perceive the direction of the vibrations. There was no difficulty in standing upright, but the motion made me almost giddy: it was something like the movement of a vessel in a little cross-ripple, or still more like that felt by a person skating over thin ice, which bends under the weight of the body.

> —*Charles Darwin*, The Voyage of the Beagle. *This entry, contrasted to Darwin's later descriptions of the destruction of nearby Concepción, Chile, illustrates the differences in the experience of a large earthquake in unbuilt and built environments. In Concepción, thousands of people were killed by falling structures.*

I HAD TO TAKE A DETOUR ON MY WAY DOWNTOWN TO THE FBI office. A water main had burst, necessitating a rip-up job with an oversized backhoe, blocking traffic on State Street, right next to one of the stops on the new light-rail train. The gaping hole threw a messy black eye right in the middle of all of Utah's hard work at looking downright brilliant for the coming Olympic

Games. As the backhoe swung a bucketful of dirt, it barely missed one of the fancy banners that had been hung out to greet its sports-hungry visitors. Oh, sorry, just a burst water main here. No, nothing. Little bitty earthquake put a small crack in it. We'll have it fixed up in a minute here. . . .

How embarrassing.

Aside from the burst main, surprisingly little damage requiring immediate cleanup had occurred along the rows of high-rise structures that constituted the main business district of Salt Lake City—a carved sandstone cornice was down here or there, some broken glass—but the place had sprouted vans with satellite dishes. Reporters and guys with big shoulder-mounted video cameras were dogging the emergency crews, hungry for any little chunk of fallen masonry or broken glass that would look really horrifying on the evening news back in Cincinnati, Palm Beach, or wherever, places all but ignorant of the realities of earthquakes, where citizens were hankering for a vicarious adrenaline rush. I spotted a CNN van, which meant I should add to that list such places as Oslo, Caracas, and Seoul.

Some of the emergency crews were hard at it, checking for signs of deeper structural damage. Quite a few citizens stood around in the winter air, shivering and gawking, and, this being the center of the Mormon beehive, many more scurried about, looking for some way to be involved in doing whatever was necessary to make their apiary once again secure.

I slipped in the back door that led up to Tom Latimer's third-story office and checked in through security. The guard lifted two fingers in a salute, my face and name being quite familiar to him by this time. The training Tom was giving me was strictly private, between the two of us only, but he quite frequently had me meet him here, and the staff had long since quit noticing my comings and goings as anything unusual. I bustled in past the office manager, dumped my down jacket on a hook on the coatrack, and slithered through the doorway into the room where Tom sat, phone to ear, his shoulders hunched up in his storm-cloud array.

He had his back to me, so I slipped in and sat down quiet as a mouse in hopes of hearing some of his phone call.

He was saying, "Right. I know that. Uh-huh. I'm going to do it anyway! Right. Your job is to get her in and out unnoticed. I know that. Right now."

When he turned around, his first glimpse of me brought a jerk not of surprise but of avoidance, as if he was . . . embarrassed. He dumped the phone onto its cradle and began to stare into some scene inside his head.

"Reporting," I said, giving him my best Junior Woodchuck salute.

"Got a job for you."

"Figured."

"Some geology."

"What?" I squinted at him trying to decide if it was Faye who had him off his stride, or something else, something to do with his work. As a working hypothesis, I decided it was probably both.

He chanced a bit of eye contact. "I want you to read some reports."

"What's the case about?"

Tom took a deep breath and let it out slowly. Then he said, "Information concerning this case is on a need-to-know basis. You do not need to know."

My heart sank. *So that's the way it's going to be.* I got up in preparation to leave.

"As a personal favor, then?"

"No."

Tom's eyebrows bashed into each other. "Listen, this isn't detective work I want done; it's geological analysis. I'd ask any number of other geologists I know around this city to do the work, but they're all—"

"Employed," I said, cutting him short, throwing my hands up in frustration. "They're out there looking for ground rupture, or plotting the orientations of chimneys that fell, or . . . or—" My hands fell into my lap as if the life had just gone out of them.

Now Tom looked at me directly. "Right. They're out looking for earthquake damage. I need a geologist. Can you help me?"

I could see too many of his teeth. He was getting mad. He didn't like to beg.

I closed my eyes and rubbed a hand over the lids, trying to scrub out the sight so I wouldn't feel sorry for him. "Sorry, Tom, but you've taught me too well. Your training has been all about keeping Emmy safe, and the first thing you taught me was never, never take on a job without knowing full well what I'm getting myself into. For all I know, this is just one of your tests. I do not intend to flunk."

I opened one eye. Tom was staring at the top of his desk again. He looked worried. I began to wonder if, for the first time since I had known him, the fabled Tom Latimer was in over his head. He wanted me safe, he wanted Faye safe, but, even more essentially now, he wanted his world safe for one brand-new passenger.

"Tom," I said. "Look, I'd like to help, really. I just—you know me, Tom. If you don't tell me what's going on, I'm even more likely to walk right into the middle of it and really get myself into trouble. So please, let's solve two problems at once. Tell me what's going on."

Tom turned his hands palms-up and shook his head.

Suddenly, it hit me. "Sidney Smeeth," I said. These two dots were easy to connect: death and a geologist. I had been here before. "Murder?"

Tom nodded. "Someone pitched her off the sundeck at her house."

I held up both hands. "Whoa! Wait a minute, Tom. You were teaching me not only to keep myself out of danger but to stay out of fights that don't have my name on them. This investigation is even outside *your* jurisdiction. I mean, she's a state employee, right? Not federal, and her home didn't just happen to be on a federal reservation or anything, right? So—"

Tom leaned forward onto his elbows and folded his hands tightly in front of him. "Right, but wrong. The murder is local jurisdiction, the Salt Lake City Police Department. But there's more to it than that."

"But—"

"But. But there's this little matter of the Olympics."

The Olympics. I pursed my lips into a ring that said Oh with no sound. Interlock four more and you've got the official logo. And hundreds of thousands of visitors, and hundreds of millions of dollars flowing into Salt Lake City. It was a huge thing for Utah, and for the Mormon Church: one long television infomercial showcasing the splendor of Utah tourist destinations, all with the towering spires of the Salt Lake temple forming the backdrop for the medals ceremonies.

Tom's lips tightened. "Right. Elite athletes from around the globe. Tens of thousands of athletes and press and support personnel already here, and more by the end of the month. Then the spectators start arriving. Remember Munich? Remember Atlanta?" He swallowed. "Remember New York and the Pentagon?"

I sat down heavily. Death and terror, and not from Mother Nature, but at our own hands. But how did this connect to the death of the state geologist?

Tom said, "We've been working on this for years, attending strategy meetings, setting up scenarios. Now this."

"A murder. But how—"

"I don't know how. That's why I need you."

"But why—"

Tom's eyes grew bright with his ferocious brand of anxiety. "*You* tell *me* why."

My mind raced. "No, wait, Tom. Unless you know something you're not telling me, which is a damned habit of yours, there is no connection between this death and the Olympic Games. Sure, it's weird as hell that the state geologist should be murdered immediately after an earthquake, and murder always has some kind of a reason—or unreason—for occurring, but what's the connection?"

He looked away from me. "There may be none. Probably isn't. But I just can't take the chance." He began to twist back and forth in his swivel chair.

I turned to make certain that no one in the outer office was near enough to be listening to us. Then, my voice down to a whisper, I said, "Come on, Tom. Spill it."

"Spill it?" Tom kicked his desk. Hard. "In fact, I have no excuse to go butting into a police investigation. So I'm sending in my most covert undercover agent. You. They'd never suspect someone who doesn't actually work for me, would they?"

I began to make some nasty connections. "Sure, Tom. Except the someone who's dating the cop. Hoping for a little pillow talk? I should get so lucky."

"No. My original request was legitimate. I just want you to chase down a few things that only a geologist can get for me. What I'm asking of you is this: Go to the City and County Building. Read a few files that are on public record. Read them like a geologist. Come back to me and report. Is that so risky? Hmm?"

I shrugged my shoulders. "You tell me. Sounds like you think that at least one geologist has already been killed over what those files can tell us."

"That's why I've assigned an agent to watch over you. I've taught you well, Em. Now, will you do it?"

"You're giving me the willies."

He pulled his lips back from his teeth like the Cheshire cat. The effect was sickening. "Please. Pretty please."

My stomach tightened with fear: images of the fallen towers in New York lived sharp as bullets in my mind, right next to the fresh knowledge that there are no civilians in a war with terrorists. "Okay."

Tom nodded, satisfied. "You got another pair of shoes in your truck? Those red boots of yours kind of stand out."

Bleakly I shook my head.

Tom said, "You need to blend in with the crowd is all."

"I drove Faye's car. My truck is high and dry by the side of the road up there, remember?"

"Ah. Well then, they'll have to do. And as to pillow talk, please do not tell Ray about this little field trip, okay?"

I shook my head as a new reality sank in. "No problem there. I haven't seen him in days, and when he does come home, he'll be too busy piloting his tribe through their earthquake jitters to be curious what I did with mine."

Tom's eyes softened. "Okay. Well, this is Agent Sampler. He's new here." He indicated a tall, burly man with a wide, close-mouthed smile who had just appeared in his doorway.

I turned around in my chair and acknowledged the man. He had a nice, broad chest and shoulders, but as I didn't need that kind of distraction just then, I didn't smile. "Front name or back? Or is that not your name, but your function?"

His smile didn't waver. "John Walter Sampler. You c'n call me Jack. Some earthquake, huh?"

"Okay, Agent Jack," I said as I rose from my chair. "Let's make tracks."

THE FILES IN QUESTION WERE AT THE SALT LAKE CITY PLAN-ning Department. They were design reports for a housing development, dated five years earlier. Huh? What did old development designs have to do with terrorism, or, for that matter, murder?

I looked up from the reports at Agent Jack, wondering what in hell I was supposed to get from reading them. Agent Jack gave me a smile that somehow now made him look kind of slack-jawed and stupid. He slipped a stick of chewing gum between his lips and began to chew. He had an easy way about him. As I said, he was a good-sized guy, rather stocky, with the kind of mesomorphic build that could be described as either muscular or couch potato—esque, depending on what he was wearing and how he was standing. When I had first seen him back at the FBI office, he had been wearing a pressed oxford-cloth shirt, snug blue jeans, and white leather athletic shoes, and had stood very straight, revealing his fitness. But he had exchanged the preppy look for a sagging, torn Utah Jazz sweatshirt and cheap, bedraggled homeboy footgear before leaving on our errand. I noticed that, after pulling the sweatshirt over his head, he had roughed his hair up even more, rather than smoothing it, and had begun to walk with a more rolling, shambling gait. In sum, he looked like a real spud. Which was undoubtedly the impression he wanted to make on everyone in the Planning Department's office: All the time he'd been in line, he had let his shoulders go round and his eyes go tepid, like he was just some dolt taking up space, and when he got to the counter, all outward evidence of I.Q. had slipped to double digits.

Catching me looking at him, he gave me a wink and straightened up for a moment; then something went click in his eyes, and they cooled down again as he slumped back into bubba pose, like the whole standing up straight thing had been a momentary aberrance caused by a crick in his back.

He had my complete and undivided attention, and I promised myself that if I ever found myself dealing with him again, I'd never underestimate him. "So what am I supposed to be looking for?" I asked him as he crowded in and began to peer over my shoulder.

Putting his lips close enough to my ear to look like he was trying to cop a midmorning kiss, he whispered, "You're the geol'gist, right? Look for geol'gy."

I flipped back and forth in the report he had given me. "This is a plan for a housing development," I said. "There's no geology in here. None at all. You sure you got the right file?"

Agent Jack slung an arm around my shoulder as comfortably as if we were a couple of low-rent trailer-park lovebirds. At a barely audible whisper, he said, "Keep it down. I have 'structions to keep you unner wraps. That's why this report is checked out unner my name; ol' Tom din't want you goin' up to the counner and leavin' your name, get it? Now, when you're done wit' that one, I've got another. But you be thorough, okay? Gotta take this nice 'n' easy."

Grumbling, I bent back over the task of reading, which, inside of five minutes, had my eyes glazing over. The report on Eastgate Acres had all the fizz of dry mud and half the palatability. I flipped through the rest of the report to check out the illustrations, found nothing interesting, and started reading again in the middle, and then near the end.

At the best of times, I'm a slow reader, and this stuff was pretty dry. No, let's call that arid. Parched. A real bore-o-rama. We're talking mud cracks. Moreover, I was beginning to feel the lack of sleep the night's events had brought about. That and not having any clear direction on the nature of the question I was seeking to answer had me in a bad mood, because at moments like that, I begin to feel like somebody else would have a clue where I didn't. In summary, I wanted to go eat something sugary and put off noticing how inadequate I felt. Anxiety-driven weight gain is an occupational hazard of the intuitive, spatial thinker.

I stretched and looked about. No doughnuts in sight. Gritting my teeth, I told myself, *When in doubt, invent a system.* Turning back to the front of the report, I began reading each heading and subheading in order, searching for anything to do with any subject remotely referencing geology, or soils, or building stone, or . . . you name it. When that didn't produce results, I started again and read the first sentence of each paragraph. In this way, I finally found a few lines way in the back of the voluminous report that referenced the kind of core sampling done for soils analyses, followed by a brief statement regarding the type of foundations that would be used on all structures larger than a certain size. The statement referenced work by Francis W. Malone, consulting geologist.

And that was it. Period, end of paragraph, end of topic. I flipped back and forth in the report, looking for the map that would give me the position of the development relative to the topography of the mountain front. When I found it, it looked like the development was right smack on top of a major break in slope, which is all it takes to raise a red flag with any geologist: it says, "possible fault." In fact, it looked like it was right near

Faye's house. That got me looking even harder at the map. "Whoa," I said softly. "Jack-o, check it out."

Agent Jack craned his neck to read it. Then he looked at me, his eyes sharpening as he read me for clues while his facial muscles continued to play pudding brain. "Wutzit mean?"

"Well, here's this big, long report with all this crap about this proposed development—all the nuts and bolts about lighting and sewer and paving and so on—just like they designed it around existing knowledge of everything any reasonable person would want to know about the area, geologically speaking. Brief reference to managing the soil type for foundation design. Not a breath on the subject of whether that soil might occasionally have some rather enormous shock waves running through it. Look at this change in topography. Any geologist can tell you that a steep slope means risk of landslides, and a change in slope can be a fault scarp. Movement along a fault can also *cause* a landslide, or it can mess up your foundations on the way to racking the whole house. Now, based on this morning's experience, does it sound smart or reasonable to talk about the soils engineering but not the geological picture that put that soil there, or the slope it's lying at?"

"Nice work," Agent Jack said, closing the report on his thumb to keep the place. "Now read this one." He slapped another one down, turned, and shuffled slothlike off toward the photocopying machine.

I stared at the cover of the second report. Another development, this time a shopping center, also past history. Same developer, Hayes Associates, Eagle Gate Tower, Salt Lake City. I dug straight to the back of the report but found only the same weaseling paragraph about foundations that the first one had sported. Instead of racked houses, this one brought to mind an image of panicked shoppers trying to find their ways out of collapsed department stores and parking structures. *There has to be a building code that addresses all this*, I assured myself. *A city built against a fault showing this much displacement can't get by without one.*

I straightened up and looked around the room, ready for the next report, now not the least bit interested in doughnuts. I wanted to discuss each new bit of evidence, to think out loud. Bubba Jack was still waiting in line at the photocopying machine, so I filled time studying the room, tapping my thumb on the table. I had not been to the Salt Lake City Planning Department before, or even to the City and County Building. I had driven past once or twice, marginally noticing the behemoth structure as I navigated through traffic on State Street. But on entering it today, I had been happily surprised—impressed, in fact. It was a big old sandstone job with elegant carvings. It was five or six stories tall, with a steeply sloping slate roof and an imposing central clock tower that reached another four or five stories above the rest, surmounted by a big green statue of a woman with her arm raised. "Columbia," Agent Jack had said as we strolled up the long walkway from the curb. "I hear she's fond of pumpkins."

"What's that supposed to mean?" I had asked.

Jack had not answered. Now I wondered if *he* was the pumpkin.

Inside, we had found a splendidly restored and maintained central staircase and hallways, spectacular limestone wainscoting, tiled floors, and gleaming period chandeliers. As I now studied the inside of the Planning Department's office, I noted that it was a degree less opulent, but as lovingly restored.

"Finding what you need?" a man's voice inquired.

"Oh, yes . . . ah, sure," I answered. I turned to look, ready to match a face with the voice. It was a friendly-looking fellow with a black beard. "Nice building you got here." I gestured at the high ceilings, the fresh paint on the walls.

The man smiled proudly. "Yes, it was all restored just a few years ago. Lucky, too."

"Lucky?"

"Well, the earthquake. They didn't just fix the paint and carpeting; they did a full seismic retrofit." He shook his head meditatively. "I got to admit, I thought like everyone else that the thirty-four-million-dollar price tag was a bit steep, but the building rode out this morning's shaker like it was just a little sneeze. Why, up to home we lost half the crockery, and there's cracks running all up along the plaster, but here? Nothing. A couple pencils on the floor. Nothing." He finished with a neat little gesture like he was flicking a little dust.

Everybody's got an earthquake story, I mused. "Yeah, it was something. Tell me more about the retrofit, please. I'm a geologist, so I'd love to know how it held up."

"Oh, you should get the guard to take you around sometime," he said. "They'll show you the base isolation system in the basement, and all the reinforcement in the clock tower. Of course, you can't take any pumpkins up there."

I was just opening my mouth to ask him what all this stuff about pumpkins meant when Agent Jack returned from the copy machine. As he closed the final ten feet between us, he went so deep into his Bubba Jack act that I was afraid his knuckles were going to drag on the floor. The city employee saw him coming and took a step backward. Bubba Jack gave him a toothy smile laced with a malevolent insouciance that suggested that he was ready to smack anyone who messed with his woman. The man with the beard melted away.

I said, "Nice work, Jack. I was just about to unravel the secret of the pumpkins."

"Jus' love workin' fer Tom," Jack gurgled.

"I can see why you two get along," I countered. "Between the two of you, you could act out all the different characters in *A Midsummer Night's Dream*."

Jack managed to hide his amusement in a stiff-lipped smile that made him look like a half-witted adolescent who'd just heard a great fart joke. "Next file," he said, guffawing gently.

In all, he showed me five files covering the two development projects, and not a one had even a paltry reference to what I'd call a geological appraisal. I compared the dates on the files, and the titles. There was a clear pattern to them: preliminary reports gave way to revised, and in the case of the project that had three reports, revised gave way to final. "So," I murmured, "any chance the developer has turned in any reports marked 'Report on Geologic Hazards,' or perhaps 'Environmental Impact?' "

"Oh yeah, we got the EIRs right here," Jack replied, dropping a final two reports on the table.

I went through them page by page. Lots on traffic mitigation, noise levels, utilities consumption, and the like, but not a word on the fact that there might just be a honking big fault running right through either project, ditto landslide potential, or any of a half dozen other delightful geologic hazards. And the housing development lay perilously close to the swanky neighborhood where Faye lived. I looked at the map a second time. In fact, it *was* where Faye lived. Suddenly, I wanted to know a whole lot more.

I turned to Agent Jack and put an arm around him. "Let's take a spin over to the Utah Geological Survey, Pa," I murmured. "Got a little ol' map or two there I'd like to take a squint at."

Agent Jack gave me a toothsome grin. "Sure, Ma."

9

MICAH HAYES SAT AT HIS SPACIOUS DESK ON THE TWELFTH floor of the Eagle Gate Tower in downtown Salt Lake City. From this rarified perch in the downtown Salt Lake City business district, he stared straight down on Brigham Young's Lion House. He could look across Temple Square and up the hill toward the state capitol, uniting the three campuses on which he operated.

He was waiting for a telephone call, and he did not like to wait, or, worse yet, to be kept waiting. Waiting was not a skill he greeted with equanimity, especially when seated, even after his now fifty-seven years spent sitting in church each Sunday morning and half of the evenings of the week. In fact, it was only by taking over leadership of the study sessions that he had come to tolerate them at all. This accommodation had ironically earned him a reputation for great devotion. Had he contemplated this irony (and had been a man capable of appreciating ironies), he might have found it humorous, given the pragmatic, rather than spiritual, basis for his church attendance. Apparent piety was simply one of the prices of doing business in his community.

It was important that he sit completely still. He made a practice of leaving his door open for an hour each day, so that his employees could see him sitting there, being still. Even though no one was peering in on him at this moment, he was ever vigilant, lest one of them wander past, wasting time, as usual. When he *was* seen by such minions, or by his adversaries, he had observed that his stillness mired them in the presumption that he was calm and in control, and control was everything in this business.

His business was the development of unused lands—God's investment in him—and the redevelopment of decayed properties—God's dividend. His business was exercising the power of his imagination in the pursuit of making money, and make money he did. Piles of it, mounds of it; enough money to make his fair and honest tithe to the church and still have enough left over to purchase every political tick who presumed to cling to his hide and try to suck his blood. It was pathetic how cheaply they could be persuaded. A pittance of campaign money here, a "loan" to cover a foolish little bet there. They were all the same kinds of boys and girls once things came down to particulars. They were all idiots. They were all whores.

He was waiting to hear back from one of those whores now, and being kept waiting was irritating in the extreme. But he knew he must play the foolish game with this one for a while longer. Little that he liked to admit such things to himself, Hayes needed this particular fool, and, as two years remained before he would make certain that the fool was not reelected, it was undoubtedly not the last time he would need him. He would use this fool and his magnified ego to back the state geologist down again so he could avoid costly delays on his newest project: a solid city block of new shops three stories tall. Too bad it wouldn't be ready for the hordes of tourists who would soon flood into the city for the Olympics, but his mall would reap the benefits of the bounty of additional tourism the Olympics would bring in its wake. The second phase of the project was ready to break ground. Time was money, and the fools set up hoops to jump through, rather than having the wit help themselves by helping him. Now they were requiring that he provide easier access to his new sports stadium to further promote the public good! What did they think—that commerce was not in the public good? It was the very essence of the public good!

Of course, by joining the stadium to the mall he had been able to get public funding, a dip into the public tax stream, so at least the bribes he must pay to push the mall project forward would not come out of his pocket. But first he had to deal with this latest resistance from the state geologist. Meddlesome woman! Hayes was almost mad enough to spit. The geologist worked for the elected fool, but the fool wasn't controlling her. All she had to do was scream "fault line" and work ground to a halt. Why did he listen to her? He need only make an undocumented phone call to secure the necessary swing of a rubber stamp, but no, this fool wanted documentation from his godless scientists. Who were also fools. Gnats. Lice. All sucking blood. All lined up with their grubby little hands out. Smeeth had told him to his face that she couldn't be bought, but everyone had a price and he'd find hers!

His right hand rose up and slammed down on his desk, making his expensive pen and pencil set rattle. Outside the door to his left, his newest executive secretary jumped noticeably. He rotated his head slightly and stared through the doorway at her back, at her narrow neck, at her birdlike shoulders. She was a perilously young thing. They were all young. By twenty-four at most, she'd be married off and pregnant, and her duty then would be to her family. How he longed for a nice impoverished divorcée with half a dozen mouths to feed—a woman who would nail herself to the desk just to keep her job. Focused. No quibbling. No bawling. But divorcées were unseemly.

What was this one's name? Tina. Hayes looked on her with loathing. The precious Tina was now slouching in her chair, examining the state of her manicure. She was slothful. She would have to be replaced. "Tina!" he roared. "Close the door!"

She jumped up and whisked the door shut like someone was chasing her with a stick.

Hayes rotated his face back toward the window and took a long, seething breath, his hour of door-open time completed for the day. Evading his conscious notice, his right hand moved and picked up the gold-plated pen from the set and began to tap it harshly against the edge of the desk, *tap-tap-tap*. *Where is he?* he wondered. *I want confirmation that Smeeth is out of the picture! Why can't he find his way to the telephone on time? He'll pay for keeping me waiting,* Hayes promised himself, now rapping the pen hard enough to leave a widening dent. *He won't cross me twice. I'll have him out of office so quick, he'll be wondering what's causing the draft!*

There was a knock at the door.

"What?" Hayes barked.

Tina's watery voice penetrated the wood. "Your lunch, sir."

"Bring it!" *Damnation,* he thought, *that makes it noon! Where is that rotting piece of carrion?*

The door opened wide and Tina shuffled in, carrying a silver tray with the offensive display of fruits and roughage his doctor allowed him.

Hayes's ailing stomach tightened at the sight of it. "Leave it and get out," he ordered.

"Um, sir?"

"What!"

"I'm sorry it's late, sir. It's just, like, everyone's all upset about the earthquake, you see, and so everything's running a little late. And, um, I was on the phone, you see, trying to get some word on that poor little baby boy, sir."

Hayes turned his face to stone in warning. He did not want to hear problems, he wanted answers! But who was this boy she was telling him about? It sounded like something he should be aware of, to be informed of because knowledge was power. "Yes, the boy," he said cagily, not making it a question, so she wouldn't know that he didn't know.

"Yes, he's in intensive care. They don't know if he's going to live. I know the Ottmeiers. They're such nice people, very worthy. I just can't understand how anything like this could happen to them, but if it's Heavenly Father's plan . . . The thing that hit him—the bookcase—it was, like, so heavy that it hurt his insides. He's b-bleeding . . . um, in-internally."

"Send some people down to the hospital to give blood," Hayes ordered. He did not say, *You can go yourself.* It was important to make the correct gesture, but that would be ridiculous. Tina was almost worthless, but what little worth she was to him, he would hang on to.

"Thank you, sir," she said, her chin beginning to tremble.

"Now, get back to work," he growled.

Tina all but dropped the tray on his desk, spun, and skittered from the room, forgetting to close the door in her haste.

Hayes was just drawing in his breath to order her to once again close the door, when he saw her draw up her shoulders coyly and tip her head to one side. What was she doing? *No doubt kowtowing to someone who is approaching her desk from the hall.*

She sniffled prettily and said, "Hello."

Undoubtedly a man, Hayes surmised. *Time for this one to be bred, if she can't keep her mind on her work!* She turned, following the visitor with her eyes. Hayes could see her lips move around her murmured words. He watched with hate-filled fascination as a shy, tremulous smile bloomed on her rosebud lips.

Tina tittered a bird song of embarrassment, curving her belly forward and her buttocks back provocatively as she leaned to press the intercom button for Hayes's phone. "It's Mr. Harkness, sir," she said, managing to make the phrase come out slightly syrupy. "He wants to know if you got a minute."

Got a minute? He was supposed to report to me yesterday! Where's he been? "Send him in and close the door," Hayes replied. *And then go pack your things. No, first call the temp agency and get them to send over someone else!*

The girl stepped aside and waved the visitor through, her hand moving through the air like a caress. She said, "Right this way, Enos," as if the name filled her mouth with honey. The doorway was briefly filled with the square frame of a man in his mid-twenties, almost tall, almost handsome.

Hayes took the measure of his most junior structural engineer. He had on a badly fitted suit of dull brownish gray fabric, and he wore his hair cut unflatteringly short, Hayes noted with approval. *Young and pliable; lots of mouths to feed.*

Without hesitation, Enos Harkness moved toward one of the side chairs that faced Hayes's desk, but he waited to be told to sit down.

"Close the door!" Hayes bellowed to Tina. The door clicked shut. He favored the waiting Harkness with a glance that trailed toward the chair to his right.

The young man missed the cue and remained standing. "Thank you for seeing me, Mr. Hayes."

The older man flicked a hand, dismissing the civilities. He continued to study the young engineer. He noted that he seemed unusually pale. Was he ill?

Enos cleared his throat. "Uh. Well, I wanted to report on the progress of the mall project, Mr. Hayes."

"Towne Centre project. Get it right, Harkness. Make the right impression." The fingertips of Hayes's right hand tapped rapidly on the top of his desk, matching the rhythm he had so recently inflicted on his pen. He narrowed his eyes, peered at Enos Harkness, and decided that just maybe this one had potential, even though he required constant reminding and tutelage.

Enos seemed as emotionally absent as if he were waiting for a bus, except that he covertly rubbed his hands against his trousers, as if the palms were sweating. "Yes, Towne Centre. I-I think that problem you mentioned is resolved, sir."

For the first time that day, Micah Hayes showed his teeth, creating a wide, tooth-brandishing display, enough to freeze anything but the uppermost animals in the food chain in their tracks. It was not a smile, but a exhibition of dominance.

Enos did not freeze, nor did he blink. He gazed vacantly out the window towards the temple. He said, "Sadly, the matter has been resolved by a death."

It was time to look piously concerned. Hayes arranged his face for the task. "Death? Whose?"

"Sidney Smeeth, the state geologist, sir."

Hayes's lips twisted on the unaccustomed verge of a smile, which he moved to cover with a cough. "Broccoli," he muttered, pointing at his lunch. "Gives me gas. Well, that's terrible, of course. Whatever happened?"

The intercom on Hayes's telephone buzzed again, and Tina's querulous voice wafted out of it. "Your call, sir."

Hayes bent toward the intercom as if it were a hated rodent he was about to inject with cyanide. When he spoke, he almost said, *Tell him he's too late.* Instead, his voice hissing like a snake moving through dried weeds, he replied, "Tell him I've gone out." He snapped his finger off the button and regarded Enos Harkness with an expression of feigned grief. "Sit down, Harkness," he said. "Tell me all about that poor woman's demise."

10

I heard the windows in the Garder store creaking and twisting it seemed to me, and then looking up at The Tribune building I could see the top of it a kind of swaying, it looked as if the cement or plaster was breaking loose from the brick. There was dust coming out in clouds from the side of the building. Everybody on the sidewalks ran to the middle of the street. Many of those who were in the restaurants rushed into the street with the napkins still adorning them—the meal was forgotten, they were seeking a place of safety. . . .

> —*Roy Worthington, quoted in the [Salt Lake City]* Daily Standard *of May 23, 1910, describing his experience on Main Street during the Salt Lake City earthquake of that date, which was estimated at 5.5, felt intensity (Mercalli scale) VII. His observation of dust coming out of the walls of the building accurately describes the disintegration of mortar during moderate earthquake-generated shaking of a brick building in which no bricks are displaced. During each subsequent earthquake, however, such bricks are increasingly likely to move, being held by only fragmental mortar, compressive load, and force of habit.*
>
> *The sand of preference used by masons is all of one size. In years past, masons used dune sand, because the winnowing action of the wind serves as a natural sorting mechanism. Unfortunately for the resulting masonry, dune sand is exceptionally well rounded. When the cement in such older buildings is shaken into dust and blown away from the sand, each brick becomes an individual projectile riding on a layer of miniature ball bearings, just waiting for the next earthquake to send it flying.*

As I led Agent Jack across the parking lot and into the building from which the Utah Geological Survey operates, I noted that its flag was flying at half-mast. "In honor of the departed director?" I asked.

Agent Jack was still playing Bubba. "Huh?" he said, looking formidably dull.

The UGS is located on West North Temple, a few miles out from downtown Salt Lake City, past a thicket of burger stands, quick-lube shops, down-at-the-heels strip malls, the Utah State Fair Park, and the concrete-lined banks of the Jordan River.

That's right, the Jordan River—not the one that flows through Israel, but its namesake, an urban park–type prettified drainage that you might miss if you weren't looking for it. No aspiring saints baptizing up-and-coming prophets here.

Anyway, the UGS has a truly wonderful salesroom just to the left of the entrance, and it was jam-packed with books, maps, reports, CDs, and all the other goozily things a geologist just drools over. Better and better, the UGS had recently been directed by a man named Lee Allison, who understood not only the need to develop understanding of the geological hazards and resources of the state of Utah but also the parallel and inextricably intertwined need to provide the information in forms that its citizenry could access. Which meant that he got his geologists to produce more comprehensible materials, and that these materials were now attractively displayed in full-color covers just dripping with eye appeal and user-friendly lead-ins.

One of the goodies the UGS provides the public, at no cost, is a series of seismic-hazard maps covering all the counties through which the Wasatch fault runs. I had to wait in line to ask the store manager where to find one. He was busy helping half the rest of Salt Lake County's jarred residents find that map and such popular tomes as *The Homebuyer's Guide to Earthquake Hazards in Utah*, which has a nice photograph of a hundred-year-old cottage sheared off its foundation by a 1989 California quake on the cover. Finally, he turned his large chocolate brown eyes on me and gave me a bright, earnest display of his brilliantly white teeth. "You need some help finding something?" he asked.

"Yes. I'm a geologist, and I'm trying to get a better grasp on the seismic picture here in Salt Lake."

The man led me around through the display stands, pointing out possibilities. "We've got the big-scale maps over here—just a few left—and you might also find something of interest in some of these." He handed me a couple of technical papers. One was entitled *Paleoseismic Investigation of the Salt Lake City Segment of the Wasatch Fault Zone at the South Fork Dry Creek and Dry Gulch Sites, Salt Lake County, Utah.* He hurried onward. "Or if you want greater detail, here's the USGS map." He handed me a folded map in the kind of plain manila envelope preferred by the federal government, on which was emblazoned *Surficial Geologic Map of the Salt Lake City Segment and Parts of Adjacent Segments of the Wasatch Fault Zone, Davis, Salt Lake, and Utah Counties, Utah.*

Agent Jack peered over my shoulder again. "Wuzzat?" he inquired.

"A geologic map," I said, passing it to him. "Geologists are not known for brevity where it comes to thinking up titles. See, here they're telling you exactly what's covered."

He ran a thick finger along the face of the map folder. "Twenty-six words," he said. "Any pictures?"

I wasn't following him. Gullible cretin that I am, I said, "Well, it's a map. I guess you could say it's all one big picture."

Jack's face lighted up with a goofy grin. "Well then, where's the other nine hundred seventy-four words?"

Definitely Jack was no idiot. Reminding myself to keep in mind that the slack-jawed bit was an act, I moved on.

I wound up selecting two reports, the USGS map, and the giveaway map published by the UGS: *Selected Critical Facilities and Geologic Hazards, Salt Lake County, Utah.* I bellied up to the counter to pay for them with my sad old credit card, but Jack slapped a twenty down on the stack and grabbed the receipt. On the way out to the car, I asked, "Does that mean I don't get to keep them?"

Jack glanced skyward. "You duke that out with big Tom. C'mon. He's waiting."

◈

"DOES FAYE KNOW you're investigating the developer that built her house?" I asked my erstwhile mentor.

Tom shook his head. "Doesn't bear on the case. Just a coincidence."

"Sure."

Tom shot me an angry look, then turned away. After a few moments, the bad temper seemed to drain from his face and he said, "Sorry, I'm . . . a bit off today. I'll admit I am concerned about Faye's house, but please keep in mind that I found out about the problem in the course of being concerned about all our good citizens' homes." He leaned back in his chair and seemed to collapse inward. I noticed how tired he looked, and how . . . unyouthful. Sensing my eyes on him, he added, "Good work on this file review. I . . . I'll call you if I need anything else, okay?"

"I'm not done yet," I said. "I'm going to work up an understanding of the local seismic picture for you, a sort of thumbnail sketch of what sort of due diligence should be observed before and during construction near the Wasatch fault."

Tom still didn't look at me, but his posture suggested that he was in pain.

Ideas flooded into my head as I spoke, and I felt an old enthusiasm rise, the cavalry scout's call to action. "I picked up a map at the UGS and I'm going to mark those developments on it and so forth. My curiosity is up now, especially after this morning's quake. I have only the vaguest understanding of what size earthquakes can occur around here and where and why and to what effect, and I'd like to know. And what exactly are the building regulations? I want to know if this developer has skipped any steps, or whether it's considered completely kosher to build in a fault zone in this town."

Tom nodded his head. "Okay. Fine. I'd be curious to know what you get."

Our eyes met. He looked worried as hell, and I knew it had nothing to do with the job at hand. I thought of saying, *It's okay—she likes children.* But I knew better than to get started. What did I know about the anxieties he must be feeling? I'd never had so much as a bad scare regarding accidental pregnancy, and I was involved up past my eye sockets with a man who practiced the most bombproof form of birth control known: abstinence. But needless to say, the whole topic had me thinking thoughts, and feeling feelings.

Tom cleared his throat, his face now devoid of emotion. In his schoolteacher voice, he said, "Procedure."

I sat up straighter and did my best to respond to his request. He had been trying to teach me to think ahead, to have a plan. To understand that having a plan was the first defense against getting myself in a jam. Trouble is, I'm not a person who plans ahead. It seems to take the fizz out of the champagne of exploration. And it just doesn't seem to apply in certain areas, such as knowing what questions to ask when going on a fishing expedition like this. Besides, preparation is tedious and boring. But I said, "Ah, I'm going to read these maps and reports, figure out what I know and don't know about the Wasatch fault and public policies concerning building on or near it. Figure out who might know what I don't know. Talk to those people. Revisit my understanding, repeat as necessary."

He tapped the small stack of maps and papers I had purchased at the UGS. "What sources will you use other than these?"

"I'll start with my undergraduate textbooks. Good summaries, but no doubt out-of-date. Move up to the university library. Maybe get into GEOREF."

"Which is?"

"On-line search engine for geoscience publications."

"How are you going to contact people?"

"I'll try the government pages of the phone book first, see who the flak-catchers who answer the phones send me to."

"What are you going to tell them about yourself? Remember, cover is one of your weak places."

"I know. If I tell the truth, say that I'm just sniffing around, I stand out like a sore thumb. But if I tell a cover story, such as that I'm a grad student at the U, then I open myself to easy cross-check of my story."

"And worse yet?"

"Worse yet, I am likely to forget my cover story, because I am at heart a lousy liar. Under pressure, I tend to remember only what makes sense, or is true, or, worse yet, I get confused about who I am. Being prone to identity crises being a problem of mine."

Tom smiled kindly, amused at my self-evaluation. "Correct. Know thyself first; then get to know thine adversary. Otherwise, thine adversary will teach you about yourself the hard way. And what's the best way to tell a lie if you have to?"

I recited, "To attach it to the truth. That way, if I'm caught lying, I can say that I was wrong on that part but see this other part is right as rain."

"Yes. So tell me again: What is your cover story?"

I thought for a moment, then laughed. "I am a geologist. I guess I don't have to tell them anything beyond that."

Tom gave his desktop a swat of approval. "Very good. But what if they ask?"

My imagination soared. "Then I'm with EBH Consultants, a small firm out of Wyoming."

"EBH?"

"Yeah, that's my initials. Emily Bradstreet Hansen. At least half of all geological engineering firms are three-initial names, very forgettable. And I am out of Wyoming. And I don't have to be making money to call myself a geologist, damn it!"

◈

I HEADED TO my apartment, figuring I'd sit and read awhile, maybe slide a peanut butter sandwich between my teeth, but, to be honest, my real reason for going home rather than to the university library was not hunger, but the hope of a message from Ray. I knew he had to go on shift in the afternoon, which meant that he was due back in Salt Lake City anytime now, so I was thinking that he might just call me. Or should I say, I was hoping he'd call. A month or more ago, a phone call at such a juncture would have been a foregone event. But things had begun to change between us. To drift. To become . . . less predictable. And not in a good sense. Our "engaged to be engaged" status was beginning to feel more like simply "stuck."

There was no call from Ray on my message machine.

Trying to tell myself that this didn't mean anything significant, I kicked off my boots, flopped down on my bed with the maps, and tried to absorb some information from them. But I soon rolled onto my back and found myself staring at the ceiling, that tried-and-true, near-featureless expanse where certain kinds of answers can be found if you can just figure out what, in fact, the question is.

My gaze focused on a crack in the plaster.

A gap had always existed between Ray and me, at least on some levels, and it had begun to widen at Christmas. On the face of things, the rub was that he was Mormon and I wasn't, but, in our case, this difference wasn't just a matter of where we went on Sunday mornings. To a couple of overly serious types like Ray and me, this difference carved down through peculiarities of lifestyle, on through habits and rituals, and right down into personal philosophies and the question of whether or not we could indeed proceed as a couple. Ray was a big-time family man. His mother, Ava, was a widow who had not remarried. Being Mormon and the only male of Ava's five children, the eldest, and therefore twice over patriarch in charge since his father's death, Ray knew that his presence—and, in fact, his authority—was required at all family events. And if family were a class you took in college, I'd get an *F*.

My mind followed the crack in the ceiling north and east into Wyoming, up the Sweetgrass River, down the Platte past my grandmother Hansen's place near Casper, and along the Front Range to Chugwater, to my parents' ranch. We had been a family, hadn't we? But a family that needed the wide expanses of the short-grass prairie to get along even as poorly as we did. My parents had gotten on best when Dad was way out in the farthest paddock, miles from the house, mending fence, and Mother was on the couch in one of her silk robes, sleeping off the excesses of another hair of the dog that had bitten her the night before. And where was I? Hiding in the barn, or out talking to the grasshoppers that dined on the forage we needed for the cattle. They never answered, just hopped away, green and yellow speedsters who didn't need words.

The few times I saw my mother and father walk out together across the ranch, he'd be looking outward across the sage brush, checking the grasses, watching for coyotes, and she would look inward, back through the early death of their son and into the loss of her own frail sense of belonging back East, where she had lived as a girl.

She had looked westward after college, thinking it would save her. He had married East, enthralled by the stiff presumptions of a culture that could measure itself back farther than a hundred years. Adventure can die a sad death if the heart is not strong enough.

And I had risen from that ground propelled only by a longing to reach for the sun. Our family had died. Like the adobe soil we tried to tame, it had crumbled, frozen by too many harsh winters, baked every summer under a pitiless sun, chewed at by the wind, and beaten under the hooves of a hundred thousand witless animals driven to the slaughter for too few dollars.

I closed my eyes, my mind going empty from the cold blast of memory. How I longed to be part of a family, and not just a small collection of hard-bitten individuals who couldn't bear each others' pain. I wanted smiles on arrival, tears on farewell, laughter at the tales of my adventures, joy in my accomplishments, a man to embrace in the dark warmth of sleeping, and, if I could believe the tingling that had been set off by Faye's early morning surprise, I wanted children. I wanted to look into their eyes, stroke their hair, and teach them what they needed to know to find more love than hatred, just as soon as I learned it myself.

Six months earlier, Ray had asked me to marry him, thinking I would convert to Mormonism and become part of his life. I'd said maybe to the marriage part of the idea, but made it pretty clear that I never had, and could see no reason I ever would have, any interest in joining his religion. It just wasn't me, and I'm a person who doesn't do things for show. But thinking I could meet him halfway, I had moved to Salt Lake City a month later, right in the middle of the summer heat. We had managed to get through the frivolities of Labor Day weekend, the circus atmosphere of family birthdays, and the observance of perhaps half a dozen Family Home Evenings (the weekly Mormon home study and prayer gathering; I'd gotten out of the rest because he was on shift for six others, and I was . . . otherwise engaged). And I had finessed the secular holiday of Thanksgiving by thinking up a reason I needed to run up to Wyoming to see an uncle. But then came Christmas. Christmas is the ultimate in family holidays, a bucketful of joy if you have an ecstatically wonderful, supportive, loving family, stressful at best if you're in the other

99 percent of reality. On Christmas, the rivets in our relationship had begun to pop.

On that date, it became clear that I was not only ignorant of the all-important family traditions but also congenitally bereft of any talent for adapting to them. I showed up in slacks, only to find Ava and all Ray's sisters in floor-length dresses and tinselly hair ribbons. I presented a little prepackaged assortment of dried fruits and nuts as the sisters proffered artistic basketfuls of home-baked goodies dripping in chocolate, the Mormon cheat street into the pleasure of caffeine. I sat mute and unmusical as everyone crowded around the piano to sing carols. I was relegated to setting the table while the brothers-in-law played with the children and Ava and her daughters laughed in the kitchen. I lifted my fork before all the prayers were said at dinner, screwed up and asked for coffee with desert, and longed for a good old cowboy shot of schnapps to calm my nerves as we cleared the special Christmas dishes and I dropped one. And all eyes focused on Ray and me as we opened each other's gifts.

I had bought Ray a ski sweater in the exact shade of indigo that flashed from his wonderful eyes. He loved downhill skiing, so I thought this might be a suitable peace offering, since I had screwed up a month earlier by admitting that I much preferred the solitude of cross-country skiing, could barely stay upright on downhill skis, and detested the congestion and high-priced show of ski resorts.

Ray had smiled politely at the sweater and awarded me a chaste peck on the cheek. His mother had made a study of an object on the other side of the room. As he handed me his gift, his sisters' postures had shifted, their heads swiveling like so many radar dishes, tracking the package, measuring it, burning holes through the paper with X-ray vision, their eyes widening and contracting as they noted that it was a big package, not a small one. Not a ring. Little smiles flickered across certain faces. I avoided Ava's eyes but stared down each sister in turn, unable to hold my defiance in check any longer. I wanted to say, *He offered me the ring last summer and I said not yet,* but such candor was inappropriate, then and perhaps forever. Reining in my anger as best I could, I managed to smile as I yanked the ribbon off the box, tore off the paper, slid it open, and saw . . . a ski sweater. A vivid, rose pink, soft, fuzzy ski sweater. Ray patted my walking cast and said, "This comes with ski lessons." I said, "Thank you" and "I love it," then returned the peck of a kiss to his handsome cheek. With stiffened fingers, I touched the mass of pink fuzz, pretending to admire its softness, but I could see only how sallow my hand looked against the color. As I set the box aside, Ray's sister Katie managed to catch my eye. Katie is the number two sister, about twenty-five years old and already the mother of three. She looked smug. "See, I told you she'd like it, Ray. You just leave that shopping to me," she purred, grandstanding her prior knowledge, her complicity. I spent the next hour trying to imagine a way to rip the putrid pink mass into strips and knot it into a vengeful noose. I even picked out a beam from which to hang a rope that I could loop around Katie's deceitful neck, and imagined her kicking as she swung. It was a long, bitter afternoon, during which I reproved myself continually for my paranoia and inability to let things roll off my back.

Extracting myself once again from the delicacies of this fantasy and touching down briefly in the present moment, I found a new crack on the ceiling of my bedroom, this room that Ray had never entered. Had this new rift been there the day before? Had the earthquake caused it?

Suddenly, I could no longer stand to be alone.

I jumped up and threw the UGS materials and my freshman physical geology textbook into a backpack along with a sandwich and a bottle of water, put on some hiking boots (I was beginning to feel self-conscious about the red ropers), and then headed out to the street where I'd left Faye's car. I was soon once again hammering all that horsepower up the hill toward her house. She would understand. She would help me through the coming hours. And she had many more immediate worries under whose weight I could bury my fears.

This time as I ascended toward her house, I took much greater interest in the surrounding topography. Surprising how much more menacing those boulders on the rampart above the development looked now that I could no longer assume that the developer had done his geologic hazards homework. Was that slope sufficiently stable to ride out a truly big earthquake, or perhaps even a springtime mudslide?

I was so involved with reading the landscape that I zipped right past the place where my truck had died without noticing that it was gone. Or perhaps it was a combination of the landscape and my need to be in the comfort of my friend's company. Or just call it denial.

And Faye was not home.

I stared numbly at her front door. If she wasn't there, then I urgently needed something to do. I remembered the maps and books. I pulled the backpack out of the Porsche and headed up the road.

It was only a short distance to the foot of the rock-strewn slope above. At the end of the pavement, I passed a parked pickup truck bearing official state of Utah plates and stepped onto a path that led into the "open-space corridor," that steepening slope I hoped the city or county officials had deemed unsuitable for building.

The ground rose steeply into arid scrub land as I followed the zigzagging trail, noting the sizes of boot and dog prints that had become implanted after the several cycles of freezing and thawing that had visited the area since the last snowfall. Something in me soon found this concentration of so many people's journeys annoying, even intolerable, and I stepped off the path, crunching through the crust of old corn snow. I stomped straight up the slope, dodging only as I reached the more sizable rocks or arrays of stunted oaks. I marched resolutely toward the biggest boulder in the neighborhood, a slab of sandstone the size of a small truck, figuring I'd sit on it and read. It lay at the edge of a great train of boulders that filled the slope immediately below the mouth of a narrow canyon above.

Somewhere in there, I realized that I was following tracks left very recently by another adult human. The afternoon sunlight glinted in gemstone flashes off the snow, an array of whiteness rhythmically disrupted by the blue shadows that filled the shallow boot prints. Laid over the icy crust of the snow were small sprays of older, more powdery snow that the boot-owner's strides had brought up from underneath.

I decided the footprints belonged to whoever had parked the pickup truck at the end of the pavement below.

It was not long before I caught up with a man about my age, who was dressed much as I was: blue jeans, hiking boots, and a down parka. He had heavy shoulders and a wide face to go with them. His nose was broad and rounded, terminating neatly over a thick beard that curled away from his cheeks. Together with his high, boxy cheekbones, the combination of nose and beard gave him the air of a kindly lion I remembered from a picture book I had had as a child. He was leaning jauntily against one of the boulders, making notes on pages fastened to an aluminum clipboard. His jacket was open down the front, exposing a plaid wool shirt and a telltale cord that led down inside his shirt toward a small round bump about an inch thick in the middle of his chest.

"Doing some geology?" I asked pleasantly.

He looked up abruptly, feigned surprise, and then set to examining himself as if he were covered with some odd substance. "Does it show, really? I mean, I can never understand how people guess so easily," he replied, in a perfect deadpan. Then he gave me a sly grin.

I smiled back. "It's the hand lens around your neck, the basic pragmatism of the attire, the 'I set my own fashion' beard, the chapped hands, the stoical use of a metal clipboard even on a cold day, the ease with which you sit on a nice hard rock. More comfortable here than on an office chair, your posture suggests. Add to that the pickup truck down the hill, the fact that I'm finding you out on a potentially unstable slope the afternoon after an earthquake, and—"

He held up a hand. "That'll do. But tell me how do you know these things, O ye who climbed out of a Porsche even though you look like you'd be more at home on a horse."

I grabbed the side seams of my jeans and dropped a prim curtsy. "Because I also am a geologist."

He somberly put his lips together and whistled the tune that goes to the words, "You can see by my outfit that I am a cowboy."

Smiling at his musical quip, I acknowledged the rest of his observation. "And yes, I've done my time on horseback. The fancy car belongs to the friend who also belongs to the house. My pickup truck fell on its sword this morning as I was driving up here to check on my Porschely friend, who was not as sanguine about the trembling of terra firma as I."

The man nodded. "Ah. Yours was the twenty-year-old beige half-ton getting towed."

I winced, then looked down the hill toward where it should have been. "I guess some chichi neighbor reported it abandoned," I muttered. "A towing bill. That's all I need."

"Imperialist swines. Need some help?"

I let out a long sigh. "No. I guess there's really nothing that can be done."

"A venerable beast," he said sympathetically.

"Just getting broken in. A mere pup."

The man pulled his cap off and held it briefly to his chest, put it back on his head, then hopped off his rock and presented me with a hand to be shaken. "Logan de Pontier."

"Em Hansen."

His hand was surprisingly warm, considering his lack of gloves and the metal clipboard he'd been handling. His beard was clipped closer than the slightly wild hair that curled over the back of his collar, and his eyes were bright green and wide-set, giving his leonine face a mystic, walleyed look. There was something disquieting about standing so close to him that I could see the subtleties in the color of those eyes. I withdrew my hand and used it it to gesture at the slope.

"What are you looking at?" I inquired.

"Oh, just checking for movement on this landslide."

"This is a landslide? It looks more like a talus slope."

"Technically, a debris flow, which is of course a type of landslide. Like someone opens up a cement truck at the top of the hill and lets it rip. Only, as you can see, the chunks here are the size of trucks themselves. Talus would be just the chunks, no finer sediment."

I looked up and down the slope at the tumble of rocks that formed a narrow, steep cone projecting from a notch in the mountain face above. "So you're an engineering geologist?" I asked. It was occurring to me that this man might be able to save me a lot of reading with a nice quick lesson on faults and the landslides they can trigger.

He smiled for the first time, a brief flexure of the whiskers that exposed more lip but no teeth. "Right again."

"Utah Geological Survey?" I asked, recalling the official state license plate on the truck.

He nodded.

I said, "Sorry about your boss."

He closed his eyes briefly. Opened them. "Yup."

I paused a moment, observing what I hoped was a proper solemnity. "So I'm a petroleum geologist by training. After this morning's quake, though, I'm thinking I ought to get a handle on the seismology of the area." Almost bungling this perfectly natural reason to be questioning him, I added, "Don't need to explain to you that I'm just good old-fashioned curious," then brazenly put forth another question. "So this is a normal fault, right?" I asked. The plane of a normal fault slants toward the valley; another way of saying it is that the plane of the fault parallels the mountain front. As the valley drops, it slides down and away from the mountains, and the mountain front is essentially the fault scarp. I point this out because some faults—called thrusts—move in the opposite direction, thrusting the mountain up over the valley, shortening the ground. On still others, the two sides grind past each other laterally.

Logan de Pontier nodded and said, "Well, yes, the Wasatch fault is normal for the most part." He pointed downhill to the west first and then uphill to the east. "Valley block down, mountain block up. But of course a fault system this large isn't just one single tear in the Earth. The Wasatch branches and breaks into segments. And, of course, it's part of a much bigger picture. It's the eastern end of the whole Basin and Range province." He made a panoramic sweep to the west with one hand. "Extensional faulting clear west to Reno. Reno's moving away from us about one centimeter per year. The rate your fingernails grow. About a third of that motion is taken up right here along this mountain front. In fact, it's what's forming this mountain front."

I translated this mentally into images. He was saying that between Salt Lake City and Reno—a distance of four hundred miles—the Earth's crust was pulling apart like a giant accordion, and that as the two towns moved away from each other, large blocks of the Earth's crust were settling, literally falling into slots along big parallel fractures, forming valleys. "So the Wasatch fault is a huge feature."

"Yes. It's about three hundred miles long, but like I said, it's broken into segments." He gestured at the Salt Lake valley. "We call this the Salt Lake segment. It's one of the more complex sections, broken into many branches." He moved his hands around to illustrate this, making a series of angled chops through the air like plates stacked on edge in a dishwasher, but then remembered his clipboard and began to sketch. What he drew was a cross-sectional view of the Earth that would only make sense to another geologist.

I smiled, amused that I could interpret his scribblings.

He said, "See, instead of just one fault plane, it steps down in sections that look parallel on the surface, but the planes can curve at depth. How it's all connected down below is a big question." He drew a question mark where the branches of the fault appeared to converge. "Wait a minute," he said, and pulled out his own copy of the geologic map I'd just bought. He unfolded it. "See, here's the nearest branch, running right along there." He pointed to a dashed line that ran just above Faye's house. The dashed line indicated that the fault was covered by surface deposits at this location. And million-dollar homes. So much for ritzy acreage.

"I thought this break in slope was one of the old wave-cut benches from Lake Bonneville," I said.

"It is. But right here, it's also a fault scarp."

Realizing the I was standing so close to such an active fault made me feel almost itchy in the soles of my feet. "So this morning's quake was one of these branches letting go?" I asked.

Logan opened another fold of his map. "Not this one. It was probably on the branch we call the Warm Springs fault." He pointed to a parallel line, this one solid, that started north of downtown and stopped just short of the state capitol.

I gulped in a burlesque of nervousness. "Well then, I'm glad this morning's quake wasn't any bigger. I was inside the City and County Building for the first time today, and I wouldn't want to have seen a seismic retrofit of that much stonework put to the test."

Logan nodded. "The City and County Building isn't immediately on the Warm Springs fault—unless it goes even farther south than I think it does—but it may go past or under a lot of the larger buildings downtown. And neither would you want to see the Convention Center, or the new Assembly Hall, or, for that matter that brand spanking new stadium cut in half if you had a quake big enough to break surface." He held his hands together to indicate the two sides of the fault, then dropped his valley-side hand abruptly—*wham*. "Nice three-foot scarp'd crack your foundation like a twig."

"How big a quake would that take?"

"Six point five or better. Maybe a seven. This morning's was a five point two. The actual rupture was downstairs a few kilometers, if not ten. Just made all that lake-bed sediment the city's built on jiggle like jelly."

"Did this morning's quake give you new information you've just added in there?" I asked. He had penciled in a section of dashes that continued the line of the Warm Springs fault to the south, from just west of the state capitol downtown toward the Convention Center and most of the other tall buildings in Salt Lake City, just as he had said.

"No, that's some mapping that was done years ago. It got left off of this map."

"Why?"

Logan de Pontier fixed his green eyes on me and gave me a probing look. "That's a good question," he said, his voice suddenly tight. "That's a really good question. Guess you'd have to call it a difference of opinion."

"A scientific disagreement?"

Logan did not answer me.

I turned and looked out across the Salt Lake valley. A valley filled with a network of cracks just spoiling to rupture. A valley in which perhaps a million people lived, most in houses made of unreinforced brick. I drew in a breath and released it. I asked, "Quake that size, how many people killed?"

"Official estimate? Up to eight thousand immediately, another forty-four thousand injured. Twelve billion in damage, six more in economic losses."

"Homeless?"

"I don't even have that number. Say also thirty percent of businesses fail within the next year. Families separated, dispersed."

We stood in silence for a while, burdened by our knowledge. Finally, I said, "But this morning's quake was a little one."

Logan's chest moved with a deep sigh. "Yes. Let's just hope it was the main event and not a warm-up for something bigger."

◈

I SETTLED IN on the rock next to Logan and asked him all the other questions I could think to ask, but after a few minutes, I had exhausted my knowledge of earthquakes and what causes them and decided to angle for a business card and call him later, when I'd read a little more.

Down below, I saw a taxi moving up the road toward Faye's house. It pulled up by her walkway, then stopped. Faye climbed out, turned, paid the driver.

"That's my friend," I told Logan. "The one who owns the Porsche and the house. I guess I'll go on down and see what's happening."

"Wait, I'll come on down with you. I'm done here for today."

We started down the trail together. As Faye started up the walk toward her house, she looked up and spotted us. Pilots have good eyes. I waved. She stopped and waved back, changed her course for the foot of the trail, and arrived perhaps a minute before we did. As I got close enough to see her face, I saw that her lips were swollen from crying, although those who had not met her before might think she was possessed of the kind of bee-stung lips women pay plastic surgeons big money to create for them. Her eyes were hidden behind a set of aviator sunglasses.

She presented one of her more formal smiles. "Hi, Em," she said. "Who's your friend?"

I made the introductions. "This is Logan de Pontier. He's a geologist with the Utah Geological Survey. He's checking to see if you're going to get a new rock garden in your living room."

Faye tipped her head forward and gave me a "Drop dead" look over her sunglasses. "What are you saying, Em?"

I made a sheepish gesture toward the hill. "Landslide."

"What landslide?"

"That landslide. Don't worry—it's not expected to come this way anytime soon. Right, Logan?"

Logan slipped into his official tone. "Technically speaking, it's a debris flow."

Faye looked from Logan to me and back again. "All I need."

For a man who had been so garrulous, Logan was quickly growing terse. "Well . . ."

Still not smiling, Faye said, "Well hell. Why don't you come on in and have a beer and tell me all about it?"

"I'd like to, but I can't." He turned toward me. "If you want . . . I could . . . you know . . ."

Faye continued to stare at us over the tops of her glasses. "Just give her a business card, Logan. I'll make sure she gets in touch with you."

I snapped my head toward her and gave her a dose of storm cloud with my eyebrows.

She indulged herself in a snarl. "Em, I am having one hell of a day. You are having one hell of a life. Mr. Fellow Geologist here has some information for me, and God knows what he has for you. We want to stay in touch with him, now don't we?"

I could feel heat and pressure building across my forehead and hoped the blush would not show.

Logan cleared his throat and quickly pulled his wallet out of his back pocket. "The UGS is in the book of course, but here's my card, and please do call if you have any more questions." Having rediscovered his aplomb, he added, "As a matter of fact, a bunch of us are getting together after work for some beer and pizza, kind of compare notes on our observations today. Be glad to have you—ah, both of you—ah, join us."

Palming his card, I said, "Thanks, Logan, but—"

"But I'll make sure she shows," Faye said, completing my sentence for me.

Logan smiled absently. "Pie Pizzeria. About six. Look for the motley crew in the back."

I jammed the card into my back pocket with considerable force and grumbled, "Make mine artichoke hearts and Canadian bacon."

11

I was in the Walgreens drugstore in the Marina District, way in the back. Stuff was coming off the shelves. People were screaming. I ran to the front of the store. There's a turnstile, and I couldn't get over it. I thought I was going to die.

—A young woman describing her experience of the 1989 Loma Prieta magnitude 7.1 earthquake. The Marina District in San Francisco is built on bay fill that was poured behind a seawall to provide ground for San Francisco's Panama-Pacific Exposition of 1915. Much of the sand for the fill was from dunes. Wind-deposited sand grains are known for their highly rounded character and unusually uniform diameter. Like a stack of ball bearings, the material is unstable and tends to settle in response to the call of gravity. It was intended that the seawall and the sand fill be temporary, and, as they were constructed prior to the inception of engineering codes, the fill was not mechanically compacted. More-over, it was, and still is, saturated with bay waters, providing the perfect conditions for liquefaction.

Over the years, the seawall has been repeatedly patched, like the Dutch boy applying his fingers to a failing dike. By the end of the seventeen seconds of shaking the Marina District experienced during the 1989 temblor, the seawall had failed in several places, and sand was erupting in liquid fountains through lawns over which, moments before, joggers had been jogging and mothers had been wheeling their baby strollers. Gas pipes broke, and whole square blocks of housing collapsed and caught fire. It is estimated that had the shaking gone on three seconds longer, the entire

ground would have liquefied and flowed through the ruptured sea-
wall into San Francisco Bay, taking housing, lawn, joggers, and
baby strollers with it.

JIM SCHECTER SWUNG HIS FLASHLIGHT AS HE CLIMBED THE last few courses of steps that led up to the top of the stadium seating. He wished he had not been quite so quick to give blood for Tommy Ottmeier. Heaven knows, the child needed it, but it had left Jim fatigued, short of breath.

He was almost to the door through which he must pass before he could start checking the trusses that supported the roof. As with each other item on his mental list, he would search the roof trusses methodically for distorted tubing, cracked welds, anything that would indicate damage caused by the earthquake. He hummed softly as he worked, certain he would discover nothing amiss, happy to be doing a job that would reassure the Olympic committee that their years of careful arrangements, ministrations, and orchestrations could proceed as planned.

Three steps from the top, he turned briefly toward the center of the stadium and gave his tired spine a series of twists, relieving the cricks that had begun to set in after four hours of searching for the trouble he knew he would not find. The earthquake had been only a 5.2, after all, barely large enough to trigger the protocol he was now following.

Below him, in a dramatic sweep, were arrayed the thousands of stadium seats that in three short weeks would be filled with excited spectators applauding, gasping, and cheering in unison. Yes, it would be a huge crowd, but only an infinitesimal fraction of the number who would like to be here. A privileged few had won the seating lottery and each had managed to pony up the obscene cost of the tickets that would enable them to attend the opening-night ceremonies of the 2002 Winter Olympic Games. Right here, in this stadium, with the beauty of Salt Lake City and the Wasatch Range for a backdrop.

He had to sit down for a minute to collect himself, to fight back the first surge of phobia that was threatening to arise. How he hated doing building inspections. He wanted dearly to return to his usual tasks back in his nice safe office. How he wished the powers that be would quit trying to cut corners on such essential protocols—in this case, assuring that the stadium had ridden out the earthquake without so much as a chink in its plaster—and hire regular staff to do the inspections. It seemed ironic to him that public buildings were still inspected by untrained staff like him, while private structures were governed by much more stringent requirements. Odder yet, this stadium was privately owned, but because it was to be used by the public for the upcoming event, he had been detailed to inspect it under the looser requirements. *At least I'm an actual engineer so I can give it a good going-over*, he thought. *Some of the schools get inspected by janitorial staff. What kind of money-saving measure is that?*

He closed his eyes and breathed deeply, as the therapist had taught him. He said his calming words deep inside his mind. *I am safe. I am on the Earth. The Earth loves me. I am safe. There now. There.* They were such silly words, but they seemed to work. And it was a good thing that they did, because he didn't want to have to take a sedative in order to handle being up on the catwalk that would give him access to the roof trusses. If he got sleepy and stumbled, it would be such a long way down.

Feeling restored and confident, he opened his eyes. Yes, the steps seemed much less steep now. *Good.* He looked out through the central opening in the roof at the tops of the downtown buildings, at the mountains beyond. The stadium was brand-new and beautiful, another testimony to the goodness of this wonderful community in which he lived. Right here, they had transformed a disused, downtrodden piece of real estate into a spectacular new community gathering spot.

It would not be long now before it would be filled for the first time. Far below him, teams of workers scurried about, busily erecting the stage and rigging the lights and pyrotechnic effects that would dazzle tens of thousands of viewers here and hundreds of millions more worldwide. This spectacular view would be right there for the whole world to enjoy, appreciate, and admire.

He rolled his head slowly left, then right, enjoying a nice series of cracking sounds deep in his neck, savoring the moment. He was proud to be in charge of ensuring the safety of all the good citizens who would come here to honor this pinnacle of what had been a great many years' hard work and sacrifice for the citizens of Salt Lake City—all the disruption due to construction as new highways, bridges, hotels, a light-rail system, and this stadium were built for the event.

How glorious opening night would be. Just down there, the runner would emerge from the entrance tunnel carrying the burning torch, then would circle in front of the cheering crowds. The light of the torch would illuminate the beaming faces of the best athletes from a hundred countries. His chest swelled with pride. His city was the site for this event. The years of sacrifice and disruption would be gone, the black eye of the bribes and kickbacks taken by the organizing committee forgotten. Yes, this was Salt Lake's moment, and this special event would honor his city.

But first, he must inspect the trusses. He had already checked the foundations, which were fine. He had checked the framework members that held the weight of the stands. They were fine. The crossbracing, all perfect. Now the roof trusses were all that remained to be examined. It was an easy job, a piece of cake. *Except for the*—He stopped. Breathed. Cleared his mind. He knew not to even think about the sense of exposure that awaited him on the catwalk.

Turning back toward the last few steps, Jim raised the tightly focused beam of his powerful flashlight and gave the roof a preliminary scan. Plenty of light bounced in through the wide center opening from the bright winter sky, but he liked to use the flashlight to focus his eye, just in case some telltale crack lurked in the one stray shadow. *Yes, yes, fine so far, just as I expected. This great structure was, after all, built by a local firm. Well, a local developer in partnership with a big international construction firm, but that's how business is done. That is how you keep as much of the profits as possible right here in Salt Lake City while still engaging a company big enough to handle a job of this magnitude.*

Jim circled slowly along the top row, dancing his beam along the steel tubing. When he came to the door that gave access to the trusses, he unlocked it and ascended a metal staircase that let him out onto the catwalk that ran through the trusswork itself. He gripped the handrails and took a deep breath, remembering not to look down, abstracting himself from the fear he would feel if he looked all the way down through the plummeting open space that was all that lay between him and the ranks of seat backs that waited, knifelike, below him. *I am on a sidewalk down on the street*, he told himself. *I am on the Earth, and the Earth loves me. I am safe.* He took a breath, exhaled.

He moved out along the catwalk, checking the first truss. He swung the flashlight beam this way and that, examining the arching ranks of steel tubing. The tubing looked perfect.

He checked the welds. The welds—

Jim swung his beam to a joint in the nearest truss, the place where three tubes met a fourth. Held it there. What he saw turned his knees to mush.

Oh no.

A crack ran clear through the weld.

Tightening his grip on the railing, he struggled to steady the hand that held the flashlight. He aimed its jiggling beam now onto the plate that had been placed there to reinforce the mammoth junction of steel tubing. Here he found a curl of paint that had been scraped loose.

Oh no. Oh no.

He forced himself to move along the catwalk, to check each

of the next three connecting plates. The first showed the same cracked welds and buckled paint; the second exposed a gleaming section that should have been covered; the next—

Oh no, oh no . . .

Jim Schecter unclipped the cell phone from his belt and raised it to his face, tried to concentrate on the way the plastic felt against his skin. He punched two buttons to dial the desk phone of his superior. It rang once, twice.

"Building Inspection," announced an officious female voice at the other end of the connection.

"This is Jim Schecter. Give me Fred Miller."

"Oh, hi, Jim. He's not here. Can I take a message?"

Jim tried to breathe, his eyes now fixated on the drop below him, every blood vessel in his body dilating, searching for the blood he had gifted as his prayer for the baby boy. "No! No, I— get the file open for the stadium, will you?"

"Don't you have that with you, Jim?"

"Yes, but—"

"Is something wrong, Jim?"

Jim's field of vision began to distort. His right eye felt as if it were coated with Vaseline. *Hell*, he thought, *a migraine. Why now?* "Hold on a minute," he gasped. He put the phone back in its holder, forced himself to stand straight, to grip the railing, to move back toward the safety of the stairs. *Why now? Why why why . . .*

Swaying as if the earthquake had returned, he reached the metal staircase and sat down, hugging the upright that braced the railing. Now the rainbows were coming, the blurry places. Not for the first time, he wondered at the people who told him how lucky he was that he got only the visual aspects of the migraine and not the pain.

A voice spoke to him from the cell phone. "Jim? Are you okay?"

He pulled the telephone back out of its clip. "Okay. I'm back." *Please God don't let her know what's happening to me. I'll lose my job!* There was a roaring in his ears. He hallucinated that it was the sounds of the crowds—the parents, the children, the relatives who had come so far to see their heroes perform—all the people who had been meant to fill this stadium, all the good citizens who had come to cheer the athletes in their triumphant entrance into Salt Lake City, his city. Now those people would not sit in these seats, would not raise the ghostly roaring that filled his ears. He forced himself to breathe, but could not draw his breath below his diaphragm. Somehow, this was all his fault.

"Jim? Okay, I've got the file."

"It's okay," Jim said. "I'm back by the stairs. I—get Miller to call me when he gets in, okay?" He set the cell phone down on the step beside him. He blinked repeatedly, trying to dispel the strange colors and warpings that danced in his vision. Head spinning, he opened up his clipboard notebook and tried feebly to make notes. The pen seemed to melt out from between his fingers. It dropped onto the page. He squeezed his eyes shut, trying to sort out the protocol he was supposed to be following, but he couldn't remember it.

"Jim?" said a voice like a gnat buzzing about his cell phone.

He snatched up the phone, pressed it to his ear, spoke. "Oh. Yes. I'm up in the trusses at the stadium. I . . . we . . . just get Fred to phone me first chance he gets, okay?"

"Fred went home with the flu."

I'll have to go home myself, Jim realized dully. *I can't go back up there until the migraine passes.*

"Jim? Do you have a message for him?"

"Yes," he said, forcing his voice to be level, calm. Forcing himself to do his job. "Tell him the welds are sheared. Not just one or two but a whole run of them. Got that?"

"Welds sheared," she repeated slowly, taking time to write it down. "Stadium. Whole run of them. Okay..." Her voice trailed off into the muffling that told Jim she had put her hand over the receiver.

"Did you get that?" he asked.

The muffling sound stopped. "Yeah. Sorry, Frank Malone's here. He's waiting to talk to the soils engineer."

"Yeah. Sure. Frank will know what to do." *Fred. Frank. Man, I'm losing it, scrambling up names.*

Jim closed his eyes, forced himself to breathe deeply. Frank would know how to deal with this. He'd clear the stadium, red-tag it. There was snow forecast, and with that additional load and just a little wind, it could come down like the hand of God and smite him dead.

12

Once Logan de Pontier had left and Faye and I were inside her house, with the door firmly shut, I lost my cool entirely. "*What* was that all about?" I demanded.

Faye's shoulders slumped tiredly as she tossed her jacket across an overstuffed leather chair. "I just came from the doctor's."

"You're dodging the question!"

"She confirmed that I am pregnant."

"As if you had any doubt. But just why in hell—"

"Pumped up like a nickel balloon."

"Faye!" She was beginning to cry again, and I was not done being mad at her.

She began to flail her arms. "Knocked up! With child! In an interesting condition! In the family way! One month gone! Gravid! Parturient!"

"Parturient?"

"Too many years of Latin. Or as the Spanish say, *embarazado*, which, most appropriately, is derived from the obvious root." She began to stamp a foot on the hardwood floor in a spot where it was not covered with one of her spectacularly huge Navajo rugs. "I! AM! EMBARRASSED!"

"But parturient? I've never even heard the word."

Faye threw her sunglasses and purse down on the floor and stalked through an archway into the adjoining dining room on her way toward the kitchen. "Technically, it is not the correct term. It would suggest that I am much further along than I am. There's another one I'll have to deal with if I keep this thing. 'How far along are you?' Shit!"

" 'This thing'?" I said, following her through into the kitchen. "*This thing?* And *if* you keep it? This morning it was a child, which, you will recall, you wanted."

I had to duck quickly to dodge a bowl of fruit that Faye now threw at me. The ceramic turned to ballistic shards as it struck the wall next to my head.

"Child? Try parasite! Yesterday I had a life. A good life. Boring perhaps, but I was in charge of it. Today I discover that I have picked up a hitchhiker, and now you tell me half the mountain is on its way down the hill into my living room!"

"Kitchen. It'll hit this end of the house first."

The fruit bowl was followed by a pitcher and two plates. When she got to saucepans and other objects unlikely to break, and it became clear that she was no longer aiming but just interested in making a lot of noise, I figured I had accomplished the mission of helping her to get mad enough to vent her feelings. At least for the moment. Sure enough, after a clattering of stainless-steel pot lids, she dropped down onto her knees, planted her face on the floor, and began once again to bawl.

I switched the gas on underneath the kettle for tea and got down next to her. Very gingerly (because I was as yet new to this business of having such a close, direct, and downright blunt friend as Faye) I put an arm around her.

She kept her face hidden. "I'm so confused," she crooned. She began to rock back and forth with the force of her emotions.

"I'd be surprised at you if you weren't."

"Oh, Em . . ."

I straightened up a little and began to massage her back. "You're a good person, Faye. You'll do the right thing, whatever that is."

"I don't want to do anything," she blubbered. I want to go back to yesterday, or last month, when I did not have this decision, or this responsibility. I want to be just dumb old Faye again, fat, dumb, and happy—"

"Skinny. No one can ever call you fat, you lucky bum."

"—and just messing around like it didn't matter."

"You can't tell me you never thought this through. That's not like you."

"Oh sure. It's easy when it's some infinitesimal statistical possibility. But now it's a baby."

"Embryo."

"Don't split hairs," she wailed. "We're talking about a life. A whole, separate life."

I stopped rubbing and kept just one hand in the center of her back. "There you're wrong."

Faye turned her head and looked at me, her face wet with tears.

"It is not a separate life," I heard myself say. "Not an independent one, at any rate. Not now, and not for years. We're not like lizards or turtles who just lay an egg and wander off. You're talking about a human child, one of the most dependent creatures to ever suck air into its lungs and cry for dinner. Hell, even calves can stand up just as soon as they're born. You're talking about an enormous demand on your resources, and you don't just get to say good-bye. Not now, not ever."

Faye's face contracted. "You're scaring me, Em."

"You should feel scared. Sure, you've got the money to do as you please. You won't be out on the street. But what you're feeling is the part that gets left out of some of the pro-life propaganda. This is going to have an enormous impact on your life, regardless of what happens. And you have a right to life, too."

Faye rested her cheek on the tiled floor. "Are you saying I should get an abortion?" she whispered.

I stared down at her, my mighty woman friend brought to

her knees, and felt a wave of something—energy, life, chi—sweep through my being. In that moment, sensing the little life that pulsed within her womb, I knew two things: that I could never end a life within me, and that the decision to end or continue was so deeply personal, so pivotal to the very definition of a woman's soul, that I would defend to the death my friend's right to end it if she must. And I would stay by her if she continued. "No. It's your decision. Either way, I would help you cry." I felt warm tears spill from my eyes.

Faye reached up and touched them, amazed.

◈

AN HOUR LATER, we were curled up in the living room with soft afghans, a dwindling plate of chocolate-covered shortbread cookies, and our second and third cups of herbal tea.

Faye leaned back against the cushions. "Imagine me a mother," she said. "I remember my own mother. She used to take me up to her room in her parents' house—my grandparents' estate—and let me play with the dolls she'd had as a girl. It was the nice part of going there. I loved it, in fact. Just the two of us, with those dolls. It was more like having a sister than a mother."

"Why didn't she bring her doll collection to her own house?"

Faye shot me a look. "She didn't have permission. You don't know my grandparents. They have their rules. You don't upset the household. You want to suffer, try pissing off my grandfather by being a child. Imagine me all done up in hair ribbons and pinafore, being seen but not heard. Hell, I didn't really exist in that house, except in that room with those dolls."

"Sounds awful. How did you stand it?"

"I have it to thank for my early interest in Buddhism. You know, thanking your petty tyrant for the opportunity to learn. Detachment. Equanimity. Understanding your adversary. That sort of stuff."

"You mean it warped you," I said cheekily.

"Yeah. I suppose it did. Oh well, the old man left me a wad of money, so I suppose I should be grateful, even if he did force me to do things his way."

That reminded me of Faye's performance around Logan de Pontier. I decided it was time to give her some heat for it. "Nice going with the UGS geologist," I said. "Speaking of 'my way or the highway,' you embarrassed the hell out of him, Faye."

Faye snorted into her tea. "Uh-uh. *He* was pleased as punch. It was *you* that was embarrassed."

"The hell. What you selling?"

"He was kind of cute."

I set my tea mug down rather hard. "Faye, I am engaged to Ray."

"Engaged to be engaged, and—"

"I prefer not to mess up what I've got, if you don't mind."

Faye reached for another cookie so she'd have something to examine as she said, "Has he called you since he got home? I noticed you checking your phone messages while I was getting the tea and cookies together."

I frowned into my mug. "No. He hasn't called."

"Did you drive by his work and see if his car was in the lot?"

"I managed to restrain myself."

"Have you called him?"

With some heat, I said, "No!"

"Oooo. That does not sound good. So I saw this perfectly nice guy coming down the hill with you, watching you like he'd never seen anything quite so nice, and I'm thinking, This could be a good thing."

"What are you talking about?" I said defensively.

"And he had nice buns. And the beard wasn't half-bad."

I munched down another cookie before I said anything more. "I didn't notice them. Ray's a tough act to beat, Faye."

"You mean follow. You should go to that dinner tonight. In fact, I wasn't kidding: I am going to take you there."

"Faye—"

She held up a hand. "And I'm not just doing this to meddle in your love life, pal. You need to make more contacts in your professional life. Hey, I'm the one who has to listen to you gripe about the temp jobs you've been taking to pay the rent, not that you've been willing to move in here, where it wouldn't matter if you paid me a red cent."

"I couldn't do that. I need you for a friend, not a landlady I mooch off of."

"Your pride is surpassed only by your stubbornness."

"You're going to need your privacy with Tom now more than ever."

"If he's still talking to me after I tell him."

I threw my head back and stared at the ceiling. "Oh, is that what this is all about. Faye, he's a cantankerous shithead, I admit, but a more honorable cantankerous shithead you would never find. And underneath it all, he's really just an old softy trying to look after the people he cares about."

"So I'll call Ray for you."

"No, you won't."

She picked up the phone that lay on the end table next to her. "What's the number?"

"No."

She punched some keys. "I need a number in Salt Lake City," she said into the phone. "The police station. Central." When she had the number, she punched it in. "Hello, may I speak with Officer Raymond?" she asked, her hand going for another cookie. "Oh. Oh, I see. No, no message." She hung up the phone and looked up at me. "He called in sick."

"Ray?" I said incredulously. "Sick?"

"The duty officer said that Ray swapped shifts with someone. Sounds more like he called in *well*, the bastard."

"Now wait just a minute! We may be having our little problems with adjustment, but that doesn't put him in the bastard category. Maybe he just couldn't get back in time, so he swapped shifts rather than take another vacation day."

Faye looked at me like she wasn't so sure.

"Ray's a nice guy, Faye," I pleaded. *Nice and romantic*, I thought defensively, remembering the time he'd taken me dancing before I'd broken my leg late last summer. *Nice and direct*, I added to my mental tally, thinking of the three times he'd driven over the mountains to Colorado to get to know me before I even came to see him once. *Nice and companionable*, I mused, thinking of countless hours we had sat just holding hands and staring out into the world together. Ours was an unspoken relationship.

She pursed her lips. "Yes, he is, Em. Too nice. His ma's got him running so fast, he hasn't got time for you."

Changing the subject from my conundrums back to Faye's, I said, "Besides, Tom already knows about your little secret."

Faye had just been putting her tea to her lips and choked on it. She slammed the mug down on the end table and bent forward to put her hands in her face while she coughed. She managed to squeeze out a strangled "Noooo!"

More gently, I added, "C'mon, you know the work he's in. He read that one like it was up in lights. Want my opinion? He's as scared as you are."

13

The only man who was enthusiastic about the earthquake from the start was geologist Irving J. Witkind of the U.S. Geological Survey, who was living in a trailer on a rise to the north of Hebgen Lake, above the Culligans and Parade Rest, while he surveyed and mapped the area.

When the first shock hit, he figured his trailer had somehow broken loose and was rolling down the hill. He charged out, intent on stopping it. From the way the trees were swaying in the absence of any wind, he knew it was a genuine earthquake. He hopped in his jeep and headed down toward the lake. He saw the [earthquake] scarp just in time to stop.

"It's mine! It's mine!" he shouted as he got out of the jeep and realized the full measure of his fortune. His words will echo wherever geologists gather in years to come. Professionally, his once-in-a-thousand-lifetimes fortune in being on the scene of a major quake meant as much as discovering an unfound Pharaoh's tomb would to an Egyptologist.

—*From* The Night the Mountain Fell: The Story of the Montana-Yellowstone Earthquake, *by Edmund Christopherson. The 1959 magnitude 7.5 earthquake was centered about fifteen miles north of Yellowstone National Park.*

MY ADVICE, IN CASE YOU EVER CONSIDER THE OPTION, IS don't ever mess with Faye Carter. Her way of dealing with stress can be ugly. Case in point: That evening, she did indeed drag me to that meeting at the Pie Pizzeria. And no, it was not a case of a pregnant woman having food cravings. She did not take bite one. She just hung there like a vulture waiting for death, insisting that I look like I was having a whee of a good time.

It started like this, the moment we reached the table:

Faye: "Hi, everyone, this is my friend Em Hansen. She's a shy geologist who wants to drink beer and whoop it up, just like the rest of you."

Me (finding no words but plenty of body English, including, but not limited to, cringing and sheepish grinning): "Gaa-uhn" (Which probably means something in Arabic or ancient Tahitian, but, freely translated from Wyoming cowgirlese, means "I feel an intense desire to sink through the floor to the center of the Earth.")

Logan de Pontier: "Hey, Em, sit down. And what's your friend's name again?"

Me (finding my voice at last, given this extraordinary setup): "Attila the Hun."

Faye (with meltingly lovely smile, self-deprecating hand gestures): "I'm Faye Carter. Attila is just my stage name."

Logan: "Ah. Great. Well, let me introduce you around. This is Wendy Fortescue. She works at the Seismic Station up here at the university. This is Ted Wimler, a *compadre* from the UGS. Hugh Buttons, director of the Seismic Station. Pet Mercer, science reporter for the *Tribune*. There'll be a couple more coming. Come on and sit down. Can I get you a beer?"

Me: "Oh God, please, yes."

Faye: "Not for me, thanks. My karma currently disallows it."

Everyone at the table seemed content enough to ignore that last remark. They shifted and shuffled around to make room for us to get seated, mercifully putting Faye in the back corner beyond the bulk of Hugh Buttons, where she could contemplate the graffiti on the brick walls if she liked. I sat at the other end of the table, across from Logan and between Pet Mercer and Ted Wimler.

I had to strain to hear Hugh, who had apparently been in the middle of giving Pet Mercer and the others an update on the earthquake situation. He was a big guy with a puffy stomach and elastic-waist pants, which made him look like a watermelon sitting in a shower cap.

"We haven't had very many aftershocks," he said. "I had expected—or should I say hoped for?—maybe three or four times as many. But what we have does begin to paint the plane of the fault."

Pet pulled an almond out of a pocket and popped it into her mouth. I noticed that she hadn't taken any pizza from the communal dish, and didn't even have a plate in front of her. She said, "I've noticed that there has been surprisingly little historic seismic activity right along the fault. Why is that?" She passed him a map showing a black dot at the epicenter of every earthquake that had occurred in Utah over the past thirty years.

Hugh stared meditatively at the map. "Yes, you've noticed our odd blank area right where the fault lies. Well, that's because all these other quakes were fairly small, but there were a lot of them. Here, for instance. That's the Book Cliffs. These are all rock bursts in the coal mines there. Tiny. But the earthquakes along the Wasatch fault, when they occur, are much larger, and the larger the quake, the further apart they occur temporally. If the fault slipped more easily, we'd have many small earthquakes for every medium one we do have. It's got to do with the fault geometry and the way the stress accumulates in the rock."

Pet nodded. She said, "You've always taken pains to explain to me that the Wasatch fault is a zone, not one discrete plane."

"Right, it's a set of fractures, and each one is in fact a zone of subparallel fractures, because a fault does not fail in precisely the same place each time."

"So which part cracked this time?" the journalist asked.

Hugh inhaled and exhaled visibly, his bulk rising and falling with the action. "The hypocenter—that's the actual point of slippage—was on the Warm Springs branch of the fault, the part that runs near downtown."

"Runs *under* downtown," Pet suggested.

Seeing that Pet was trying to get the director of the Seismic Station to make a statement he was perhaps not yet ready, from a scientific standpoint, to make, I asked, "Where was the epicenter?" *Epicenter* was one of the terms I had spent the previous hour brushing up on in my old physical geology textbook. The epicenter of the earthquake was that point on the Earth's surface immediately above the area of slippage; the rock would not fail on the line where the fault actually came to surface, because the Wasatch fault plunges into the Earth at an angle, dipping away steeply to the west.

"Just west of downtown," Hugh said. "Out toward the UGS, in fact." He smiled jauntily over toward Logan de Pontier and Ted Wimler. "But in deference to our esteemed colleagues there, we're not calling it the UGS Quake."

"You mean, in kindness to Sidney's memory," Ted said dramatically.

I turned and looked at Ted, a rather slight man who parted his limp hair down the middle. His eyes were too close together for the width of his soft face. I wondered what his exact relationship had been with the deceased state geologist.

Hugh Buttons tipped his head to one side and averted his eyes sorrowfully.

Wendy Fortescue, the seismology tech, rolled her eyes and groaned. Pet Mercer's eyes snapped her way.

I saw Logan's eyebrows tighten downward. They were rather heavy, and quite expressive, giving him a brooding look when he did that. "It's been one hell of a day, eh? She left two kids, although they'll of course go live with their dad, and—"

"A fine woman, and an excellent scientist," Hugh said, his voice thickening. "A tragedy."

Ted said, "Everything must be a shambles up at the house there, Wendy."

Wendy drew one knee up toward her chest and said, "I haven't been home."

Logan asked, "Has the funeral been scheduled?"

Hugh Buttons said, "Tomorrow morning."

"So soon?" someone asked.

"She was Jewish."

Pet Mercer glanced back and forth, taking in everyone's reactions. I realized then that she was watching them with the same kind of intensity I was, and, unless I misjudged, with much the same sort of intent. "Tell me about Dr. Smeeth, Wendy," she said softly. "I understand that you roomed in her basement apartment."

Wendy said, "I've got nothing to say. I don't want to be in the funny papers. You reporters are all a bunch of maggots."

Oblivious to Wendy's coarseness, Ted said, "I can tell you this: People bad-mouthed Sidney, said she was a troublemaker. But I thought she was the best boss I've ever had. She gave me every opportunity. She encouraged me with all my ideas. I—"

"This isn't all about you, Ted," Wendy growled.

Artfully not looking at Pet, Hugh said, "I'd prefer we discussed this at another time. We've all had a long day, and I'm sure . . . ah . . . that Pet here has some more questions before she has to go to press with her story. We don't want to keep you, Pet."

Avoiding looking at Pet, each person averted his or her eyes in a slightly different direction. I began to get the idea that, even as cute as she was, Pet Mercer was considered a bit of a piranha where science news gathering was concerned. She was slightly built and perky, and her hair bounced as she wrote, and it was clear that she used her diminutive appearance to put her interview subjects off their guard, but that this group had been treated to that trick once too often. She said, "Yes, I do need to get to press, Hugh, but, if you'll forgive me, Dr. Smeeth is part of the story. Ted, you said people called her a troublemaker. Could this trouble you're talking about have anything to do with the contention that existed between her and the governor's office? I have sources who say there was quite a dustup between them two days ago over the Towne Centre project. Can you give me more on that?"

Ted cleared his throat in preparation to give her a dramatic answer, but before he could speak, Hugh Buttons said, "Dr. Smeeth served at the pleasure of the governor, Pet. She was a fine scientist, and stringent in her interpretation of her mandate. Naturally, there would be places where she would rub against any person whose job it is to make political decisions. It is the nature of the game. It is . . . I want to say almost unavoidable, but, damn it, Pet, I don't want to go on record saying anything like that, because it's so obviously the case that it comes off sounding contentious."

Ted had found his voice. "Yeah, but in this case, it was more than a little disagreement. Hell, I heard her——"

Logan said, "That's enough, Ted. It's not our place to get mixed up in politics. Remember, our job is to report findings, not create policy."

Pet watched each man carefully. As she did so, her hand slipped into a pocket, produced a raisin, and popped it into her mouth. She chewed it quickly, like a chipmunk.

Ted closed his eyes indignantly. "Logan, there is a time and place——"

Logan barked, "But not here, and not now, and not mixed up with the earthquake. This is an important chance for us to get the word out about seismic risk, and we're not going to confuse it with some crap about political infighting that'll make us look like a bunch of idiots. We are *scientists*." His thick eyebrows had lowered again.

Ted shut up. If I had been on the receiving end of that look, I think I'd have stayed quiet for a week.

Pet threw down her pen. "Okay," she said, "you guys are dodging me again. Come on, why shouldn't scientists create public policy? I mean, who better than the people who really understand what's going on? Look what happened with the extension of the Salt Palace. Some say that the county just shopped around until they got the geological opinion that fit their game plan. Now we have another project even closer to the known trace of the fault. No, it's worse than that. Today's data say it's right *on* the fault. So why aren't you guys screaming at the tops of your lungs?"

There was silence at the table for perhaps fifteen seconds, during which time nobody ate and several people drank.

Ted stared into his pizza morosely.

Pet caught Ted's eye and mouthed the words *I'll call you.*

Ted's lips curled eagerly.

Pet blinked at Ted, evincing obliviousness to his reaction.

Hugh said, "The problem is, Pet, that there is a difference between theory and fact. That the crust of the Earth cracks and slips along gigantic shear planes is a fact. We can observe directly that it does so, or, where exposures are good, where it *has* done so. Unfortunately, the exact location and intensity of tomorrow's slippage is not known. Tomorrow's slippage is a matter of theory. A theory is considered good if it predicts events, and is discarded if events occur that refute it. Prediction is another matter, as we have been explaining. Prediction is the application of common sense to observed facts—if it has always snowed in December in the past, we presume it will snow in December again—but in the case of geologic hazards, its utility is quite limited. The future of the Earth's crust is absolute—stresses will build up and faulting will occur—but our specific knowledge of that future is no better than an educated guess. We can gather historical and carbon dates from past faulting events and calculate statistical averages that tell us about how often faulting occurs at a given location, but an average interval is a mathematical result, not a schedule. Using satellites, we can now measure the motions of the Earth's crustal plates, but observing a build-up of stress does not set a date for the moment it will be released." Hugh took a bite of pizza, shook his head, and chewed. "Besides, Pet, science is most accurate when it is unemotional and rational, and politics is anything but that. Politics must strive for the best for the most. If as a scientist I must decide who will benefit from my observations and whom to exclude from benefit, my thinking is immediately clouded."

Pet for once looked flummoxed. "Well, okay, moving on, then. Have you come up with a name for the quake?"

Hugh smiled at Pet in a fatherly way. "I'm glad we're back on stable ground, not to make a seismic joke. In fact, Pet, it doesn't have to have a name. It wasn't that big an event." His smile turned wan. "Let's save a name like 'the Salt Lake City earthquake' for the big one. Sorry to downgrade your earthquake, and I don't mean to suggest that it's not newsworthy, but you'll recall that we've had three others in the five to five point five range in the past hundred years around Salt Lake City. Use it for its educational value. Talk about what the big one would be like by contrast."

The reporter scribbled madly. "Okay, good," she said. "But really, Dr. Buttons, it's got to have a name. This was a big earthquake for a lot of people. Like the Ottmeier family, whose infant son Tommy was fatally injured when the bookcase fell over on him." Her sharp eyes focused tightly on Hugh's face, watching for his reaction.

Hugh Buttons closed his eyes, drawing himself inward. "Please don't ask me for a quote on that, Pet."

Faye interrupted from the far end of the table. "Little Tommy died?" she asked. "I—I didn't hear about that." Her complexion had paled.

Pet said, "Well, he's not dead yet, but I hear it's imminent. Wow, what a news cycle this one is becoming. All the extra press personnel who are here already for the Olympics are completely ravenous for the human-interest stories. The parking lot outside the hospital looks like a display yard for media vans with jack-up satellite dishes. ABC, CBS, NBC, CNN—everyone's down there. And the blood bank's going wild. You know Salt Lakers— when there's an emergency, every last one of us rolls out in support."

"So you're in hog heaven," Logan said.

Pet gave Logan one deft bat of her eyelashes. "Well, Logan, I suppose I would be if that were the trough at which I fed. But I'm a science journalist, and I'd rather focus on the science. Report the story behind the story, the educational bit that might just help people be a little more intelligent about how they go about living in a huge earthquake fault zone."

Ted Wimler leaned toward Faye. "The parents put the kid to bed below this humongous oak bookcase that was already leaning into the room, they had so much on it. So much for bookish people being smart, huh?"

Wendy Fortescue whipped her narrow little face his way and said, "Shut up, Ted."

"How frequent are earthquakes around here anyway?" I asked Logan.

"That depends on the size of quake you're talking about. Felt earthquakes? One like today? About every forty years around here."

Pet said, "Yes, I'm aware of the earlier quakes that were big enough to get your attention. Let's see: 1910, 1949, and, if you count the one over by Magna, 1962. And Salt Lakers felt Montana's Hebgen Lake seven point five quake in 1959, and the seven point three Borah Peak, Idaho, quake in 1983. I've looked them up on your UUSS Web site. I found the 'Personalizing the Earthquake Threat' section and read the accounts you posted from the old newspapers. Great stuff. And there must have been smaller quakes, too, right? So it sounds like you begin to have some data. So tell me, what do the data tell you?"

Hugh shifted in his chair and took a sip of beer. "We have anecdotal data, yes, but remember, our records only go back a hundred and twenty-five years. Our seismographs were pretty primitive in 1910, and even though the recording equipment had improved, the instrumentation network was still scanty in 1949, so while we could triangulate the epicenter of those quakes, we couldn't get much resolution on the subsurface picture. Even now, we're struggling to get a more three-dimensional picture. Funding, it's always funding. Seismographs and telemetry cost money."

"Amen," said Logan.

Hugh continued. "And again, the local quakes we're talking about are fairly moderate-size ones—the five to five point five range. Like Logan says, the recurrence interval—that calculated average—for those is well under a hundred years. But Logan here can also tell you a lot about the big presettlement earthquakes—the sevens—that this segment of the Wasatch has seen in the last few thousand years. Always remember, for every whole number larger on the Richter scale, thirty-two times more energy is released. So a seven would release almost one thousand times more energy than a five. Those are the ones that we truly need to worry about. We'd be looking at a lot more than just a few chimneys down, and, ah, so much more than the one casualty."

One thousand times bigger. I wondered what, if anything, would have been left of Mrs. Pierce's house after that level of shaking.

Logan bunched his eyebrows again. "I gave you the publications on that, Pet," he said, "and you should talk to the emergency-preparedness people again to get that from a human angle. Hugh, tell her more about today's event. You said you've begun to paint the slippage. So is it official? Did the movement occur south of 600 North Street? If it's down on a latitude with the survey, that puts it six blocks south of that at least."

I listened sharply, remembering the map we had looked at together that afternoon. Salt Lake City's street-numbering system is excruciatingly practical, in a weirdly original kind of way, like a lot about its Mormon founders. The street is called 600 North— the 600 is not an address, and there is no North Street—and it's right between 500 North and 700 North. The quirks of the street-numbering system formed the basis for my suspicion that the men who designed Salt Lake City were all engineers, and not one of them a closet poet. But then, Mormonism has always struck me as a religion designed around expediency and practicality, with an answer for every question and a contingency for every eventuality, and no quarter given to spoilers like chaos or entropy or even ambiguity. Which was part and parcel of my disinterest in joining it: as a geologist, I see ambiguities in everything. Or perhaps it's my ability to perceive ambiguities that makes me good at geology.

But I digress. Logan had a gleam in his eye that said he was highly interested in Hugh Buttons's answer. And the degree of his alertness had reminded me of the missing fault line he had added to his USGS map. What had he said? The dashed, or "approximately located," line had been on an earlier map but had been left off the 1992 edition?

Hugh replied, "Yes, we are confirming that the Warm Springs branch of the Wasatch fault does continue south of 600 North. We're showing movement spanning from 100 North to South Temple." He shot a quick look at Pet Mercer. "Again, Pet, that's not a very big earthquake. A ground-rupturing quake, a six point five or a seven, would have ripped loose several kilometers north to south."

"And if we had ground rupture," I said, still trying to get a handle on the scale of such events, "what would be the vertical throw created by that size quake? How big a scarp would we see?"

Hugh took another sip of his beer. He focused tightly on the foam at the top. "Again, Logan's your man. What's the rate of vertical movement, Lo? A millimeter per year, right?"

Logan gave Hugh a look that said, *You know damned well what the rate is,* but said, "Yes, that's our best estimate, but that's an average. These things don't go off like clockwork. Earthquake prediction is, as you said . . . well, not truly possible. There are too few data—too few observations—and an average is a mathematical construct, not an observation of nature's pattern. And as Em is suggesting, movement on the Wasatch comes in large jumps, sudden releases of stress that are rare by the standard of human experience. Say the recurrence interval—that's how often you get an event that size on this segment of this fault, Pet—is a thousand years. In fact, the interval is one thousand three hundred and fifty years, plus or minus two hundred. Do the math. That would give you about a four-foot-high scarp running down the middle of West Temple from north of the capitol clear down past the Convention Center. Or worse, because you get back-tilting and antithetic faulting. The place is ripping apart, not just moving up and down. The kind of vertical offsets we see when we are able to cut a trench across the fault are in fact ten feet or more."

Pet twisted this way and that in her seat, taking notes with great concentration. She hadn't slipped any nuts or raisins out of her pockets in quite a while. "Okay," she said, "so that would crack a few foundations, right?"

Logan leaned forward onto the table, his green eyes wide with amazement. "You have a quake that size on this fault, it won't matter what's built across it, Pet. Every building within miles not built to Code Four will be badly damaged, if it isn't outright flattened, and we're going to be a whole lot more worried about the dead and dying than about any kind of real estate. We'll have kill rates up to thirty percent. Utilities will collapse, food and clean water will run out, the hospitals and the doctors and nurses that staff them will be under piles of rubble, and we won't be able to bring in supplies or triage personnel because we'll have bridges down all over the place and the airport runways will be submerged under water draining east from the Great Salt Lake. And even if that water weren't as salty as all hell, it wouldn't be potable, because it will be laced with that tailings pond crud Kennecot's got stacked up behind those levees that are going to breach."

◆

IT'S POSSIBLE THAT Faye's lack of appetite had more to do with Logan's description of a "big one" than with her little hitchhiker's affect on her digestion, but I made up for her gastronomic shortcomings by putting away four pieces myself. The Pie does a good pizza, and I am a glutton when it comes to that all-American combination of Italian ingredients.

Several more geologists joined us before the last crumb and string of melted mozzarella vanished from the table, but I forget their names. They discussed the observations they'd made that day, often stepping around Pet Mercer's questions so they wouldn't be quoted before they were ready, but they did keep the conversation lively by telling war stories about other temblors they'd experienced, where they were during the 1989 Loma Prieta quake, or the latest they'd heard concerning the debate over the geologic setting of the Republic Day quake in India in 2001. Like I said, everybody has an earthquake story, and it wasn't long before they got into volcanic eruptions, landslides, and flood stories.

Out on the sidewalk, as the party began to break up, the subject of recreation suddenly supplanted seismic hazards. A tall blond consulting geologist named Tim or John or something, who had joined the pizzafest late, asked Logan, "So, are we still on for our annual Seismologists on Skis adventure? Or does an actual seismic event supersede swilling beer and skiing?"

"You're right, I got so wound up in that shaker that I forgot."

He looked around at the others. "When were we going to do that?"

"This Wednesday," Wendy said. "Day after tomorrow. I think we'd better postpone. I don't want to miss any aftershocks. And . . . you know . . ."

"Hey," the tall blond man said, "now that Pet's out of earshot, did you hear that Frank Malone dug a trench down at the new mall site this morning?"

"He didn't!" said Logan, appalled. "What, did he have to get out of his truck for that?"

"Got right down into the trench, I hear. And didn't find a thing."

"Figures," said Logan. "He couldn't find his ass with both hands and a roadmap. Didn't phone us, either. Wouldn't want anything so complicated as a second opinion stirring up controversy, now, would he?"

The blond man shook his head in disgust.

I cut in. "Malone," I said, thinking the name sounded familiar. "Who's he?"

Logan looked out from under his eyebrows. "Oh, just another engineering geologist of easy virtue. Don't mind us. We can't afford to cut trenches very often, but he gets the big bucks from his clients—you know, developers."

"You mean he digs trenches when they're getting ready to put foundations in for big buildings and like that."

"Yeah."

"Doesn't the state or the county require that the UGS pass judgment on things like that? I mean, doesn't he have to call you when he's cutting a trench?'

"No, not usually. Not unless the Building Department gets nervous and says he has to get a second opinion, but that doesn't happen very often. We just wish to hell the slimeball would at least give us a squint at his trenches while he has them open.

Hell, we'd do half his work for him, scrape down the sides and all, but he doesn't call."

"Give up, Logan," the blond man said. "Malone wouldn't want you looking into one of his trenches. You might see the fault his client doesn't want him to see." To me, he said, "It's rare as hell to get a look underground at a downtown site. And this one was right on trend with the Warm Springs fault no less, and he cut it just hours after the earthquake. I hear he had it backfilled by lunchtime."

Hugh Buttons maintained a diplomatic silence. "Well then, it sounds like you ought to go skiing. The fault will keep," he said. "Fun as this quake was, I keep telling everyone it isn't the big one, so life goes on."

Ted frowned. "But we're in mourning. Sidney—"

Logan said, "I think Sidney would rather be remembered from the ski slopes than think of us glooming about town. Let's go on up there and slice some powder for her, okay? Besides, if we wait until next week, all the people coming in for the Olympics will be crawling around up there like maggots. If we don't go now, we may as well wait until March."

The blond man said, "Sure, but let's give it another day. How about Thursday?" He looked around at everyone. A quorum nodded assent. "Where?"

"Alta," said Logan.

"Alta?" Wendy cried in her surprisingly harsh voice. "Alta don't allow no snowboarders!"

"Precisely why we want to go there," Logan informed her. "Come on, Wendy, you can raise the level of your game for just one day, can't you? Besides, you snowboarders spend all that time in prayer. Seems your prayers should be answered by some real skiing."

Wendy screwed up her face pugnaciously. "What you mean prayer, asshole?"

"I mean you're always on your knees, darling. You got no control over that thing."

"Fuck you!"

Logan flexed his eloquent eyebrows. "Is that an offer?"

"In your dreams, frog boy."

"Well then," Logan replied, wandering along the sidewalk, "off to bed, perchance to dream."

Wendy gave him a quick jab in the gut, then grabbed his shirtfront, pulled him down into range, imposed a kiss on his lips, turned, and strode off. Several other members of the party roared with laughter. Ted Wimler pouted and whined, "Hey, where's mine?" unintentionally seeding more laughs.

Logan said good night to the rest of the party and fell in step next to Faye and me, slowly strolling up toward the corner, which looks out toward the natural history museum and the University of Utah campus. "So," he said, "anyone here for skiing Thursday? We're supposed to get some new snow tomorrow. Should be good."

I said, "I don't—" but Faye rammed me in the ribs with her elbow.

"We'd love to, wouldn't we, Em? What time, and where do we all meet?"

I said, "Sorry, but I just got my leg out of a cast."

Faye said, "Precisely why you need to get up there and get your confidence back."

I opened my mouth again to object that confidence was not the issue, but Logan cut me off. "I'll pick you both up," he said, his eyes dancing with amusement. "Say nine o'clock. At your house, Faye, or shall I find you before that, Em?"

There it was, the big opening, where I was supposed to give him my address and phone number. I looked into his eyes. They were interesting eyes. Another time, another place, I would have been jumping up and down like a puppy, but just then I wanted to be looking into indigo blue eyes, and from a much closer range. "I'll be at Faye's," I said sadly.

Just then, Pet Mercer came bounding up the sidewalk. "Logan, don't run off!" she called. "I've got something you're going to be interested in!"

"What?"

She caught up to us, not even breathing deeply. "Want to tour the City and County Building with me tomorrow? A guy from the county is going to inspect it, see how the seismic retrofit held up in the quake." She gave him a very special smile.

Logan looked embarrassed. "Um, well, I've seen it already, Pet."

"What part?" she asked, undeterred. "You mean the base isolation system, don't you? That stuff in the basement. Well, have you ever been up in the clock tower?"

Logan lowered his eyebrows and considered Pet carefully. He seemed to be trying to decide how to answer. Clearly, this was ample bait, but, just as clearly, she did not want to get involved. "Well, Pet, I . . ."

"Oh, come on, it'll be great. I hear it's scary!"

"Pet," he said, lowering his voice, indicating that his words were for her only. "I appreciate your interest, really, but I think that after Sidney's service tomorrow, I'm just going to go home and sit."

Pet refused to be brushed off. "It'll be quick. Come on, have you ever been up in the tower? This is a terrific chance for someone in your line of work."

Logan's face clouded with conflicting feelings. It was clear that he wanted to do this but felt he would be misleading Pet in a social sense. Pet was just winding up to deliver her next volley of wheedling when I did a crazy thing. I said, "Sounds really great. Can I tag along, Pet?"

Pet looked at me and blinked. Obviously, I was not the fish for which she was angling.

I shrugged my shoulders. "I mean, I'd jump at a chance to go up that tower. I was over there today reviewing—" I snapped my mouth shut. I had nearly spilled the beans, almost told them what I'd been doing at the City and County Building for Tom Latimer. What had I been thinking? Or had I just not been thinking? Surely this was why Tom was so concerned about my chances for survival if I kept on getting myself involved with forensic work.

Pet was quick. She had seen me bring myself up short, and for the moment, she was more interested in me than in Logan. "What was it you were doing there?"

"Oh, nothing," I said. It sounded lame even to me.

Logan watched me, deep-set green eyes unwavering. "So much for rehabilitating your leg. That's a long climb up that tower."

Out of the corner of my eyes, I saw Faye twist her lips to one side, a kind of "you hopeless jackass" look.

"Sure," Pet said brightly. "You come, Em. I'll meet you in the main lobby, by the guard's desk. Two sharp tomorrow afternoon. Don't be late."

IT WAS ABOUT 8:00 P.M. BY THE TIME I HAD DROPPED FAYE back at her house—she insisted I keep her car again—and had returned to mine. I wanted to race inside and check my answering machine for messages, but Mrs. Pierce caught me on the front porch.

"I've been worried sick about you," she said. "Where have you been?"

I stared at her, goggle-eyed. "Huh?"

"You were going to check in with me after you found out what had happened in the earthquake," she said.

"Oh. Yeah. Well, I did come back, Mrs. Pierce, but you were out, I guess."

Mrs. Pierce raised an eyebrow, letting me know that my guess was wrong.

"Well, anyway, I found out that there's really not much to worry about," I said, wondering how true that statement was. "I talked to some geologists from the Utah Geological Survey, had dinner with them. The head seismologist for the Seismic Station at the university was there. They all seemed to be digesting their dinners okay. So I think everything's pretty much okay."

Mrs. Pierce wasn't ready to let it go that easily. "Well, did you hear about that poor little baby?"

"Yes, Mrs. Pierce. It's awful."

"Mm-hmm. I knew his grandmother in school. I feel so sorry for his family."

I wondered what it would be like to belong so deeply to a city that could so easily think like a village.

Leaving my landlady to contemplate her connection to her cosmos, I hurried upstairs in search of a message from Ray. There was none. I lifted the receiver to make sure my phone was getting a dial tone. It was.

Ray had always been a man of few words, but his silence had always before held deep communication. I thought of all we had been through together in the year and a half we had known each other—two murder investigations, travel across three states; he had saved my life and I had saved his; we had thus flowed into each other's lives and psyches, filling in each other's lonesome spots, sharing a quiet that had come to mean more than words— so why did the silence now seem so heavy, and fill me with such foreboding? I thought of the gentleness with which he enclosed my hand in his, the scent of his breath as he leaned near to kiss me, the sound of his heart beating each time I leaned my head against the broad, warm expanse of his chest.

About there, I began to lose control. Gone was my last shred of dignity, my carefully planned program of waiting for Ray to call me. I picked up the phone and called his house, knowing that I would sound pushy and petty, and knowing also that if he was indeed sick, I risked waking him and just plain pissing him off. But when the line connected, I heard only his answering machine, with his terse recording: "This is Ray. Please leave a message."

I almost didn't. Instinctively, I knew that I was already in a cat and mouse game, and I wanted to run to the nearest hidey-hole: good old silence, but reminded myself that I was an adult having a relationship with another adult, and briefly found the courage to say, "This is Em. I . . . haven't heard from you, so I'm wondering if you're okay. Please call."

I hung up the phone, lay down on my bed, and managed to stay there all of five minutes before phoning Faye. It's hard to stay mad at a woman when she's the only true pal you've got in town.

She said, "Why don't you call Ava? I mean, it was his mother he was traveling with this weekend, right? You can say you're concerned because you haven't heard from him. Which is true."

"Okay," I said weakly.

"Confront it," Faye said, her tone communicating both sadness and frustration. "Ava's a decent sort. She won't dump on you, will she?"

"Right. No. I don't think so."

I hung up and dialed. The phone rang once, twice, three times before someone answered it, but instead of the solidity of Ava's mature, brisk, measured tones, I was greeted by Ray's sister Katie. "Hello," she drawled breathlessly.

I was startled to hear her voice, but then I remembered that the previous week she, her husband, and her children had moved in with Ava. They had been renting a house not far from her while they built their own house, a very large one. Ray had told me that there had been unexpected delays, but I suspected that Katie's lavishness had simply run them out of money. I said, "Oh, hello, Katie. You sound out of breath."

"I've been out jogging," she said. I could hear a small voice in the background, a child calling, "Maaaa-*meee!*"

"Hush!" Katie snapped. To me, she cooed, "What can I do for you?"

"May I speak with Ava, please?"

"Oh, is this Em?" she purred.

I knew she'd known it was me, so why was she asking? Had I missed some social nicety that she could now rub in? "Yes," I said, starting over. "Hi Katie, this is Em. As I said, I'd like to speak with Ava, please."

"Well, she's here," she said, again drawling. "And so's Ray. . . ."

I froze. What was she up to?

"We've just had Family Home Evening," she informed me, stressing the "we." It was an insinuation, as in: *And you weren't here.*

"Oh." I had in fact forgotten, given the events of the day, that it was a Monday, the day each week when the Raymond family gathered for dinner, prayer, religious study, and what have you.

"So you couldn't *make* it," she continued, managing to make it sound like an indictment of my non-Mormon status. "Are you taking another of your little *classes?*"

I took a deep breath, trying to quell my acute sense of not belonging. I decided that ignoring her question was the best policy, much as I wanted to take her accusations apart piece by piece and feed them to her with vinegar. "So you're done now. May I speak to Ray, then?" I asked, struggling to keep my voice level.

Katie giggled. If I hadn't known better, I might have thought she was drunk. "No, Ray's in the *middle* of something, Em," she informed me in a voice as stealthy as a cat slithering through tall grass. "But why don't you just come on up? We have plenty of cake, and I'm sure he'll be ready for *you* by the time you get here."

◆

IDIOT THAT I am, I got back into Faye's Porsche and drove to Ava's house. It's a big spread up on the east side of Salt Lake City, southeast of the university. All the way there, I argued with Katie in my head, explaining to her why my relationship with Ray was none of her business. Wishing I would pass a gas station so I could stop and do some nervous peeing. Praying that I was doing the right thing. Certain that I was not.

By the time I reached Ava's house, clouds had begun to gather, obscuring the moon. I got out of the car, hurried up through the icy darkness past the family fleet of bright, shiny new SUVs and minivans to the bright beacon of the porch light, and rang the bell.

Katie opened the door almost instantly, as if she had been waiting for me by the door, ready to spring on little rabbit Em. She greeted me with a big smile and a little half hug. If I hadn't figured out by then that something was up, that would have been a tip-off; in all the months since we had met, she had never once favored me with even the slightest physical touch.

"Uh, hi," I muttered.

Two small tow-headed kids ran up to her, one chasing the other with a headless Barbie doll. "Get away!" one screeched at the other. "Maaamy! He's hitting me again!"

Katie eyed her children, her lips drawn into a straight line. "Children, you behave or you'll answer to your father when he gets home!" she hissed.

"He never gets home!" the doll-wielding child wailed.

Katie slapped the child soundly on the bottom. "Go to bed," she ordered.

The child turned white and disappeared around the corner, holding the doll across her rump.

Horrified, I began to step away from the fracas.

Katie stepped toward me, snatching me up like a hovering mosquito. "Come right this way," she said, slipping her hand behind my elbow and all but dragging me toward the kitchen. My stomach turned to clay, and I began to doubt even more strongly whether coming had been a good idea. Then halfway to the kitchen, I heard a sound I had not heard in weeks—or was it months?

It was the sound of Ray laughing.

I stopped in my tracks.

Katie drew me onward. I yanked backward. Katie smiled and caressed my arm. I now heard Ray's voice, soft, kidding with someone—he who was so serious, he who seldom spoke. His voice was playful, teasing, almost giddy.

I faltered, uncertain what to do. I wanted to see Ray, to run to him, to take refuge in his embrace, but simultaneously knew that that kitchen was, just then, a dangerous place. I braced my feet.

With one more tug, Katie drew me through the archway into the kitchen.

There stood Ray, his back to me, an apron tied around his waist. He was drying a plate. Now he set down the plate, tossed the dishtowel casually over his shoulder, and slipped his arm around the waist of the young woman next to him.

Drew her to him.

Put his lips to her soft pink ear.

I turned and ran.

15

George Hungerford, foreman at Hebgen Dam, and Lester Caraway, his assistant, were awakened by the major shock and within moments recognized it as an earthquake. With their wives, they hurried to a water gage downstream from the dam to see if the river flow showed that the dam was leaking. As they neared the gage, Hungerford heard a roar. He glanced up to see a wave of water about 4 feet high moving down the river. Fearing that this meant the collapse of the dam, he returned to his house on the highway above the gage and tried to telephone a warning, but the line was dead. The two couples then drove toward the high ground near the dam and arrived there at about 11:55 P.M.

The moon was obscured by dust, and it was very dark. The water had withdrawn from sight, but they noticed that the downstream side of the dam was wet. Then, before they could see it, they heard water again; it was coming down the lake. They climbed out of the way and watched the water rise, overtopping the dam by about 3 feet. After 5 or 10 minutes it receded, then disappeared from sight. "All we could see down the dam was darkness again," Hungerford recalled.

The crest of the dam was again submerged in 10 or 15 minutes, but this time by less water, and the water receded sooner. In all, there were four surges over the crest. Between them, Hungerford and Caraway could see no water on the upstream side, even once when they ran out onto the dam. The water in Hebgen Lake had been sloshed about like water in a bathtub, and it continued to oscillate, though less violently, for at least 12 hours after the quake.

—*Irving J. Witkind, U.S. Geological Survey, describing the seiche that*

occurred in Hebgen Lake during the 1959 earthquake. A seiche occurs
wherever an earthquake shock is transmitted through a lake or large river.
Seiches have been observed to transit Great Salt Lake consequent to earth-
quakes, sometimes cresting the levees across which the trains and highways
run.

TUESDAY DAWNED SLOWLY. IT WAS SNOWING HARD, THE PER-
fect icy cloaking for my mood. Not having anywhere I could
think of to go, and having no one to do it with even if I got
there, I pulled the covers over my head and stayed in bed.

I had found scant sleep in the hours between 2:00 and 6:00
A.M., and since then I had lain awake, tense as a rabbit scenting
coyote on a turbulent wind. The best I could do was to try not
to think, but even at that battle, I was losing.

Losing. I was losing Ray.

Why? And who was that woman in his mother's kitchen? And
whose idea had it been to invite her there? Ava's? Katie's? His?

I tried to remember what she had looked like. She was taller
than I, I thought, and her hair had been . . . pale brown. No,
blond. Try as I might, I couldn't remember much about her, but
at the same time, I did have a very strong impression of her. She
had stood straight, and yet softly. Everything about her was soft
and pliant. Yielding. Cooperative. Willing. Everything I was not.

And she had made Ray laugh, and whisper in her ear. Or had
that been a kiss?

For the hundredth time, I rolled over sharply in my bed and
crammed the pillow over my head. I was wired and angry, frightened and distraught, but I could not manage to cry.

THE PHONE RANG at about ten o'clock. It was Tom Latimer.
"Can you come with me for a few minutes this morning?" he
asked. "I want you to run a make on some of the people who'll
be attending the state geologist's funeral."

"Oh, that's all I need," I told him. "I'll just waltz into a funeral and start pointing them out to the FBI. That will endear me to them. Really put the salsa into my attempts at professional networking."

"You won't even have to get out of the car."

"Whatever."

I was just climbing out of the shower when the phone rang again. This time, it was Ray.

"Em," he said with his usual terseness.

"Ray."

There was a pause. "You phoned."

Now I waited. What should I say? What could I say? Finally, I said, "I didn't hear from you. There was the earthquake and all. I was worried."

"Oh, right. Are you all right?"

A flash of anger heated the top of my head. *All right? Me? Hell no! I am a shambles, but it doesn't have a thing to do with that earthquake! It has to do with the man I love only asking me as an afterthought how I fared in it!* Forcing my voice to a level tone, I said, "Yes. No trouble at all. I dropped by your mother's last night to check on you all, but you seemed busy."

"You *did?* I—"

"No, I didn't stay. It was Katie's bright idea. You were in the kitchen with . . ." I almost said *your friend.* But that would have been spiteful, and spite was beneath me. This was Ray I was talking to, not Katie. The Ray who had asked me to marry him. The Ray to whom I had made certain promises. One of those promises had been that, while I was as yet unready to consent to a marriage, I would open my heart and mind to a growing relationship. Gritting my teeth, I reminded myself that part of being open meant being willing to hear an explanation, and, hopefully, hear that I was wrong.

Ray said nothing for the space of four heartbeats, then: "Oh. Yeah. That was an old friend from Saint George. I was helping her with the dishes."

A thing I've never before seen you do, I wanted to say, but again I held my tongue. *And neither have I heard you make such excuses.*

There was a pause; then he said, "Em, is something wrong?"

I didn't answer. I couldn't stand to say, *Yes. I saw you touch another woman. I saw you laugh with her.*

Ray's next words came with a soft purr. "Come on, you're my tough girl. A little earthquake didn't get you worried, did it?"

The irony of his words almost made me swoon. I could not think of a thing to say.

After awhile, Ray ended the silence by saying, "Okay. Well, I'm glad you're okay. You just take it easy, okay? I have a lot to do before going on shift today, so I'd better go."

Go? Faye's words rang in my head: *Confront it.* I blurted, "I think we should get together."

Now Ray was silent.

I said, "When do you get off tonight?"

"Well, late, and—"

"How about tomorrow?"

"Uh, too much going on at work."

"How about Thursday? You usually have Thursdays off."

There was another pause. "Yes. But I have to . . . ah . . . I promised Katie I'd take her skiing. Her husband, Enos, has been working so hard lately that she never gets to go."

Take Katie skiing. Sure. "Skiing," I echoed. "At Alta."

"How'd you know?"

"Just an unlucky guess." *Which confirms that I will tell Faye and Logan I will not go skiing with them.*

Or maybe you should, dingbat. What is this? Em is not allowed?

If I go but don't tell him I'm going, he'll think I'm just there because of him. But I could of course go and just avoid him, stay on the bunny slopes. He'll be on the expert runs and I'll never see him. Or he'll see me with Logan . . .

Now you're cooking with gas!

As I tied myself in knots trying to figure out how to play the situation, there was continued silence from Ray's end of the line. I felt opportunities slipping away. The opportunity to be willing. To be exactly what he wanted me to be. To be who I was and just say good-bye. *The big goodbye.*

Finally, Ray's voice came on again, this time more direct, less evasive. "Right. I think you're right. We need to get together. I have my break at six tomorrow evening. We can meet at the Pie."

16

In my eyes there abides the face of a stricken man, perhaps a fireman, whom we saw carried into a lofty doorway in Union Square. His back had been broken, and as the stretcher bore him past, out of a handsome, ashen young face, the dreadful darkening eyes looked right into mine. All the world was crashing about him and he, a broken thing, with death awaiting him inside the granite portals, gazed upon the last woman of his race that he was ever to see. Jack, with tender hand, drew me away.
—*Charmian London, on the devastation caused by the April 18, 1906, San Francisco earthquake*

WENDY FORTESCUE HUNKERED DOWN IN THE PEW AT THE synagogue. She wondered if Jews called their benches pews. Here in Salt Lake City, everything was all screwed up. It was the only place she knew where Jews were called Gentiles. But that was a Mormon thing, and this funeral was Jewish.

She didn't like funerals, Jewish or otherwise, because she didn't like being part of a death. She particularly disliked this one, with everybody pumping her for information about Sidney's death, and asking why the police were so interested in talking to everyone.

Because it's a murder investigation, she wanted to tell them, but the police had told her to keep her mouth shut. There was crime-scene tape covering half the backyard of the house, so they couldn't keep her ignorant of the situation. But keeping her mouth shut was no problem. About the last thing she wanted to do was go blabbing anything about the facts of her living situation or, in fact, anything else about her personal life to much of anybody. Wendy knew she had a loud mouth, but it wasn't a big mouth. The distinction lay in an examination of what exactly came out of her mouth; she could have told them that if they'd asked. A bigmouth was someone who couldn't keep things quiet. A loudmouth was someone who had no compunction against stating what was on her mind.

Take weepy Ted Wimler, who was sitting in the men's section. Ted was a big mouth. Always wanted to be the big gossip reporter, the one who knew what was cooking with everyone. But Ted was not a loudmouth. If something was on his mind, it was stuck there forever. He had the consciousness of a gnat. But Wendy knew she was a loudmouth, because if someone asked her opinion of Ted, she'd open up her mouth and give it: He was a whining, self-pitying insect. And so-so in the sack. Too quick on the trigger after too much time getting the mechanism cocked, as it were. If she was ever sorry for indulging herself in a quickie, it was that one.

Now, Logan de Pontier, on the other hand—who was sitting next to Ted—he was worth taking time with, but he wouldn't *give* her the time. Oh well. Wendy took in the robust, whiskery presence of the geologist she'd most like to screw. She wondered, not for the first time, what was ticking up inside that boy's braincase. The thing was, he wanted a relationship, not a sex partner, and that meant not just curiosity but companionship. The long pull. The whole enchilada.

Logan had seemed interested in that Em Hansen chick, the one who had turned up at the pizza thing with Ms. Long Legs with the attitude. Whatever. But Hansen had not been interested in Logan, so maybe the old boy'd need a little relief sometime soon. Of course, he hadn't called her when things had fizzled between him and Sidney. Wendy smiled. This was one of those little things she wasn't supposed to know about, but when you live in someone's basement, you may as well be an ant crawling around underneath her table. Or under her bed. Although things hadn't seemed to progress past dinner between those two. She had to hand it to old Sidney, because she was just that: old. The dew was off the lily. Forty-eight if she was a day. Ten years older than Logan, minimum. What had he seen in her?

And old enough to be Ted's mother, if you went by his emotional age. What a jerk. Left notes for her all over the place— stuffed into Sidney's mailbox, jammed into some trite little potted plant or another. What level of professionalism was that? It was crap, that's what it was.

Wendy stretched and yawned. The service was droning on and on. Out of the corner of her eye, she measured Hugh Buttons's response to the proceedings. Fidgety. Huh. Usually, he seemed more doleful, playing out his "world's on my shoulders" gag. Not for the first time, she wondered if it had been Hugh who had stayed with Sidney the night before she died. But if it had been Hugh, she would have thought he'd be showing a little more emotion. Of course, the real question was not who had spent the night, but who had circled back and killed her. Woof. Creepier yet, she might even have been there when it happened!

A buzz like a jolt of electricity zapped through Wendy's brain at the thought of the actual murder, and she shook herself to discharge it. She didn't want to think about it. Didn't, didn't, didn't. It was good that Sidney's kids had been with their father that morning, across town, where he lived with his new wife, a less pushy woman. Good, good, good.

Wendy noted that Pet Mercer was sitting not far away. Now, that girl was up to something. Sure, as science reporter for the *Tribune*, she had interviewed Sidney several times, but that didn't mean she had to attend her funeral. Had Pet, with her prodigious knack for digging, figured out that Sidney hadn't just slipped?

Wendy had watched her carefully out in the lobby before the service. Pet had moved systematically through the crowd, nabbing people with questions.

Wendy recognized a policeman among the mourners. The good-looking, athletic one with the incredible buns and thighs. He had come around the house and interviewed her again just before the funeral, all trussed up in his navy blue uniform. Now he was in street clothes, obviously trying to blend into the crowd, little that a hunk like that could hope to blend with the rest of these bozos. What was his name? Raymond, that was it, Officer Thomas B. Raymond. He had "Mormon" written all over him: presumptuous, distracted, and hum-baby, how clean and healthy these Mormon studs could be!

Up in the front pews, just behind the blubbering family members, Wendy checked out the official lineup, or rather, the lineup of officials. Those to whom putting in an appearance is a political act, not a personal one. Maria Teller, director of the state's Department of Natural Resources, Sidney's boss, a butt-kissing buck passer if ever there was one; she was there to look good, in lieu of the governor himself. A couple guys from various state agencies, a few county and city goons. She looked around at Officer Raymond to see if he was hip to that deal. Gonzo. Zip. Nope, he was staring at some other doorknob kind of guy, a younger guy, a slide rule and pocket protector type of guy in a bad suit, who was sitting at the other end of her row. Now, who in hell was he? She'd seen Pet Mercer try to hit on him before the service, and he'd all but turned into smoke as she approached. He seemed familiar. Was he a relative of Sidney's? No, wrong ethnic group, too white-bread, too goy. Oh, now she remembered; he was a young hopeful in local party politics, a real hard-on, who looked like he was being kicked into the job.

Mercifully, the service was now ending, and everyone was rising to his or her feet to watch respectfully as the family of the departed filed by. She stood up and watched Officer Raymond bird-dog his quarry. Sometimes it was downright convenient to be short, because people just didn't see her watching them.

Wendy threaded her way quickly through the clogged aisle, hoping for just a glimpse of the good officer's buns in motion. *Yeah!* He was tailing the other guy all right. *Yipe! Dodged out of sight!*

Wendy moved up behind the man Officer Raymond had been watching, hoping to catch a little whiff of who he was and what he was doing there. This was going to be tough. He seemed to be alone. He wasn't talking to anyone, even seemed to be avoiding drawing attention to himself. Damn, this called for extreme measures!

Several minutes later, when Wendy had escaped to the safety of her car, she dipped her hand into her coat pocket and drew out a handful of business cards. Took a look at each one in turn. Smiled. Yes, she had sure scored when she slipped her hand into the mystery man's pocket! Here were five or six of his business cards, all fresh and crisp, like he'd just put them in there that morning. Of course, he didn't seem quite enough to be the type who knew to carry business cards, so it was probably his wife who had put them there: Here, dearie, don't forget your business cards, you never know whom you're going to meet, gotta make those contacts and haul home big bucks so I can be queen of the cul-de-sac!

Wendy had to squint to read the guy's name, because the card was one of those corporate jobs where the company's name is much more important than the jerk who does the work. It read *Hayes Associates, Salt Lake City, Enos Harkness, Structural Engineer.*

Hah! thought Wendy. *Just as I thought, an engineer. But what's an engineer got to do with Sidney's death?*

❖

MICAH HAYES SAT resolutely at his desk, enduring his open-door hour, rapping his pen sharply on the edge of his desk. Through the doorway, he observed the back of Tina's bowed head and mentally auditioned several of the dismal fates he thought might await her. She was an imbecile. Anyone could see that; it showed in her insipid smile, her hopefulness. Hayes knew there were Bible verses that suggested that God looked after people like her, but he knew better. It was people like him who looked after people like her. Tithers. Taxpayers. *Because all too often*, he thought seethingly, *the Tinas of the world suck up the tithe money. They're too quick to marry, and five kids later, they're on their own, wondering what hit them. And then people like me, who pay the lion's share of the tithing, see our money drain into the sands of welfare as those children grow up and make equally idiotic choices. Money the church could have spent building new temples, using firms like mine. The very best form of recycling*, he decided, with a slight tightening to one corner of his mouth that would have become a smile if his contemptuousness had not stanched his sense of humor. *But here's a thought: I could propose to the church that my firm build special housing for them. Yes, that would be good. I could reuse the plans for those condominiums I put up near Park City, save costs. Just simplify the plans a bit. Downgrade. Leave out the hot tubs the Gentiles like to bask in. Two bedrooms, but with bunk beds . . . yes, and an enclave of the disadvantaged would provide the low-wage workers needed for so many businesses, perhaps even a steady source of the divorced mothers I need to have sit right where Tina is now sitting. Got to catch every advantage from the upswing in population and visitation this city will have now that the Olympics are here to advertise its credentials. But meanwhile, I move forward with the mall. . . .*

Outside the door of his office and across the reception area, the elevator doors opened, revealing a tall dark-haired young woman who stood with one foot turned outward in a vampish posture. Micah Hayes knew her, although wives were discouraged from coming around the company and interrupting their husbands. *Katie Raymond—no, I keep forgetting that it's Katie Harkness now—come to check up on her husband's progress.*

Katie enjoyed a healthy dose of the Raymond family beauty, but these particulars of her looks were lost on Micah Hayes. Being an unsentimental man, his lack of response to the kittenish sexual heat that flickered behind her well-groomed exterior had nothing to do with the fact that he had known her since she was born. As he did with all people on whom his gaze fell, he examined her only to evaluate how she might be useful to him. He reviewed in a fraction of a second his earlier assessments of her to see if anything had changed. *Proud,* he had decided long ago. *Far more ambitious than her husband. A pity she was born a female. Might have been able to form a personality that brutal into a good right arm.* If he had been capable of carrying his entire evaluation into consciousness, he would have added, Patrician in all the most presumptuous ways. High gut-level intelligence, unperturbed by the consumptive forces of intellectuality. Instead he thought, *Unusually pleased with herself today. She's up to something. Look at the way she flaunts those breasts, like money she's about to spend.*

Katie scanned the reception area before stepping out of the elevator, saw Hayes's open door, saw him staring at her. She smiled—no teeth, eyelids half-lowered—stepped off the elevator, and advanced toward his doorway. "Good morning," she said. "How nice to see you today. How are things going?"

"Fine, and thank you for asking," he answered, slipping into the display of deep dignity that served so well when dealing with the ladies and less guileful men of the church. "Tell me, Katie, what brings you here today?"

Katie tipped her head forward slightly and took him in from the top of his balding head to his belt buckle, past which the desk obscured him; then her eyes continued to pan downward, as if could see right through the wood.

Hayes would have found this action disconcerting if he hadn't considered such displays of presumption a flaw that, in the transparency of its calculation, indicated his advantage. *She's decided she can handle me. Let her keep thinking that.*

"I thought I'd take Enos to lunch," Katie said. "It seems that's what I have to do if I want to see him." She offered Hayes a coy, pettish pursing of her lips. "You keep him so busy." She tugged lazily at her gloves and slowly pulled them off, revealing long, tapering fingers as supple and expressive as a dancer's legs. She was attired today in a long white coat made of a good-quality synthetic that approximated polar bear fur. The collar stood up next to her dark hair, setting it off to brilliant effect.

Below the hem of her coat, Hayes could see the last few inches of her shapely, muscular legs rising from a pair of high-heeled shoes that matched the purse that hung casually from one shoulder, its black strap sunken into the softness of the fur. He mentally tallied the cost of her ensemble, knew that, with their—how many, two? Three?—children, Enos's salary had not covered such expenditure. Was it a hand-me-down from her mother?

Her mother. Ava Raymond. That reminded him: He had not been in touch with her lately, except for the usual nods at church. He must phone her, offer the customary civilities. It was good business to stay on such terms with one's silent partners, and helped to keep them silent. In Ava's case, it assured her that her share in the corporation was being well cared for. And care for her share he did, because her prosperity was of course his, as well; but caring for her—the widow of his former corporate treasurer—also increased his stature in the eyes of the church, which was his greatest customer. Her departed husband, Thomas Raymond, Sr., had been a great asset to Hayes: scrupulously honest, yet incapable of detecting deceit in others. The perfect clean-faced boy to put in the front office, tallying up the numbers where everyone could see him. Back when Hayes Associates was young, Micah had given him stock options in lieu of salary advances, and it had paid off in the form of a handsome home, everything a widow could want or need, and an education for each of the children, not that the church would have let them go hungry. Too bad Thomas junior had become a policeman instead of a precise numbers man like his father, or an engineer like his brother-in-law. Little Ray had grown up to be as hardworking as his father, and twice as earnest. He could have used him. And here was one of Ray's sisters, just as bright, but of little worth to him because of her gender. As an ultra-devout Mormon, she must stay home until her children were grown, and she had not even finished producing them yet.

Katie had not sat down, having not been asked, and was beginning to look restless. He considered inviting her to sit, but found it more to his advantage to keep her standing. "You're right, I do keep Enos very busy," he said, letting a faint trace of fatherliness lace his tone. "But be thankful that Enos is such a hardworking husband. After all, you have that great big new house to pay for. How's that going, by the way?"

"Fine." Her answer sounded brittle.

Just as I thought. Cost overruns. Her ambition is being thwarted. This, I can use. Against the husband. Now to turn up the heat. He said, "Enos is not in just now."

Katie's smile hardened and her eyes turned to flint. "Oh? Did you send him out somewhere?"

"No. He asked for the morning off. As you say, he's been working very hard, so I gave it to him."

Katie's posture congealed like a layer of cooling fat. "Well," she said stiffly. "I'll just leave him a note, then."

Exactly, because you can't stand to be kept waiting, Hayes observed, knowing the symptoms entirely too well.

JIM SCHECTER SAT on the edge of his bed. He was perspiring, even though he was cold. He could see the moisture from his hand on the telephone, which he had just replaced on its cradle. A night and all morning spent lying down had done nothing to restore him to a sense of calmness.

He could not believe what he had just heard. Had he misunderstood? He had called to double-check that his discovery of the cracked welds in the stadium roof had reached the correct ears, and had been told—could he truly believe this?—not to file a report. That everything would be handled quietly, so as not to worry the public. But how could repairs possibly be made in time? And it was snowing, loading the roof, and there were people working in there now! Had Satan stolen their minds? Salt Lake City would probably lose one small citizen to this earthquake; did they want to lose thousands?

His head pounded. His vision swam. Somehow, he had to keep going. Do the next inspection. Which, O God, was the City and County Building. Which meant climbing all those unprotected stairs into that godforsaken clock tower.

◈

FRANK MALONE EXTRACTED the plastic toothpick from his Swiss army knife so he could dislodge the corned beef that had gotten stuck between his molars. It was hard to accomplish this while driving, but he felt a certain urgency to get where he was going.

It was an unexpected but very fortunate payoff for all his time spent hanging out making friends at the Building Department that he had been there when that call came in from the inspector who'd found the broken welds in the new stadium. Otherwise, he might not have had enough warning to get away before people decided that he was someone they needed to talk to. To demand answers from.

Off to Cabo for a while. Do a little sportfishing. Work on the tan. Too cold here in Salt Lake in the wintertime anyway. Best to be unreachable until the dust settles and some other poor fool is strung up instead of me. Some fool who stays in town. The politicians were so predictable: All they wanted was a hide to tack up on the city gate, someone to point at and blame for the fact that their damned $50 million sports arena was a dud. It didn't matter whose hide got tacked, so why stick around and look like he was volunteering? Hell, the news media alone could bog him down for days with their phone calls, and the resulting publicity could set him back for months on the profit schedule. They, too, would move on down the line until they found someone to sensationalize, someone to blame. They didn't understand science, didn't understand that he was in the business of stating opinions and making interpretations, not guaranteeing answers. *The fools should know that. The developers certainly know it; hell, if they don't like my interpretations, they just throw my reports into the circular file and shop for ones they like. It happens all the time.*

"So don't blame me," he said out loud. "Blame the developers." *Or the regulators. Or the idiot public that sits around waiting for someone else to take responsibility. Hell, I wouldn't sink my investment dollars into a fault zone. Or a floodplain. Or a tornado alley. Or a shoreline. The list goes on. Geologic hazards are here to stay, and the damned fools keep thinking they won't be the ones to get caught. But not me; I'm going to Cabo.*

He, Francis W. Malone, was not going to get caught. Just as with the new mall project next door, he had called the disturbed ground under that stadium a case of liquefaction, not fault slippage, and he was entitled to that opinion. Besides, short of the big 7.0 it would take to rip the Warm Springs branch of the Wasatch fault to surface, no one was going to be able to prove his interpretation wrong—otherwise, the data were going to stay buried as deep as the quake itself—so why stick around and try to defend it? It was a witch-hunt they'd be wanting, and he was just an old jive geologist.

As a professional courtesy, he had, before leaving, put a call through to his client, Hayes Associates, and spoken to the big man and the big man only. Hayes had been grateful for the trip-off, and gratitude was bankable. It meant more jobs with nice big fees. And all so easily accomplished.

17

A baker who was on his way passing through the city and county building grounds, looked at the big clock to see what time it was, and when he looked he forgot all about the time. The big tower was swaying back and forth. The baker looked again and rubbed his eyes and the swaying motion continued.

—*"Tremblor Incidents Tersely Told"* an eyewitness account of Salt Lake City's 1910 magnitude 5.5 earthquake reported in the Deseret Evening News, *May 23, 1910*

THE RED SANDSTONE BULWARKS OF THE SALT LAKE CITY AND County Building rose before me. I paused a moment to enjoy it this time. It's a gem, an architectural delight snatched from the jaws of tear-down-and-rebuild-itis by a seismic retrofit.

As you approach the formal entrance from State Street on the west, you're looking at five or six stories (depending on what you count) of ornately carved and fenestrated red sandstone. It is elongate north to south, and the barrel arches above each door and most windows peg the style as Romanesque Revival. The walls rise to a splendid array of round and square turrets and cupolas capped by steep slate roofs, needlelike finials, and statues of heroic ladies. According to the free brochure from the guard's station, the square central clock tower tops out at 250 feet above ground level. Stacking all that rock was a real job of work. It took three years to build a railroad spur to a quarry in the Kyune Sandstone, cut the rock, haul it one hundred miles to Salt Lake City, and raise it into place. The Kyune Sandstone was chosen because it was soft and easily carved. The main sections of the stone that forms the walls were left rough-hewn, forming pleasing horizontal shadows, but around every door and window, it sprouts smooth columns and patterned friezes, geometric textures, and classical curlicued acanthus leaves. According to the brochure, most of the stone was cut by masons whose names are lost to memory, but the myriad creatures that peek out from around its arches were done by a sculptor named Linde, who caught the likenesses of everyone notable, from American Indians, to Spanish explorers, to early pioneer men and women. He added gargoyles for fun, and Mormon beehives, and mythical sea serpents said to have inhabited Lake Bonneville. He signed his artistic statement by adding himself, slipping a self-portrait in between the words *City* and *County* on the north face.

And that's just the outside. The inside has been completely restored, right down to the last inch of bird's-eye marble wainscoting, tile, gilded picture frame, and chandelier. It is opulent. It is delicious. Unlike the austere spaces and cold lines of so many modern civic structures, it is warm and welcoming, yet dignified. Mature. Venerable. Stuff like that.

Pet was waiting for me at the guard's desk in the main hallway, just as she had said. She seemed bursting with energy and excitement. "Em! There you are. I just phoned you to make sure you were still coming." She waved her cell phone. "This is Jeremy, the guard who's going to take us through the building," she told me, gesturing toward a young man built like a whippet.

I nodded to him, wondered if he'd gained his sinewy physique from running up and down the clock tower several times a day.

"The inspector isn't here yet," Pet said breathlessly. "I called his office to make double sure, and the secretary said he should be here soon. He took the morning off, she said. Something with his health. I hope it's not his heart or lungs, because I hear it's a long way up that clock tower."

"So we're really going up that tower?"

"Yeah. Cool, huh?"

The guard said, "No pumpkins, y'hear?"

Pet gave him a wink. "Gotcha."

I was just about to ask why everyone seemed so sensitive about pumpkins, when the building inspector hove into view. I knew it had to be him because he was dressed in the simple, no-frills attire of a civil servant and he carried an aluminum clipboard. He was a slightly overweight man in his mid-forties, thinning hair, pasty face. I wondered if he was entirely well. He shuffled up to the desk and said, "Jim Schecter." He offered a hand to shake. It was cold and clammy. "Which one of you's the lady from the *Tribune*?"

Pet said, "That's me. And this is Em Hansen. She's a geologist, came along to get a firsthand look at a seismic retrofit job."

The man turned toward me, his eyes widening noticeably. Then he did a double take and put his hand over his heart with relief. "Oh. You mean for this building. Yeah, it's already done."

"So there's another building that needs one?" Pet asked.

The man flinched and clamped his mouth shut as tightly as a child trying to avoid a spoonful of medicine.

I said, "I'll bet half the older buildings in Salt Lake need it to one degree or another. If only a chimney brace, or fresh pointing on the bricks."

Pet kept after the inspector. "What other building needs a retrofit?"

The inspector avoided looking at her. When he spoke, his voice quavered with anxiety. "Let's . . . uh, get started with this one, see how she's held together." He nodded to the guard and started toward the stairs that led to the lower floor.

He took us first down into the basement. As the guard un-locked the door that led down underneath the main staircase to the building's nether regions, Inspector Schecter (I wonder if he ever got teased about that) said, "This part of the retrofit is called a 'base isolation system.' The idea is that the engineers have isolated the building from the movement of the ground it's sitting on. It was quite a job to do this. It was only the second or third building to have it done."

I asked, "Have any of them been put to the test yet? I mean, does the system really work?"

The inspector turned and looked at me with his jaw hanging open, like he'd never thought to ask this question before. After a moment, he surreptitiously rubbed the palm of his free hand on his pants leg. I noticed that it was trembling. His gears seemed to have jammed again. He took a breath, exhaled, and closed his eyes for a moment as if in meditation. When he opened them again, he seemed to make a point of not looking directly at me.

I glanced at Pet. She looked my way, raised one eyebrow. She was catching all of this, too.

The guard stood by the open basement door, looking expectant.

Fixing his gaze resolutely on the floor, the inspector pulled a heavy metal flashlight from a holder on his belt, clicked it on, twisted the head of it to focus the beam on the floor, and then followed its light through the doorway and down the stairs.

At the foot of the stairs, we were greeted by a large framed blueprint of an elevation of the building. In fact, there were two renderings of it: one showing it in a stationary position, and the other depicting it horribly bent to the shape of a sine wave by the force of a titanic shock being applied from one side. One glance at that picture and I knew exactly what the engineers who designed the retrofit had been worried about. "That's gross," I said.

The inspector seemed to stick to the floor again, then found forward gear one more time and stepped through a final door, which the guard had now unlocked.

The building guard nodded. "After seeing that thing, I wouldn't want to be down here unless they'd done the retrofit."

Pet and I joined the inspector in the subbasement. It was a cramped region, little more than a glorified access to an immense crawl space that extended the length of the structure. We were standing in a small pocket where there was barely room to stand. All around us were the dusty, gray bowels of the building, a grid of heavy concrete beams running this way and that. The ground was strewn with rubble. I looked more closely, trying to discern what the inspector was aiming his light at. It appeared to be a large cube of black rubber, about a half meter on a side.

"What's that?" Pet asked.

"That's what this building's sitting on now," Jim Schecter told her. "There are four hundred and forty-three of these." He danced his light through the gloom, showing us the repetition. Then he aimed it at one of the posts that used to support the incalculable tons of stone that rested over our heads. It had been sawed through.

"Ohhh, that's cool," Pet said. "Wow, how did they do that?"

The tool used had cut two-inch-diameter cylindrical holes side-ways through the post, leaving a row of concrete teeth above and below a horizontal cut. "Rock drill," I said.

Pet put a hand on the inspector's arm and turned him more fully toward the cut post, away from me. "Tell me about it, please," she said, her voice soothing, encouraging.

He took a deep breath and said, "It was quite a feat. They braced each section, then made these cuts." He gestured with his flashlight as if it were a drill.

"Wow," Pet gushed. "This is so fascinating. And old," she added reverently. "Our forefathers did such a job here."

I almost groaned. She was playing the Mormon card.

The inspector took in a deeper, more prideful breath. "Yes, and they were frugal. Just look at this." He skipped his flashlight beam over to a place were the concrete formed a sill. There were bits of iron hanging out. "Look at that. An old railroad rail. And that, an old pipe. They used whatever iron they had available. Acted like rebar."

I realized that while I seemed to be putting this man on edge with my blunt questions, Pet was pouring on the charm, coddling him, pumping him for every bit of information he had. I decided that it was best if I faded into the background and let her do her work.

The inspector led us from the basement up through several rooms, where he was apparently checking for cracks in the plaster or along the grout in the flooring tiles. He found none. Along the way, he had the guard take us into the council chambers, a large dark red room set up with a gallery of oak chairs looking up toward a long, raised desk where the council sat. It was trimmed with oak wainscoting and a simple but elegant coffered ceiling, from which was suspended an array of gilded chandeliers, all in the pleasing open style of a century and more past. Along the back wall hung a life-size portrait of Brigham Young in a broad carved oak frame that more than rivaled the ornamental ruckus of the outside of the building. "There's the man," Schecter said proudly as he faced the portrait. "Not just a great spiritual leader but a great engineer."

From the third floor, where the council chamber was located, the guard and the inspector took us by elevator to the fourth floor, then up the fire stairs to the fifth. At that level, the inspector took us through the base of the clock tower and out a door that opened out onto an ice-encrusted catwalk that led along the peak of the steeply pitched slate roof of the north wing toward one of the building's two flagstaffs. I stepped gingerly onto the walk and looked down onto the slates below. From that angle, the roofs looked like knives. There were nice meaty railings along the catwalk to hold on to, but still I thought it prudent to turn around about halfway and go back inside, and it did not escape me that the inspector had not strayed from the doorway.

Here Schecter turned to Pet and said dolefully, "It's a lot more stairs from here. You sure you want to see it?"

My legs were already aching, and not just the one that had so recently been in a cast. I had to face it: I had been hobbling around so long that I was out of shape.

Pet once again put a hand on Schecter's arm. I half expected her to say, Whither thou goest, but she said only, "Please lead onward," and gave his arm a reassuring squeeze.

The inspector held the door and waved us through, again avoiding looking at me.

We had to duck our heads as the guard led us under a big heating duct. We then turned, climbed a steel staircase about a story and a half up to a trapdoor, heaved it open, and stepped up through it.

We were now inside the main volume of the tower. And, I should say, inside the clock. Understand that the tower is about forty feet square and has a huge clock face on each side that's at least ten feet across. So how big are the clockworks driving all those big hands? Well, you could put them in your pocket, except for the connecting rods. Rising from the floor to a fist-sized cluster of gears was a steel rod not much bigger around than my thumb. The gears were about the size of silver dollars. They drove four more rods, each again about the diameter of my thumb, one going to the inside of each of the four clock faces, so that all hands turned in unison. The whole rig was so surprisingly undersized that I felt like I'd seen under a big man's shirt and found out that he was a midget wearing a giant's clothes held outward by toothpicks.

Near the central rod sat a small hydraulic tank with four arms coming out of it. Attached to each was a slim cable that rose up through the open center of the tower toward the ceiling, which was fifty or sixty feet overhead. I didn't have time to wonder what the cables did, because the guard and Pet had already started up the long steel-grid staircase that cranked at ninety-degree turns all up inside the empty interior space of the tower.

I turned and looked at the inspector. His face had turned ashen. "I'll follow you," he said hoarsely. "So I'll . . . um, be behind you. You know."

"Yeah."

Let me admit something here: I don't like that kind of staircase. I prefer my stairs with opaque treads, not grillwork, and please give me risers. And I like stairs to be fixed firmly between two solid walls, and a ceiling a reasonable distance overhead will do nicely. This baby just cranked right up through open space, nowhere touching the walls, and now it wasn't just Jim Schecter who was feeling a smidge uncertain.

I told myself, *Going up won't be so bad, but coming down will be a bitch.* I gripped both handrails and headed on up.

Twenty or more feet up, I remembered to look at the walls, which were rough-finished and braced with a network of modern steel beams, shot through with enough bolts and whatnot to make an engineer weep for joy. I decided that while I still had to go back down these stairs, I would at least survive if the big one hit before I got there.

We were almost up under the ceiling when I heard a whirring sound, and all of a sudden those arms on the hydraulic gizmo started to move and, *BONG BONG BONG BONG*, bells somewhere above our heads began to chime, so loud that the fillings in my teeth almost fell out. The only reason I did not suffer hearing loss was because we had not yet crossed up through the ceiling to the next level, where the bells were. Four of those big Liberty Bell jobs. I was thankful that we had not arrived any earlier, or my auditory nerves would have been pureéd.

We stepped out now onto a wooden floor. It was old and splintering. The steel staircase we'd been climbing was new, part of the retrofit, but here we passed on to the antique goods, a crotchety old wooden job that cranked steeply upward through a narrowing space underneath the pinnacle roof of the tower.

The guard turned toward Pet and me. "You sure you want to go up there?" he asked.

"What's it like?" Pet asked, almost bubbling over with enthusiasm, as if she were asking for a clue regarding the contents of a birthday present.

"Dunno," the guard said. "This is as far as I've ever been. I hear they're kind of creaky." He looked doubtfully up toward the roof. As he took an experimental step across the floor, the edge of one board splintered under his weight. He looked back at us, eyes wide.

Pet turned to me, her grin so wide I thought she might bust her face. "What do you think, Em?"

What did I think? I thought that what waited below was a return trip down stairs I didn't like, on legs that were already like jelly. This new flight of stairs looked worse than the others, but at least they led upward, and I never like to start a job and not finish it. "Well, we've come this far," I said.

"Right," she said. She turned to the guard. "Onward!"

The guard started the final pitch of the climb. The stairs in fact did not creak, or not much, and I'm pleased to report that the handrails were nice and meaty, but by now, we had climbed over one hundred feet vertically, so the going was more of a trudge than a merry scamper.

At the top, the guard heaved open another trapdoor and briefly stuck his head up through the hole. As he stepped back down to make room for us, he said, "Don't go all the way out, okay?" Then he winked and added, "And no pumpkins."

Pet and I climbed the last few steps together and peeked out over a low wooden railing.

The air was clear and bracingly cold. We looked out into the realm of angels and airplanes, a glimpse stolen from the life of a bird. I wanted both to cower and leap.

It was all too dizzying, too distracting, too wonderful. I felt on top of Salt Lake City, truly at ease with it for the first time. It was a beautiful city, sparkling and ringed by mountains. I breathed in, taking it to my heart.

I thought of love. I thought of Ray.

I thought, *If Ava could see me now, she'd know I'm the one for Ray*.

Then I wondered, *Where'd that idea come from?*

I got no answer.

Pet was saying something, something about getting to the top at last, but stopped in the middle of her sentence and said, "Hey, where's the inspector?"

I turned and looked down. I saw the building guard at the first landing below us. I followed the turns of the stairs down from there, down to the bells, the wooden floor, and the trapdoor below us. No Jim Schecter. "Perhaps we'd better go check on him," I said. "He didn't look so good earlier."

I forced myself to look only at my feet. The guard descended before us, turning, turning, stepped down onto the floor, then down onto the steel stairs. I concentrated on his head, and on my feet, on the sensation of the handrails against my hands, submerging my fear of the depths that yawned beneath me. I stepped down onto the open grillwork of the steel stairs, began the descent through space. The sky above had been home, but this was hell. In here, wings could not help me if I fell. In here, the requirements of safety had been met, but not the visual equation for security. In here, I felt that I was falling, and far below, at the last landing of the turning stairs, I saw the crumpled body of the inspector of buildings.

18

THE INSPECTOR WAS NOT DEAD, NOR WAS HE INJURED. WHEN we reached him, he was panting and perspiring freely, but he waved us off, whimpering, "Go, please. It'll pass. Please."

Pet took his hand and felt his pulse. Her eyes widened with alarm, but in the calmest of voices, she said, "There, there, we wouldn't leave you like this. Guard, please go get a doctor. Em and I will stay with Mr. Schecter."

The guard turned to go, but the inspector called him back. "No! No, I don't need a doctor. I just . . . I need to get home."

"Can you tell us what's the matter?" Pet asked.

"No. I'd rather not. It's . . . a silly thing. I'll be fine. I always am. I just . . . need a few minutes is all."

"Do you have medication you take for this?" she asked.

"Um, well . . . yes."

Pet gave the guard a pert little smile. "Can you get Mr. Schecter some water, please?" As he turned to fill her request, she sat down, lifted the inspector's head away from the hard, cold metal where it rested, and cradled it against her bosom. I eased out of sight beyond the inspector's line of vision. As his eyes closed in the comfort of her kindness, she put a finger to her lips to indicate that I should keep quiet. She murmured, "Well, you had me worried for a moment there, Jim, but I see now that you're just fine, aren't ya? Tough work, this inspecting business." She patted his hair smooth. "So, do you have these attacks often? My dad had them. My, how he hated it. Laid him out for days sometimes."

"The poor man." Schecter sighed. "Did he find anything that helped? Any of the sedatives? The analgesics?"

"No, but he'd let me hold him just like this sometimes, and if I spoke really quietly and kept things nice and dark for him, he'd feel better after awhile."

"Yeah, dark helps. Just got to cut down the stimulation, that's all. But after yesterday . . . I don't know . . ."

"You had one yesterday, then," she said confidentially. "How frightening."

"Oh, yes. It was terrible."

"But you're such a brave man," she whispered. "What could have frightened you that much?" She patted his cheek, smoothed his shirt.

"I can't tell you," he said, barely above a gasp. "Strictly confidential, I was told."

"Of course," she murmured. "Please, don't say a word." She began, ever so slightly, to rock him. She even hummed a soothing tune.

After awhile, as if in deep torpor, he said, "I was doing okay with the height. You believe me, don't you?"

"Of course . . ."

He opened his eyes and looked imploringly up at his elfin guardian. "It was the cracks," he pleaded.

"In the wall?"

"No! In the roof! The welds!"

"Yes, of course. That would have terrified me, too."

"And all those people are going to be so disappointed."

"It's terrible," she agreed. "The opening games."

"Brand-new stadium," he said, a tear leaking from underneath his closed lids.

❖

"SO THE BUILDING Department's red-tagged the new stadium which was going to be used for the opening ceremonies of the Olympics. You knew that coming into this meeting, right?" I asked Pet after we had gotten the inspector safely into a taxi and then had gotten ourselves to a place where the two of us could talk. I had said I was hungry, and she had offered me a handful of nuts and raisins. I had allowed as how I was not a squirrel, and that any combination of beer and Mexican food would do nicely. Pet had taken me south of town, to a place called the Lone Star Taqueria, a quirky little joint with a new spin on the use of fish and cilantro in Mexican cuisine. Pet was beginning to look like my kind of woman. I ordered a sampling of the house fare and we each ordered a long-neck Corona.

She took a pull at her beer. "No, I didn't know, and no, it hasn't been red-tagged. Jim thinks it should be, but if I read him right, he reported it and nothing happened. He phoned his office to report his findings, but he was told to lose his notes. And this is all confidential. Remember? The poor dear had himself tied in knots trying to keep the secret he so badly needed to lose."

"Then how did you peg the location that quickly?"

"Oh, I don't know . . . public buildings . . . acrophobia . . . that narrowed the field. It had to be somewhere with a big drop. I didn't consider the stadium right away, because it's privately owned. It should have a different inspector. But as soon as he started talking about disappointment for lots of people, I knew he meant the Olympics, and the new stadium west of Temple Square was a likely subject, because it's sitting right in line with the Warm Springs branch of the fault. Beyond that, call it instinct."

"You're good."

Pet smiled, pleased with herself. "Damned good, to be precise."

I raised my burrito *de carnitas* in recognition. I was famished. I had ordered enough to keep me going for a week.

Pet spirited a raisin out of a pocket and nibbled at it.

I pushed a taco *de pollo asado* across the table at her.

She said, "Well, just to be polite," and took a bite, and then another. She added, "I'm so good, in fact, that you're going to tell me what you were doing at the City and County Building yesterday."

I lowered the burrito back to my plate. "Sorry."

"Ooooo. Another secret, huh?" She crunched down on her taco and moaned.

I smiled at her. "Give up, Pet. I'm not a sweet old engineer with a fear of heights. I don't crack that easily. I don't have acrophobia or—what was that other one again?"

"Agoraphobia. Fear of open spaces. That means the guy's not only afraid of heights but that he'd much happier in a box with the lid taped shut."

"You know all that because your dad really had it?"

She took a sip from her beer. "Never met my dad."

I laughed, nearly choking on my own *cerveza*. "Sorry again, because that's not funny at all."

"Oh, I don't know about that. It makes it handy when I need to invent someone who's just like whomever I'm trying to pump. I'm not blinded by the truth that way."

And you pass yourself off as the pert little reporter from the Daily Blah, I thought. "So somebody's trying to keep a lid on Jim Schecter's findings. Who? Developer? Politician?"

"I don't know. I intend to find out, though."

"You said the stadium was privately owned. So who owns it?"

"An investment group. It's part of a big package of urban redevelopment. They get federal, state, and local redevelopment funds—you know, grants-in-aid—if they improve the place, but to qualify, they have to include a feature that's in the public interest. Like a symphony hall or a museum. This particular group wanted to put in another huge shopping mall—a cultural mecca if ever I saw one," she said dryly, "so they stuck it to the stadium, which they built first, right next door. It's a clever scheme. They want a sports franchise, so they need a stadium, but stadiums are expensive. And they want to put in their shopping mall, but they need to have a feature in the public interest. So they put the two together, making sure they have the stadium in time for the Olympics, and tell the city, 'See? You okay our development, and you can have a brand-new stadium for your big show-off event. How much more in the public interest could you want?' So the political bosses tell the Building Department to give it the go-ahead. And the developer is happy as a skier in deep powder, because now he's got public money subsidizing both the mall and the sports franchise."

I said, "But the truth is, or should be, that if that stadium's unsafe, it can't be used."

"That's the way I read it too."

"Then why help keep it secret? Hell, if that roof falls in on how many thousand spectators, that's a black eye the city would never recover from. In fact, there should be a big red tag on the front door barring entrance. And you're telling me there's not."

"Not according to everything I had from the Building Department up till ten minutes before we met the inspector. Unless you got something I missed when you went to Planning yesterday."

Evading her probe, I asked, "When did he inspect the stadium?"

"Yesterday. Monday. Earthquake day. That would have gotten a man like him pretty wound up all right. And then someone told him to keep quiet about it. Imagine."

"I wonder who got to him."

"Got to his boss, you mean. It's probably grounds for dismissal, if not a felony, to leave something like that unreported. Or it should be."

I took a bite of my taco *de pescado*, the house specialty. It was a choice little morsel with shredded cabbage, tomato, fresh cilantro, onion, and lime nestled on a soft white corn tortilla and slathered with jalapeño mayonnaise. It was delicious, although under the circumstances my enjoyment of it was abstract. I was beginning to feel personally responsible for the safety of a great many people. "What exactly are you working on, Pet? It's not just a follow-up on Monday's quake, is it?"

"I'll tell you if you'll tell me."

"No can do."

She shrugged her shoulders.

As I took another draw on my beer, I mapped the deception in her elaborately innocent face, read the tension in her shoulders, read the runes of her hands, which now curled so tightly around her coffee mug that the knuckles were bleached. I thought, *We both love the science in this story, but earthquake alone don't make us that tense. No, you've found something all too human in the middle of your story.* "I get it," I said slowly. "You're trying to figure out who killed Sidney Smeeth."

Pet's smile crimped up tight as a little raisin. "Then you are, too."

"What are you talking about?"

"The police haven't yet released what they know. You've forgotten that the unwitting public still thinks her death was accidental. So your connections confirm that it was murder. That's terrific."

I sank my face in one hand, then snapped it up again. "No. I—I didn't know until you just told me. Oh, how surprising—"

"Cut it out, Em. You're a lousy actress."

"Wait a minute; how do *you* know it was murder?"

Pet bit into her taco. "I was on my way up to interview her when the ambulance pulled up. They said it was an accident, but

I waited awhile in my car, writing up my notes. Okay, I hid and watched. I saw them put up the crime tape."

"You were going to interview her. Why?"

"Because she is—was—the state geologist."

"No, there was more."

"Because they cut off her TV interview."

"Which she had staged in front of the new stadium."

"Correct."

"So here's the question," I said. "Who's they?"

"That's what I'd like to know. Okay, so I've given you something; now it's your turn. Who told you? Was it that cop boyfriend of yours?" She wiggled her eyebrows at me.

I wondered what to say. There was no way I was going to tell her about my FBI connection. I could tell Pet that I'd heard it from Ray, because he was city police, whose jurisdiction it was to investigate the murder. That would cover my tracks with Tom Latimer, whose interests went far past the termination of one life to the protection of tens of thousands. But saying that Ray had spilled the beans would get him crosswise with his bosses, if they found themselves reading it in the *Tribune,* and that would be very bad for our relationship. I decided on the slipperiness of another nonanswer. Let her presume what she would presume. "How did you know I was dating a cop?" I asked.

"Like you say, I'm good. And this is a small town. It didn't take me long to dig up the connections. Okay, I have a friend who covers the police desk. She remembered your name from the dinosaur job you got involved in, the one where you met Ray. You were something of a celebrity for a day or two there, little that you let yourself be interviewed for our paper. Like I say, it's a small town."

"Not that small."

"Well, okay, Ray was at the funeral, and—"

"Sidney Smeeth's?"

"Yes, and his brother-in-law. Quite the family affair."

That made my head spin. What had Ray been doing at Sidney Smeeth's funeral? "What, is he working the case?" I looked askance at Pet, who was sipping at her beer, looking even more elaborately innocent. "You're fishing," I said. "Quit messing with me."

"Okay, okay. I know Ray's sister Katie." She gave me a look of sympathy.

Now I put my head all the way down on the table and groaned. "Katie," I said into my plate, "my guardian angel."

"Yeah, I thought she was a real bitch, too, first time I met her. Clear back in grade school."

"Wait—how did you know I was at the Planning Department yesterday?"

"I asked the guard if he'd seen you before. Evidently, your red boots made an impression on him. But don't change the subject. Katie Harkness is one of my very favorite bitches."

I vowed right then to leave my old red ropers in the bottom of my closet forevermore. "Listen, I have to give Katie the benefit of the doubt. It's serious business between me and Ray, and—"

"You've got to be kidding! You're not a Mormon, and the Raymond clan are as Mormon as they come. Wow, this is incredible!"

I stared at Pet, wondering how she'd gotten off on a spree of gossiping, but then realized that she was just using a gossipy tone as a way to try to railroad me into spilling my guts. "No sale," I said.

Pet moved meditatively back to her taco, applied a little more of one of three salsas the waiter had provided, and studied me for a while. "I like you," she said, "so this I'm giving you for free. Watch out for Katie. She doesn't play by the same rules you and I do. You and I like to know the truth. The truth doesn't matter to Katie. She just wants to be in control."

"You mean she wants to be a good Mormon, and I don't fit that picture."

Pet shook her head. "No, that would be her mom's department. Katie's agenda has nothing to do with the church. Katies are born into every religion. She's just a jealous, grasping bitch who only feels secure when she's making the decisions for everyone around her."

"Wait a minute. Jealous? Manipulative, I'd say. Proud to a fault. But jealous? What's she got to be jealous of?"

"An older sister who's prettier, and a younger sister who's more talented, a sister younger yet who gets to be the darling. A brother who gets crowned king. I don't know, maybe she was just born with a tin can for a heart. Maybe her mother wasn't ready for another baby just yet. It doesn't matter. Jealous people are like paranoiacs. They're feeling inferior and have to have someone to blame it on. If there's nothing real around to hang that feeling on, they'll simply find something. So Katie's found you, or should I say added you to her list. You must drive her wild."

"What are you talking about? I'm no beauty. I've got no money, no influence. Why should she be jealous of me?"

"Oh, Em, you'd make her nuts simply because she can't control you. You get it? People like her feed on family structure. They're like vampires. They need everybody to hold still so they can get their big red drink. The more rigid the family, the better. Her family confuses her pushiness with support of the family interests. Just imagine: If someone comes in from outside who perturbs that structure, she's got to make that person go away. Particularly a truth junkie like you."

"Truth junkie. What are you talking about?"

"It takes one to know one. You want the truth, and you'll risk everything to get it. People like Katie want order—with them at the top—and they'll suck the blood out of anything in their path to maintain it. They'll tell themselves—and you—that they're the big victims, working their tails off while everyone else loafs. And they lack the capacity to see that their precious orderliness isn't even in their own best interest, let alone anyone else's."

I leaned back and took Pet in from a wider angle. Her little poppet eyes had grown wide and fierce, and both of her hands had tightened into fists.

Pet looked away, out the window at the cars passing in the street. Her mouth ran on with her. "Yeah. Control is more important to them than truth. More important than love, because they wouldn't know love if it jumped up and kissed them. But it doesn't jump up, because everyone around them is either cringing or in deep, deep denial. They keep pushing people away from them, even while they're trying so damned hard to hold on. Their hunger for power and importance is insatiable, and it makes them mean. Then it all becomes a big game to yank the rug out from under the people who have disappointed them. They'll bad-mouth their own daughters one minute and then try to extort special treatment for them the next."

My jaw was hanging halfway to my knees. Who knew that beneath Pet's perky exterior beat a heart filled with such rage? And what had provoked it? I said, "You seem to know a lot about this."

Feeling my eyes on her, Pet forced her hands to open, but they quickly contracted back again. She glanced at me, looked away. "Let's just say I've known a lot of Katies."

"I'm sorry to hear that."

"It's no matter. I have a good job, and I'm going to have a great life."

Going to have. What about now? I wondered.

We said nothing for the space of several heartbeats. I watched her chest rise and fall with her breath. Watched her hand dance lightly on the table, saw it dart out and grasp the remains of her taco and whip it up to her mouth.

I said, "So you've known Katie since school. Does that mean you're a Mormon, too?"

"I'm drinking beer, aren't I? The term is *Jack Mormon*, dear heart."

"You can go in some doors but not others."

"Precisely. And control freaks *love* keeping doors closed."

Instinctively, I asked, "Tell me about her husband, Enos."

Pet winced.

So that was it: Katie had beat Pet out for a husband.

Pet's spirits seemed to wobble for a moment, but she recovered quickly and said smoothly, "Yes, I've known Katie since when, and Enos, too. He was supposed to become somebody, be the big engineer, but then Katie got her mitts on him. He was never brilliant, but he was a hard worker, did his missionary year, worked his way through college, all that, so he should have been okay."

"Poor boy?"

"No, his folks had a little money, or they could have at least helped him, but they believed in tough jobs to build tough men. Kinda harsh."

"The Raymonds have money."

"Yeah, Ray senior was treasurer of the company. Did very well for them all."

"So, did Katie marry down?"

"Katie married someone she could *control*."

"He seems happy enough," I said, pushing her.

"Happy? He never knew what hit him. She latched onto him so fast his head spun. She insisted that they not wait to get married, that they have babies immediately. He crumpled under the strain of trying to do school and work and become a father at the same time. That's what Katie wanted, see, so that's what she got. Crank out the babies as fast as you can, because that's the big badge of honor in our community. But it wasn't enough for her that he worked as a humble little guard at the City and

County Building. Night shifts. Imagine trying to do college and family and work nights. The minute he graduated with his degree in engineering, she booted Enos into the family business, real fast-track job, lots of responsibility but almost no experience, but it pays the freight. I guess he's done his best, but he sure doesn't laugh anymore. She even wants him to run for political office! She has a big plan. First county commissioner, then—"

"Wait. Laugh? Enos?"

"Used to be a real cutup. You think I'm kidding? He used to kid me that I should come on down and he'd take me up that very same clock tower we just climbed."

"Enos? He doesn't strike me as the romantic type."

"Liked to do it, you know?"

This time, I did choke on my beer.

Pet said, "Oh, you'd be surprised. He was fun and romantic and—now he's just stressed. Gone real secretive. Doesn't come around to see his friends anymore," she added, as if it were an indictment.

"Well, parenthood alone can do that, right?" I said, still playing the Devil's advocate.

Pet gave me a "you fool" look. "Well, don't say I didn't warn you." She reached over and polished off the last of my tamale. "Now, give."

"I'm sorry. It sounds like you already know more than I do."

She eyed me carefully. "At least tell me why your geologist pals clam up around me. What am I doing wrong?"

I shook my head. "Nothing. You're just an outsider." Glad to turn the wheel toward safer ground, I continued. "Geologists gossip with one another but clam up around people who aren't their professional colleagues."

"Talk about paranoid," she said.

"It's not that. It's the nature of the work, and the training. Geology's a close-knit community, but more importantly, it's a community of people who speak a special language. We all know what constitutes a presumption in our language, and what's a fact, so we don't have to label them separately when we're together. We can let our hair down and chew on ideas. But ideas are exactly that, just speculation, and we're not allowed to speculate in public. It's against the rules. We might set off a panic. We're dealing with information that can influence people's lives, or even whether they live or die. You're the last person we'd want to shoot our mouths off around."

"But I'm a science writer. I understand the difference between fact and conjecture."

"Yeah, but you're trained in journalism, not geology. Geology is a very qualitative science, full of incomplete or ambiguous data. We speculate all the time around one another, think aloud. That's how we work. Exchange ideas, then go out and test them. But our mandate is different. We're trying to get at the story, but we're not trying to sell papers. We wait until an idea has been tested into a good, solid, predictive theory before we announce it to the press, because again, the public doesn't understand the difference between an idea and a fact, not to mention a theory. You want me to start giving you some examples? A meteorologist in Missouri gets a little gaga with age, but that doesn't erase the ink on his Ph.D. diploma. He gets to playing with numerology and decides that one-two-three-four-five-six-seven-eight-nine spells *earthquake*. So he announces: 'On January second, at three-forty-five P.M., there's going to be a magnitude six point seven quake that will kill eight hundred and ninety people.' The press picks it up, reports this guy's prediction and people go nuts, because he's a Ph.D., so he must know, right? No matter that his Ph.D. isn't even in geology."

"Then why not educate the public? That's my job, right? You'd think your pals would love to talk to me."

"Sure, that's part of our job, especially folks who are in the public sector—Hugh Buttons, Logan de Pontier, Sidney Smeeth—it's their job to get the information out there, so we can help the people we're mandated to help, but at the same time, we have to push our observations and data through rigorous analyses and colleague reviews before we launch it into the public sphere. Otherwise, we might go off half-cocked and cause more harm than good. That's why public employees are told to 'state facts but not create public policy.' We're supposed to leave policy making to the elected officials, because they've got a lot of political footballs to juggle. It's a real bugaboo."

"That didn't seem to stop Sidney Smeeth."

"No, it didn't."

Pet said, "I applaud her. She really knew how to get her issues into the press."

"Yes, but you're also thinking that it looks like her media savvy got her killed. So now maybe you understand another reason why other geologists won't talk to you."

"Not even about something as important as seismic hazards? Hey, I'm trying to educate a public that's living right on top of a killer fault in unreinforced brick houses!"

I said, "First off, you called it a 'killer.' "

"Isn't it?"

"That's editorializing. Or anthropomorphizing. And inaccurate, Faults don't kill people, falling *buildings* kill people. This city lies entirely within Seismic Code Four; but almost nothing here is built to that strict a code."

"People can't afford to build to Code Four."

"Now you're a politician, not a scientist. Aren't you going to tell them that their lives are at risk below Code Four?"

"But drawing attention to the fault gets the facts about risk across," Pet countered. "Then the citizens can make informed decisions."

"Does it? You're college educated and interested in the sciences, an easy sell. But do you really understand what is meant by risk? We talk about earthquake probability—how likely it is that one will occur in a given place within a given period of time—but earthquake risk is a measure of how likely it is that people will be killed if the earthquake occurs."

"Oh."

"Where's the greatest seismic risk in the U.S.?"

"California, right? Or Alaska?"

I started listing the numbers I'd read the day before in my geology text. "No. Probably Boston. One good shock through that area, with all that unreinforced brick, and wham. Or Saint Louis. Neither city has earthquake protection in its building code, and yet the most destructive earthquakes on historic record have occurred not far from them. Boston: Saint Lawrence River, 1663, Mercalli magnitude ten—that's like a Richter seven. Devastating if it happened today. Boston, *wham*. Half of New York, too, I'd imagine. Or the 1886 quake that knocked down Charleston, South Carolina. Saint Louis: shaken by New Madrid quakes, 1811 and 1812, both magnitude eight or worse. The ground accelerated so fast that it snapped the tops off the trees. And yet the average citizen does not think of Saint Louis as a big seismic zone. In California, everyone braces for the earthquakes, and every revision of the building code decreases risk. In Saint Louis, they have diddly."

Pet was silent for a moment, thinking. "Thank you. You clarified my thinking on that point. But still, the main point is to get people thinking about these things."

"No, the tough part is getting them not just thinking but also educated, so that they *understand*. People don't seem to understand that the Earth's crust is continuously under tremendous stress, and that there are certain places where it's likely to snap. California, sure. Alaska. Salt Lake City. There are places where the stress is minimal, and we worry about other things instead. And there are *other* places where we don't even *know* it's likely to snap, because while we don't have *historic* records of movement, Mother Nature may have been winding up the spring for eons. And Congress just cuts the budget, thinking it's not important to have scientists out there studying these things, that God won't let it happen here, or that we'll all be dead from pollution or viruses when it does happen, or who knows what!" Noticing how strident I was beginning to sound, I leaned back in my seat and took a long pull on my beer. "The Earth's crust is being moved by convection cells in the mantle," I said more calmly. "We're riding around on a big heat engine. The flywheel goes clear to the center of the Earth. There's no amount of wishful thinking on our part that's going to make it stop."

"You're talking about plate tectonic theory," Pet said briskly. "The Earth's crust is broken into large and small plates that are driven this way and that by those convection cells in the mantle, the molten layer below the crust transferring heat from the core outward. See? I know this stuff. The plates stretch apart, as here at the Wasatch fault, or they collide and push upward, as the Himalayas."

I added, "Or they grind past each other, as the San Andreas fault in California. Or one slides under the other, as the Juan de Fuca Plate diving under the North American at Seattle. But the human mind cannot comprehend things happening at such immense scales except in the abstract. We think in a scale as long as our arms, or the lengths of our feet. We're just scrambling around trying to make a go of it over the few decades we're alive, always much closer to the edge than we like to contemplate."

"But geologists are good at that abstraction. You eat ambiguity for breakfast."

"Yes," I said. "We deal with ambiguity and uncertainty, and for the most part, we do it qualitatively, not quantitatively. That makes it even more difficult to get our points across. If geology were a more quantitative science, it would be easier, because while most people don't really understand numbers, they've at least been taught to respect them. When we give a statistician all the carbon fourteen data we can regarding how many episodes of fault rupture we have and how long ago they occurred, he crunches them through a preset formula and comes up with an average number of how often a quake that size occurs. The public thinks that means they know how likely they are to get hit by a magnitude seven earthquake. They believe it out of hand. When engineers deal with uncertainty, they also put a number on it, and even though that number is conjured out of thin air and dressed up with a fancy title—an 'uncertainty coefficient,' or something like that—people get real impressed. But most of the work of geologists is qualitative, because we're dealing with things that are so large or so long-term that assigning numbers is sometimes meaningless. So we say things like, 'We're building houses in a fault zone. Don't you think we ought to build them stronger, or perhaps build somewhere else?' And everyone accuses us of being simpleminded. Give them a number—say 'On average, we'll only get a magnitude seven quake here every twelve hundred years, and the last one was maybe a thousand years ago'—and they figure they've got two hundred years to go, and feel all comforted, like they've got the picture straight."

"So what would you do?" Pet asked.

"Well, for one thing, I won't build a house in a fault zone."

"But you rent an apartment in one." Pet smiled sardonically. The expression looked odd on her perky little face.

"Yeah," I said. "Seems like I'm a risk-taker after all." I stared into my beer, trying to take comfort the soft reflection of light off the surface of the brew. "In order to see what we see, we also have to know that we don't quite see it perfectly. We perceive the imperfection of our own understanding. And that's necessary, because it keeps us from going off half-cocked, like I said. But it also forces us into an odd kind of humility. It's a funny package, huh?"

"You're like a bunch of lizards, each hiding under his own little rock."

I laughed at the image. "We're born to see things in four and five and six dimensions at once, and it makes us a little apprehensive. Ambiguity can be anxiety-producing. We see our own capacity for error, see the incompleteness of the incoming data. So we appear hesitant, reclusive, while all the time we're the only ones who can hope to resolve the questions we're grappling with. When will the next earthquake strike, and where? What, therefore, should be the policy regarding construction of homes in Salt Lake City? Or Boston? How much oil is left to fuel the cars and trucks on which we depend, and where is it? What killed the dinosaurs, why are the coral reefs in the Caribbean dying now, and will similar events kill us?"

"All right, but yesterday morning, the Warm Springs branch of the fault slipped, and the earth shook. How ambiguous is that?"

"It isn't," I said. "And it is. Where's the fault?"

"Well, it's . . ." Pet paused. "Oh. Yeah. You're having to interpret where it *is* most of the time, not just when it's going to slip."

"Uh-huh, and that spells dollars and cents, because it means that we're uncertain how to prepare for life in a fault zone. How long before it slips again? Are you going to make everybody build to the expense of Code Four even if the big quakes might not come around except once every twelve hundred years? That's over fifteen times our lifetime. Do the math. It's a sticky mess. And finances are finite. If you have only X dollars to spend on seismic renovation, do you spend it all on one or two structures, or do you spend a little bit on all of them? And do you close schools because of the risk of what might happen to the buildings?"

"You sound like a politician," Pet said.

"I just try to understand the problems they face," I answered. "That way, I don't get riled enough to kill one of them."

Pet smiled. "*Now* we are back on a riddle we *can* solve. Dr. Smeeth."

" 'Screaming Sidney,' I've heard her called."

"Not your typical geologist."

"No," I agreed. "She was much more vocal than most of us. But a damned good geologist, from all I've heard about her. And, as director of the UGS, she had to take a lot of flak from above."

Pet nodded. "Okay, so Sidney Smeeth answered to the governor—through Maria Teller, the director of Natural Reserves—and neither of them have training in the sciences. What do you suppose that does to the mix?"

"I don't know. I guess you'd have to look at what she was answering to them for—her exact mandate, that kind of thing."

"Fair enough. The state geologist is there to manage the exploitation of the state's mineral wealth, and guide examination of things like geologic hazards."

"Landslides," I said. "Earthquakes. Swelling and liquefying soils."

"Precisely," Pet said. "And we have all of those right here in Salt Lake County, as well as most of the state's human population. In support of public housing but perhaps contrary to public safety, we also have a mandate to develop the 'built environment' of the state."

"A mandate?"

"Yes. Building and planning departments work with people who are building. If no one was building anything, the Building Department would not exist, because they make their income by charging fees for writing permits, not by keeping land undeveloped. When you think about it, it's a conflict of interest to put building and planning in one department."

"Do you have a specific development in mind?" I asked.

"Well, the new stadium, like I said, and the mall it's attached to. The Towne Centre project."

"Hmm. Yesterday's earthquake put the stadium to the test. It flunked. And the seismic record Hugh Button's getting may reveal the exact location of that branch of the fault, turning a dashed line into a solid one."

Pet nodded. "Makes you wonder why that dashed line was deleted in the first place, doesn't it?"

I pulled back, insulted. "You think a USGS geologist would leave a line off a map for political reasons and the UGS would follow suit?"

"Lots of hands touch those maps."

"Now you are sounding paranoid."

"And you are sounding naïve."

I said, "That deletion of a dashed line is a perfect example of a geologic controversy. One geologist thinks the fault stops somewhere north of town; another looks at the same evidence and says it marches right on through." I took a sip of beer so I could momentarily hide behind the bottle. "Who put that interpretation into the UGS seismic map anyway?"

"I hear that the infamous Frank Malone had a hand in it."

Frank Malone, the engineering geologist whose name appeared in one of the files Tom had me read. Now is when I definitely begin shutting up! I told myself, but I said, "The same Frank Malone who digs trenches but won't let anyone see what's in them? What's he got to say for himself?"

Pet replied, "Interestingly enough, I can't reach him for comment. He is not answering his telephone calls."

"Well, there are talented geologists and there are not-so-talented geologists," I said, evading her gaze by looking out the window.

"Oh, sure," she said. "The geologist clams up again."

"I'm sorry."

"Don't be," Pet replied, the annoyance in her tone putting the lie to my apology. "If I can't get what I need from a geologist, I think I know who to ask."

Embarrassed, I took advantage of the call of nature to take a break from our conversation and headed for the rest room. When

I came back, Pet was just finishing up a call on her cell phone. Her tone was much more terse and aggressive than it had been. "I want to ask you about the cracked welds in the new stadium," she was saying into the phone. "Fine, off the record. What I tell my editor depends on what you tell me. Uh-huh. Right. *And* I want to talk to you about Sidney Smeeth. Yeah, I have a lit-tle suspicion that you have something to tell me about all that. Mm-hmm. What? Well, okay, eleven will do nicely." She listened a moment longer, then said acidly, "I understand perfectly."

"You get hold of Frank Malone?" I asked when she put the phone down.

"Perhaps. Let's just say someone who'd know more about that fault and that stadium than you."

That hurt. "You're getting kind of rough there, Pet."

Pet covered her reaction with a final long sip of her beer. At length, she put down the bottle and gave me a deeply probing look, all fluff and playful artifice gone. "I suppose I should say I'm sorry. But this is too important."

"I can respect that. Just be careful."

Pet shook her head dismissively. "No, you're being careful, and that's fine for you, if you must. But let me tell you, being careful doesn't get you there. Being careful is staying home and doing what mommy tells you to. Being careful is watching it all happen and not doing a damned thing about it. Sometimes you just have to open up your mouth and report what's happening."

That sounded to me like the bull was charging, only I wasn't sure if Pet would find a matador or an abattoir on the other side of the red cape. And with that thought, it occurred to me that Tom's cautionary training was finally beginning to take hold. I said, "Well, if you don't like being careful, there's also being reasonable."

"And what's that supposed to mean?"

"I don't know. I'm right in the middle of trying to figure that out myself."

And that was it. Pet went to wherever she was going, and I went home. I phoned in a report to Tom, telling him everything I had just learned. He thanked me for the information but took points off for my being such a sieve. I defended myself by saying that at least I hadn't blabbed that I was working with the FBI. He said that I had that part straight anyway and to cut the nonsense and make myself scarce next time Pet Mercer came looking for me. I said I would, but I wasn't entirely sure I meant it. I suggested that he have a talk with her, and he said he would first thing tomorrow.

After hanging up the phone, I ate a solitary late-evening snack, climbed into bed, did some reading, and eventually got some sleep. How I wish that Pet Mercer had done the same.

19

THE CLOUDS DIPPED LOW, FILLING THE NIGHT AIR WITH freezing fleece. Pet Mercer stood in the parking lot beside her car, waiting. As she waited, she smiled. Even though the mercury was nearing zero, the air was full of rich aromas. She could smell a story. Her story. It was big. She could almost smell the ink on her Pulitzer, could see it hanging in her cubicle at the *Tribune*, could . . . She arched her neck backward, staring up into the streetlamp that bloomed in the thick snow that sifted down over her head. The snow was falling faster now, the big soft flakes obscuring everything but the lamp, her car, and the surrounding twenty feet of pavement. Her search had mounted to a crescendo, gaining rapidly in the last few hours. What she had gotten from the geologists had clinched her theory. She had made the perfect phone call at the perfect moment, caught the right person off guard, ready to talk, and now here she was, waiting for him to come and spill it all to her under the cloak of darkness and in the silence of the falling snow.

In ecstasy, she opened her mouth to the falling crystals and let them melt on her tongue.

Pulitzer. *L.A. Times, Washington Post,* maybe even New York . . .

Her ear pricked to the sound of the approaching motor. Was that him?

She straightened her neck, then looked down. Snow was just beginning to collect on the blacktop.

The sounds of the approaching car grew, and she could see a brightening where the glow from its headlights roamed hungrily through the falling whiteness. Now she could see individual beams, now the form of the car. It was a Ford Explorer. She laughed to herself. How predictable. He was driving the most common vehicle in Salt Lake City.

As the vehicle pulled up next to her, she noticed that it was not exactly like every other Ford Explorer in town. This one had something mounted on the front bumper. It looked like a sheet of plywood, or . . . no, it was cardboard. How odd.

The driver's window slithered down. "Pet? Pet Mercer?" a man asked.

Her heart beat even faster. "Yes, it's me," she said brightly, going into her act. "Thanks for coming."

"Okay. Yeah. Um, sorry about this. I—"

"It's okay. I haven't been waiting long."

"Yeah. Just . . . just let me get this thing parked," the man said. He put the vehicle in reverse and rolled quickly backward, cutting his headlights as he went.

Pet lost sight of him in the snow. She looked down at her feet. The tire tracks had come quite close, but they were quickly disappearing in the gathering whiteness. The sound of the Explorer's engine seemed to have receded quite far. Now she heard it change gears. Why was he parking so far away? The engine was idling; now its sound indicated it was in forward, coming back her way, now accelerating.

Why? What?

Pet's quick little brain spun quickly, recalculating her conclusions, spurring her feet to move, but she was wearing the wrong shoes. The leather soles slipped on the frozen pavement, and she went down just as the Explorer barreled into her, crushing the fleeting light of life from her tender body.

20

The fire made its own draft. . . .

By Wednesday afternoon, inside of twelve hours, half the heart of the city was gone. At the time I watched the vast conflagration from out on the bay. It was dead calm. Not a flicker of wind stirred. Yet from every side wind was pouring in upon the city. East, west, north, and south, strong winds were blowing upon the doomed city. The heated air rising made an enormous suck. Thus did the fire of itself build its own colossal chimney through the atmosphere. Day and night the dead calm continued, and yet, near to the flames, the wind was often half a gale, so mighty was the suck.

> —*Jack London, "The Story of an Eyewitness"* (Collier's, *May 5, 1906), describing the devastating fire that consumed San Francisco immediately following the April 18, 1906, magnitude 8.2 earthquake that was centered in Olema. The quake burst water mains, causing cisterns to drain, leaving firefighters without hope of battling the blaze. By contrast, as the result of far better planning and preparation, only about two square blocks of San Francisco burned following the 1989 magnitude 7.1 Loma Prieta earthquake.*

WHEN I AWOKE WEDNESDAY MORNING, IT WAS SNOWING hard. The mood suited me: total isolation under a blanket of cold. Unable to stand the idea of being alone in bed, I jumped up, showered, dressed, and trotted down the stairs to see if there was a copy of the *Salt Lake Tribune* I could read. I hoped for a follow-up story on the damage the earthquake had done to the stadium. Knowing what I now knew, I wanted to see how this would be reported. I wanted to read Pet's words. And I thought when I was done basking in my insider's knowledge, I'd read up on the legions of elite athletes who were now arriving in the Salt Lake area to acclimatize for the coming Olympic games. They were powerful, beautiful, and astonishingly grounded people, and I felt none of that. Like all the rest of creation, I hoped to pick up a little vicarious splendidness just by reading about them and goggling at their pictures in the paper. Or at worst, I thought I'd flip to the editorial page and see what Pat Bagley was doing with them in his cartoon.

I didn't subscribe to the paper, but I had found that one of the other occupants of the apartment house in which I lived often waited until evening to read the paper, which left it available to me during the day, providing I was respectful and returned it to the porch in the same condition in which I had originally found it. Or close enough to. I had never actually asked, but no one had come pounding on my door to complain.

Today, I found the paper in a snowdrift, which meant that I was going to have to thaw it and dry it before I read it, folded it up again, and put it back on the porch, because it had been put out there warm and the snow it landed on had thawed and frozen to it as it had cooled. No matter; I needed to keep busy, right?

Right, so I stuck it in my oven while I fired up my midget travel iron, which is all the iron I can stand to own. Then I laid the first section flat and began to iron it dry so it wouldn't wrinkle. Well, the point of all of this is that I usually don't read the front section, it being a chronicle of events too ephemeral to interest a geologist, but because I was working it over with the iron, I actually read the front page.

The first headline read SALT LAKE GRIEVES LITTLEST CASUALTY. It seemed that, after two days of valiant efforts to save him, little Tommy Ottmeier had died. The report was that his weeping parents had stood by his bedside as the life-support equipment was removed, committing him to God's care and asking that he meet them when the day came that they would follow him to the next life. A funeral would be held. I noted that it was planned for the church at the same stake—what Mormons call a parish—as Ray's family attended. I try not to read such things, as it seems an invasion of privacy, but this time I couldn't help it. I had connected this infant with Faye's, and I found myself fighting back tears.

I read onward. The article included moving testimonials by those who had known little Tommy, and who knew and revered his parents. Mercifully, it limited its recitation about the short-sighted choice of a sleeping area that had led to the child's death, but by the same token, said nothing about the mechanics of earthquakes, substandard building practices, or corporate greed that had contributed to the casualty. I figured that at least a summary about earthquakes ought to have been there. Pet could have dashed off a box with one hand tied behind her back.

I scanned the page, wondering where her story had gotten buried. Above the fold, there was another pump-up article about the arriving Olympians, this time featuring their reactions to arriving at a place that had just thrown its chimneys into the garden. I was pleased to know that all the healthy young jocks from California and other places more frequently known to shake had taken it in stride, and I tut-tutted sympathetically as I read that this year's great American hope for figure-skating gold had clutched her teddy bear tightly when she heard about Tommy Ottmeier, but overall the article left me feeling more impatient than gratified. In fact, I would have put the paper back on the front porch in disgust if I hadn't by then opened it up far enough that I was committed to ironing it so that I could refold it correctly. As I continued ironing, I finally looked below the fold.

In the lower right-hand corner of the front page, I found Pet Mercer's face looking back at me.

She was easy to recognize, since I had seen her so recently, but I had to look twice to believe it, because it didn't make sense. It was her all right, right down to the pert hairstyle and bright, observant eyes.

I scanned the headline over her face, thinking that she must have won some award and that her employer had decided to crow about her on the front page, but instead the headline read SCI-ENCE REPORTER FOUND DEAD.

The words so thoroughly stunned me that I straightened up and looked around my small apartment to make sure where I was, and where all other solid objects were, as well.

Everything was still right where I had left it.

I looked back at the paper. Read the day's date. It was correct. I had not slipped into a parallel reality.

Finally, I read the story:

Salt Lake Tribune science reporter Amelia "Pet" Mercer, 26, was found dead shortly before midnight Tuesday in a parking lot near the state capitol. Mercer was pronounced dead at the scene. The cause of death is believed to be vehicular manslaughter.

Mercer had worked for the *Tribune* for five months. She was a graduate of the University of Utah and held a M.A. in Journalism from Columbia University.

The owners and staff of the Tribune are deeply shocked and grieved at her loss.

"We're putting everything we've got into the investigation," said Salt Lake City Police Department detective Arnold Haas.

It went on from there, talking about what a promising reporter Pet had been and so forth, that she'd been destined for greatness, loved by all, but there was not a single additional bit of hard information regarding where she'd been found, why ~~she~~ she'd been there, what had happened, who might have done it, or when, except that it had happened some time before midnight.

Which meant that I was probably the only person who knew anything about what had led to her death.

I slapped down the paper, unplugged the iron, and dialed Tom Latimer's number at the FBI.

◇

"SHE WAS DIGGING into Sidney Smeeth's death," I told him twenty minutes later in his office. "I told you that last night. So this has got to be connected."

Tom closed his eyes and rubbed the space between his eyebrows. "How I hope and pray you're wrong," he said. He opened his eyes and tried to smile, but he was not fully in control of his mouth, and he wound up looking like he was fighting off tears. Perhaps he was.

Not a good moment to go out of commission on me, Tom, I decided, then mentally whipped myself for my selfishness. Tom was my friend, and he had a whole lot more on his mind than what happened to be bothering me.

I got up and closed the door. Leaning with my back against it, I asked gently, "Is there something else you need to talk about, Tom?"

He examined me distantly, as if I were something lovely and admirable but inanimate, such as a statue on display in a museum. I examined him right back, marveling at how remote a truly brilliant intellectual can be about his emotions.

I sighed, wondering how he and Faye were going to muddle through the challenge they had created for themselves. Last week, they had been two sexually satisfied adults who seemed to enjoy each other's companionship. Now they were like a couple of superannuated kids who'd just pushed the wrong button on their toy rocket ship and found themselves on a foreign, potentially hostile planet. He seemed to have shrunk into himself, like a little boy caught sitting in his father's chair.

"Tom?" I said.

"It's okay, Em," he said pleadingly. "You can open the door. Please."

I stayed where I was.

He got up and opened it himself, returned to his seat, cleared his throat, then pressed onward. "Now, about the Mercer case: Let's review what you know about what she was working on."

I told him again about the pizza dinner Monday evening, detailing the way she had pushed for information and who had worked hardest to stonewall her, and why. Hugh Buttons, the Seismic Station's director, had seemed pained but on the spot. Logan de Pontier had been brusque. Wendy Fortescue, the seismiology tech, had kept her mouth shut. And Ted Wimler had been a drama queen. We reviewed our observations about how each of these people had behaved while entering the synagogue. Then I told him again about the tour of the City and County Building, and about our chat over tacos and beer.

Tom said, "So Mercer was asking about Sidney Smeeth's relationship with the governor, and she was interested in earthquakes. Anything else?"

"She said something about the Towne Centre project. Does that ring a bell?"

Tom nodded. "Yes, but I'm not going to say anything more for now," he said. "Please don't push."

I took a breath. I was beginning to get the picture now. Whatever was going on involved some kind of buy-off, some kind of cover-up. Large-scale developers and possibly high-level politicians. That old cocktail: people with a lot of money mixing it up with people with a lot of power, all interests fully vested, blinders on, no one looking out for the fact that they were building in an earthquake zone. "How did Pet die?" I asked. "The paper said 'vehicular manslaughter.'"

"She was run over. Twice."

I winced. Once might be manslaughter, but twice was murder. Accomplished by a person or persons who also threw public servants off their sundecks, or hired someone to do it, and both times managed to do so without being seen. He was right: I should keep my nose out of this one.

Tom continued. "Thank God the murders aren't my jurisdiction. I hate that kind of stuff. Leave me the paper trails to be followed, the nice cold brutality of fraud or the lasciviousness of interstate theft, but spare me the personal stuff."

I thought, *Now we're getting down to it*, but I said, "Running over someone with a car in a snowstorm sounds plenty cold and brutal. And so does heaving someone off the deck of their house. But maybe it's also stupid. I mean, the deck job might have been done on ice, where they'd leave no footprints, but didn't the vehicular job at least leave tire tracks?"

Tom nodded. "Police say the preliminary evidence is some kind of SUV or truck, a common chassis with very common tread. Whoever did it planned ahead enough to wear gloves and put some kind of covering over his—or her—boots. And it was snowing hard. There were only the vaguest footprint impressions around her and leading up to her car, which had been systematically searched, the contents turned over, her files standing up on edge, very tidy."

"A cold, brutal, methodical killer. Not my idea of a dream date, either."

"This is of course not to be discussed."

I knew Tom meant that I was not to tell Ray that he had passed me the evidence. "Don't worry," I said, looking away. "I barely ever see Ray these days. When I do, it's to discuss exactly that fact, not chitchat about murder cases, of which he would disapprove of my interest in the first place."

Now it was Tom's turn to sigh. "Sorry to hear that, sport."

I glanced quickly at him, trying to discern whether this really was news to him, or if Faye had told him all about it and he was just being decent. It didn't matter, really; the two of them were the people I trusted most in Salt Lake City, next to Ray . . . or perhaps now even more than Ray. I was sure they had their system about these things. Of course, I didn't discuss Faye with Tom, and only indulged in discussing the friendship aspects of Tom with Faye, never the business in terms of our friendship. It was a matter of propriety.

I moved back over to my chair and loaded myself into it. "So. What's my assignment?"

Tom tipped his head. "I can't assign you anything else; you know that. I bent the rules as far as they would go just asking you to read files for me. I appreciate your bringing the infor-mation about Pet Mercer around, and I'll see that it gets to where it needs to go without your having to make a trip down to the cop shop to give evidence. And of course, if you hear anything more, I'm your man. But things are heating up, Em, which is precisely the time for you to lay low, right?"

"Right," I said, thinking, *You dirty dog, Sidney Smeeth was a stranger, at best a distant colleague, but Pet Mercer was on her way toward becoming a friend of mine. Not twenty hours ago, we were peeking out of clock towers together and comparing notes like com-rades in arms. We ate together, Tom. And even if I hadn't come to care about her you've just told me that whoever killed her went through her files. Her notes, Tom! She had notes from her conver-sations with me! And my phone number and—and now you're telling me to stay out of it. Get real!*

◆

AS IF THE morning's events weren't enough to tie me into emo-tional knots, I had my dinner date with Ray to prepare for. I passed a long, tense afternoon trying to read about earthquakes, even though I had other schoolwork to do for the classes I was taking. As you may have surmised, I didn't have a temp job that week, so I should have been concentrating on catching up with some advanced math and a second semester of both undergraduate chemistry and physics, which I did not take in college but needed if I ever hoped to get a master's. My undergraduate degree was a B.A., not a B.S., so those two courses hadn't been required. I skipped them, figuring I'd just be going back to the ranch anyway, where math and chemistry didn't get much past counting cows and laying out a little mineral cake. This had been a bad plan, considering that my dad had died and I had been unable to work things out well enough with my mother to return to the ranch, but I valued the fact that I had instead taken philosophy and creative writing, which had helped me think more broadly and communicate those thoughts.

But now I had to bite the bullet and strengthen my credentials. The few geology jobs that came open were going to people with advanced degrees. I had researched the idea of training as a forensic geologist, which was what I had begun to call myself, but aside from a course by that title at certain schools that happened to have a forensic geologist on the faculty, there didn't seem to be an established curriculum. The specialty appeared to be staffed by geologists who loved puzzles and had advanced degrees, with concentrations in geochemistry and sedimentology, and minors in law enforcement. So I had a way to go, if I could stick it out. As I lumbered along trying to beef up my grade point average and correct those chemistry and physics math, I wished I was ten years younger and still on the family payroll, because those temp jobs were getting in the way of studying.

And now I had reason to believe I was on the list of a cold-blooded killer who had murdered two women in as many days.

And my love life, which had brought me to Utah, was getting painful enough to make me want to leave. I was beyond the point of anxiety with Ray. In fact, I was now all the way past worry to full-fledged panic. When he called at the last minute to change the restaurant, I was somehow not soothed, even though he had upgraded from a pizza joint to upscale bistro. The restaurant on the ground floor of the grand and lavishly old-fashioned Inn at Temple Square to be precise. It was newly renovated for the Olympics, all hip and "Euro," but it was still a deeply Mormon establishment—not a Budweiser in the place.

When dinnertime finally arrived, I put on that damned pink sweater and combed my hair, then headed downtown. I found Ray parked just down West Temple, sitting in his squad car, talking on his cell phone. Which meant it was a private call. He was smiling. When he saw me, he ended the call abruptly and his smile turned into an abstracted version of the Mona Lisa's.

At least he's not scowling at me, I decided, trying to think positively. *Well, up in the saddle and nose into the wind, cowgirl. It's time for the roundup.*

Unfortunately, another part of my consciousness went over the same evidence and decided I was a fool. *Right*, it sassed me. *What do you think you're doing here, Em? It's over. You've been bucked off this horse. You lost your grip on the saddle and landed on your butt, and you ran from his mother's house like your boots were on fire. You were right the first time. You should have kept on running.*

This man has asked me to be his wife, I answered myself self-righteously. *That's got to mean something.*

Oh, sure, it means something, but what? Remember, he's a Mormon. His own grandfather probably had more than one wife. He's a widower, but he still wears his first wife's ring. That little tête-à-tête you witnessed in the kitchen was probably an audition for wife number three. Or two, if you keep playing hard to get.

The door to the squad car opened. Ray stepped out and strolled toward me, elegant even in his standard-issue uniform, his snug hips rolling that incredible way they did when he wanted to say hello without words. He moved up close to me, touched my cheek, smiled pensively. "Hello, love," he said. He seemed distant and sad, almost dreamy, but the words rang in my heart.

And I felt a tugging in those parts of me that are most female. More than a year of pent-up longing seemed to burst from my seams. All reason instantly vanished as I saw again what it was about this man that had drawn me to move clear across the Rockies to be with him. If he'd asked me to jump in the backseat with him then and there, I would have unbuttoned my blue jeans on the way.

But he didn't. He didn't even kiss me hello, being out in public and all that. Instead, he took me by the elbow and ushered me down the sidewalk, around the corner, through the lobby of the hotel, and into the restaurant. I immediately rued wearing the pink sweater, even if Ray had given it to me. What had I been thinking? I tugged at the hem of my down jacket, wishing I were dressed as cleverly as the other women in the place.

A young woman with a spine like a dancer's showed us to a seat by the windows that looked out over Temple Square. I began to worry even more.

We sat down and ordered dinner. Being gently raised at least as far as restaurant dinners went, I followed his lead and asked for soup and salad. It was clear that he was trying to keep the costs down. Which added to my confusion. I wondered, *Why has he brought me to such a swanky place? I'm not the flowers and chocolates kind of girl when it comes to accepting apologies; a simple "Sorry" does fine. And doesn't he know it blows the effect if he brings me somewhere expensive and then orders down? Or is this the big farewell, carefully orchestrated in a venue where I'll feel constrained against pitching a fit?*

I had rehearsed a whole speech. It went something like this: *Ray, we've been spending a lot of time apart lately, and I am concerned. Yesterday evening, when I went to your mother's house, I saw you behaving affectionately with another woman, so naturally my concern increased, and I ask you to explain what was actually going*

*on there. I am here in this town to build a middle ground with you,
and I reaffirm that intention. Right now, I'd like to know if that's
still your intention, as well.*

So much for practicing in front of the mirror. Try reciting an
overblown bunch of syllables like that when you're so scared that
it feels like there's a hand closing around your throat. Instead, I
said nothing.

We waited for our salads, not making eye contact, the con-
cussively loud music crashing around us like rocket fire. I was
torn between getting up and running away and simply digging a
hole through the floor and crawling into it. And all the while,
Ray kept glancing at the entrance to the restaurant. It was perhaps
three minutes before I cracked and started trying to make small
talk over the noise. "Nice place. I've never been here. The menu
looked good."

"I chose it because my brother-in-law's supposed to be here,"
Ray said.

Well, that remark sure pushed me back over the edge between
intimidation and anger. I am pleased to report that I found my
dignity before I put my mouth in gear, so instead of yelling, *You
bastard!* I said almost calmly, "Ray, that hurt."

He quit watching the entrance and looked at me for the first
time since the sidewalk, said, "Oh. Sorry."

I was not going to be ignored now. "You seem more than a
little distracted. Mind letting me in on things?"

He drummed the table lightly with his fingertips. "Fight between Katie and Enos."

"*What?*"

~~Tom~~ _{RAY} seemed startled by my anger. He said, "He's not getting
home enough."

Sounds writhed in my throat like snakes. I wanted to tell him
about what pet Mercer had said about Katie, say, *See, I'm not the
only one who thinks she's making trouble,* but, ironically, the only
words that made their way out were, "I know how Katie feels."

Ray gave me a withering look.

I removed the napkin from my lap and began to refold it. "I don't deserve this," I said, almost shouting to be heard over the music and laughter that boomed all around us.

"What?" He looked mystified.

My hands froze in the middle of the job with the linen as my brain now tripped me up with the half baked social etiquette of the half-reconstructed soul. *Right, I have to spell it out or I'm just being passive-aggressive. I have to use an "I" message: When you do X, I feel Y, and I wish you'd do Z. But I can't think of a thing, except, When you put your arm around another woman, I feel like shit, and I wish you'd suck eggs.* Wobbling on the edge of a meltdown, I took a deep breath, found my voice, and said, "Ray. Something's up—or should I say down?—between us, and I think we ought to talk about it. I moved to this city to be with you, and . . . that's not turning out to be easy. Your rules say I don't go to your house and you don't come to mine. At your mother's house, we have no privacy. I have to come to a public place to have a very private conversation with you, not that you're a talker anyway, and hey, I'm a private person, too, okay? So listen: I'm not an idiot. I am an observant person. Something's wrong. Let's get it out where it doesn't fester."

Ray stared at me. He looked scared, or tired, or some combination of the two. "You're right. I'm sorry. I've had a lot . . . going on."

"Like what?"

But Ray had forgotten me again. His eyes had darted again to the entrance of the restaurant and locked, his neck stiff as a hunting dog's.

I turned and looked, too.

Katie's husband, Enos Harkness, was just walking in. I personally wouldn't have noticed him, even though I had met him many times; Enos was a straight-arrow sort of guy, an engineer for some big firm. And when we were together, he had always said even less than Ray, and with about one-tenth the effect. But on this occasion, with Pet's confidences freshly in mind, I saw him as if for the first time, and the thing that went through my head was, *Pet thought this guy was a party boy?*

Enos had caught the hostess's attention and was on his way to the long counter where singles were served when Ray jumped up and cut him off in the middle of an aisle between tables. Ray cut a shoulder between Enos and the hostess and stepped in close to talk to him, his neck ramrod-straight. Enos avoided eye contact with Ray. He stood uncannily still and stiff, his buttocks tightened up to the size of apples. Words flew back and forth between their emotionally masked faces, a real guy thing. It was like watching a couple of cigar store Indians trade insults about whose cigars were bigger, except that I was well enough acquainted with both of them to know that Ray was blistering mad and Enos was nothing short of terrified.

The young female who was trying to seat Enos stood by, looking blank. *Mormon*, I decided. *Not that they'd employ anyone else here. But I have no doubt. She is pretty in a made-up, conformist, self-deprecating sort of way, and I want to SCREAM!*

Enos suddenly turned and broke for the door. Ray did not follow. He stood with his hands on his hips, burning a hole in his brother-in-law's back with his eyes.

Remind me to never truly piss this man off, I told myself. *He'd reduce me to ash.*

It was only as Ray moved back toward our table that I realized that he had gotten up so fast that he had not even put down his napkin. Now he arranged himself in his chair again, spending an extraordinary amount of time flattening the napkin back into place. "Excuse me," he said. "What were you saying?"

My heart sank down through the floor. He had not invited me here to visit, much less to sort out our differences. *He brought me here to trail along while he looks after family business!*

Now fully deflated, I leaned back in my chair for half a minute, studying the faces of the people at the tables around us, their clean, close-shaven Mormon faces, their feeling of belonging, their air of separateness from any world I knew or understood. Wheels were turning within wheels, and I was not even part of the machine. I wanted to say, *Who was she?* but knew that I had to trust Ray unswervingly or not at all, and if there was no trust, it was simply time to pack it up and go home, wherever that was.

Ray was preoccupied, and it had little or nothing to do with me. Something was askew in his family but I was beyond guessing what it was. For all I knew, the woman in Ava's kitchen really had been a childhood chum, and maybe Katie really didn't have it in for me, but had invited me to her mother's house because she wanted any distraction that would get her mind off the fact that her husband wasn't coming home often enough. For a moment, I felt her pain.

So in answer to Ray's question, I said, "It's nothing. Or at least, nothing that can't keep." I picked up my fork and jabbed it into my salad, which a very efficient waiter had just slid in front of me.

Ray nodded. "Sorry, Em. Things are just a little busy right now is all."

I hoped and prayed that he was right, and that tomorrow, or next week, or, at worst, next month, as the days grew longer and winter began to lose its grip on my heart, things would be better.

But as I pierced the cherry tomato that garnished my salad, it seemed to bleed.

21

I was on the eighth floor of the Starbucks Building. Someone was already under my desk, so I held on to a post. It went on a long time. I thought I was going down.

> —*Jon Engle, describing the February 28, 2001, Nisqually earthquake that rocked Seattle. The 6.8 quake's epicenter was thirty-five miles southwest of that city, and its focus, or actual area of slippage, was thirty miles below surface in the subduction zone between the Juan de Fuca plate and the North American plate. Hence, its destructive force was greatly dampened relative to surface structures. Luck was also with the citizens of Washington because there had been little rain recently, and the quake therefore set off relatively few mud slides. The time of day when it occurred was also important. In Seattle and Olympia, falling bricks and cornices crushed parked cars, but, because the quake hit midmorning, before patrons had migrated from their well-constructed office blocks to restaurants in precode brick buildings, no one was killed.*

My orchids began to dance. I was ecstatic. I thought, I was just preparing for an earthquake this morning, and here's one now.

> —*Susan Oliver, describing the same earthquake, as experienced in a one-story wood-frame building in Port Angeles, twice as far from the epicenter*

IN THE MORNING, I GOT MYSELF UP EARLY AND PULLED ON my thermal underwear and the tightly woven wool pants I wear cross-country skiing. I scrambled up some eggs, guzzled down some orange juice, brushed my teeth, piled on thick socks, a turtleneck shirt, a wool shirt, and a knit cap, grabbed my down parka and a pair of mittens, stepped into my pack boots, and headed for Faye's Porsche, which was beginning to feel like home. I was gettin' real good with the shifter, as one of my father's ranch hands used to say, and I loved the way the thing got up and went.

Logan was already at Faye's house when I got there. He had Ted Wimler with him. Faye had shown them into her kitchen and had introduced them to Tom Latimer, and they were all sucking up some swanky coffee and a pile of pastries. Faye, needless to say, was eating nothing, but neither was she running to the bathroom to barf. Which was something of a relief. I had been concerned that Faye was going to say, Sorry, I'm not feeling well, and send me up the canyon alone with this gang of relative strangers. Perhaps her morning sickness knew what her overheated little brain currently did not—namely, that there was such a thing as pushing your pal Em too far.

Logan was in good humor, and I heard him laugh for the first time. It was a rich, committed kind of laughter, straight from the gut. The fact that he was wearing a crisp white turtleneck brought my eye to the rich, wavy hair that went into short, tight curls at the nape of his neck. I caught myself thinking, *Not bad.* I find that when a guy isn't quite perfectly groomed I feel closer, even intimate. I mentally slapped myself on the wrist. *You're getting too old to drown one failed relationship in another one,* I told myself, *and if you don't want the one with Ray to fail, try keeping your mind on making it work.* My heavens, I can get stern with myself.

After a couple of pastries, I decided to vent my spleen a little by bringing up a topic that was not so jolly. "So," I said. "Did everyone read about Pet Mercer?"

Logan stared into his coffee cup. "Awful," he said.

Ted Wimler opened his mouth. "Two deaths in just two days! I tell you, something's going on!"

"Three deaths," Faye said in a voice suddenly gone faint.

Tom went stiff, his eyes on Faye.

Ted got out his metaphorical crying towel and said, "That's so sad. I hear there's going to be this humongous funeral observance for him. At first, the city wanted to downplay it, but the whole thing has become such a media circus that they're pulling out all the stops."

"I suppose it will serve some good," Logan said. "You know, publicity and all that. Even if all we can get is a few sidebars on better earthquake preparedness. With Pet gone, we sure aren't going to get the coverage we need to educate the public the way we need to."

Tom watched them both closely.

Ted took a deep breath and was about to start in again, but Logan said, "Well, we're here to have fun. So let's talk about something else."

I shut up. Perhaps it was just those curls at the nape of his neck, but I didn't want to annoy Logan by bringing up any more sad or contentious subjects. Which left me feeling more than a little confused. For all I knew, Logan had killed Sidney Smeeth, and possibly Pet Mercer, as well. What had Pet said? They had been involved, and something had gone wrong. And Ted was certainly a strange one, but in an idiotic way. Of course, I had no idea what either man's motivation might be for doing anything so bloodthirsty, but I was no longer an ingenue in the business of detection, having learned that the most deadly variety of murderers had a way of hiding in plain sight. So I took a nice long look at Logan, wondering what brewed beneath those fierce eyebrows of his. Could it be a killer? *That's nuts*, I told myself. *You're being paranoid. Whoever killed Sidney Smeeth probably had some connection to whatever big-time fraud Tom Latimer's digging into, one far beyond my specialty or reckoning. It'll turn out to have nothing to do with geology. Besides, Pet told you she was going to speak with someone other than a geologist the night she died. Didn't she?* I tried to remember her words, but I could not.

"So," Logan was saying, "ready for some gliding over the frozen medium?"

Faye seemed to be in no hurry. Logan genteelly tried to hurry her by heading out to the driveway to load her skis onto the rack on top of his vehicle. When that didn't get her through the front door, he came back into the kitchen and said, "Let's get going."

Faye replied that we were waiting for one more person.

I gave her a *huh?* look, and was just opening my mouth to ask her what kind of crap she was up to this time, when Agent Jack Sampler pulled into the driveway in a beat-up BMW with skis on the rack.

Faye asked, "Is this him, Tom?"

"Yes." Tom, who had been kind of lying in the weeds through all of this, led the way out into the driveway and introduced Jack to Faye and Logan and all the rest, adding finally, "Jack would like to tag along on your skiing trip. That okay with you guys?"

Okay? Well, how were we supposed to say no?

Jack was smiling like he had just been let out of an asylum for the mentally peculiar for his first field trip in twenty years. He was dressed just fine, Mr. Smooth Skier, but he suddenly seemed very big. It was a bit like being handed a large untrained dog to care for. I wondered, *What do I do with him?* And, *Does he come with a book of instructions?*

Logan put on a poker face.

Faye said cheerily, "We can all ride in your vehicle, okay, Logan? Or should we take Jack's?"

This was about the breaking point for me. I had had about enough of Faye and Tom running my life for me. They were good friends, and I didn't like confrontations, but I have my limits. I said, "Gosh, Faye, seems like you're getting really good at fancy footwork. Why don't you and Jack just waltz along behind? Hell, even Tom might like to come."

Faye stiffened.

I grabbed Tom by the elbow and dragged him out of earshot. Keeping my voice down as best I could under the circumstances, I said, "Tom. Why is Jack here?"

"He wants to go skiing. Show him a good time, okay?"

"Nonsense!" I whispered. "You're up to something!"

Tom's smile drained into a look of sobriety. "Things are a little stirred up in your geological community just now, Em. I don't need to point out to you that these men you're about to spend the day with knew both of the women who have been found murdered in our fair city in the past few days. But don't go connecting any dots. Just go have a good time skiing."

"The hell."

Logan's eyebrows had risen halfway up his forehead as all this transpired. He looked over toward me and seemed to read my exasperation. He said ever so politely, "We already have most of the gear on mine," and started opening his rack to take Jack's skis.

Logan was driving a nice functional Ford Explorer, like half the rest of Salt Lake City drove. His had Mardi Gras beads wrapped around the gearshift, a nice layer of dried mud and gravel on the floorboards, and miscellaneous rock samples in the drink holders. I felt right at home.

So, all loaded up, and with Creedence Clearwater Revival blasting out of the CD player, we headed on down the mountain front to Little Cottonwood Canyon, which is a narrow thing with DON'T PARK HERE FROM OCTOBER THROUGH MAY signs all along the road to mark the avalanche chutes. We soon arrived at Alta, which is at the top of the grade. The sun was shining, there were six fresh inches of snow on the slopes, and there was not a cloud in the sky. I should have been ecstatic, but, as I said, I don't much like to ski downhill.

First off, there's the fitting in issue. I did not. I did not own my own equipment, and I wasn't dressed like the rest of the crowd. Faye was in a one-piece suit of some sort of expensive stuff in the color of the sky, shot with red and yellow accents. Logan, Ted, and the others from the pizza dinner—who were waiting for us at the lodge—were decked out in various sorts of modern snow gear, not a shred of which was made of wool. Only Wendy Fortescue even halfway approached my déclassé dowdiness, and that only because her gear seemed to be made up out of spare parts and because her color sense clashed with her skin.

So that was point one against downhill skiing. Point two was that I was really bad at it. But I was now committed to a day of it, so I tromped through the ski-rental shop, bought a lift ticket, and got in line with the rest of the gang to ride the lift farthest to the east.

Faye chose it. She said it supplied a good warm-up slope. Having orchestrated things this far, Faye also managed to shuffle things around enough that I rode the double chair with Logan, which left her making small talk with Agent Jack. From what I could see by craning my neck around and staring back at them, she was uncertain of his companionship and contemplating having words with Tom when she got home. Her maneuver further backfired when I took a fall coming off the top, right in front of Logan and all the others, who were waiting for us at the top of the lift. Logan said something conversational, like "Been a while?" and helped me up, then made two lovely moves to get out of the way of the gathering crowd, displaying the fact that he was a damned good skier. Quick and at ease. I followed as best I could, trying to remember what I had never known about the sport. I managed to stay upright all the way to the bottom, but wore down some tooth enamel en route.

For the second ride up the lift, I managed to maneuver my way into sharing a chair with Wendy Fortescue, figuring that as long as I was going to suffer through this day, I could at least be gathering information.

"Enjoying the snow?" I asked brightly.

Wendy twisted around in the chair and stared at me. "Are you some kind of a fruitcake or something?"

I stared back at her. "No. I was hoping to get you to talk about Sidney Smeeth."

"Nothing to say."

"I understand. But I have a question for you nevertheless. I'm wondering why Dr. Smeeth chose the new stadium for a backdrop when the TV stations were doing the breaking news about the earthquake. Just before she died. I was wondering if she mentioned anything to you that morning before heading down there. Anything about going down to check it for cracks, for instance."

Wendy stared at me for several more seconds before speaking. "Okay. I guess it's no big secret. She had it in for the developers."

"All developers in general? Or the one that built the stadium in particular?"

Wendy grunted. "That one would do nicely, don't you think?"

"Why so?"

"Aw shit, they put moment frames in that sucker. Even after that didn't work in Northridge. Fuck that shit. Real brain trusts, huh?"

I figured she was referring to the 1994 Northridge, California, earthquake, but I had no idea what a moment frame was. Trying to look like I knew all about them, I said, "So, Sidney had already decided that building was at risk?"

Wendy snorted. "At risk? Those damned welds cracked in the first high wind. It was just coincidence that she'd gotten in there and had a look the day before the quake. God, she was pissed when she got home. I could hear her screaming into the telephone, right through the floor."

"Oh," I said. "You know who she was calling?"

Wendy stared at me blankly. "Some stiff or another at the county offices, I imagine. That's who she usually beat up on."

◈

WE ALL STAYED together for another two runs, after which time it was clear that most members of the party were restless to go to the top of the mountain and do some real skiing, and certain others, specifically Faye, needed to head for the bathroom to vomit.

"I'll wait for you here, outside the lodge," Logan said.

Agent Jack lurked right next to him, making no pretense about his presence. He was not here primarily to ski, and neither was he making sure Faye was all right. He was baby-sitting me. It was time to make it clear to Jack that I didn't need a nanny, and to Logan that I was not his date. "No, you fellas go on with the others," I said firmly. "I'm going to work on the basics. You go on up and carve yourselves some mountain."

Logan's brow knit briefly and then unknit. He said, "Okay, but let's get together later on. Meet here for lunch at eleven-thirty, avoid the rush."

"Fine."

Logan left. As I watched him glide away, I thought, *Em, you are an idiot.* That thought was underscored ten seconds later as I turned and saw Ray arriving from the parking lot. With Katie. And Ava. And the "friend" from Saint George. I was out of my bindings and into the lodge quicker than a coyote with its tail on fire. I completely forgot about Jack Sampler.

"Faye," I gasped when I'd finally found her, having somehow navigated a staircase with my feet locked up in those iron maidens they call ski boots. "Ray's here."

She was bending over one in a line of sinks, rinsing her mouth.

She looked slightly green. "Ung," she grunted. "This could be interesting."

"Noooo, no no no no. Interesting, I do not need. Ix-nay on the interesting-ay."

Faye gave me a long, grouchy look. "Of all the juke joints he had to—"

I spoke quickly. "Fact is, I knew he was coming here today. He said he was taking his sister Katie. But I figured they'd be at the top of the mountain already and I could just stay down on the beginner's slopes and stay out of trouble. But it's worse. He's got his mother with him, and—" I almost gagged on my words, because just then, Ava walked into the bathroom.

When Ava saw me, she came to an abrupt halt, stared at me, then straightened her jacket, gave me a prim smile, and, with evident discomfort, murmured, "Em, how are you. I thought you didn't like skiing, dear."

So that's how this is going to be, I decided. *I'm going to be held accountable for being in a public place where she does not want to find me.* I thought of saying, Don't worry, I won't mess with your precious son, but I figured that such candor would about tear things, if there was anything left to tear. So instead, I blurted out something more factual, which was, "This was Faye's idea. You remember my friend Faye?"

Faye straightened up to her full five-foot-ten and turned to face Ava with an austere smile, one queen to another. "Good morning, Ava. I didn't know you skied," she said, her eyelids suddenly grown heavy. "What fun. Perhaps you'd like to join us. I've brought Em up here to socialize with some of my geological colleagues, a memorial to Dr. Smeeth. Em's getting quite involved with this earthquake thing, you know."

Faye's words had a surprising effect on Ava. She flinched and shot a nervous look my way. Whatever had caused that reaction, she quickly covered it. "Oh. How interesting. No thank you. I just needed to . . . ah . . . get some tissue." This she did, grabbing a strip of toilet paper out of the nearest stall as quick as a chicken nailing a june bug. She waved it at us as if to prove that was what she had had in mind and scarpered. Zip. Vanished. Gone.

Faye narrowed her eyes and folded her arms across her chest. "Now, is it just me, or did you-all notice anything funny in that behavior?"

"Hmm. Dunno, but if all she wanted was to swipe a bit of TP, then why was she taking her jacket off and unzipping her swanky bib overalls on the way in here?"

Faye smiled like a cat. "Why, Emmy B., you're a right 'un. It looked for all the world like Mizz Ava was in some kinda hurry getting herse'f ready to pee, and here she done run for it the minute she seen you."

"No, the minute you said—what was it you said?"

"Something about geologists. Or earthquakes."

"Yeah." I started to laugh giddily.

"What's so funny?"

"I must be flunking Buddhism one oh one, because I'm having this nasty thought: I want to see Ava trying to take that first run still needing to relieve herself that badly."

Faye pursed her lips, still watching the doorway through which Ava had appeared and so quickly disappeared. "Even Buddhists have their days, dear heart." Then she turned and looked at me. "And not to confuse the uses of the word, but if you're thinking that, then I'd say you're a little bit pissed yourself."

I found I could not meet her gaze. "Yep," I said through my teeth. "More than a little bit."

"Figured out yet who you're pissed at?"

It is not always easy being Faye's friend. I considered ignoring her question, but I reached down inside and took a look at that burning coal I called a heart and said, "I am mad at Ava, and I'm not sure why. Hell, I'm mad at the whole damned family." I took a breath. "And at Ray."

"You figure out yet what you're going to do about it?"

The image of a fleeing rabbit zigged across my brain. "No," I answered. "But whatever it is, I reckon I'm going to have to do it soon."

22

THE THING WAS, I HADN'T TOLD FAYE YET ABOUT THE woman I'd seen Ray flirting with in Ava's kitchen. Because old friend, new girlfriend, or whoever the woman in the kitchen was to Ray, that was exactly what he had been doing with her, and that was a humiliation I had to face. I hadn't told Faye because, even though she was a dear, dependable friend, there had been a limit to the amount of confession my pride could endure all at once. Hell, the evening before, I hadn't even been ready to admit the truth of Ray's behavior to myself.

"Faye," I said as we ski boot–hobbled up the stairs from the bathroom together, "there's something I got to tell you. Let's go into the restaurant here. I'll spring for the tea."

"Great. Let's sit out there on the deck."

"Noooo. Inside. Out of sight."

Faye said, "Listen, Em, you have every bit as much right to be here as he does."

"That is currently not the point." We were at the top of the stairs. There stood Agent Jack Sampler, bubba turned ski dude, waiting for us. For me. I gave him a weary flick of a smile.

He nodded.

"Gimme a minute, Jack," I said.

I sat Faye down and got the teas. When I had maneuvered

myself into another chair at the same table, I told her about the scene Monday evening in Ava's kitchen.

Faye began to nod her head in wide arcs, very slowly. "Ooooooh, now I see. If Ava looks that squirmy, you think it's because the 'friend' from Saint George is out there with Ray and she doesn't want you all to meet."

"Precisely. They're out there all right. And neither do I want to meet them. Faye, I'm not tough enough. And there's more." I told her about the uncomfortable dinner with Ray the evening before, and about his confrontation with his brother-in-law Enos Harkness.

Faye shook her head side to side and said, "Weeeeeeeird."

"Yeah, and now Ava's jumping like a cat on a hot griddle when she sees me, and running for the high timber when you say something about earthquakes. I have no idea what this all means, but I'm telling you, instinct tells me to play it kind of cagey just now."

"Gotcha."

"Yeah. So let's send Agent Jack here up the hill to get a pail of water or something and go sit in the car until we're supposed to meet Logan and the others at eleven-thirty. Ray and his family will have cleared out of the lower slopes by then, because they'll no doubt have their lunch at the upper lodge, halfway up the mountain. Much more romantic," I said, unable to keep a trace of bitterness out of my voice.

Faye was looking out the window at nothing, or so I thought. Her eyes had taken on a thousand-yard stare. "No, I'm staying here. We came in Logan's car, remember? And he locked it. But listen, you and Jack go back up the east lift and get some practice in, try to have fun."

"But what if—"

"No, I really don't think you have that particular problem to worry about at this instant. What's Ray's poisonous sister look like? I've never had the pleasure."

"Dark, like Ray. Almost his height. Athletic build."

"Any of his sisters blond?"

"No."

"How about Honeycup Saint George?"

"Blond, shorter, softly shaped. A real pink-and-powder blue type. Why?"

"Because someone answering to that second description just got on one of the other lifts with Ray. They're going for the upper mountain, just as you said. You go back up the lift to the east."

"But what if they change their minds and come down that slope? Faye, I can't see him here, especially not with her!"

She picked her fanny pack up off the floor, pulled out a trail map for the ski area, and consulted it. "It looks like . . . they could possibly do that, but it's highly unlikely. Look, you go on up the east lift. Take Jack. He's trained in everything from body-guard to lounge lizard, by the looks of him, and it's obvious he's here to look after you. For some reason that you and Tom are not telling me, I might add. I'll just sit out there on the balcony and keep an eye on things."

"But what if they do come down the same slope? Faye, I'd shit little green nuggets! She's all pink and blue and blond and I'm the bag lady who got loose in the smart set."

Faye patted my hand, then opened the pack and pulled out what looked like a little transistor radio with a fat antenna a few inches long. "Take this. I'll have its mate." She showed me that there was another still in the pack. "Set it for channel . . . let's see . . . twelve. Privacy code . . . ten." She fiddled with the dials, bringing the numbers up bright and clear on the displays. "Yeah, that doesn't have any traffic on it. You turn it on here, set the squelch there. Carry it in your breast pocket. If I see them coming down the hill, I'll give you a holler."

The thing suddenly spoke to me, but the voices were faint. "Who's that?" I asked Faye.

"Don't know," said Faye. "Here, if that bothers you, I'll change the channel. How about good old thirteen?"

"Isn't that bad luck?" I asked bleakly.

"No. But everybody else thinks so, so we'll probably have it all to ourselves. These things are getting popular on the slopes."

I hefted the little radio, still uncertain.

Faye unbuckled her boots and put her stocking feet up on another chair. "You'll be better hidden on the beginner's slopes, and God knows, you need the practice. Me, I've got a date with a saltine cracker and a crossword puzzle." She unfolded a sheet of newspaper out of her pack, pulled a out a short pencil, and bent to her work.

"You sure figured all the contingencies," I snarled.

She didn't even look up. "Someday you'll thank me. Now git."

I was starting to get as steamed at Faye as I now felt at Ava. However well intended her harebrained scheme to improve my love life or broaden my professional network had started out, she now had me up a canyon with no personal means of escape, looking stupid in bad ski clothes and falling off of chairlifts, and with no one but the unnerving Jack Sampler to look stupid with because she had the tummy crummies. Without saying good-bye, I headed for the door. Agent Jack fell in a few paces behind me as I stomped out onto the deck of the lodge.

It being my day for bad luck, I took one stride outside the door and bumped right into Katie. Literally. *Wham.* Dropped the damned radio. I was so awkward in those ski boots that it took me a moment to squat down and reach for the thing.

Katie was dressed in fuchsia from head to toe, but was still in her street boots, so she was quicker than I was, quicker even than Jack, being another of the Raymond family athletes. She ran five miles each morning, and it showed. She was as trim and muscly as a sprinter. She bent down and snatched the thing up before I could get my hand even six inches from it and examined it with interest. "Very fancy," she said. "These radios are all the rage now. I didn't think *you* would have one."

I forced myself to take a deep breath before replying, during which time I got past my urge to say, Go piss up a rope, but, mentally chanting one of Faye's mantras about putting myself in my opponent's shoes, I told myself that Katie was probably . . . threatened by me, so I managed to say nothing. *This woman's husband had to be disciplined in public for not coming home often enough. And she's had to move back in with her mother. She's on edge, spoiling for a fight. I won't give her one.*

Agent Jack sidled up next to me and measured Katie up and down. He said nothing. Just then, I was damned glad that he was big and burly and, for the moment at least, downright presentable.

Katie ignored Jack and looked *me* up and down. "Nice outfit, Em," she drawled. "Why aren't you wearing that nice pink sweater I had Ray buy for you for Christmas?"

Again, I said nothing. I do admit that I indulged myself in snapping my sunglasses down from the top of my head to the place where they belonged. No reason not to look as intimidating as possible.

Katie still held the radio. She said, "Let me guess. Ray told you he was coming up here, so you had to tag along, huh?" She still ignored Jack Sampler. Clearly, she was not as easily cowed as her mother. She was going to hold on to my radio and keep on dishing out barbs until I said something back. It took everything I had not to react. But I decided that there was no harm in seeing if the words *geologist* and *earthquake* would have had the same effect on Katie as they'd had on Ava. I took one more deep breath and said, "No, that's not how it is, Katie. I'm up here with a bunch of geologists." This got no particular reaction from her, so I added, "Who study earthquakes."

Jack Sampler now reached out one of his big meaty hands and

locked it around my upper arm, reminding me that I was skating pretty damned close to topics I was not supposed to discuss.

Now Katie could not avoid noticing Jack's presence, and I wondered how she was going to play it. Would she threaten to tell Ray that I was there with another man? No, her gaze shifted to the hand that gripped my arm, but she still refused to look him in the eye. She said, "You mean you're hanging out with the guys who think Heavenly Father's going to open up a big crack in the ground and swallow Salt Lake City." She laughed unpleasantly. "Yeah, Enos told me about that earthquake stuff. Well, maybe that's going to happen, but not until *we*'re done with it."

She had emphasized *we* not to include me, but to indicate the Mormons, the Church of Jesus Christ of the Latter-Day Saints. She was testifying to her belief that the Earth was in its latter days, its last millennium, or whatever the particular spin was. The Earth would be destroyed and some would go to heaven and the rest of us . . . well, *pfft.*

I didn't need to take a deep breath this time. For all the impact her words were having on me, I may as well have been watching a barking dog on closed-circuit TV; her intentions might be questionable, even frightening, but her beliefs were merely disturbing.

Now Jack spoke. "Thanks for picking up her radio," he said. He reached out a hand, palm-up.

She dropped the radio onto it, still refusing to look at him.

"Thanks," he said, and began to draw me gently but firmly away.

Following his lead, I lumbered ungracefully across the deck and away from the lodge, stepped into my bindings, picked up my poles, and headed for the lift. Foolish me, I thought I'd won that round. I did not know yet that Katie was carrying an identical radio.

◈

As I SAT down in the chairlift, I turned to the center, it being an old center-pole lift, and gave Jack a nod. "Hello," I said. "Thanks for the help back there."

"Hello to you," he replied, making light of things. "The name's Jack Sampler, from Howe's Bayou, Louisiana. Just up here for a spot of skiing. You?"

"Em Hansen. Chugwater, Wyoming. Just up here to bruise my—oh, you know the parts."

Jack chuckled. "Not much of a skier—is that what you're trying to say?"

"Rotten. In fact, I hate the sport."

This seemed to tickle Jack Sampler back into bubba mode. "Well now, that's great. I like an honest gal. Well, why'n't you ski with me for a while? Maybe I can show you a thing or two."

I said, "Mr. Sampler, sir, I'm so full of vinegar just now, I'd probably curdle your whole day."

"Nonsense." His tone shifted back. "So who was the chick with the nasty disposition back there by the lodge?"

"Katie Harkness. My boyfriend's sister. She never has liked me."

"Is that Harkness of the Salt Lake Harknesses?"

I squinted at Jack, trying to figure out what he was really up to. "Damned if I know. Her husband's name is Enos. Why, you grow up around here and learn to hate him in Eagle Scouts or something?"

He shook his head. "No'm. I done growed up in Mudlump, Mississippi, like I said. It's right down the road from—"

"Okay, that's enough." I turned my face away, stared into the rocks and leafless aspen trees past which the lift was now carrying us.

Jack gave me a friendly elbow in the ribs. "Lookee here, there's an art to skiing. First, you got to enjoy the ride up the mountain. Here, take your sunglasses off so you can see the true color of the snow. Yeah. I like them blue shadows on the sparkly white. Ent it purty?"

I did as he said, and smiled, even though the glare hurt my eyes and the cold made them tear. We were high up now, passing the upper limbs of a grove of evergreens. Down below, the snow did indeed sparkle, and the icy air seemed to stand like mute spirits between the trees.

Which in turn made me melancholy in a new way, as it brought to mind the people who had lived here ages before my fellow whites came and broke the quiet with our progress. I wondered what the valley had been like before it was carved up for ski trails and jacked full of monsters like Katie in brash synthetic clothing and discontented people like me, whisking along on iron seats through the silence of the trees. I decided that the Indians most likely never saw the mountain with snow on it. The Indians might have padded through here in moccasins, hunting mule deer in the summers, but through the frozen months, the mice and the trees would have had the mountain to themselves. Had the trees and tiny rodents felt the giant earthquakes Hugh Buttons spoke of? What would that have been like? In the winters, strong shaking might have loosed avalanches, but there would have been no one here but the mice to suffer. The ancestors of these trees might have swayed, and a few rocks might have rolled from the heights, but there were no brick homes or soaring skyscrapers to fall on the first Americans.

Jack was still talking. "See, in that pine tree there. Nice little chickadee. They stay all winter. Sometimes you can get 'em to eat outta your hands."

I watched the little bird flit from one branch to the next. It stopped and tipped its head to get a better look at us as we went by. "I've had them land on my hand when I was cross-country skiing," I countered, "but not here where there are so many people."

"True enough. So that's what's eating you? You don't like people?"

"I don't like the woman who isn't my sister-in-law," I answered. "Ms. Personality. The one you just got a load of."

Jack tipped his head like a chickadee himself. "Well then, it's a good thing she ain't your sister-in-law."

I sighed. "Maybe."

Jack gave me a smile. "We're almost to the top. Tips up," he said, raising the tips of his own skis. "Stand up when I say."

I did, and glided easily off the top of the chair.

"Now, let me see what you got," he said. "I used to teach this stuff back in my ski bum days."

I showed him. I planted my feet about twelve inches apart and parallel and started down, twisting my skis into a snowplow wedge every time I tried to turn, leading mightily with my downhill shoulder. After we had descended through the first meadow, I stopped and waited for him.

He came to a sedate stop and considered me. "Not bad, not bad. Except those poles aren't just for ornament. You got to plant them, and turn around them. Like this, see?" He demonstrated. He moved nicely for a big guy.

I tried it too, approximating his form.

"That's good. That's good. Now, let's work on keeping your shoulders faced straight downhill. This ain't no place for the football tackle. So you prefer cross-country skiing, huh?"

"Yeah," I replied. "Cross-country skiing goes somewhere, not just up and down, up and down; it's goal-oriented, like me, not process-oriented, and it isn't a fashion show. It offers privacy, nice views, and plenty of exercise." I laughed. "And on cross-country skis, I never get going fast enough to hurt myself when I fall."

But now I was actually being taught, and in spite of myself, I began to learn. And enjoy it. By the third run I took with Jack, he was clapping his gloved hands in congratulations. "Now here's the next little tip," he called as we started off the top the next time. "Keep you hands where you can see 'em!"

"What you say! That feels all off balance." My sore leg was getting tired by then, and I wasn't sure I could do much more.

"No, ma'am! You're off balance the way you *are* skiing. Now keep both mittens where you can see 'em and see if it don't help!"

He was right. Suddenly, I was truly on my skis, whizzing down the slope, my boots close together, my butt swaying to and fro, bouncing over the bumps like a regular ski bunny. I laughed and fell, then got up and skied again.

At the bottom of that run, Jack clapped me on the shoulder and drew me toward the next lift down to the west, saying, "Time to get you on some steeper slopes."

Experiencing a sudden panic, I said, "Wait a minute," and pulled Faye's radio out of my pocket. I was about to press the talk button, when I spotted Faye sitting out on the deck of the lodge. I pointed at the second lift.

Faye gave me a thumbs-up. Then she held up both index fingers, jiggled them along to indicate a pair of people walking, and pointed farther west twice. *Ray and female two lifts over,* she was saying. *Go ahead.*

"Okay, Jack," I said, and we got in line.

Just then, I saw Logan cruising down the slope. He waved, and I waved, and, as this lift was a triple chair, he joined us and we settled in for a nice swing up the mountain. In fact, I was looking forward to showing off to Logan what I had just learned.

But it was on that ride up the mountain that Katie dropped her bomb.

23

I went down to the Marina District [in San Francisco just after the earthquake] with a friend who lived there, and I did a stupid thing. I went with her into her house. It was like going into a fun house room, not a square angle in the place. . . . I wound up bringing a number of people home with me, because they had no place to stay; so I had strangers living in my apartment.

A thing they don't tell you is that it's not over right away; it's just the start. There are aftershocks, and things keep falling down. I remember a few days later watching the TV in my apartment. They were showing people being evacuated from their houses, carrying their bedding, their clothes, because their houses were about to slide down the hill. The thing was, I was watching that scene on TV and I looked out the window and there it was, right next door.

—*Cassandra Shafer, recounting the aftermath of the 1989 Loma Prieta earthquake*

"I DON'T KNOW IF I TOLD YOU THAT LOGAN'S AN ENGINEER-ing geologist," I told Jack as the chair swung away from the loading point. "He goes out looking at landslides and earthquakes and such." I did not tell Logan what Jack did.

Jack gave Logan a "Hey, dude" smile, as if he were just Joe ski bum making small talk. "Yeah, I felt that shaker we had the other morning. What went wrong? I thought you geologists got that earthquake business all figured out and fixed up."

Logan nodded. "You bet. Superman had a little time on his hands after his last movie, so we've been having him go round and stick rock bolts through all the big cracks, keep things from moving so much. We just hadn't gotten to the Wasatch yet."

Jack chuckled appreciatively. "Just as I thought. All's you really need is the right glue."

"You're so right," Logan agreed. "The right glue, and we need to repeal the laws of thermodynamics. All that claptrap about heat flux downstairs setting up convection currents that keep pushing those crustal plates around and causing earthquakes. Damned law's no good, and I say if a law's no good, throw it out. Get on with things."

I tipped back my head and smiled, tickled by Logan's indignant summation of plate tectonics theory. I was having fun in spite of myself. The day was looking up, even though my bum leg was beginning to stiffen up from the ride up a longer lift ride.

Then my jacket pocket began to talk. The radio said, "So, Jenna, how are you liking skiing with my brother? Are you having a great time or what?"

The voice was somewhat faint, but I knew it instantly. It was Katie's. Jenna? That wasn't one of her sisters, and it sure wasn't her mother. There was only one person it could be: the woman from Saint George. And the brother was, of course, none other than my engaged to be engaged sweetheart, Ray.

I began to claw at my mittens, trying to get the right one off so I could plunge my hand into my breast pocket and turn the radio off. Or turn it up, key the microphone, and scream something I was damned well not going to be sorry for. But my mittens were suddenly like bales of hay, and I didn't want to drop my ski poles from the lift. Worse yet, we were within two towers of the upper end of the lift, and I'd soon have to see if I could once again get off without killing myself, death and murder being very much on my mind. *Katie memorized my radio channel and set hers to match it,* I realized. *It must have taken her this long to find the mysterious Jenna and change her channel, too, without Ray noticing. Because that's precisely how Katie does things, underhandedly and with stealth!*

As the connections between the erosion of my relationship with Ray and Katie's obvious complicity in it—the unflattering sweater at Christmas, the importation of the "old friend" from Saint George, and now the radio—began to click together in my mind, I heard Jenna's reply. First, she giggled. "Oh, he's a wonderful skier, just like you said, Katie. I'm so glad you suggested I come back to Salt Lake with you all. I'm just having a wonderful time!"

"Terrific!" Katie exulted. "And I'm not kidding, you should really move up here. I'm *sure* I can get you a job at Hayes Associates, Ray's having a *wonderful* time skiing with you, too; I can tell by the way he *smiles*. I haven't seen him so happy in *months* and *months*. And you know the family just *loves* you!"

My heart was racing. I had my right mitten off finally, but now the zipper over my pocket was jammed. And there was no more time to turn off the radio, because we had arrived at the unloading position. I stuffed my mitten in my mouth and grasped my poles, ready to jump off the lift and race to the bottom, where I hoped to find Katie's car and jam the points of the poles into her tires.

"Well, you've been right so far!" Jenna's chirpy voice exulted from the front of my jacket. "It's being just the perfect day! Oh! Here he comes now! He's so *beautiful* on skis!"

"Oh, I *know. Isn't* he?" Katie crooned.

Overhearing the conversation, Logan said, "Stupid bimbos get on the radio and yak. Mind turning that thing down, Em?"

"I'd ruv to," I told him inelegantly through the clenched mitten. "Trutht me on this." I shot off the top of the lift, off balance on my stiffened leg, scanning wildly for a place where I could stop and get at the offending radio.

"I'm talking to Katie!" Jenna's voice warbled from my jacket. "Got anything to tell her, Ray?"

Oh God! I thought, *Don't say what I'm afraid you're going to*—

Ray's voice came over the radio. "I owe this day to you!" he said, with more cheer than I had, in fact, heard from him in months.

I skidded awkwardly to a stop, stabbed my poles into the snow, whipped off my other mitten, dropped both of them on the ground, and yanked at the zipper on my breast pocket. Just as I was about tearing my jacket apart to get at the offending radio, a kid in a racing helmet careened past me and I began to slide forward wobbling on my bad leg. I slipped over an edge, hit a rock, and fell, tumbling sideways like an eggbeater through half-whipped meringue. Even in the confusion of the fall, I could hear Katie's deceitful voice prattling on. "You've been so *lonely*, Ray. Two years since your wife died, and no one's given you a moment's happiness except *you*, Jenna. You're his *miracle* sent by Heavenly Father."

I lay on my back, no dignity left, no sanity. I yanked the zipper up, down, and got it loose. Wrenched the radio out of my pocket. Threw it as hard and as far as I could.

Logan skied to a stop next to me and leaned down on his poles. "Are you all right?" he asked, his great dark brows crushed together into one short line. "I mean, darling sweetheart, I asked you to turn the damn thing off, but I didn't mean—"

Jack had now arrived on the other side of me, and he lowered himself to the ground all in one motion. His face was tight with concern. I looked up into his eyes, tried to take a breath, but found that I could not control it. It was stop breathing entirely or break into tears. I held my breath and shook.

"Take it easy," he said gently. "I used to be a medic once, back in the before times. Tell me where it hurts."

I realized that it did in fact hurt. Badly. "My ankle," I said miserably. "The right," I added as Jack began to press and probe at my legs.

Logan's face had vanished from my field of view, and I thought, *Makes sense. Why hang around a loser like me?* I lay on my back, staring up into the sky, amazed that it was still blue. I felt Jack's hands supporting my leg, and a distant, painful throbbing in an ankle I no longer wanted to own.

"Can you wiggle your toes?" Jack asked.

High above me in the sky, the tiniest puff of a cloud floated into view. I tried to wiggle my toes. Couldn't find the will to do so. Logan's face reappeared. He showed me that he had found the radio, showed that he was turning it off, pantomimed shooting it with a pistol. "Shall I call Faye on this thing?" he asked, trying to think of some way to comfort me.

I shook my head vehemently. I didn't want Katie to know that her arrow had so keenly found its mark.

"Call the ski patrol," Jack said, his voice completely changed from the down-home good old boy to that of a man used to being obeyed. Switching back, he smoothed my hair and said, "You just lie still, sweetheart. You've had about enough for today anyhow."

24

I WAS LUCKY THAT MY ANKLE WAS ONLY SPRAINED.

That was what I kept telling myself all the way down the mountain, riding behind a ski patrolman on a growling, stinking snowmobile, but I didn't feel lucky at all. I felt cursed.

I begged everyone else to go back up the mountain, insisting that I could take a bus home or something, but by the time the patrol was done with me, it was past two, Faye had been ready to leave for hours, Ted seemed pleased as punch to be able to quit early, Jack was sticking to me like glue, and Logan was damned if he was going to let me ride a public bus when he had brought me in his car.

So off we went. We dropped Faye off first, and, as I needed someone to blame for my ineptitude, I was glad to see her back. Jack hopped into the car he had parked at her house and followed the rest of us to my place. When we got there, Logan and Jack made a chair for me with their arms, and I let myself be carried up the stairs as Ted scrambled along behind.

Mrs. Pierce was aghast to see three men helping me up to my apartment. "Exactly what is going on here?" she demanded. Then she saw the brace on my leg. "Oh. Well. But I should come along to supervise."

I was more than a little bit perturbed to discover that Mrs. Pierce thought she could impose such rules on my residence. I almost asked her why she had waited four months to tell me, but then I realized that I had never brought a man upstairs before. Ray had never come up to my rooms. The matter had not previously been put to the test.

Ergo, and with a mixture of fury and a bitterness I could no longer deny, I told my landlady, "With respect, Mrs. Pierce, my apartment is not big enough for that many visitors. Besides, I'm too old and dissipated for a chaperone to do me a damned bit of good. And trust me, none of them is staying. My apartment is a mess and I'm—" I had almost said, *I'm not staying, either.* I let it hang. Beyond anything else just then, I could not believe that I had been foolish enough to move to Salt Lake City in the first place.

Once up in my apartment, the men got busy getting me comfortable. "Sure you don't want me to make you an appointment to get that x-rayed?" Logan asked.

"I am certain," I said. *No X rays, no Rays, no nothing. Just leave me here to suffer in peace.*

Jack tidied the bed, got me up on it, and arranged everything remotely resembling a cushion under my head and back and wounded foot.

Ted got busy making me some tea.

Logan checked out my refrigerator and cupboards to make sure I had food in the place, and then started washing my dishes.

"This is humiliating," I said.

"If you'd be so kind as to quit fighting it, you might find you like it," Jack said in a voice that would suit a British butler. He had run down to his car and returned with an EMT kit and was now undoing the temporary brace from my ankle.

Ted brought me the tea and a plateful of cookies, put them down on the bedside table, and brought the phone over where I could reach it. Jack worked my pants off over my wounded appendage, leaving me in thermal underwear that looked a bit like the pajamas I wore as a kid.

Jack's hands were sure but gentle as he worked. He peeled the sock off my foot, produced an elastic bandage and some adhesive tape, and began to wrap it. "Doesn't look like it's going to swell too badly," he commented.

"You play football or something?" I asked.

"How'd you know? Must be my artistry with the bandage. That, and I was a medic in the army. I wasn't just making that up."

Logan was watching from the kitchenette. "What do you do now?" he asked, finally getting around to wondering about Jack's particulars.

I smiled cheerfully and waited, ready to hear what kind of story Jack was going to produce. So far, I had seen at least three regional varieties of consanguineous good old boy, a butler, and an army medic, so what was it going to be this time? A college student working his way through school as a nightclub strip act? Idle rich? Door-to-door Bible salesman?

"I'm a field agent with the FBI," he said matter-of-factly.

"Cool," said Ted.

"Oh," said Logan.

Ted's face lighted up. "Hey, so maybe you're into figuring out who killed Sidney Smeeth," he gushed. "Wow! Hey, so you tagged along skiing 'cause you were hoping one of us would say something that would be, like, a clue, and then you could pass the information on and—"

"Who ever said she was murdered?" Logan asked.

"Ted did," Jack replied.

"Of course she was," Ted said.

"You're paranoid," Logan insisted.

"Anyway, that would be a matter for the city police," Jack said, keeping his eyes focused on his bandaging job. "I'm just stationed here in Salt Lake, but I go all over. And the FBI seldom gets involved with murder cases."

My, my, but Jack was good. He had made it sound like the

Sidney Smeeth case was the last thing in creation that would interest him. In spite of myself, I began to take notes regarding technique and style.

Ted took the bait hook, line, and sinker. "But you *should* be interested in this," he continued. "Because it *is* murder, And more than that, much more."

My estimation of Ted's intelligence had just tripled, gullible or no. Or was there something much darker about his interest? Was he like a firebug who shows up in the crowd of spectators while the firefighters try to douse the flaming house? I held very still, hoping that Logan wouldn't tell him to shut up.

Jack kept his attention on my ankle. He'd just finished up with the elastic bandage and was now putting my sock back on over it, tickling my toes as he went.

Logan's attention flicked from Jack to Ted and back to Jack. He seemed content to listen.

As Jack had still not risen to his bait, Ted said, "Look, this is how I've got it figured: Sid directed the Utah Geological Survey, sure, but she wasn't just an administrator. No. She was all over the place. In Washington just last week, meeting with senators and congresspeople. Getting crosswise with the ones who want to open up the national parks and wilderness areas for oil exploration. Lobbying the Department of Energy about that and high-level nuclear waste. Pissing off the Indians who want to charge big bucks to have it buried on their reservation. Getting on the Religious Right for teaching creationism in schools and calling it science. Oh, and she was death on the state of earthquake preparedness for the Olympics. Climbing up everybody's butts about planning and all. Ripping the mining interests a new asshole about the tailings ponds just west of the airport that would have failed Monday if the shock had been any bigger or had gone on just a little longer. Hell, the list goes on and on. I mean, so what do you say?"

Jack had pulled the sock off my other foot and now began to

222 ♦ *Sarah Andrews*

rub it. "Well, I dunno," he said doubtfully. "There's lots of people as gets mad at others in the course of their work, but that don't mean someone's gonna kill 'em for it."

Oh, so it's going to be Bubba Jack again. I put down my tea and sank blissfully into the pillows Jack had put under me. He was not only good at taping ankles; he was a master at rubbing feet. He had found my great weakness in life. I prayed that he would string Ted along for hours.

Logan caught my eye. He was beginning to smile tartly, like something was very, very funny.

I squinted one eye back at him, trying to tell him, *Yeah, this is pretty good, so don't interrupt.*

Logan grinned.

I grinned back. This was fun. I hadn't let myself flirt in ages. Just then, Jack hit an especially fine spot and I groaned. I thought, *If Mrs. Pierce only knew.*

As if reading my mind, Logan said, "Keep it down, Em, or your dragon lady downstairs will call in the Vice Squad."

"Vice, I do," Jack said, getting into the game. "Just love busting up something nice and naughty. I can see myself giving testimony now. 'Mrs. Pierce, dear, yes, I observed the defendant to be enjoying that entirely medicinal foot rub I was giving her. It was dis-gus-ting. Throw her out on the street.' "

I sighed. "Guilty as charged."

Jack gave my foot a final pat and stood up abruptly. "Anything else you need before I go?" he asked, a certain resonance in his voice.

Go?

Ted was on his feet instantly. "Hey, wait! I mean, there's more! Maybe I could take you for a beer or something. I mean, we're all back early, and—"

"Sure, why not?" Jack said, as if he were doing Ted a big fat favor. "And maybe you can teach me more about that glue you guys use to keep them rocks together, too."

"That's my department," Logan said. "Ted's the one that busts the rocks. I'm the glue guy."

❖

FIVE MINUTES AFTER they left, Tom Latimer telephoned. "My condolences," he said.

"For what?"

"Your ankle. Your love life. Katie should be shot."

"Did Faye tell you?" I demanded. This was the limit. I had about enough privacy left to clothe a gnat.

"No. Jack called on the cell phone just now to report. He's on his way to have a beer with Ted someone and . . . let's see here; I wrote it down. . . ."

"Logan de Pontier. Cajun engineering geologist. You want to know his favorite color? Taste in pizza? Because that's all I've got. And I don't know why you're calling me. I'm out of action. I'm—"

"He told me about the bit with Katie and the radio."

I had to press my lips together so I wouldn't cry. I was glad that Tom was only on the telephone, not in the room. At the same time, I wished he was there to pat me on the back and tell me it was all going to be okay.

Tom said, "Listen, my advice? Get something to wrap your mind around. You just took a hell of a blow. You're going to be there for a while with nothing to do. That would drive me nuts. So put your mind to the information you have already. See if you can spot the pattern in what you have. Connect the dots. Then give me a call, whenever." His voice went deeper, more gentle. "And call even if you don't have anything to tell me."

His caring was the hardest to take of all.

❖

FAYE SHOWED UP a couple of hours later. As she ushered me back into bed, she said, "I've decided that I have watched you beat up on yourself long enough. Here, I've brought you a book to read."

"What's that for?" I asked, staring at it. *Waking the Tiger*, by Peter Levine. It was looked suspiciously like a self-help book.

"For your ankle," she said. "And for the leg you broke last summer, and everything that broke inside your mind when that happened, and when you got shot at before that, and threatened, and crashed helicopters, and almost crashed airplanes, and for all those times you came off your horse barrel racing. Not to mention every time your mother . . . wasn't there for you."

"A *book* is going to fix all that."

"It's a book about why the human species has so much trouble dealing with things that frighten us. A friend told me about it. Read it. It might apply."

"Thank you, Doctor," I said grumpily. "Have you read it?"

"No."

"Then you read it first."

"I've got other things on my mind," Faye said, and quickly changed the subject. "I have to hand it to old Jack-o. That boy can really put two and two together. He meets Katie just once and figures out that's her voice over the radio and what she's up to. Pretty good, huh? And he seems to like you." She wiggled her eyebrows.

My blood boiled all over again. "This is great. Tom and Jack and who knows who else are sitting around down there at the FBI offices discussing what set ol' Emmy off so badly that she's got to take a dive and screw her ankle up. Hey, but this is the FBI we're talking about; they specialize in invading privacy. I suppose they've got a tap on my phone. Or is that your department?"

Faye pulled the straight-backed chair away from the small dining table that doubled as a desk and sat down. "Sarcasm does not become you," she informed me.

My ankle had begun to ache in earnest. "Listen, Faye, this is really the limit. I know you've got things on your mind you'd rather not think about, but making a project out of micromanaging my life instead has got to stop. Both you and Tom. And Ray. I mean, who died and made the bunch of you king, anyway?"

"Sorry."

"It seems everybody's got an agenda for me these days. You want me to become a social butterfly, Tom wants me to become Sherlock Holmes, and Ray wants me to become a Mormon housewife. Or not. No, Ray wants me to dry up and blow away so Miss Perfect can become his Mormon housewife. Start cranking out a passel of little Raymonds, keep the name going, fill up the rest of the portrait wall at Ava's house."

"You're right, I've been a controlling shit." She stared at the floor.

"You're damned straight you have!"

Neither of us said anything for a while. It was a strange moment, me all jacked up with a bad ankle and she nauseated from an unplanned pregnancy. "We're a pair," I said finally. When she didn't reply, I added, "I suppose you've come for your car keys. Did you have to take a cab again? I can give you the money for it."

She shook her head. "No. The car's at my house, remember? And I have a second set of keys. Did you get an estimate on your truck yet?"

I laughed mirthlessly. "No. It was towed. I haven't even called around to see where it is. I consider it my ex truck."

Faye continued to stare at the floor. "Well, you keep the Porsche. You'll be driving again before I will. I mean, unless . . ."

"Is that the deal? You haven't been driving because of the nausea?"

She squirmed in the chair. "Yeah. That, and . . . well, right now I don't really trust myself. It seems too dangerous to get behind a wheel."

About then, I finally figured it out. "Ohhh . . . I get it: You've lost your self-confidence. Here you're the big hot pilot, all in control, and you can't even control what's happening in your own body."

She didn't argue.

Trying to make it sound lighter than it felt, I said, "So you're scared even to drive a car, let alone fly an airplane, but why not distract yourself by controlling Em's life? Go ahead, everyone else seems to do it, and she never complains."

"Hardly ever. That's why you're in so deep with Ray's family."

I let that sink in awhile. "Ouch," I said.

"You should have made a stink a long time ago," Faye suggested. "Probably before you moved here. Not that I'd prefer you hadn't come."

"Want some tea?" I asked desperately.

"Nah, even herb tea makes me puke these days."

"That's the pits," I said, glad to have the topic off of me.

"Oh well," Faye said, letting out a long, shaky breath, "I know a cure."

Her words hit like a bolt of lightning. "Wait a minute! You're not talking about getting an abortion? I thought you said you wanted this baby!"

"I want *a* baby. Not necessarily *this* baby."

"Damn it, Faye, you don't get to pick and choose. Next thing, you're going to be one of those assholes who's injecting genes so you'll get Einstein on a football scholarship."

"But she's got to play piano like Rachmaninoff," Faye parried.

I reached out and swatted her knee. "So that's not it. What is it? Ohhhhh, I get it: Tom doesn't want the baby. Oh, I'm so sorry. I shouldn't have made fun."

Faye shook her head. "No, that's not it, either."

I reeled in my hand and closed my eyes. "Faye? Dear friend?

I'm trying to be understanding here, and, like, figure this out, but help me a little, okay?"

In a tiny voice, Faye said, "Tom hasn't said anything because I still haven't told Tom."

"What?"

"I—I can't. I keep opening my mouth, but nothing comes out."

"Well, why not?"

"I don't know! Oh hell, I know exactly. I'm afraid he's going to be upset. I'm afraid he doesn't want the child. I'm afraid he doesn't want to be a father. I'm afraid—"

"You think he'll leave you?"

She looked up. "Why would that be a problem? No, in fact, you may have struck on something here."

"Faye, you're not making sense."

"I'm being droll. I . . . um, love Tom, but it would not be the end of the world if he left."

"Are you serious?"

"Well, it would simplify things. I could just raise the kid and make a life out of that, and that would be okay, right?"

"You tell me. No, that sounds like selfish bullshit. Think of the kid, and all that. So that's not it. So you tell me why you want him to leave."

Faye began to shake. "Because I don't want to raise a kid with a daddy who might get killed any minute, that's why!"

I reached out and grabbed her arm. "Faye, listen. He could take early retirement. God knows, he's old enough."

"Thanks a lot!" she said hotly. "I'm not getting any younger, myself!"

"So now you're arguing the other side of the issue, saying you need to have this child because you hear the clock ticking down. No way, Faye. I'm not telling you that you should have kept your knees together until Mr. Perfect came along, but didn't you at least think about this before you and Tom went to bed?"

"Well . . . sort of. In an abstract sort of way. A . . . a long time ago."

"Like maybe when you were eighteen, and a freshman in college, and thinking you'd like to go to bed with the first guy you fell for, and in your eighteen-year-old wisdom you decided that come what may, you could deal with it. And, as you haven't been caught until now, there seemed little reason to revisit that decision."

"You're lethal, Em."

"No, I just have a pretty good memory of what adolescence was like myself. But hey, now we're almost twice eighteen. Life seems a bit more precious now, doesn't it?"

"Yeah."

"Yeah."

She sighed. "So what am I supposed to do?"

"Tell him."

"I can't."

"He already knows."

"I know."

"He hasn't left yet."

"That's what scares me."

"Let him love you."

Faye looked up. "What are you talking about? Of course he loves me!"

I shook my head. "Define love. He feels strong, warm, happy feelings toward you, yes. He's made love to you. Now let him make love an active verb. I hear it's what all couples have to face if they stay together long enough. It's a lot of work to love someone. It's a choice. A devotion. You have to give up your pride, and your privacy. Be willing to give in. Compromise. Hey, think of the word's roots: 'promise together.' You're the one who took all that Latin."

Faye thought about this for a long time. "But I'd also be doing all that for the child."

"Same but different. One relationship is adult to adult, the other parent to child."

"It was simpler when it was just me, the house, the Porsche, and the plane."

"I know." I didn't point out that it was in fact her, the house, the Porsche, the plane, and the trust fund. That seemed too harsh.

"But what about Tom?" She asked. "Do you think he's good for it?"

It was my turn to think. "I don't know. But it's his child, too. Half the responsibility is his."

"Yes. But half the choice?"

"Now you're getting on marshier ground. I'm just suggesting you talk to him about it. Let him support you in this. Like he's already doing, I might point out."

WE WERE INTERRUPTED by a knock at the door. Faye got up to answer it. I was just opening my mouth to say something witty about being in Grand Central Station, when she pulled the door open and I realized that it was Ray.

He was standing there in his uniform, hands jammed deep into his pockets. His radio squawked. His patrol partner stood behind him, looking acutely embarrassed, and behind him, peering around his shoulder, stood Mrs. Pierce, looking snippy.

Ray caught sight of my bandaged ankle. "What happened?" he asked, his face shifting confusedly from imminent thunder to partly cloudy.

Completely startled to see him there, I said, stupidly, "Nothing."

Faye said, "Well, hi there, Ray. I was just going."

Ray turned bright red.

I groaned. "I think he wants you to stay, Faye."

Ray squeezed his eyes shut.

Faye looked over Ray's shoulder out into the hall. "Don't worry, Mrs. Pierce, Officer what's-your-name, I'm here to chaperone these fully grown adults. You can go on back down to your apartment." She pulled Ray into the room. "I'm going into the bathroom to run some nice loud water," she told him, then added, "Better talk fast, Ray, we live in a desert." As she moved to close the door, she leaned out through it and called, "I said no, Mrs. Pierce. Sideshow not open today!" Instead of stepping into the bathroom, she headed out into the hall and proceeded to usher Mrs. Pierce and the other policeman toward the stairs, closing the door behind her.

Ray shot a look as dark as eagle's breath at the door and then turned it on me.

"What?" I said indignantly.

"I don't appreciate being summoned by your landlady," he said tightly. Then he looked at my ankle. "What happened?" he asked again. This time, it sounded almost like an accusation.

Furious, I jumped off the bed, landing hard on that foot. My leg buckled out from under me with the pain. Ray's expression again flip-flopped from rage to shock and sympathy as he stepped forward to catch me, but I grabbed the edge of the bed and waved him off. "No," I said. "You stay right where you are."

Now Ray looked confused and anxious.

"What," I spat, "now I'm getting indignation? Try looking through the glass from my side. Mrs. Pierce calls you to tell you I've got men up in my room, and you have the gall to come over here and give me shit? Where did 'Em's a grown woman, Mrs. Pierce, and there's no law against having guests' go?"

Ray blurted, "Did you have men here or not?"

I glared at him. Was he jealous?

He said, "And how do you think that looks?"

If I had been a rattlesnake, I would have been coiling by then, ready to strike. "It looks like I sprained my ankle, Ray, and it looks like a couple of nice gentlemen helped me up to my apartment, made me a cup of tea, and bandaged me up. Just exactly what part of that justifies your anger or presumption or invasion of my privacy?"

Ray's normally ruddy skin turned white. "What happened to your ankle?"

"I fell down skiing," I growled between clenched teeth.

Ray's face darkened again. "How is that *my* fault?" He threw his hands out in confusion, asking the four walls of the room to explain this to him.

I took in one mighty inhalation, ready to tell him, ready to blast him about skiing with another woman, ready to skin him alive for cooperating with his hideous sister, about—

A funny little connection began to form in my head.

His sister. Enos. "Ray? Enos works in the family business, right?"

"Enos has nothing to do with this!"

"Oh? But what is the name of the family business?"

"Hayes Associates. Answer my question!"

My mouth opened again. "Your family's wealth comes from that—" Suddenly, the feeling I'd had—that I was unworthy of his family—fell out of my heart, and a more impartial—and more separate—reality trickled in. My universe had shifted slightly, and I didn't feel like I had to be nice about his family anymore. By the same token, I noted that I didn't hate them as much, either. I took a breath. I heard myself say simply, "I fell down skiing. At Alta. I was not there because of you. But I fell because I heard your voice over the radio. You were talking into one just like it, which your sister Katie had set to match the frequency of mine. You said—"

Ray's dark indigo eyes grew wide with horror. "What in God's name—"

"You were thanking her for what a good time you were having. With . . . Jenna, I think her name is."

Ray's face went slack. I wondered if he might begin to flow, like rubber.

My thoughts wavered, swinging wildly between the roiling source of terrible hurt that stood before me and the itty-bitty cushion of abstraction that was beginning to formulate in my mind. As if someone else were speaking, I said, "Don't you get it, Ray? Katie's manipulating you."

Ray peered at me like I was some strange insect he'd found on his salad. "You think . . ." He left it hanging. "You take it easy on Katie, Em. She's been under a lot of stress!"

My mind whizzed back and forth, now observing Ray, now escaping from the horror of what was happening between us, now soaring up past feeling anything, hiding in my head, the perennial observer, never involved. Now piecing together something Pet Mercer had said. Something about . . . Sidney Smeeth's funeral. About seeing Ray and his brother-in-law there. *Tom said to think this through*. Did "brother-in-law" mean Enos? So confusing, in a family so large. But why would they attend that funeral, and why together?

Ray was saying something. "Yes, I had a *good* time skiing. It was *fun*." He was leaning forward, glowering at me.

About then, I remembered that I was in the middle of a fight with the man I had hoped to marry. I felt wobbly, and cold and tingly, almost as if I were falling through the darkness of outer space toward a planet I no longer wanted to inhabit. "I'm not *fun?*" I asked, with the little wisp of breath I managed to force up through my tightening throat.

Ray's eyes were almost black with feeling, a wild mixture of anger, frustration, and fear. "You're so *serious* all the time!"

I began to lose my sense of what was vertical. I was still holding on to the edge of the bed, so I sat down on it. *Ray. Thinks I am too serious. What in hell's name is happening here?* "Get out," I said.

25

. . . The firm and stable mass of the earth trembled and shook, and the sea withdrew, its waves flowing backward. The sea floor was exposed, revealing fishes and sea creatures stuck fast in the slime. Mountains and valleys that had been hidden in the unplumbed depths since the creation of the world for the first time saw the beams of the sun. Boats were left stranded in these newly created lands, and men wandered fearlessly in the little that remained of the waters, collecting fishes with their bare hands. But then the sea returned with an angry vengeance. As if resentful of its forced retreat, the sea roared and rushed through the seething shallows, dashing through every open space and leveling countless buildings in the cities and wherever else they are to be found, so that amid the mad discord of the elements the altered face of the earth revealed marvelous sights. For the great mass of waters, returning when it was least expected, killed many thousands of men by drowning; and by the swift recoil of the eddying tides a number of ships, after the swelling of the wet element subsided, were found to have been destroyed, and the lifeless bodies of shipwrecked persons lay floating on their backs or on their faces. Other great ships, driven by the mad blasts, landed on the tops of buildings (as happened in Alexandria), and some were driven almost two miles inland.

—Ammianus Marcellinus, Roman historian, describing his experience of the earthquake and tsunamis in A.D. 365 that leveled the city of Kourion, Cyprus, knocked down the lighthouse in Alexandria, and devastated ancient Mediterranean civilization

AFTER CLOSING THE DOOR FIRMLY BEHIND RAY'S RECEDING back, Faye was kind enough to stay until ten. She ordered Chinese food delivered, but neither of us ate much. We played double solitaire. We talked about everything but the irresolvable turmoils that had both of us wondering if we would survive the night.

That night, I did not sleep. Or very little, anyway, and what sleep I got, I cannot call rest. Exhausted as I was, I fell asleep quickly, but did not stay asleep. I awoke after an hour, or at most two, then lay awake far into the waxing hours that touch the wrong side of dawn. As it finally began to grow light, I began drifting off again, but what sleep I found then lay in sick, uncontrolled oscillations shot with horrifying dreams, like riding the crest of a freak wave in a cold, dark ocean.

Let me tell you about insomnia.

I know it well. Have had it again and again, in so many of its forms. The can't get to sleep, mind racing form. The awake from two until five, feel like shit when the alarm goes off at seven form. The so buzzed that sleep is something that comes in narcotic blanks between jolts of wakefulness form. The list goes on. But this one was different. This one was a corker. This was the big kahuna of all sleepless nights. This was: Sleep won't save you, Em; your life is crumbling.

I was thirty-five years old, I was living in a bed-sitter on a dwindling bank account, I had no job, no real prospects, not even the guarantee of further education, and I had just shot my prospective mate out of the sky.

I could not sleep because I was scared. Right down to the core. Past it. I felt like the fault that ran underneath Mrs. Pierce's house had let fly the big one, flattening a city of a million souls, except that this fault ran right through me. It had opened up inside me, and there was a gaping hole through which life as I knew had disappeared.

My ankle hurt terribly, and, having been so stoic that I'd refused to see a doctor, I had no painkiller stronger than aspirin.

The pain soon took on a life of its own, not growing huge or insurmountable, but making my foot seem like a separate entity that had come into the room to sit like a ghost at the other end of that limb I used to call my own. And yet it was also me, looking back at me, telling me the terrible truth about myself.

Em, it said, you shouldn't have tried to build your life here. Now it is broken, damaged beyond repair. It's not just your ankle, or your love relationship, or the world you live and move in. This uncontrollable chaos you call life. This place where stadiums have lethal wounds in their roofs. This place where people who try to change that are slaughtered like rabbits. And worse. This is that and everything else, too, all the horror of human existence swirling like a whirlpool into that hole you call a life. This is the big telegram, but it's not from some friendly creature called God; no, it's from the guy who's really running the show, and he's not your friend. He's an engineer with the heart of a bureaucrat, the jig's up, and the unfunny joke's on you. You thought this was all going somewhere nice, that all your sprained ankles and broken legs and concussions and shredded heart strings were teaching you something, taking you somewhere important, some big next step, but life's not really like that—get it? It's not wine and roses, no big romance, no road to triumph, and you're not special. It's just the gaping death's-head, dear heart. Rot. Degeneration. Give up. You're just a chemical factory waiting to reproduce, like your friend Faye. Swap your genes out quickly into the next generation and get done with it. It's not even laughable. It's not even so organized as to justify your grief.

I'd felt despair before, but this was far beyond that. This was icy, bottomless fear at its corrosive worst. This was: Suicide won't even fix it, and opium won't ease the pain, so just get down on your knees and weep.

Crying is an amazing thing. They say water is the universal solvent, but I say it's tears. They carry messages from the brain to the child who lives beneath it. They teach her that her pain is real. In rolling over her skin, they give it shape.

It took hours of feeling so freaked that I wanted to puke before those tears came, but when they did come, I began to face a few things, and I entered a small, quiet place deep inside, where things didn't exactly seem better but where my suffering was less.

In that place, I faced the fact that Ray wasn't going to love me the way I needed him to love me.

I faced the fact that I was tearing myself to shreds trying to fit into his world, and everybody else's, for that matter, and that none of it was working for me. And that I had no idea what other world I could try fitting into next.

I faced the fact that life was tenuous, and frightening, and that I was not in control of it, or when it happened, or to whom. Nor was I in control of Faye's womb, or Tom's seed, or old brick houses, or the restless ground on which they stood, or a whole community of people who lived in ignorance and denial of the devastation that was coming with the next big snap of the thin crust of solid Earth on which we were all just trying to live.

And I faced the fact that I was deeply, viscerally angry about all of the above, even though being angry wasn't going to change anything.

With that, my feelings became unstuck and began to move. Call it a nervous breakthrough.

I drew up a list, first inside my head and then, finally sitting up and turning the light on, on a pad of paper. On that paper, I first listed all the things I did not want to know, such as the facts I named above, the big mortality chunk. Then I listed the wishes that had been driving me without my admitting them. My wish for a happy family. My wish for children to love. My wish for magical deliverance from feeling scared and crappy most of the time.

Then I made a list of unfinished business.

That list was much less consistent and more miscellaneous,

being a mixture of things that had to do with me and things that did not, but it went like this:

ACTION ITEMS

(Underlining those words seemed to help.)

1. Figure out who killed Sidney Smeeth, Pet Mercer. (Same person?)
2. Clean house emotionally.
   a. Ray
   b. His family
   c. My family
   d. Life, the universe, and everything
3. Quit getting hurt instead of getting the point (physically, emotionally).
4.

I couldn't think of a good number four, so I put down the pad of paper, picked up Faye's book, and read until dawn, taking special note of everything it said about insomnia.

26

There were several large aftershocks. During one of them, my husband called down the stairs, "That was a three point four!" A few minutes later, I heard on the radio, "That aftershock measured three point four." I was very impressed. When Doug came downstairs, I asked him how he had known, and he said, "Madam, I was on the toilet, and when my balls are swinging free, I know these things."

—*Mary Madsen Hallock, recalling the 1969 Santa Rosa, California, earthquake*

IT WAS SNOWING AGAIN, AND THE HEAVY CLOUDS DELAYED the dawn. I had put down the book and turned out the light to watch it arrive, but it came like gray flannel, barely discernible.

I lay in bed, staring at the thin crack that ran across the ceiling. It was visible even in the darkness, like the cavern into which my life had fallen. It reflected my pain. I held on to the pain, stabbing myself with it to stay alert, to avoid being fooled again by my wishes and needs. Ray had chosen his family over me. I wondered only why I felt so surprised.

I promised myself that I would maintain the mental high ground, and not again lose sight of reality—that Ray was stuck in his family, that they had no real place for who I was—no matter how painful. It was over with Ray. I did not belong. That was abundantly obvious, but there was still some emotional stickum holding me invisibly in place, making me hope he would call and say I was mistaken. It was like cosmic flypaper, and it had in its grip not only my feet but also my self-confidence.

In the past, I had used mental exercises to distract myself, so I could slither back to sleep, but this morning, the only puzzle I could conjure involved the deaths of Sidney Smeeth and Pet Mercer. They were like ladies floating in the lake, their unseeing eyes open to the sky. Submerging that image, I dived in myself and swam into the depths of their mystery. *Tom said I should connect some dots. Dot connecting is a good thing. It raises the unconscious to consciousness. It throws light into shadows.*

I began, at last, to piece things together. I had seen Sidney Smeeth being interviewed on the front steps of the new stadium. She already knew that the roof had been damaged. The stadium had just been hit by an earthquake, so she knew that it would soon be inspected. She tried to say something about it, but she was cut off by someone in the control booth at the TV station. Had that been a coincidence? And what had she been about to say?

The broadcast of her interview had been interrupted, and not to switch to something more . . . earth-shattering. What did that mean? TV stations answer to their owners, and owners have agendas. Might someone have been trying to muzzle Screaming Sidney?

From the stadium, she had gone home and been murdered.

Tom Latimer had sent me to read files. I had found evidence of shoddy or nonexistent geologic hazards reviews for major developments.

Jim Schecter had indeed inspected the stadium roof, had found cracks in the welds, and had been told to keep his mouth shut.

Pet Mercer had figured out that Sidney Smeeth's death had been not an accident, but a murder. She had gotten Jim Schecter's stifled report out of him. She had made a phone call to someone who "would know." Then she, too, had been killed. Was the timing of her death coincidental, or a decisive blow meant to keep her quiet?

There was one obvious commonality that might connect almost all those dots: Hayes Associates. They had built the stadium. They—or their consultants—had prepared the reports Tom had had me read. And Sidney Smeeth had, according to Wendy, set her cap toward kicking developers in the teeth.

From there, things got stickier.

Enos Harkness worked for Hayes. Enos was a structural engineer, the kind of guy who specifies what type of steel goes into a building, and what type of trusses. Ray had been housed, fed, and educated on money that flowed from Hayes Associates. And Enos Harkness was his brother-in-law. Enos was the dreaded Katie's husband. And Enos had not been home much lately.

Could Enos have been sent by Hayes Associates to muzzle Sidney Smeeth? No, that didn't make sense, or not enough sense to spell murder. But it did make sense that Pet Mercer's telephone call would have gone to Enos, and in no time at all, she, too, was dead.

What could Enos have to hide? Had he gotten himself stuck in a web of corrupt building practices? Had Sidney Smeeth threatened to expose him? Could it be that simple, that personal?

No. Tom Latimer was investigating a scheme that went much deeper, and it involved bribes on a scale that Enos Harkness could not possibly have conjured. Besides, he was only an engineer, an employee. The big money would change hands much higher.

But he was an employee of a company owned in part by Ava Raymond, his mother-in-law. Ava, who turned tail and ran away when she heard that I was interested in earthquakes. The rest of Faye's words to Ava floated back to the surface of the lake. She had mentioned Sidney Smeeth!

It was dizzying; every time I connected two dots, Enos was somewhere along the line.

Enos, Katie's husband.

Katie, whom I wanted to see boiled in oil.

I told myself, *Your judgment is clouded, Em. You're seeing things. And while you're at it, you were trying to get disentangled from this family, remember? So think about something else!*

So then, what should I do?

Tell the police and let them do their job.

But Ray is the police.

Then tell Tom. Let him deal with it.

But if Ray's brother-in-law is behind the killings, it will be a terrible embarrassment to Ray.

Yes, it will. Why do you care?

Because I do, damn it!

Nonsense. You're just trying to be a hero. You think that if you save Ray by tipping him off, he'll realize that you're right and he was wrong. You think he'll take you back—no, more foolish yet, you think he'll abandon his family, his religion, his way of life, and magically turn into something or someone who could live with you. Good one, darling; what does that look like?

I can't argue any of that.

But still I asked myself, *Should I go to Ray about it?*

At length, I decided, *Yes, but leave yourself a back door, Em.*

WHEN THE SUN had risen and the rest of humanity was up and about, I got to work.

First, I phoned Tom Latimer and made an appointment to see him later that morning.

Second, I phoned Ray. I had decided, as a matter of courtesy, that I would inform him of my concern that his brother-in-law was involved somehow in the murders. That way, he could do what he would—probably just laugh in my face, but at least then I would feel that I had done the noble thing, and even false pride was some kind of pride.

I hoped that I would get his answering machine. On his machine, I could be detached, efficient, smart. When he listened to the message, he would wonder how he could have been so stupid, and, as it was too late for reconciliation, I could bask in the knowledge that he was a fool who was painfully aware of his foolishness.

I felt surprisingly calm as I counted the regulation four rings that preceded his brief message, and barely swerved when I did, indeed, get the infamous beep, and not the actual man. Taking a deep breath, I told his electronic proxy that I was sorry to have spoken to him quite so sharply ("Get out" seemed to fit in that category), that I hoped we would in time become friends, and that I had something important that I needed to talk to him about.

Third, I phoned Faye to tell her that I had survived the night, and to inquire about her own mental health.

"I'll live," she said gloomily.

"You got a paper in front of you?"

"The *Tribune*. Why?"

"When's Tommy Ottmeier's funeral scheduled?"

I heard Faye suck in her breath. "Em, I don't even want to think about dead children right now, if you don't mind!"

"Good. Sorry. But it's important."

I heard pages rustle. "Saturday. That's tomorrow. Two P.M. Why?"

"Because I have five aces up my sleeve. Is your airplane fueled up?"

"I told you, I'm not flying."

"Even if I copilot?"

She didn't answer right away. "What do you have in mind?"

"A quick trip to Reno. They can take care of one's marital status quickly there. Or are you and Tom still being stuck?"

After another pause, she said, "I'll think on it."

◈

FOR MY NEXT trick, I had to figure out how to get around on my sprained ankle, in the snow, and without a vehicle. If I'd still had my wandering truck, I might have tried it, but there was no way I was going to risk stacking up Faye's Porsche when I couldn't even take enough weight on that foot to make it down the stairs. Fortunately, being a procrastinator by trade, I had not yet gotten rid of the crutches I used for my broken leg before my original cast was replaced with a walking cast. So I got them out of the closet and hobbled around my apartment a bit, remembering how to use them. I hobbled into the kitchenette and took a photograph off the refrigerator and put it in my pocket. It was my one picture of myself smiling into the camera as part of the Raymond clan. A summer snapshot. A picnic. Lots of uncertain laughter on my part. But every living member of that extended family stood or was being held, babes in arms, within the frame of the photograph.

Next, I called a cab, then went downstairs to the front porch to wait for it.

❖

I HAD THE driver take me to Ava's. Unannounced. And wait. I told him I would tip extra if he would roll down the window and witness the conversation I was about to have. He did so. I walked up the flagstone path and mounted the front porch. I rang the bell, praying that my timing was right. I wanted to talk to Ava while Katie was still out for her morning run.

"Hello, Ava," I said, when she opened the door.

She pulled back in uncomfortable surprise.

"I won't be staying," I said. "I won't even come in. I just wanted to ask you a question."

She thought about this for a moment, her face hanging in a pensive sadness. Then she said, "Certainly, dear," although she seemed to utter the words more to mollify me than to express anything akin to affection.

I took a deep breath. "Is Katie here?"

"Out jogging. Ask your question."

"Exactly what form did Sidney Smeeth's threat take?"

Ava's eyes glittered. "I'm not at all certain what you're asking," she said.

"Was it just that she was going to expose Hayes Associates for the cracked welds in the stadium roof? Or was she going to make it specific to Enos, for having specified the trusses?"

Ava stood a long time looking at me, watching me as if I were part of some action occurring across the street from the house—a fire in a trash barrel, or some kid writing graffiti on the neighbor's garage. Then she stepped back solemnly and closed the door.

◈

I HAD THE driver take me next to the University of Utah campus and drop me at the Seismic Station. The building had an elevator, which was great, and Wendy Fortescue was in, which was lucky, because I hadn't phoned ahead. I knew that the tough part was going to be getting her to talk to me, so I had decided to just go up there and shove.

"I understand you live in the basement apartment at Dr. Smeeth's house," I began.

"I ain't talking."

"That's fine. I have just a couple more questions."

"You deaf?"

"Look, I know it was murder. I'm just wondering about a few things, like—"

Wendy's eyes got real little, and her lips drew up as tight as a raisin. She said, "Listen, Em. I'm not known for my social skills. So if you want to stay in one piece, I suggest you buzz off while you've still got one good leg to stand on."

"Just tell me the parts that are public record."

"Go read them at the cop station."

"I got my reasons to avoid that location, and I think you know them."

A wry smile rippled across her little face. "Yeah. I heard Mr. Beautiful got hisself another squeeze."

I took a long, deep breath and stared at her levelly. It was unpleasant to discover that my geological colleagues had been discussing my relationship to Ray in my absence, but she had in the process told me a lot—namely, that she knew who Ray was. I took an intuitive leap and said, "So. The good officer Raymond has been around to question you."

"Yeah."

I tucked this information firmly into my data bank. "I'm going to let you in on something free and for nothing, Wendy. If you told Ray anything at all, you got yourself snookered. When he talked to you, he wasn't on duty."

Her eyebrows went down like a freight elevator. "Bullshit. I know official business when I step in it. He was wearing the blue. I've had cops climbing all over me." Then she smiled, apparently savoring that image.

"Not bullshit. He may have shown up in uniform, but here's something he didn't tell you: He's not working Homicide."

"Then why'd he question me, smart-ass?"

"I'd like to know that myself. Let me guess: He came around the morning of the day after the murder."

"Yeah."

"He's working evenings, Wendy."

Her jaw descended. Fury began to contort her face. She tipped her head back and stared at the ceiling. "Okay, ask your questions. I will answer them if you'll leave immediately after."

"I'll do my best. Give me the scene: Who found her? Where? When? How did the killer get in?"

She let her breath out in a huff. "Pet Mercer found her. She had come to do an interview. She found . . . Sidney . . . below the deck. It's a twelve-foot drop, with the slope, onto rocks. Sidney liked to use her deck, because it's a great view of the Salt Lake valley. I imagine she had left the front gate unlocked so Pet could get in. I don't know. It was about six-thirty. She'd been dead half an hour or more. I was taking a shower."

"You'd just woken up?"

"Are you nuts? You think I could sleep through an earthquake? Get real. When that quake hit, I got up and ran down to the station here to make absolutely certain everything was running. You know, ogle the strip charts. It was better than sex. Then I ran home to get a shower and some breakfast, because I knew it was going to be a long day at the Seismic Station with all those media geeks staring over my shoulder."

"So you wouldn't have been looking out at the deck—or out from underneath it because you were in the basement—when she was killed. When was the last time anyone interviewed her there?"

"Huh?"

"It's not a trick question. When was the last time anyone interviewed Sidney on that deck?"

"A day or two before. She was doing a series on geologic hazards. She liked to do her arm-waving bit."

"So that's how the police knew that the railing had been intact until the murder. She would not have had TV crews out there without a railing, and the station that shot the previous interview had the tape showing it in place. And no ice, I'll be willing to bet." I pulled at my lip as I thought it through. "So he took the railing out and poured water on the deck. What a dumb shit. Like he thought that would fool anyone."

Wendy looked at me sideways. "You say 'he.' How do you know it wasn't me, for shit's sake?"

"Police grilled you, huh?"

She snorted.

I ignored her bitterness, said nothing about how frightening it must have been to see her landlady dead and then get grilled by some homicide detective. If I'd said that, she might have cracked, and I wasn't yet ready to have the real Wendy, the soft thing that lived inside this hardened shell, show herself. For the moment, I wanted her to stay tough, and spit out the story free of emotional embellishment. So I changed the subject. "The deck squeak much?"

"Like a fool."

I thought out loud. "So you would have heard it if things had actually come down that way anyway. And he wouldn't have dared set it up like that if he'd known there was a downstairs apartment. Too risky."

Wendy stared at me.

"But wait," I said, beginning to perceive a hole in my own logic. "You would have heard him rip that railing apart. So what aren't you telling me?"

Wendy finally took her hand off the mouse she had been using to plot P and S waves when I first came in. She rubbed her eyes. She said, "Listen, you're welcome to your fantasies. What happened to the railing? You got me. I was in the fucking shower. I'm god damned glad I didn't hear it. Pet found her, and now Pet's dead, too. I saw nothing. I know nothing. I don't know about you, but I like staying alive."

I began to ask a scattershot of questions, hoping to hit something. "Is the only way onto the deck through the house?"

"Go see for yourself. I gotta get back to work. It's the sucky part of staying alive."

"What's the address? It's not in the phone book."

She stared at me blankly for a while, then gave it to me, her tone flat.

"Was she bloody?" I asked, now ready to press her over her emotional limit if I had to. "I saw a body after it had taken a big drop once. Pretty gruesome."

Wendy peered at me like I was some bug on the stage of a

microscope and she had been set the task of examining me. She opened her mouth and said, "She didn't die from a fall." With that, she turned her face back to her computer. Her narrow little shoulders followed, and I found myself staring at her back.

I asked ten or a dozen more questions but got no replies. Within the world of Wendy Fortescue, I was a bug that no longer existed.

There was a loose thread here, dangling, teasing me, but I couldn't quite grasp it. I decided it was time to get out my photograph of the Raymond family. I stuck it under her nose. "That's Officer Thomas B. Raymond," I said. "Right?"

"Right."

"Who else looks familiar?"

Wendy shot me an acid look. "Great, I got snookered by an off-duty cop. Now his shit-heel girlfriend is giving me the full-court press. Go fuck a duck, will you?"

I jabbed my finger at Enos' face. "How about him?"

Wendy's sharp little gaze slid down toward the photograph and back toward me. "Yeah."

"Yeah what?"

"He's been around." Her face had gone stiff. After a moment she said, in a much smaller voice, "A real lover, that one. And if you don't leave right now, I will call security."

◈

IT'S A GOOD thing that Salt Lake City cabs are relatively cheap. I called one to take me to Sidney Smeeth's house next.

I had the cab wait, and it didn't have to wait long. The tall iron gate out front was locked, and there was no way I was going to try any fence climbing with a game ankle. What I did learn from that lap around the track was that there were plenty of places to hide nearby if you were interested in ambushing a state geologist, and that once inside the gate, an intruder could not be seen from the road.

I turned and looked up the hill. I hadn't been paying much attention as the cab drove up to the house, but as I stood there, watching the fat white flakes of snow settle on the fancy landscaping across the street, I realized that Sidney Smeeth's home stood on the road that led uphill toward a posh neighborhood I knew well. It was the neighborhood where Ava Raymond lived. And at this time, while their expansive, expensive house was being constructed, Enos and Katie Harkness lived there, too.

◆

I HAD THE cab drop me at the *Tribune* office, where I identified myself to the security guard as someone who wanted to speak to whoever was taking over Pet Mercer's stories. I was shown into the newsroom, a newly remodeled place with a blue Mac computer in every cubicle. The place was buzzing with activity, especially the zone right underneath a special sign that read OLYMPICS.

A tall, lanky fellow named Bart came over to talk to me. He was almost as reticent as Wendy Fortescue—more used to asking questions than answering them.

"Thanks for seeing me, Bart," I said. "I'm here because I was working with Pet Mercer the afternoon before she was killed."

Bart's eyes lit with sudden interest. "Tell me."

"We went up the clock tower at the City and County Building. It was pretty wild. We were looking at how the seismic retrofit fared in the quake."

"Cool," said Bart, beginning to smile in a way that I suppose was meant to put me at my ease and keep me talking. "Can I get you a cup of java? Then maybe you can tell me why you're here."

For once in my life, I turned down a free cup of coffee. "Thanks," I said, "but I'm kind of in a hurry. The thing is, I've been feeling a little bit jumpy ever since. You know, murder and all; I was wondering if she had her notes from that afternoon with her. Because whoever killed her might have, you know, ah . . . seen them and, like, gotten my name. The police won't tell me. I'm, ah . . ."

Bart nodded. "Scared." He led me to Pet's desk. It was empty. "Did the police take away her stuff?"

"I suppose."

"Damn. Clean as a whistle. Unfortunately, negative results don't mean that the killer doesn't have my name. Did they take her hard drive?" I wrung my hands and glanced around furtively, trying to convince him that I was scared witless, which was not entirely an act. "Or are you on a network?"

He took the bait. He flicked on Pet's computer, tickled some keys, brought up some shreds of what she'd been writing. He scrolled down, searching for my name. "Nothing," he said.

Not exactly nothing. I was able to read a few lines over his shoulder, grabbed a few phrases. " 'Steel tubing,' " I read out loud. The next term sounded like something Pet had said. " 'Moment frame.' Wait—don't turn that off. Are those notes from the new stadium?"

"Looks like it." He moved around in the file. "Yeah. Looks like she was talking to one of the designers."

She had indeed. I saw the name I was looking for: Enos Harkness.

I PHONED THE UGS from a sidewalk phone booth and asked to speak with Logan de Pontier.

"Em," he said. "How's the ankle?"

"Better, thanks."

"I'm glad to hear from you. Want to go out and catch a movie tonight?"

I gave myself a brief moment to consider the option, to ask myself whether I trusted my judgment around men any better than I had the night before. With a sigh, I answered, "Can I take a rain check? There's . . . a lot going on just now."

"Okay," he said uncertainly. "So, to what do I owe the honor of this call?"

"Tell me about moment frames."

There was a pause. "You mean as in structural engineering?"

"Yeah."

"They used them in Northridge. That's in California, near L.A."

"I remember. Big quake back in '94."

"Exactly. That put the concept to the test. A lot of them failed."

"Why?"

"Well, the idea is that the moment frame is flexible. You build vertical members, which are designed to sway with the motion of an earthquake. That way, you can design for bigger openings in walls, or wider spans in a roof. This is as opposed to the braced frame, which has cross-members at forty-five-degree angles, or near that, designed to take up an earthquake by standing rigid."

"And the moment frame didn't work in Northridge."

"Remember all those photos of collapsed buildings?"

"Right. So the moment frame wouldn't be used anymore?"

"Well, not entirely. It's often a cheaper way to build, because there's less steel in it, so I suppose there are places where it's a good idea. Big spans with no supports right beneath them, like certain roofs, or big archways."

"Like perhaps in a place like Salt Lake City, where the seismic building code is less stringent?"

"You're quick, Em. But even here, it depends on how they're constructed. I'm sure that some of them perform as expected."

"How come the moment frame works sometimes and not others?"

Logan said, "The problem is that the metallurgists keep coming up with better steel."

"How is that a problem?"

"Well, you see, the welds used to be the strongest part of the structure. The moment frame idea was that the tubing would take up the flex. You know, sway side to side. Now the tubing is stronger than the welds, so at Northridge, that's where the structures failed."

"And a roof truss would sit on top of a moment frame?"

"It could. Yeah. Like in the new stadium. Shitty design. I understand that the architects designed it differently but that the builders changed it."

"Is that unusual?"

"Sadly, no. Changes happen all the time. Sometimes for the best, sometimes not. This time, I'd say the builder was being cheap."

"So if you're an engineer who has specified moment frames in this city, and you're running for public office, and your welds crack in a stadium, say, that's just about to be on nationwide— no, international—TV, you might think your deal was going down if someone like Screaming Sidney Smeeth found out about it."

Logan laughed unkindly. "That would depend."

"On what?"

"Whether our engineer was connected. You know, a Mo."

"Mormon?"

"Yeah. The bottom line is that bottom line with that gang."

I let that hang in the phone line an extra heartbeat before replying to it. "Come on, isn't that a bit of a generalization? I mean, it's a family-oriented religion."

Logan grew quiet. "You a Mormon, Em?"

"No."

"Well, let me tell you about some religions. They're big on what I call compartmentalized intellect. They believe in family and goodness, and charity and all the other virtues on Sunday, and for every other occasion when it behooves them to think the think. But on Monday, when they go to work, they walk a different walk, even if they don't talk a different talk. And it all goes down as pragmatism. Guy down the hall here? A geologist like you and me? He believes in evolution and a four-point-five-billion-year-old Earth Monday through Friday, and on Sunday? It's Adam and Eve, honey. And he doesn't even blink."

"What about engineers? The kind who engineer buildings with moment frames in earthquake zones."

"Now you get into another form of rationalization. Engineers can engineer around just about any hazard you can name, build you a building that can survive anything but a direct hit by a nuclear weapon or Haley's comet. A titanium sphere comes to mind. Do you want to live in one of those?"

"No. But who built the stadium?"

"Hayes Associates. Been putting up ski condos in avalanche chutes and housing developments on landslides for ages. The land's cheaper. But this time, with the Olympics coming to town, they went for something much more expensive and technically challenging. And their outside investors were much bigger players. International money. And getting back to what I was saying, you understand, don't you, that survivability and usability are two different things. Survivability means that the people inside live, although the building itself may be damaged beyond use. Red-tagged. Have to be demolished. In the case of a large public building, the builder and his investors could be out millions of dollars."

◈

AT TOM'S OFFICE, I pulled out my notes and settled in at the other side of his desk for some serious work. "I don't know who's behind your fraud case, because you haven't told me what or who is being defrauded, but I have an idea who's killing women who try to expose certain essential details of your case."

Tom leaned forward onto his elbows. "I'm all ears."

"First, you tell me exactly how Sidney Smeeth was killed."

Tom drummed his fingers on the desk for a moment, thinking. "You first, then me."

I glowered at him, then decided that if all else failed, I could simply climb up onto his head and peck at him like a mad duck until he held his part of the bargain. "Well, it's pretty simple. It's the fault. A big fat line on a map. It runs right through all of this."

"I don't disagree," he said. "But everybody knows there's a fault in Salt Lake City."

"Oh, sure, they know there's a fault, but they don't know what that means. And it's so easy to ignore, most days."

Tom nodded.

I said, "You had me read Building Department files for Hayes Associates. They built everything from condos and housing to the new stadium, and they're just breaking ground on a shopping mall next door to it. Every one of the projects I know about, including this new one, is on or near a branch of the fault or some other geologic hazard. The other thing they have in common is that the geology report was done by a guy named Frank Malone, who does not command the respect of his peers."

"You're saying that a positive report can be bought."

"A scientist can be straight arrow and brilliant and still come up with the wrong answer from time to time, but this guy ignores or downgrades the geological hazards on his sites routinely. And surprise, surprise, when things get hot, he leaves town."

"I'm following you. So you think this guy's our killer?"

"No. Opportunists don't generally kill their hosts. Sidney may not have been happy about it, but she was part of a system that keeps the Malones of the world employed."

"Can you enlarge on that?"

"Hazard. Risk. Public policy. There's always a gap in there the Malones can exploit. In this case, it's seismic hazards, an earthquake fault. Anyone who builds on that fault, or near it, is at risk of being hurt or killed when the fault breaks loose and the building fails. So we have scientists who study the hazard, but they are enjoined only to advise, not set policy. It's the politicians who set policy, who say how a building may be built, or how close to the fault, and so on. The problem is that politicians are at best trying to hit a happy medium between accommodating the risk and accommodating certain pressures such as economic resources—how much can we afford to spend on housing, or public structures. Or the fact that people started building here—and got quite attached to this place—before they had a clue that there was a hazard."

"And how does that spell murder?" Tom inquired.

I rubbed at my face with my hands. "It doesn't, not directly, because people seldom have to kill one another over politics anymore. God knows, we're all so used to corruption that we don't even call it that anymore, so what's to cover up? You just send the spin doctors to work and then go on about your merry career. But this time, someone killed a scientist. And a reporter. So it's logical to think that one was going to expose some corruption and the other was going to report it, right?"

"Keep going."

"Well," I said, "then the thing is, you have to look at the mechanism by which the big guys spin things."

"Which is . . ."

"Stick it on some underling and hang him out to dry. Say, 'He did it. I knew nothing. Oh, how horrible.' Hang him, work out your outrage on him. Ignore the fact that I'm building more buildings that will collapse on people. Don't face the fact that I've paid off a lot of politicians for the privilege of building unsafe buildings. Deny the sickening fact that the politicians have rationalized the whole damned situation to the point where they think it's fine if some nameless number of the population is stupid or ignorant enough to get killed in an earthquake. Because, hey, most politicians think in such short-term intervals that they aren't even interested in what a magnitude seven quake can do to this city. That's a low probability. That's tomorrow, or the next century. That's someone else's risk. The politicians are too busy. They're spending fifty percent of their time worrying about getting reelected, and the other fifty cutting deals for the fat cats who got them in there in the first place."

Tom beamed at me. "Why, Em, where'd your idealism get to on this lovely morning?"

"Climb off."

"I meant that as a compliment. It's high time you grew past such optimism. It can be quite limiting when we're trying to see into the dirty, shortsighted little rationalizations so many people live by. Take it from one who's never fully grown out of it himself. So, who's our culprit?"

I readjusted my foot, which was beginning to prickle with constricted blood flow. "I'm not sure yet. All I've got is an idea, not even a theory. I need more information first. More data. It's time to give, Tom."

He didn't answer for a moment, then said, "Okay."

"Good. First, Sidney Smeeth. Method of demise."

Tom watched me carefully as he said, "Strangulation."

I closed my eyes and took a deep breath. So that was why Wendy wouldn't talk. Strangulation is such a personal form of killing.

I pressed onward. "Second, you told me that whoever killed Pet did a tidy job of going through her papers. Did he take her notes from the conversation she'd just had with me? Did he take her cell phone? You can find these things out. I can't. I'm lying low until you catch this guy. But—"

"You say 'he' and 'guy.' You want to stay safe, Em? Give me a name."

"I will if I have to. No, trust me, I *will* tell you, but this time, I absolutely don't want to be wrong."

"Why?"

"Give me that much, Tom!"

"Is this Em the idealist getting on her white horse?"

"I truly hope not. Please, Tom, let me eliminate a few places where I might have gone wrong in my thinking. Just a few questions."

Tom sighed in frustration. "You know I can't tell you everything I know. I've gone too far already."

"Yes and no will do nicely. First, does Hayes Associates always build in the same political districts?"

"No. They go all over the state. Sometimes into adjoining states."

"But the fraud you're looking into involves cutting corners."

"Yes."

"Questions about whether or not building codes were sufficiently followed. Payoffs. Corruption that leads deep into government."

"Yes."

"And it's the government officials as much as anyone whom you want to get."

"You know me well."

"And that is why you used me. You wanted to make sure there weren't many FBI cooks stirring his broth, because you don't always know whom to trust. Word could get out that you're looking into certain people, and they might destroy the evidence you haven't even figured out to look for yet."

Now Tom leaned back in his chair and nodded. His gaze had gone distant.

I said, "You were working with Sidney Smeeth on this, weren't you?"

He did not deny it.

I said, "She knew that Hayes had politicians on the take, but she couldn't prove it."

Tom shook his head. "It was worse than that. Hayes had her boss in his pocket, and her boss was telling her to can it."

"You mean he was going outside and using a consultant's analyses instead of using her people."

"No, I mean she was being told to shut up."

I let out a long, low whistle. Now Sidney's rage began to make sense. It was one thing to disagree with someone like her and another thing to discard her work, but telling her to not do her job at all would be like dousing her with gasoline and teasing her with a burning match. "And let me guess: Hayes, or somebody he knows well, owns the television station that cut her off the morning of the earthquake."

Again, Tom was silent. He had found something far outside his window on which to focus his gaze.

"Ever get tired of this, Tom?"

"Heavens yes."

"About ready to retire?"

He thought a while before answering. "It has occurred to me more than once. Any particular reason you ask?"

"Just wondering. So you must really trust Jack Sampler. Where'd he come from?"

"I'd trust Jack with my life." He laughed. "I borrowed him from Washington. Told him if he'd help me with this project, he could at least get some skiing in. Best laid plans and all that."

"Sorry I fell down and ruined his pay-off. Why haven't you moved in with Faye, Tom?"

Tom's head snapped back a fraction of an inch. "What's that got to do with—"

"I want to know, Tom."

Tom's face went dark. "You're out of line, missy. We were talking murder here, and now you're—" He broke off, sputtering mad.

"Just answer, please. In fact, it kind of fits with the whole story, don't you think? It's about housing, eh? She's got that huge house, and you live in an efficiency apartment no bigger than mine. You're up at Faye's most nights anyway. Why not just move in?"

Tom inhaled a lungful and let it out slowly, struggling to control himself. Not looking at me, he said, "It is precisely that huge house that deters me from suggesting any such thing."

"Too close to the debris flow?"

"No. Too big. Faye's a wealthy woman; she can afford whatever strikes her fancy, but . . ."

"But you can't?" I said it as kindly as I could.

Tom stared out the window again, his eyes shining with anxiety, his mind wandering through a region of pain.

I watched him, surprised that I had managed to knock the great master so far off his pins. He had completely forgotten about fraud, and murder, forgotten about everything but the sad, lonely territory of his heart.

At length, he shook his head. "It's not how much more she has than I have. You must know by now that I'm far too arrogant to be cowed by a woman's net worth. That's not it at all. It's the wastefulness involved. She doesn't need all that space, and neither do I. Not even both of us, or—It's grotesque. I . . . I just worry that we live on different scales is all. No, let me say it directly: It is not in my philosophy to live beyond the carrying capacity of this planet."

Oh. I had not realized Tom was such an environmentalist, but on contemplation, it fit. He was Zen through and through, to the point of parsimony, and everything had to integrate with that principle. I said, "Don't you think you guys could get past that, Tom? I mean, have you discussed it?"

Tom made a fist out of one hand and ground its knuckles into the space between his eyes.

I said, "I'm sorry. I'm really intruding. I—"

He sighed again. "No, it's okay, Em. God knows, I do it to you. Yes, we could probably get past this, or I fervently hope so. The thing is, it's kind of a delicate time to be discussing such things, don't you think?"

It was, and I didn't have a ready answer that would make it anything other. So I said, "Okay then, back to the other stuff."

"Anytime you're ready." He sighed.

"Did the police find Pet's cell phone?"

"Why? Did she call you on it? Hell, then your number would be on it! Christ, if our killer picked it up . . ."

"Yes," I said, relieved that he understood. "And if the police got it, they'll already know."

"Know what?"

"As I said: I think I know who killed Sidney and Pet." I felt my resolve slipping away. My bubble of detachment burst as I contemplated all that I had hoped would bloom between Ray and me, in the garden of the life I had hoped to build with him.

"You have proof?" Tom asked.

Proof. That was always the problem: The game of detection was played on a field that was tilted in favor of the person willing to forgo any semblance of ethics. "I . . . I'm sorry. I'm just not sure yet." In a smaller voice, I added, "I think I should talk to Ray."

Tom indicated the telephone on his desk. "One call. Then I am putting you under wraps so you can't test your damned hypothesis the hard way."

I bit my lip. "This will be personal."

"I thought that was *over*," he said. "I thought you'd finally gotten yourself clear." He clipped his words, exasperated, unwilling to tell me how little he thought of my relationship with Ray, or the fact that I still seemed to think I had one.

"I owe him this much, Tom."

"Why? Because he's a cop? You think he's got to save face? He's not even working Homicide; what are you trying to save him from? You're afraid that Hayes is going to embarrass his precious family? Or is it the humiliation that you've figured out something he missed again? You want my opinion? He's not even that talented at walking the beat. He's quick, yeah, and athletic, but he gets the blinders on every time it comes down to seeing what's really going on. Em, you—"

I held up a hand. "That's enough."

Tom looked like he was about to burst.

I thought of telling him that he had it wrong, that it was Ray's personal entanglements, not the professional or financial ones, that had me wanting to warn him, but telling Tom would have been . . . telling. "When I know, you'll be the very next to know," I said. "I promise."

Tom shook his head in disapproval. He said, "I'll get Jack to take you home. And he will stay with you."

27

I can handle earthquakes intellectually, but emotionally, when the ground wiggles around . . . that's bad.

—*Dave Greene, engineer, recalling various earthquakes in Long Beach and San Fernando, California*

JACK TOOK ME TO MY APARTMENT AND LEANED AGAINST THE refrigerator while I dialed the phone, doing his best impression of a mild mannered unassuming refrigerator magnet.

Ray answered on the first ring. He sounded breathless. "Em! You got my call."

"What call?"

"On your machine. How soon can you meet me?"

I pushed aside the book that I had set down on my answering machine early that morning as I prepared to stare at the ceiling. Sure enough, the message light was blinking. It had not occurred to me to check for a return message from him. That meant that I had not really expected him to call me back. Or that a significant part of me had hoped he wouldn't.

What was going on inside of me?

I pushed the message button. Ray's voice came out of the mechanical memory. "Em? Honey, I—I'm sorry about last night. Please, I need to talk to you right away. Call me, okay?"

He was sorry? I had wanted to meet with him, for reasons of

unraveling things in a civilized manner. I wanted to cleanse myself of him, and, even more, of his family, of Enos and Katie and all the rest. But now *he* wanted to meet with *me?* What did that mean? Wariness flooded through me.

Best to get it over with.

"Em? Honey?"

I said, "I can meet you now. Where?" There it was, the usual issue: no privacy. He wouldn't come to my place, and I wasn't to go to his. No wonder we'd never sorted things out.

Ray said, "Are you home? I'll come by and get you."

A car date. I looked up at Jack, who was now standing at my tiny stove, pouring himself some coffee, looking at ease and at home. I said, "Okay. . . ."

◆

JACK SAT ON Mrs. Pierce's porch glider, swaying gently. "So let me get this straight: Y'all want me to let you get a head start with Joe cop, and I'm a s'posed to follow a fair distance back. You think Tom would like that?"

I was antsy, nervous. I would have been jumping from foot to foot if I'd had two feet to stand on. "Yes," I answered. "I want your protection. Get it?"

"This is your almost fiancé, and you need protection from him?"

It stunned me to realize that that was entirely the case. On some level, I was now afraid of Ray, and it wasn't just because of Enos. I said, "Come on, he's going to be here any moment! I think you'd better make yourself scarce."

Jack grinned, a toothy "bubba with a bad attitude" grin. "Disappear? Naw. I was thinking of doin' the big brother act, kinda scare him a little."

"Look, I can't explain this, expect to say that even though I almost . . . married this guy, and, um, we had a fight and all, the thing is, I think I owe it to him to . . . you know . . ." I couldn't say, I owe it to him to warn him that I think his brother-in-law is a murderer, because warning people of such things isn't quite smart. So why was I in such a heat to tell him?

Jack said, "Maybe you aren't all that done with him yet."

Just then, Ray drove up. He was in his own vehicle, his Ford Explorer, but he was dressed for work, ready to go on shift. I swung my crutches out and hobbled down the porch.

Jack followed. Opened the car door for me. Helped me up. As I buckled myself in, he draped one meaty arm along the roof of the car and leaned in to give Ray an ominous grin. "Hi, bub. Jack Sampler's the name. I'm with the FBI, and I'm assigned to baby-sit this peach. Just so's you know, I'll be following. And I don't like jokers."

Ray's eyes were dark as midnight. In classic Ray form, he gunned the engine rather than express himself in words.

Jack made kissy lips at him, then backed away and shut the door.

Ray pulled away from the curb rather more quickly than was usual or necessary, then drove up to the top of the university campus, where we could get a view. There, he turned the Explorer around to face the Salt Lake valley, parked, and cut the engine.

I looked over my shoulder. Jack had taken up a position about a hundred feet away.

Ray closed his eyes and bowed his head. His lips moved briefly. Praying. Then he spoke aloud. "Em. I apologize for last night."

"I forgive you," I said. The words came out surprisingly easily, yet they didn't seem right. I felt immediately that I had betrayed myself.

"So we'll go on from here," he said.

The moment took on the surreal quality of deep, wordless dreaming. The kind with dark holes and falling. Ray and I had broken up. I had stayed awake all night to prove it. So what were we doing here?

"I've asked you to marry me," he continued. "And I want my answer now."

My eyebrows rose so high, I could have worn them as barrettes. "You still want me to marry you?"

"Yes."

"Mormon-style."

He shook his open hands toward me in frustration, as if I were being purposefully stupid. *"Yes."*

My pulse quickened. Part of my mind careened sideways as I tried to sort out the source of my fear. "Ray, I have no interest in joining your church. I'm sorry."

He closed his eyes and bowed his head again.

"Is that what this is about?" I asked, my mind stumbling for connections. "You want to know if you're a free man, so you can go after Jenna?"

Ray opened his eyes and shot me a "Huh?" look. He seemed genuinely surprised.

That rocked me. Had I misunderstood the whole situation? I fought internally to reassert what I had seen with my own eyes, but my bubble of detachment had been hit by a hurricane, and suddenly my reality was only a shrinking subset of a partial truth that was rapidly falling apart. My words coming out so stridently that they sounded defensive even to me, I said, "Come on, Ray. I told you that Katie switched your channels on those radios so I'd hear. And I saw you flirting with Jenna up at your mom's. You were doing dishes with her, for crap's sake!"

Ray stared at his hands. Took a breath. Let it out. "Em, I'll admit that I've noticed Jenna. She's very sweet. But I want—"

"You want some kind of an Em with a Mormon retrofit. Sorry. No can do. No adapter plug. No, it goes even further than that. Your religion is incidental. I don't belong in your family, because the part they have in the drama for me is cast for a blonde who does dishes. Ray, you and I are friends, but I can see now that that's as far as it's ever going to go with us. You're an inextricable part of your family, and I . . . I'm not interested." Once I got started, the words had just tumbled out. They fell away from my lips. They were gone.

Ray's eyes had gone wide and vacant.

I felt like I'd just killed a fly with a baseball bat, which is as much as to say, Ray looked so tender and crushed that I couldn't understand why I was so angry at him.

Struggling for control, I forced the conversation back onto the rails I had intended. I said, "But I do need to talk to you about your family. I feel I owe it to you."

He didn't reply. I wasn't even sure he was still listening.

I started to open my mouth, but he stopped me.

"No," he said. "You do belong. Everybody belongs. God's love is great enough. You just—"

"No, Ray. God isn't running your family. Your sister made that clear to me."

Ray clamped his hand around my wrist. "What do you mean?" he demanded. "Em, you're always picking on Katie! She loves you. She's willing to have you as a sister!"

He had never before touched me in anything but kindness or affection. A coldness shot from my wrist to my heart. I said, "Oh come on, Ray, she *hates* me!"

Ray let go of my wrist and set his face in a remote and shallow smile, as if he was remembering some petty, nearly forgotten affront he had proudly ignored. He said, "Oh, now, Em, Katie doesn't hate you! Where did you get an idea like that? Really, I think you've spent too much time alone." His voice was oddly cheerful. It didn't even sound like him. It was as if someone else were speaking.

"Ray, she's taken a dim view of me from the start. And she—" I stopped. What was the point of debating this with him? He had denied my gut sense. Denied it out of hand, without a moment's consideration. It was as if the Ray I loved and admired had become a polyp extending from something large and unthinking. I felt sick, as if he'd hit me in the stomach. I wanted to get out of the car and run as fast as I could, wave my hands, get Jack to catch me on the fly as he accelerated from the parking lot. But I did none of this.

And that scared me most of all.

I closed my eyes, blotting out his smile. I didn't want to see him anymore. Didn't want to want him any way. Because I knew now that he didn't know me. Couldn't acknowledge my knowing, or my intelligence. At the same time, I felt like groveling at his feet and begging him to understand me, to accept me.

I felt Ray's hand on my wrist again. It slid up my hand and closed around it. With his other hand, he uncurled my clenched fingers, and slipped a ring on my third finger. He leaned close and kissed me on my ear. His breath was warm, and I could smell the scents I had come to associate with love at its most painful. I said, "I can't."

"My family would miss you. *I* would miss you."

I opened my eyes and looked into the indigo blue depths of his own. I began to tremble. He had installed a ring, the symbol of eternity, completeness, love, inclusion; and with it, a burden of guilt and rigidity under which I could not stand. I wanted to wear that ring, and at the same time, I wanted to rip it off, even if it took my finger with it. The shock of that loathing brought me to my senses. Fighting mentally to free myself, I said, "Ray. I have to tell you something. But I think you already know it."

"Know what?"

"About Enos. And Pet Mercer. And Sidney Smeeth." As I said this, I finally realized why I had felt so compelled to tell Ray of my suspicions. I wanted to see his reaction, know if I was correct.

Ray's pallor turned red, then white. In a tight, frightened voice, he asked, "How did you find out?"

My heart constricted. I suspected Enos Harkness of murder. I had thought that Ray suspected him, too, but I had not wanted to believe that he *knew*. The ring felt hot and tight, as if it were shrinking down, threatening to cut my finger. I began to cry. "Pet told me she knew him. Figuring out the connection with Sidney Smeeth was tougher. Her house is just downhill from your mother's—and, well, there are so many ways to slip in and out of that place unseen. But still I couldn't see the involvement. I mean, it didn't make sense. But I put two and two together. You said he hasn't been coming home. The cost overruns on their new house. Katie's . . . Pet called him the afternoon before she died, Ray. I was sitting right there. His phone number—or Hayes Associates—would be on her cell phone. They hold the last ten or more numbers dialed. Did the police find it at the scene?" I wanted to ask, Does Enos have the phone, and her notes? Will he come for me next? But I despaired that Ray would answer me even if he knew.

"You know I can't tell you that," he said. Ray had closed his eyes. He let go of my hand and grasped the steering wheel, rested his forehead on it, too. This was the real Ray, the familiar Ray, even if it was a Ray who was harboring a deadly secret. "No, Em. No cell phone."

As I saw the depth of his pain, my loathing slipped away as I remembered the love I had felt for him. I felt mean and guilty. Apologetically, I said, "Then I heard that you two were at the funeral together, and I . . . began to wonder."

"Enos and I weren't there together," he said, his voice constricted. "I was tracking him. I suspected." Then he said, "Are you sure, Em? Did you see something?"

"No," I said, honest to a fault. "My evidence is circumstantial. That's why I brought it to you. I thought—"

"You did the right thing, darling." He raised my hand to his lips and kissed it.

"So you'll take care of it?" I asked, almost begging.

"Yes," he whispered. "I was going to do it this afternoon, on my way to work."

With relief, I thought, *You were looking for proof before you'd turn in your brother-in-law.* And with sadness, I realized, *Before your tear your family to pieces.* "I underestimated you," I said. "I'm sorry. Oh, Ray, I'm so sorry."

He lifted his head and looked out through the windshield at the falling snow. His face was wet with tears.

28

When the Loma Prieta quake struck, I was in the BART tunnel, underneath San Francisco Bay. The train stopped. The lights went out. I was alone in the dark with strangers. No one knew what to do. Nobody came.

Time passed. We decided to walk out. We didn't even know whether we were closer to Oakland or San Francisco. The only illumination was from emergency lights spaced so far apart that I had to walk into deep shadow from one before I reached the light of the next.

I can never ride the BART again. I feel that Mother Earth personally betrayed me.

> —*Anonymous, a very shy woman who suffers extreme claustro-phobia, who, three days after the earthquake, found the courage to unburden her soul to a roomful of strangers*

"Get it off! Get it off! Get it off!" I sobbed.

"Hold still, damn it!" Faye commanded. "A little soap will do it, but you have to quit thrashing!"

We were standing over the sink in the bathroom of her master bedroom suite, she holding my finger, the one with Ray's constrictive ring on it, under running water, and I—well, I was flailing. Out of control. Losing it.

I fought to hold my hand still while she soaped it. It took everything I had.

Gradually, Faye worked her fancy facial soap under the ring, into the swelling that was causing the pain. She turned the ring, working the stone back to a position where it wasn't going to gouge my flesh as she worked the offending circlet of metal off my hand. "How'd he get it on there in the first place?" she asked, grunting slightly with the effort. "I mean, this must have been a humdinger of a struggle to get on."

"It was cold out, and I hadn't worn my mittens," I explained. "So my fingers had kind of shrunk. It went on easily enough, but then I—well, I had my hands balled up into fists trying to . . . ah, deal with Ray, and then when I finally got out and, you know, made my excuses—shit, Faye, the guy had just asked me to marry him again! I couldn't just run away. I got into Jack's car and tried to get it off, but it wouldn't come. I started yanking at it, and . . . the damned knuckle swelled up."

"Well, what else do you need to know? I've never seen such a perfect metaphor for ambivalence when it comes to marriage."

I started to cry again. "There's no way in *hell* I'm going to marry that guy!"

"That much is clear. But some little bitty part of you seems to be a-hangin' on, darlin'." She regarded the ring. "Hmm. I could cut it."

"Oh, that would go over nicely. I can just hear myself. 'Here, Ray; here's your ring back. Sorry about the nicks I put in the diamond while I was breaking your symbolic circle with my trusty hacksaw.'"

Faye pursed her lips in appraisal. "I was thinking of tin snips. Hacksaw might take your hand with it. Hey! That's perfect! You can give him your hand in marriage, and keep the rest of you for you!"

I started to growl.

Faye looked me in the eye. "Now you're talking. That's wolf for 'Back off.' It gets the message across nicely and gets that 'scared woolly lamb' look out of your eyes. Let me get some ice." She disappeared down the hall to the kitchen.

That left me staring at myself in the mirror, checking out the new, predatory Em Hansen. The effect seemed more lunatic than canid to me, but then, wolves have always been fond of howling at the moon.

The image of wolves in the high mountains in winter formed in my mind. Snow. Cold. Hunger. Resolve crumbled as I felt the frightened lamb underneath, saw her fear looking out through my eyes in the mirror.

I looked at the ring. Was Ray the hunter and I the hunted? How had he found me in the frozen landscape of my life?

As I asked the question, I saw its answer. He had followed the trail of my longing. My longing for stability, for family. For that elusive sense of fitting in and being part of what seemed normal. He had followed me as easily as a predator follows the blood of a wounded animal through the snow.

But was fitting in truly normal, or simply what most people do? Was I most people? Or was I born to a separate path, a life beyond the obvious?

Yes. My challenge lay off that map, on a territory dimly lighted, and it was my job to break the darkness as best I could. Perhaps that would stop my bleeding.

Certainly it was time to quit whimpering and take the leap out of known territory.

In the mirror, I saw a new Em, a traveler in a land where anything was possible, even bliss.

Jack poked his nose around the corner. "Having trouble?" he inquired.

I smiled. "Got a ring stuck. They teach that in paramedic school?"

"Sit down on the floor. No, better yet, lie down. Now hold your arm up. Fingers straight." He stepped around me, sat down on the toilet lid, and grasped my wrist, holding my arm at full stretch. "Relax," he said. "Jack-o gonna make you a free woman again."

"You were listening," I said.

"It's my job," he replied, his attention politely centered on my swollen digit. "Occupational hazard when it hurts peoples' feelings. Hmm, baby, you really done it to this one. I was wunnering what you was up to in the car. Looked like you was tryin' to open a bottle of champagne, only you didn't have no bottle." He leaned forward and rubbed my hand up against his cheek.

I laughed hesitantly, choking on all the goo that was still sliding down the back of my throat from crying. With my right hand, I took a swipe at my nose.

"Use your sleeve," Jack said. "It's much more absorbent."

I began to see why Tom Latimer felt he could trust this guy with his life. He was like a sentinel at the gate, with a no-guff, nonchalant attitude.

Faye came back with a package of blue ice and began to pack it around my hand, which Jack had moved away from his face the moment he heard her coming.

A few minutes later, Jack had the ring off my finger, and I stood up and rinsed my hands. Faye cleaned the soap off the ring and took it out into her bedroom, where she found a velvet box to put it in so I could return it in style. She produced a jeweler's loupe from a drawer in her bureau. This, she put to the rejected bit of jewelry, taking its measure. "Good-enough quality," she declared. "Modern cut, no family heirloom here, but at least Ray's no cheapskate. Wait—hold the phone." She had turned the band, read the inside. "Oh, great. This has another woman's name in it. 'Lisa, love for eternity, Ray.' So he's into wash-and-wear engagement rings, is that it?"

I covered my face in embarrassment.

"You got any beers in your fridge?" Jack asked Faye, beating a well-timed retreat.

"You know the way," she replied.

When he was out of earshot, I told Faye, "Lisa was his first wife. She died." The words seeming to stick to my tongue like lumps of dry plaster. "They're practical, these Mormons."

"I wonder what Lisa was like," Faye mused.

"Pretty," I said. "I've seen pictures at Ava's house. Average height, brown hair, a little heavy through the thighs."

"Like you."

I turned away. "Let's talk about something else."

"Like how you're going to give this back to him?"

"Parcel post," I suggested, the image of the wolf reassembling in my mind. "Seems I can't communicate with this guy worth beans, so why make another scene? He'll just tell me I'm nuts and push it back on me."

"He's that scared."

"Scared?"

"Yeah, without you, how's he supposed to deal with that family of his?"

"No. No, you're not going to lay that on me. I am not Ray's savior. I was not put on this earth to—"

"Seems like you've been doing a damned good job of it, though. He asks you to marry him the first time, and what do you do? You move here, set yourself up in an apartment, dodge his family when you can, take any number of knocks from them when you can't, and keep on bouncing back for more like one of those inflatable clowns with sand in the bottom. Then he gets to say to his mother, 'An heir? You want an heir? Hey, I got me a girlfriend right here, and just soon's she's ready, we's gonna cook y'all any number of heirs.' "

"That's crazy," I said, but even as I said it, I saw that she was right. I was the impossible girlfriend. He could laugh with Jenna, whoop it up, have a fine old time, and risk nothing. I was the holdout, his safety gasket. By committing himself to me, he committed himself to nothing. "Perhaps he'd had too much put on him too early. I mean, his dad died when he was still a teenager, and *wham*, he was the man of the family. Then he marries Lisa when he's nineteen. And, well, I always had the impression he liked her and everything, but that she was more like a pal. It was Ava who told them to get married."

"Now you're making excuses for him," Faye said.

I didn't reply. I was too busy trying to remember the new land I had glimpsed, the one where no blood left a trail through the snow.

"Come on, Em, time to cut the cord."

Just then, we heard a car pull into the driveway. Faye stiffened. It was Tom.

I looked at her. "And what about you? What's *really* keeping you from marrying Tom?"

Faye's face went blank. Her mouth opened. Numbly, she said, "The minute I marry, my trust fund ends."

"Matures?"

"No, ends. Kaput. End of cash flow. No more poor little rich girl."

"But Tom has money! And you could get a real job."

Faye's eyes were wide with fear. "I—I—it's not as simple as you think! I—it's always been there. My grandfather set it up. Sexist bastard. The idea is I'm supposed marry rich. Someone like 'us.' Discourage gold diggers. It's like a curse . . . glue . . . but I can't let go."

"You could just live together!"

Faye began to claw at her face. "No! Not Tom! Haven't you noticed? He won't take a key to the house. He doesn't even keep a toothbrush here! He won't even put his fucking car into my garage, Em!"

I considered pointing out that he *had* put his fucking something into her something else, but figured that it wasn't the moment to help Faye get down on Tom. She was clearly terrified, and needed just the right kind of snap to send her flying beyond the gulf of fear that separated her from her lover.

We heard the sound of the doorbell, then footsteps as Jack crossed to the front door from the kitchen and opened it.

I said, "What does the money represent, Faye?"

"What do you mean?" she whimpered.

"It's not granddaddy that you're having trouble letting go of. Is it the security, or do you have that money confused with who you are?"

"I'm *scared*, Em! I don't want to go home, but neither can I throw away the key."

I suddenly saw a Faye I had never met before. A little girl Faye, a ghost Faye, an angry little girl playing with the dolls at her grandparents' estate. She looked out at me through my friend's eyes and said, *This is the only place I'm happy, and I will not leave!*

In that moment, I came to know the splintering of the soul that can happen when a family constrains a child from finding her true self. Faye couldn't let go of that trust because her family had buried her in it; a precious part of her had gotten caught in its amber. She had confused it with their love.

Speaking gently to that child, I said, "Perhaps if you give up this thing you can't live without, you'll find that it's precisely what's been keeping you from getting what you truly need."

Faye's face crumpled into tears. "Maybe you should listen to yourself!"

Tom appeared in the doorway, still wearing his heavy winter coat. He had an odd kind of smile on his face—shy, hopeful, a little bit mischievous. He looked only at Faye. "Hi, love," he said softly. "How you feeling?"

"Good enough," she replied, quickly pulling herself as much together as she could get.

"Go for a walk?" he inquired.

Faye looked at me, then back at Tom. She raised her shoulders slightly and dropped them. In a tiny voice, she said, "Okay."

He put a gloved hand on her elbow and led her down the hallway to the door. Faye put on her ski parka, gloves, and a fuzzy hat. As the two were heading out the door, Tom asked, without even turning around to look at me, "Em, how far do I have to go to get past that debris flow?"

"Go uphill about a hundred yards, then contour across the slope until you run out of big rocks," I said. "It's a conical thing, feeding out of that chute straight uphill from the house. But don't worry, it's not likely to move today. Ground's frozen. You're safe unless we get a big quake while you're up there."

Tom paused with his hand on the doorknob. "I don't want to take any chances," he said simply, pulled the door shut, and left.

◆

I GOT MYSELF a beer and joined Jack by the picture window at the breakfast table, where we had a ringside view of Faye and Tom's progress up the hill. The snow had stopped falling for the moment, but the sky had gone cold and gray, and the whiteness that coated the ground had lost its brilliance.

My two cerebral friends followed the path up through the boulder train for a short distance, then cut northward. Holding hands. Walking slowly, meditatively. They began to converse. Now and then, one of them would pause, head bowed, and think for a moment, then say something to the other, who would by then have stopped to wait and watch. Finally, long after they were free of the rocks that delineated the tumble of earth that waited precariously above Faye's house, Tom went down on one knee in the snow, held his hands up toward Faye in supplication, and asked her a question.

Faye raised both hands to her face and placed the palms together, her thumbs touching her mouth and nose. Without breaking their union, she drew her hands down to her breast, pressing them into the yogic mudra that honors the heart. She was smiling, her face shining brightly enough to make the earth glisten on a moonless night.

29

JACK AND I DRAINED OUR BEERS AND VAMOOSED. IT SEEMED a good time to be somewhere else, to be giving Tom and Faye a little privacy.

We went back to my place first, but we didn't stay. I was halfway up the stairs, thumping along on my crutches, when Mrs. Pierce barreled out of her downstairs apartment and addressed my back.

"Consider this notice of your eviction," she said. "I don't allow my girls to have men up in their rooms."

I thought of informing Mrs. Pierce that I wasn't one of her "girls," but I bit my tongue. And I thought of telling her that Jack was actually a cross-dressing roller derby queen, then thought better of that, too. I even considered asking Jack to flash his badge and recite something from the local renter's laws. I tossed that idea, as well. Who cared what the law said? If Mrs. Pierce didn't want me—not just the me who left trails of longing in the snow but the larger, more complete me—in her house, then I didn't want to be in it, either. "I'll be out as soon's I can find another roost," I answered evenly.

Jack gave his own interpretation of the law by picking me up in his great strong arms and carrying me the rest of the way up the stairs and across the threshold into my apartment, cackling like a madman.

Riding in his arms felt good. It felt joyous. I laughed with all my body as he set me down on my bed and kissed me on the forehead. I arched my back on the pillows and said, "Thank you, most kind and noble sir."

"Want me to bring the law down on her?" he inquired.

"Nah. I think I just outgrew this place anyway."

I was still laughing when I looked at my answering machine. I said, "Oh, look: We got us a telly-phone message." Thinking nothing could daunt me just then, I punched the play button.

The message was from Katie. Her voice sounded exuberant. "Ray told Mama, and Mama told *me* the happy *news!*" she had chirped into the mechanical ear. "Well, *I* think this is a cause for *celebration*. There's a funeral tomorrow, as I'm sure you know, so we're tied up until late afternoon, but let's get you up here for *dinner*. Now, don't you worry about a *thing*. I'll arrange all the food, and all you have to do is get yourself dressed. Ray will pick you up. Say six o'clock. Great! Give me a call, okay?"

You could have knocked me over with the proverbial feather. I grabbed up the phone and dialed Ava's number. Katie answered. "Katie," I said, shaking with rage. "It's Em. Just what the fuck do you have up your sleeve?"

"Oh, *nothing*," she cooed. "Just welcoming you into the family, dear."

I could get no sounds through my windpipe for several seconds. Finally, I spluttered, "Well! I take it you haven't heard from Ray yet about Enos!"

Katie let out a smug snort. "Oh, that. Em, dear, you have to understand, a wife can be open-minded about her husband's interests in other women."

"Interests?" I squealed. "*Interests?*"

"Really, Em. Ray told me that you tried to tell him that Enos had been *unfaithful* to me. Of course that's not *true*, but so what? Even if he was you don't think that would *matter*, do you?" With each word, her voice heated a degree. Alternate meanings seemed to slither through her words like poisonous snakes.

"Is Ray there?" I asked, my throat constricting.

"No. He has gone to work. He *works.*"

And I lie around and take up space, I thought, anger once again edging ahead of fear. "Listen, Katie, I—*thank* you for your invitation, but I won't be available." I was descending quickly to her game of using one statement to make another. Then suddenly, what she had been saying hit me; Ray had not announced that Enos was a murderer; he had told his family that the man had been committing adultery! Ray had misunderstood everything I'd told him. I rewound the tape of memory and replayed it, this time hearing all the double entendres.

I dropped the phone into its cradle without bothering to say good-bye. I swung my feet over the edge of the bed and stared straight at Jack in horror.

Jack studied me with intense interest. "What?"

"I'm rethinking the conversation I had with Ray in the car. I— I asked him to deal with his brother-in-law. He said he would. And I . . . and he . . . I suppose I never once said murder . . . you know, being polite . . . but I thought he *understood.*"

Jack arched one eyebrow. "Did you mention both women?"

"Yes."

"And Ray went home and accused Enos of adultery."

"Yes. Or . . . that's what Katie just spat back at me."

"Then that means that Enos isn't our killer," he said simply. "Either that or your boy Ray's in some weird, weird space."

"Why?"

"Because Ray's a cop, Em. He thinks his brother-in-law is guilty, but not of murder, and murder has certainly occurred. You can't name murdered people around a cop and have him think adultery unless he knows your suspect is innocent. And that means that Enos has an alibi. Or worse, maybe your pal Ray is playing some kind of mind game on us all. Are you sure *he* didn't kill those women?"

"Maybe he's in denial." I suggested, knowing as I said it that I was being absurdly hopeful.

Jack said, "If he's that far from reality, I guess it's a good thing I helped you get that ring off."

I began integrating this new piece of the puzzle. "But Ava got all jumpy around me when I mentioned earthquakes and Dr. Smeeth and Enos, and she wouldn't talk to me this morning. She *knows* something."

"She has a huge share of that company, Em. You think she doesn't know what's going on there? Come on, she's no room-temperature IQ."

My stomach sank through my socks. "I don't like this, Jack. This means we can't rely on Ray to be a good cop and lock Enos up."

"You still think it's him?"

"Yes. The tidiness with which they were each killed. Those killings were engineered. And each was about to expose him." I stared at the floor. "I know how to make sure if it isn't him."

Jack shook his head. "You can't take any chances, Em."

I began to tremble with fear and rage. "Chances? Somebody out there is killing women who know too much about the projects Enos Harkness works on, and I'm the next logical target."

Jack put an arm around my shoulder. "Come on, Em, I'll take you to my place. You can stay there until this clears up."

"I'll go with you," I said. "But I can't hide. If I'm the prey, I'll draw the wolf wherever you put me."

Jack's lips set into a straight line.

I said, "I just realized something."

"Tell me."

"If I'm the bait, then we are in charge of the trap."

"What are you thinking?"

."The Ottmeier funeral is tomorrow. Everyone who is anyone in the Mormon community will be there, and that will include all the Raymonds; and unless I misunderstand the way business is done in this town, Hayes himself will also attend. We'll have to get Jim Schecter to help us, and get the use of the clock tower at the City and County Building."

For the first time, Jack looked truly worried.

30

I saw waves coming up the street and the power lines. A child tried to outrun them on his bike, but the street threw him down. Then a wall hit me.

> —*Jean Schnug, recalling the February 9, 1971, magnitude 6.5 earthquake in San Fernando, California*

As he waited in line to pass through the doors into the foyer in front of the sanctuary, Jim Schecter wished he had worn a hat. Saturday had dawned bright but windy, the very wind he feared might further load the weakened roof of the stadium, and the wind presaged another front with yet more snow.

A harsh gust whistled around the entrance of the church, sticking its cold fingers into the faces of the gathering faithful who had come to offer condolences to the friends and family of little Tommy Ottmeier. The place was mobbed; Salt Lake City's Mormon population was mourning as a community, as the integrated, faithful hive Brigham Young had envisioned, and Jim Schecter felt proud to be among them.

He did not feel proud of the TV cameras and the reporters who had set up in siege along the sidewalk. They were unseemly. They were offensive. They were like vultures preying on the dead. Tommy had gone to be with Heavenly Father. It was a time of celebration for his departed soul, not an opportunity for mawkish voyeurism. His family, celebrants though they might be, must still live with the loss of his precious company.

In unguarded moments Jim did wonder how Tommy's parents must feel; they were, after all, negligent in having put such a heavy bookcase next to his bed, but then again, the earthquake might just as easily have occurred during the daytime, and the child could have been playing in the wrong place at the wrong time and have been killed all the same.

The crowd inched forward. Jim passed now out of the wind and into the warm interior of the building. *At least the wind might blow some of the snow off the roof of the stadium,* he mused.

He wrenched his mind from the thought of that roof. That's what his doctor had taught him to do—not to dwell on things. Obsessive thoughts could bring on an attack, and that was to be avoided at all costs. It was okay to go to Tommy's funeral, because that was a positive thing, a celebration, but he must not think about things like that roof.

Or Pet Mercer.

Until I get a chance to deliver my message, he reminded himself.

Dear God, there's Enos Harkness, the structural engineer who specified the roof truss design that failed!

Jim hurried into the sanctuary and sat down as quickly as he could, following the ushers. There, he began his breathing exercises, bringing the thudding in his chest back down to a trot. Ah. Okay, it was ebbing.

The row filled in beside him, and then the one behind. He heard familiar voices threading in and out through the murmuring that rose and fell all around him as those gathered took their seats for the service. He heard a woman's voice—Velma Williams, he was pretty sure—speaking to . . . he turned. It was Ava Raymond. *I must deliver the message,* he reminded himself. *Follow my conscience.* He glanced back nervously. It was good fortune that she'd been seated so close—by God's will!—because that meant that the man he must address was there, too!

"I hear it was shoddy workmanship," Velma was saying.

Ava did not answer. Her jaw was set in anger.

"That bookcase was built in," Velma continued, making a study of the way her words sawed at Ava. "It shouldn't have fallen."

"The service is starting," Ava replied harshly.

Built in? Then it wasn't the parents' negligence! Jim reined in his galloping anxieties. *I can wait until afterward to deliver the message,* he decided. *Have to. The service is starting.* Then his eyes widened. At the far end of Ava's row, moving in late past her string of beautiful daughters and grandchildren and her handsome son, Micah Hayes was just taking a seat.

MICAH HAYES ARRANGED himself in the pew next to Ava Raymond, preparing to think about something else for the time it would take the congregation to dispatch their feeble grief. Then he would leave as quickly as possible.

He looked around at the faces of the congregation, measuring their reaction to his presence. Something was wrong. He was an important, prominent man, and a visitor at this Stake. They should be looking honored that he would favor them by attending this funeral.

He had seen eyes tracking him as he came up the aisle, heard grumblings, a pointed comment here and there that Tommy Ottmeier had been struck by a built-in bookcase in a house constructed by Hayes Associates; see, there is Hayes himself. . . . This was nonsense of course. *He* had not built that bookcase. In fact, at no time in recorded history had he, Micah Hayes, ever held a hammer. That was filthy work for menial underlings.

The service began, arched over the sadness and joy of the occasion, then drew to a close. Micah Hayes's thoughts had skated away. Were elsewhere. On his stomach. On other prospects. On a new property he had acquired near Park City. It was quite near an avalanche chute, but no matter; he knew which gears to oil in order to get the variances he needed to build his next farm of faux châteaux there for the Gentiles who were flowing in from out-of-State. They wouldn't be looking uphill towards the avalanche potential, only downhill toward the bars.

At the end of the service, the congregation stood and waited to file from the church; the family first, from the front row, then each row in turn following them down the aisle. As the pew in front of Hayes emptied out, a man stopped abruptly, turned, and stared at him. The man's eyes bulged with anxiety. His skin was the color of paste.

"Mr. Hayes," the man said. "I am Jim Schecter. I work for the county. I'm . . . an engineer."

This is the limit! Hayes thundered inside his head. *The fools are attacking me at church!* He fought to keep his face blank, his manner impassive.

"I inspected the roof of your new stadium," the man was saying, his voice now rising and tightening, as if he was about to cry. "I—I think you know what I'm telling you." He cleared his throat, glanced backward along the row of people he was keeping waiting in the pew.

Hayes turned and looked also. The entire Raymond clan had taken note, all eyes and ears focused sharply on the interchange. Hayes could see the whites of Enos Harkness's eyes clear around his pupils. Katie's eyes were half closed, her lips curling upward. Ava was focused in fury on this . . . engineer. Hayes looked back at Ray, whose eyes were blank, unreadable.

The man squeaked, "I . . . was wondering if you'd . . . ah, like to see what a seismic retrofit can look like. I'm . . . um, going to the City and County Building to do my inspection there. I invite you to come along. Six o'clock this evening. I . . ." He paused, gulped, stared at his feet, his hands, his agitation growing. "There will be a geologist along as well, meeting me there. Her name . . . her name is Em Hansen. She says she has something to tell you about the feasibility of your new building site. The Towne Centre project. Right next to your new stadium!" Suddenly, Schecter's face contorted with anger. "I know you used your influence to silence Sidney Smeeth. You should be ashamed! And that bookcase! Unspeakable!"

Hayes blurted, "You're raving!"

Schecter struggled onward, beginning to stutter, although he looked like he might faint at any moment. "I've . . . I've told M-miss Hansen to come a little later. Six-thirty. So you and I c-can talk first. M-maybe there are things sh-she doesn't need to know about. Do you understand me?" He stopped speaking. His eyes gaped even wider. He seemed to rise up on his toes as if threatening and at the same time, begging for comfort, an answer, admonishment.

Hayes fixed a commanding look on the man. "I'm sure I don't have time for such twaddle," he grunted.

"Six o'clock," Schecter said, his voice going into a sing-song of recitation. "The building will be locked. The guard won't be there—called away, I understand—but I'll leave the east door unlocked for you. Remember that. East door." With that, the man departed, almost leaping from the end of the pew like a flea.

Which is what you are on the hide of mankind, Hayes decided, rage filling the whites of his eyes with a tracery of red. He turned and looked behind him. Dozens of people had heard the interchange, and not a one now looked friendly.

◇

WENDY FORTESCUE STARED into her monitor, adjusting the crosshairs along one more small aftershock that represented the release of perhaps a dinner table-size area along the Warm Springs branch of the Wasatch fault. She had a bad feeling. That bad feeling had lingered with her all week, had grown rather than lessened. The aftershocks just weren't significant enough. It was too quiet, just like the whole Salt Lake segment of the fault had been since long before they began to record seismic activity. She feared with every bone that the fault was winding up for something much, much larger than it had dealt out on Monday.

Big quakes—ground-rupturing quakes—had, in pre-European times, ripped the Wasatch fault systematically, and doubtless would again. The towering steepness of the Wasatch Range, and the repeatedly torn apron of debris flows and alluvium that flanked it, attested to that. But those giant temblors had always shaken a landscape that had no structures, no buildings that could collapse. Wendy knew with certainty that when the next giant struck, buildings would fall. The older homes would collapse, their chimneys toppling through roofs as outer walls crumbled. Hospitals would fall, and civic buildings. The City and County Building might ride it out, but the state capitol, with all its countless tons of massive crystalline rocks, not braced by seismic retrofit, would be demolished. Perhaps the dome itself would plummet on the legislature, squashing the damned fools who refused to fund its retrofit. Highway bridges would collapse, and roads would split, making it impossible for emergency vehicles to do their jobs; and the airport control tower would rack and runways would crack, thwarting the arrival of aid. Power would fail, and water supplies would dwindle as lines and underground pipes ruptured. And far west of the city, Great Salt Lake would slosh like a bathtub, ricocheting shock waves from one side to the other, generating inland tsunamis that would crest the levees. And, as the valley slowly tipped to accommodate the addition of several new feet of real estate, that lake would flow eastward, flooding first what was left of the airport runways and next back up the waters of the Jordan River and City Creek, inundating the city itself. The brave new spruced-up center of the city would be hardest hit as its older brick and stone buildings tumbled, and businesses would close under the strain of interruptions and the cost of rebuilding.

She thought of the thousands—no, tens of thousands, perhaps hundreds of thousands—who would die, and of all who would be sick, and hurt, and homeless. And she wept.

31

I HOBBLED UP THE STEPS TO THE MAIN GUARD DESK IN THE City and County Building, past the splendid travertine wainscoting, across the intricately patterned tiled floor. I had taken my time coming in from the sidewalk, where the taxi had dropped me. I went slowly, making certain that if anyone wished to see me, they would. The bulletproof vest I wore beneath my down parka was making me sweat, and it was difficult to swing my crutches, but just now comfort was not foremost in my mind.

Once past the guard's desk, my progress became somewhat easier. I boarded the elevator, tensing as the doors opened. I got off at the fourth floor, for fear my enemy might be on it. I proceeded to the stairs that would take me up to the tower.

At the door to the stairs, I tapped three times, then once. Heard two faint taps in reply. I opened the door.

Jack was inside, waiting for me in the darkness. He moved up the stairs ahead of me as silent as a wraith.

My heart pounding in my chest, I distracted myself with thought. *Now he's a ninja. A new Jack Sampler persona for the archives. What next? A dipsomaniac granny carrying a birdcage?*

At the next door, he whispered, "Ready?" He tugged at my vest, making sure it was firmly in place, then checked the metal collar I wore beneath my turtleneck shirt.

"As ready as I'll ever be," I whispered back. I smiled. I was not concerned about bullets from someone who used their hands to strangle or a SUV to crush, but the weight of the bulletproof vest felt comforting, as if Jack himself were wrapped about me.

"Radio?" he whispered.

I tapped my breast pocket.

Jack pointed over his head. "Jim's already up there."

"Good," I whispered. "How's he doing?"

"Not so good," Jack replied. "But he's a little guy. I can carry him down when we're done."

"Ray?"

"It took a little persuasion, but I got him here."

"What did you tell him?"

"I didn't tell him anything. I called his superiors and requested his services. He's up past the bells, on the wooden part of the stairs. Above Jim. Hiding where Enos can't see him."

"He has the radio?"

"Yup."

I shook my head doubtfully. "He's a good cop. It's a shame. Anything happen yet?"

"No."

"Hayes?"

"No show."

"As expected. He sent Enos?"

"Enos came. He's up there with Jim."

"Did he use his keys to get in?"

"No. He knocked. Jim opened up for him."

"Then where are the keys?"

"Exactly. I covered things as best I could, but this place has way too many doors and staircases. Watch your back."

"Who's protecting Jim?"

"He's wearing a vest, too. And Ray's up there, remember." He smiled wryly.

"Jim's taking too much of a chance."

"He welcomed it. Seemed to perk him up."

"Okay," I said. "Any more visitors, you make like a ghost and let them through."

Jack glanced at his watch. "Show time," he said, and gave me a little kiss, again in the center of my forehead. It was a friendly thing. An affectionate thing. An intimate thing. Something that seemed to happen naturally between us. "Remember," he whispered, "don't go up above the clock faces."

I waved one crutch a half inch. "Not on a bet."

He opened the door.

I stepped through.

I hobbled up to the next level and ducked underneath the air duct. Waited, staring up at the thin steel rods that drove the hands around the mammoth faces of the clock. I lowered my gaze and turned slowly 360 degrees, checking out every shadow and blind angle in the place, taking special note of the two doors that led out onto the catwalks along the roofs, leading to the twin flagstaffs. If cornered, I must remember not to feel tempted to run out onto one of those. With the steep pitch of the roofs, it would be a quick trip down five stories to the walkways below.

"Hello?" I called.

High above my head, I heard Jim cough. "Em Hansen?" he said, his voice bouncing down the cold face of the masonry.

"Yes."

"I'll be down in . . . five minutes," he said uncertainly.

A minute ticked past. I heard their low conversation. Enos and Jim, discussing engineering. Was I dreaming?

Two minutes.

Nothing. Jim and Enos had completed their discussion of the seismic retrofit. Jim asked about moment frames, as I had suggested. Asked if indeed Enos had been the one who had specified the frame for the new stadium. Enos said he had. He sounded calm, though somewhat dejected. Hardly murderous.

Three minutes. Enos's voice still droned on, just talking. Did that mean he was innocent of both murders? Had I misgauged?

Was he hoping to catch me after Jim left, or ask to meet me elsewhere? Ray thought him innocent, so deeply that he had misunderstood my assertions. The puzzle must fit, but perhaps with the pieces in a slightly different arrangement.

From which direction would the attack come?

I glanced all around me, watching, wishing my eyes could slide around the sides of my head. Glanced again at my watch. Wondered whether my precautions had been sufficient. Considered pressing the button on the radio, just to hear it squelch above me, just to make certain Ray could hear what I thought he would soon hear. But I didn't want to give away his position.

Four.

After another furtive look at my watch, I glanced overhead, checking again to make certain that no one could drop anything on me. I was clear. But it was not the stairs overhead that worried me most.

Thirty more seconds ground, one at a time, deep into my skull. *It's taking too long. It isn't working!*

A tick. A whirring noise issued from the hydraulic tank, and the arms above it began to move, rising, pulling, moving the long steel cables that rose high overhead, where Ray waited. As the armatures began to descend, the bells chimed, ringing, clanging, filling the dark column of space with sound. Under the cover of their titanic noise, I saw something from the corner of my eye: the door to the catwalk that led to the flagstaff opening, the flag whipping against a dark sky, framing a silhouette—

Fast, coming like a bullet—

I dropped one crutch, whipped my hand for the radio, pushed the button, knowing its sound would be lost in the bells. Fear cut through me like ice.

The bullet resolved into a shape—

Katie!

She flew at me from the shadows, hands up, teeth bared, growling, her fierce strength and jealous beauty focused on my throat.

I opened my mouth to scream Jack's name, but the bells swallowed my small sound like a furnace consuming a moth.

I lunged sideways, fell—

She landed on me, her full weight writhing on me, eyes afire, pelvis grinding in ecstasy as her hands closed around my throat—

Jack yanked her up so hard that I came with her, tugged to my knees.

She whirled, arms windmilling, clawing like a cat.

I hit the button again, screamed "Ray!" though my knotted throat.

Jack whipped Katie's muscular frame into a wrestling hold.

I struggled to my feet, staggered, caught my footing, leaned onto the crutches.

I heard footsteps thrumming along the steel catwalk and down the stairs. Enos coming. Ray at full gallop. Jim stumbling along behind.

Enos arrived first. "Katie!" he moaned, "Stop! Please! For the love of God!" Then, to Jack, he cried, "What are you *doing* to her?"

"Arresting her," Jack said, his voice strained as he continued to fight her astonishing strength.

"Let her go!" Enos screamed. "*I* killed Pet Mercer, not her! Take *me*!" He fell to his knees in agony. Bent his head. Locked his hands over his cranium. Began to sob.

Ray hit the bottom step and charged into the melee. "Katie!" he screeched, a big brother scolding his baby sister. "You're not supposed to be here!"

Katie suddenly slumped against Jack, the fighting cat transformed in a blink to a pathetic kitten. "Ray! Make them stop it!"

Ray lunged at Jack.

My crutch was still in my hand so I swung it. Got him right in the shin. It made a very satisfying smack and he went down hard.

Ray rolled, grabbing at a leg bent in pain. He stared up at

Jack, who was now handcuffing a thrashing, growling Katie to the steel bracing of the stairs. Ray whined, "What are you *doing*, man?"

"Arresting your little sister for the murder of Sidney Smeeth," Jack said almost calmly. "Although I'm gonna hafta add on the attempted murder of Em Hansen. Naughty girl, Katie; mustn't do."

Ray looked up at me. He looked again at Katie. He looked lost.

Katie's face twisted into a mask of hatred. "*Kill* her, Ray!" she roared. "Use your *gun*. You're a *cop*. *You* know what to do! She *attacked* me. Look! You saw her! She just *assaulted* you with her *crutch!* Are you going to take that from a *woman?* Kill her, Ray! She wants to change *everything!* She wants to break up our family! *Take* from us. Take from *us!* You have to *kill* her, Ray! *Kill* her! KILL HER!"

"And why did you have to kill Sidney?" I asked. "Did she threaten to expose him? She almost said it all, exposed your husband right there on nationwide TV, a ruin to all your years of planning, and pushing, and hating. Or was it just the joy of knowing you could do it? There you are, a dog off the leash. Everyone thinks you're out jogging for your morning exercise. And there she is. The meddlesome bitch is opening her gate. One instant and you're through the gate . . ."

Katie's face twisted further, knotting around her teeth in a snarl. "You spawn of the devil! I've worked *hard* to get Enos positioned! It wasn't *easy* with a hopeless fool like him, but I got him in there. Got him a job. Had to push him every *inch* of the way! Who *cares* about a few cracked welds?" She began to kick at Enos. "You couldn't just get up there and paint over those cracks? What's the *matter* with you? It's the *system!* You've ruined everything! I worked *hard!* I've got *sweat equity* in this city!"

Enos hung his head and absorbed her blows.

"And Pet?" I asked.

Enos looked up at me but didn't really see me. "She said she *knew*," he said miserably. "I couldn't let her put Katie in the paper, could I?"

I looked at Ray, who now lay sprawled out on the floor, almost relaxed, his eyes glazed. "Let's go home now, Katie," he said very softly. "Let's go home. Mama's got dinner ready."

◈

KATIE AND ENOS rode away in the back of a squad car with lights flashing. The members of the media who had arrived to chase the radio calls watched them go, cameras flashing into the night, like a bad dream gone Disneyland.

I stood on the sidewalk in front of the City and County Building, leaning on my crutches, rubbing at the bruises on my neck that Katie had managed to put there in spite of the protective collar. I was almost glad for the pain, as it cut through my weariness and confusion, reminding me that what I had thought to be true was true.

Jack put a hand on my shoulder. "Okay for now?" he asked.

I nodded.

"It's gonna hurt worse later. We'll get you some rest. Quiet. When you're safe enough, you'll get the shakes, and work it out of your system. Then you'll be better by and by."

Jim Schecter stepped up closer, a shy man ready to take flight. "Thank you," he said. "I'm sorry that you got hurt. But I'm glad to get the story out. At last."

I smiled and nodded. "Keep up the good work," I told him. "People don't like to be caught at their games, but it's a job worth doing."

His lips curved into a smile, even though his eyes still registered pain.

Now Ray stepped toward me.

Jack faded back, taking up a position on the front fender of a car a polite distance away.

Ray said, "You're wrong, Em. Katie really liked you. Family's everything to her, and she wanted you in it."

I brought one finger up and poked at my ear to test my hearing. At length, I said, "Ray, that just doesn't make sense." Then I took the little velvet box out of my pocket and handed it to him. "Here. This doesn't fit me, Ray. It never will. Find a woman the right size, okay?"

"Maybe you could see a therapist. You need family," he said in a small voice. "Everybody needs family. It's more important than . . ."

I looked on him with infinite sadness, wishing our friendship could have ended any other way, yet relieved that it had indeed ended. Finishing his sentence, I said, "Than life itself?"

32

A bad earthquake at once destroys our oldest associations: the earth, the very emblem of solidity, has moved beneath our feet like a thin crust over a fluid;—one second of time has created in the mind a strange idea of insecurity, which hours of reflection would not have produced.

—*Charles Darwin*, Voyage of the Beagle, *from his journal entry made after experiencing the devastating February 20, 1835, earthquake that reduced Concepción, Chile, to rubble*

"HOW'D YOU KNOW TO USE THE CLOCK TOWER?" FAYE ASKED as we settled ourselves into the cockpit of her twin-engine Piper the next morning.

I turned around and smiled at Tom and Jack, who were already breaking into the supply of single-malt scotch Faye stocked for those who needed Highland courage to fly in light planes, or who, like these mongrels, just liked it better than water. I said, "Pet told me that Enos had a set of keys from back when he was a building guard. Apparently, he liked to take the ladies there. So I guessed that Katie would know about them, too."

Faye laughed. "A good Mormon girl like Katie?"

"Katie's one of those people who make their own interpretation of the rules, Faye. And I figured the setting would appeal to her flair for the dramatic."

Faye was still laughing. "So you thought it was her all along?"

"No, I suspected Enos. Except that it seemed too pat. So I started looking around for someone a little crazier, and what can I say?"

"I have to hand it to you. You took Ray right to the manure pile and rubbed his nose in it."

"Damn it, Faye, he took himself there!"

Faye noted that I wasn't yet ready to see humor in this topic, so she busied herself, putting on her headphones and adjusting the microphone, covering a smile.

I put on mine, too. I said, "He kept acting like *I* was the one who didn't get it. It was making me crazy. I tell you, it's a curse seeing things the way I do. People don't like knowing what I see in this crazy world."

Faye's voice now arose inside my ears with the oddly crystal-line intimacy that headphones create. Her tone was quite sober. "Most people go along to get along, Em. It's so much easier." She began going through her pilot's checklist, tapping gauges and throwing switches.

"Are you suggesting I do that?"

"Not for a minute. What would I do for company?"

"Check."

"I'm impressed that you're not any madder at Ray."

I thought about this for a moment. "Oh, I'm mad all right. I'm furious. But not at Ray. At myself. The problem started when I got what Ray was offering mixed up with what I thought he really wanted."

"And what was that?"

This was what I liked most about talking with Faye. She asked all the right questions, and they always pushed me to that next level, where my wandering thoughts came together into little rungs on some cosmic ladder. "I know that I wanted something larger and more flexible. I still do. And Ray wanted me. I don't care what you say, there must be a part of him that wanted what

I want. He just couldn't imagine going there."

"And what is that thing that's larger and more flexible?" Faye asked. There was a longing to her voice now.

"We're talking about family, right? He comes from a tight one that offers tremendous security if you'll just toe the line. I came from a small one that's been disintegrating and getting smaller all my life. Which is better? And how do you measure that?"

"I'd say that if I had to compare you to Katie, you'd win hands down," she said. Out her side window she yelled, "Clear prop!" and fired the first engine.

"But that's not the point."

"Then what is the point?"

Again, I had to think. "I guess it's got something to do with the difference between the family and the individual. If the family has no place for individuals, then it's a monster that forces the individual to be less than she is." I thought about Ray. "Or want something other than what he wants. If you can't be who you are, you can't grow. The family tacitly says, How dare you grow beyond us? Submit to our rigid, limiting behavior so we don't have to deal with all the questions you are raising."

"And if the individual can't tolerate the constraints of the family?" Faye asked.

"If the family is abusive, then the choice is easier. Then you have to leave, because if you stay, you become part of the abuse."

"But what of more normal, well-intentioned families? Families like Ray's, that hold back his growth, or his freedom to make his own decisions?"

"They offer the golden handcuffs of importance, or belonging, or. . . ." I avoided looking at her. "Or money. But tell the truth: if anything is wrong, it just festers."

Fay sighed. "Like Katie's jealousy. I still can't see how you tolerated Ray's family as long as you did."

"They're nice people, Faye. Most of them. And they kept saying, Come on in; we'll give you everything you truly need. I kept thinking that *I* had to adjust to *them*. There's always a Them."

Faye sat quietly with me for a moment, a friend comforting a friend. Then, deciding that we had taken that topic as far as we could for the moment, she said. "You were telling me how you knew it was Katie."

"She always seemed to be looking for someone to pass her bitterness to. Imagine how lonely that makes her, what pressures that must build up inside her. Nobody can get near her, not really, not even her children. It's kind of sad, when you think about it."

Faye started the second engine. Then whistled softly into her microphone. "Em, you knock me out. The bitch tries to kill you and you talk like she gave you a flu bug."

Just then, Tom leaned forward from the first seat behind Faye and kissed her neck. "Are we going flying, or are we going to sit here all day while you ladies chat?" he inquired, raising his voice to be heard over the engines.

I turned and smiled at him. And at Jack. Jack gave me the kind of smile you might see on a very well-fed lion who was preparing for a nap in the sun.

Faye covered her microphone and shouted to Tom, "Hold your horses, hotshot." Then, back into the microphone, she told me, "Well, at least Tom and I finally got it figured out. Thanks for the assists, Em."

"My pleasure."

A cloud of worry crossed Faye's face. Then she put her hands on her abdomen, and her expression softened into amazement, then wonder. "I just hope we can have the kind of family that can be elastic in all the right ways. A group of individuals sharing a life and love, that's what I want."

"That's the ticket."

Tom reached over and tousled my hair. He shouted, "Em, it's going to take at least another ten lifetimes for you to get it all figured out, and a certain baby's not going to wait that long. Let's get going!"

I yelled back, "Tom, you look happier than I've ever seen you."

"He should," Faye said. "Because I'm gonna marry him today!" Smiling happily, she began switching the radios so she could ask for her clearances.

I said, "Now you'll be counting pennies, just like me. I hope you don't hate me tomorrow."

"Comparative poverty—a brand-new adventure. You're right, Em, money can be a box, just like a bad family." Then she gave me a wink. "Besides, I've managed to get a few things in my name."

"The house?"

"No, that belongs to the trust, and it's no loss. Tom is right: We should live closer to the earth, and not just strip it."

"The airplane?"

"You think I'm stupid? This has always mattered more to me than the house. Unfortunately, it's not altogether paid for yet, but where there's a will . . ."

"And you do have a strong will." I laughed. "It's not going to be easy, I expect. You two. Married."

"Nah. Wouldn't be any fun if it were. But like you say, love isn't just a feeling. It's the actions you take." She gave my hand a squeeze. "And that goes for friends, too."

I covered sudden tears by pretending I had something in my eye.

Faye asked for a clearance to taxi for takeoff. It was granted. "Want to taxi us over to the runway?" she asked.

Grinning through my tears, I released the brake and took us

down the taxiway, gliding along past Hudson Aviation and the Air National Guard ramp. I pulled the plane to a stop in the take-off queue the end of the runway, tucking us in between a KC-135 Stratotanker and a Beechcraft Baron. There, Faye began to go through her final checklist. Before switching over to the tower frequency to ask for takeoff clearance, she said, "You know, as screwy as things were between you and Ray, you had something real together. Too bad he had to play it safe."

Now I sighed. "Safe doesn't get you to the top of your soul's mountain." I thought about the tender life that beat inside of Faye, and the tender love that surrounded it. I said, "I just hope there's an adult male waiting for me if I ever get to the top of mine."

"Chances are," Faye said. "But there's no way to find out unless you give it a try. A lot cracked loose that morning the earth shook underneath that fancy house I was hiding in. It's time to give up on the guarantees of family and risk making one of my own." She toggled her radio microphone switch and contacted the tower. She asked permission to take off. It was granted. She smiled at me. "Let's go see what's out there for us," she said.

"Yes," I agreed. "Let's fly."

She taxied into position, ran up the throttles, and began her takeoff roll. Halfway down the runway, the little plane lifted, taking us high up into the air, where we could see much farther, and more clearly. And, as we banked and turned away from Salt Lake City, I looked back on that lively crust of civilization and saw for the first time what a thin veneer it was. I saw it now as the ephemeral gathering it was, just like a family, trying its best to stand on changing ground, and it occurred to me that, just like the face of this restless Earth, families change. They grow, and break apart, or collide, or grind past themselves. And, like the earth, these changes are driven by forces much larger, deeper, and more mysterious than I can ever fully know or understand. And all of this at last seemed right, and good, and at the correct scale with the cycle and majesty of life and death and love.

Author's note

There's an unwritten rule against preaching personal politics within the text of a mystery novel, or there should be. That's why I try to present the various sides of the issues du jour in the Em Hansen stories and leave judgment to the reader. But I do have opinions. So I indulge in writing an author's note. Please bear with me and allow this old geologist/mystery writer a word or two on a topic that I hold near and dear.

The issue is the need to support scientific research; for example, investigations into the locations and activity of fault planes. To persuade you of the importance of pure scientific research (not to be confused with corporate-sponsored research, which has a product-oriented agenda), I must state that the plot of this book was derived from a true story. In that true story, no state geologist was actually killed, but one was compelled to quit his job when he was told to keep his mouth shut regarding the construction of a public building over the possible—many would say probable—location of a geologic hazard. The names and particulars are herein changed to protect the geologist—whom I consider an ethical hero—from a slander suit. I find it frightening to note that those who muzzled this man got their way and built their building. If a large earthquake hits Salt Lake City within your lifetime, you'll witness the results of that folly.

It is an established fact—not a theory—that geologic hazards such as earthquakes and resultant tsunami are real and much,

much bigger than we are. We cannot control them, we can only plan our lives around them by preparing for them and by trying to mitigate their effect. On a slightly different front, we find that we have exacerbated natural hazards such as climate change and disease-carrying intercontinental dust clouds, and we have not as yet fully identified all of their causes or been able to predict their effects.

So what are we to do? My urgent recommendation is that we publicly underwrite the careers of as many honest, independent-thinking geoscientists as we can find. This means supporting public and private institutions that employ these persons. I am talking about colleges and universities, certainly, but more specifically the federal and state geological surveys.

My first job in geology was with the U.S. Geological Survey in Denver, Colorado. I was paid almost nothing, but had the finest apprenticeship available. There were a few idiots there, to be sure—deadwood on the taxpayer's dole—but most of my colleagues had extraordinary minds, and some were bona fide geniuses. All exchanged much handsomer incomes for the government's modest ones just so they could spend their time advancing the science. The most important thing they did was think independently of special interests. If they had a major flaw, it was that they fell short on educating the nation on the magnitude of the contribution they were making. As a result, their budget was cut, and they can no longer do anywhere near as much for us.

Perhaps, before reading this book, you were not aware that the geological surveys existed. We need to recognize that our geological surveys are a precious resource, and we need to act lest they be marginalized and budget-cut out of existence. In order for them to be fully effective, we need to protect their mandate to report their findings in the public arena regardless of the agendas of special interest groups. Yes, this means tax dollars, and to some special interests, lost opportunities, but this is truly one place where dollars spent up front are earned back one-hundredfold as they spare lives, homes, businesses, and the ecosystems on which we all depend.

With thanks for your attention,

Sarah Andrews
August 8, 2001